Time
Turner

M.A. MOREA

Coventry Press Ltd.

Coventry Press Ltd.
Somers, New York
http://www.coventrypressltd.com

ISBN-10: 0988439697
ISBN-13: 978-0-9884396-9-6

First Edition: Coventry Press Ltd. 2014
Editor: Tina Winograd
Cover Design: Cover Couture

Printed in the USA

Alice: "How long is forever?"
White Rabbit: "Sometimes, just one second."

~Lewis Carrol

PART I

Chapter 1

Rowen?" A soft knock followed my mother's voice outside my bedroom door. "Don't you think it's time you got up?"

I didn't answer.

Rolling over, I took the covers with me, peering across the satin edge of my duvet at the clock on my nightstand.

Another knock let me know she didn't appreciate my plan to sleep in the remaining weeks prior to the official start of my collegiate life, not when summer in the Hudson Valley was chock full of diversions, and that included the quaint river town of Sleepy Hollow. Our village may be best known for the Headless Horseman and Halloween fun, but in the summer the streets came alive with weekends full of history, music, and theater, including an annual jazz festival and large scale productions like *Pirates on the Hudson*, not to mention boasting the biggest farmers' market in the county.

"Rowen? Gran is downstairs...."

I closed my eyes, muffling a whispered expletive. Clearly my mother had let me slide long enough.

My door opened a crack. "Are you ignoring me on purpose or is it your plan to spend the rest of this beautiful day in bed?"

"I heard you on your first knock. It's summertime, Mother." I rolled onto my back, my arm thrown over my brows to avoid eye contact and the unhappy set to her mouth. "And that means for the first time in ten months I get to sleep in, and after the last

eight of those ten, I think I'm entitled." I wasn't in the mood for a lecture, so I kept my arm where it was.

Her exaggerated sigh told me she wasn't having it. "Rowen, no one, least of all me, would dispute this year has been horrific, literally. However, you've become a recluse and I won't allow it."

"I spend time with Hunter."

"Yes, but since he left to visit his father in California you've barely stepped foot out of your room, let alone out of the house. Thank God he's on his way back."

I jerked my arm down from my eyes. "When?"

Mom shrugged, bending to pick up my dirty clothes from the floor. "I talked to his mother this morning. Britt said Hunter and his dad quarreled about him not attending USC or something. Clearly his father wants him to stay out west, but Hunter wants no part of it. The boy called Britt to book him a flight home a.s.a.p."

I sat up, covers dropping to my lap. "They must have argued after we face-timed last night." I stared at nothing, chewing on my lower lip. "Did Britt say when he was getting in?" I asked, finally acknowledging my mother with a direct look.

"Tonight. I wrote his flight information on the notepad beside the kitchen phone, along with driving directions to the airport." A knowing smile tweaked the corner of her mouth. "After a long flight and a fight with his dad, I thought he might like a happy surprise when he lands."

A full grin, wide enough to match my mother's, spread across my lips. I threw my legs over the side of my bed and hugged my middle. I missed Hunter so much. He left for the coast the day after we graduated. That was weeks ago. Three weeks to be exact, and one week since the memorial for Talia and Mike.

I glanced at my yearbook still open to the inside spread dedicated in their memory. Pain, fresh and as sharp as ever,

pierced my heart. Regardless of what anyone said, there was no escaping the guilt gnawing at my insides. They were both dead because of me.

My mother picked up my yearbook and closed the hardcover, stowing it in the top drawer of my nightstand. "Enough." The word was both a directive and plea. She turned toward me still hugging my middle, but this time for a different reason. The pain in my chest made it hard to breathe.

"Mom…"

She shook her head hard. "No, Rowen. It's time you listen to me. You think I don't know how hard the memorial was for you? Especially with Hunter away? Talia was one of your best friends. Since her murder you've clung to Hunter, and barely at that. You shut everyone out, your grandmother and me included.

"We're worried, sweetheart. We were there, too, just as involved as you in untangling the warnings behind your bloody visions. What happened was beyond anyone's control. The root of that evil is gone now, and the collateral damage in its wake is something none of us will ever forget. You can't bury yourself along with Talia and Mike. If you do, evil wins, and that I can't allow."

I didn't reply. My mother was there when everything unraveled, yet she still didn't understand. I never told her about the weird conversation I had at Talia's gravesite with the cemetery caretaker or how he cocked his head, his milky eye color flashing to a candy blue for a split second. I never told anyone, not even Hunter.

Itchy witch.

The caretaker had called me that when his eyes changed. Itchy Witch was Tyler Cavanaugh's pet name for me and only because he knew I hated anything attached to my family's witch roots.

I sighed, lifting my head to the concern in my mother's eyes. "I'm okay, Mom. Really. Except for Hunter, not one of my

friends will ever understand the evil that touched us that night in the cemetery. I know I have to let everyone think Tyler murdered Talia and Mike in a drunken rage, that he assaulted Jenny, but you and I know that's a lie. I have to listen to their gossip and innuendo when they haven't a clue what happened." A rough exhale replaced my sigh, my eyes searching my mother's face. "You want to know the worst part?"

She looked at me, her expression heavy with care. "Rowen, don't..."

I waved her off. "I can't defend him, Mom." I lifted a hand, letting it drop. "I can't say a word about what truly occurred that night."

She stepped toward the bed and laid her hand on my cheek. "I know, baby, but people like their truths in neat, explainable boxes. The alternative scares them too much. It's much easier to believe Tyler is on the run than an evil entity possessed his body and soul." Her eyes met mine, her regard soft. "It's up to you if you want to pit your truth against theirs, but you're the one who never wants to give Sleepy Hollow any more reason to hate us and our Wiccan ways."

What if I hate myself?

I dropped my chin. "I know, but..."

Truth or not, images from last Halloween engulfed me. How could I forget the evil that showed its face and flexed its supernatural muscles to keep two hundred years of secrets and lies buried? How Hunter and I discovered the real truth behind the fate of the headless horseman and had finally set his soul to rest?

She slipped her fingers beneath my jaw, lifting my gaze to hers. "Don't. I know you believe Tyler replaced the Hessian soldier as the wronged spirit in the Old Dutch burial ground. Gran and I have been canvasing every book we know, even making inquiries into some of the darker covens on ways to bring him back." She shook her head. "Everyone says the same thing. Tyler was taken because blood called to blood and unless

blood calls him back, it can't be done. Even if we had the necessary sacrifice, the spell required is so dark and so inherently evil even Gran won't touch it, despite her knowledge and control."

I blinked, realizing I had wrapped myself in my own guilt and grief to the point I couldn't help anyone, let alone myself. "Guess that makes us the *Unwicked* Witches of Westchester, huh?"

Mom laughed. "Now that sounds more like my girl." She took my hand and pulled me from my perch on the end of my bed. "Get cleaned up." A soft shove and a love tap on my butt directed me toward the bathroom. "When you're dressed, come downstairs and have something to eat. Gran has an early birthday present for you."

"Birthday? Unless she's planning a world cruise or something to give me a break from her spell classes, I don't want to know."

My mother picked up my duvet and fluffed it, giving me her *you know better than to question Gran* expression. The look was so dead-on it was almost comical.

I snorted. "Last year her big surprise was telling me my aura was bleeding. Maybe this year she'll tell me the stars have aligned and I'm destined to be Miss New York."

She folded the downy coverlet and draped it over my footboard, surveying the rest of my messy room with a small frown. "Get moving, smarty pants. Ten minutes," she instructed tapping her wrist.

Mom closed the door behind her, and I stretched, one last yawn giving up the ghost on my last vestige of sleep. Gran was up to something. *My birthday? I didn't think so.*

Eighteen. It didn't seem possible, but there it was looming right along with the college dorm shopping I had yet to start. To the casual observer, my future seemed bright. Except for the little hiccup of having two friends die and another ostensibly trapped in a purgatorial no man's land, I had a lot going for me.

In spite of my heavy grief, I managed to earn a decent scholarship to a good school…and of course, there was Hunter.

A derisive snort left my mouth. Defying evil and setting old wrongs to right while nearly dying in the process makes for quite a bonding experience, either you end up marrow deep in love, or psychotic. Considering the residual nightmares that played behind my lids each time I closed my eyes and my self-imposed seclusion, crazy was still on the table. Mom was right. Holed up in here, I was half way to being Miss Havisham from Dickens's *Great Expectations*.

I stripped and turned on the shower, stepping into the spray, trying not to think about my mother's ten minute mark. Not that she would hold me to it, but Gran would. Something was up for her to be here on a weekday afternoon, birthday gift or not. Then again, Gran had reasons for everything she did.

I washed my long, dark hair, giving my curly locks an extra shot of conditioner in the lather, rinse, and repeat. Summer was no one's friend when it came to frizz. Finishing up, I slicked a quick layer of baby oil gel over my wet skin before reaching for a towel.

I avoided the sink as much as possible these days, choosing instead to brush my teeth in the shower. Most of my friends thought it weird or gross, but they never had visions of blood pouring from their bathroom tap.

After wrapping my hair in a towel, I shrugged on a three-quarter sports bra and a pair of terrycloth shorts before wiping a hand through the steam gathered on my mirror. Condensation dripped in small rivulets down the glass. I peered at myself, running my fingers over my high cheekbones in the streaky reflection. My face was thinner, but with all the sleep I'd forced on myself lately, at least my dark circles were gone.

I took my makeup bag from the drawer but put it to the side. It was just lunch with Gran, so no need to primp. I'd save the effort for later and towel dried my hair instead, smiling in

anticipation of Hunter's face when he saw me waiting at the end of the gateway.

Dropping the damp towel on the vanity, I lifted my head and pushed the tangled mess from my eyes. A wide toothed comb made fast work of the snarls in my hair as I decided what to do next. I wound my rapidly curling hair and held it with one hand while I searched for my clip.

A tinkle of wind chimes jerked my attention from my narcissism. I had one hand on my head holding my hair and the other flat against the wide midriff band on my top. My stomach flip-flopped because I knew the sound didn't belong in my bathroom. I pushed the door open and checked my bedroom windows hoping for my own neat, little box of truth. Nope. Both windows were shut tightly and the telltale hum from the central air the only discernable sound.

My hands shook and my stomach clenched against the familiar spike in adrenaline. I pressed my lips together. *Collateral damage? Try post-traumatic stress disorder for the rest of my life...*

Annoyed, I let out a rough exhale through my teeth, dismissing the sound as imagined and turned back to the task of taming my hair.

The wind chimes tinkled again, only this time the sound was accompanied by the scent of smoke. Not a fire and brimstone stench, but a pleasant campfire aroma thick with a sense of peace and woodland solitude. I closed my eyes, ignoring what I knew was not a hallucination.

Whispers called my name, the voices as subtle as a summer breeze.

Oh God...

From the visions that hit months ago, I knew God had nothing to do with it, and I cringed. The lilt from the chimes became frenetic, their pitch increasing in volume and speed. The air around me whipped and blew in a torrent. I covered my ears, my hair dropping to my back as my shoulder muscles

bunched against the blasts sending my curls flying around my face, the still wet ends stinging my cheeks.

My back was to the mirror, and I knew whatever or whoever caused this used the reflective glass as its portal.

"Enough! You've got my attention, now what do you want?" I shouted, my voice lost to the squall.

The wind stopped and the chimes resumed their fairylike serenade. Whoever or whatever heard me despite its tantrum in a tempest. I turned, swallowing hard against my rising fear.

I thought about Gran. She heeded the cosmos, acknowledging the supernatural played by a different set of rules, yet never discounted her own power and strength of will. I was from the same unbroken line, and the universe needed to remember that as much as I did.

"Rowen..."

I exhaled the breath caught in my throat.

"Look at me, child..."

I opened my eyes to find a pale blue pair staring back at me from the mirror. My stomach clenched again, but at least I didn't flinch. I refused to allow myself to be an otherworldly pawn...again.

The eyes were clear but the face obscured, as if peering through smoke or fog. Wisps blurred most of the features, yet I caught a glimpse of steel gray hair poking out from beneath soot-smudged white lace giving the impression my visitor was female. Her eyes crinkled and I knew they did so in an acknowledged smile.

"It is time..."

Layered whispers formed the words and the woman in the mirror turned, her hand beckoning me from the glass, but the vision went dark before I could respond. Different set of rules, remember?

Outside, my mother's footsteps took the stairs two at a time, and I heard Gran's voice yelling after her from the kitchen.

"Rowen! Are you all right?" She shoved my bedroom door open and found me standing with my hands clutched over my stomach. She sniffed the air, her eyes scanning me completely before shifting to the mirror. "What happened?"

"I...I don't know exactly. I think it was a spirit of some kind."

She stepped in front of me, holding her hand over the mirror. Her gaze narrowing as her fingers closed into her palm.

"Do you smell that?"

I nodded. "There was smoke in the vision."

Mom frowned. "Downstairs. Now."

I swallowed. It was clear Mom wanted Gran to weigh in on what she sensed from the glass and a feeling of foreboding crawled over my chest.

Chapter 2

Gran scrutinized me, reaching out to push my hair behind my ears. "Tell me exactly what you saw."

I knew her touch held a dual purpose. She smoothed my fears but at the same time tried to get a bead on whom or what came through. I told her everything, leaving nothing to chance. Sins of omission were never a good idea when dealing with the supernatural, especially with entities strong enough to punch a hole between worlds.

"The spirit beckoned you, and that's all?"

I nodded, knowing Gran didn't need me to elaborate. She was simply mulling over the facts, weighing possibilities and probabilities.

She glanced at my mother and then at the calendar on the wall. "Well, Litha is this weekend, but I can't see how that would help manipulate the veil. It's not that kind of a sabbat."

"Litha? I don't know who is worse, you or Mom. Can't you just say the summer solstice like everyone else?"

Gran eyed me but didn't reply. I had slowly accepted my place as the newest addition to our family's practitioners of the white arts, but right now I didn't need another reminder. The visions were enough.

"Whoever came through didn't give us much to go on." Gran made a face. "I hate it when they're cryptic." She blew out a breath, her complaint more for herself than me or Mom. She

eyed me again. "This spirit, did she try to reach through the glass or touch you?"

I shook my head.

Chewing the side of her cheek, Gran repeatedly unfolded and refolded her paper napkin. In her quick, clipped movements I could see the likelihoods examined and discarded. She stopped, lifting her preoccupied gaze from the table. "The spirit called you by name, and all she said was 'it is time'...and you're sure there was no underlying sense of menace?"

I paused to run the scene through my head again. "Yes. I'm sure."

She picked up her iced tea and took a sip. "Perhaps this was nothing more than an awakening. It certainly sounds like one, yet..." She didn't finish the sentence. Instead she glanced at my mother.

"An awakening?" I echoed, bringing Gran back to the point.

I shifted in my seat, fidgeting with my placemat, uncomfortable with the fact Gran had let her words trail off. The woman was nothing if not definitive, and her passing hesitation left me uneasy.

She nodded. "A metaphysical *welcome to the club* courtesy of a long line of charmed ancestors."

"You're kidding."

A smirk pushed one side of Gran's mouth up. "Ask your mother." That smirk turned full on grin and Gran lifted her chin toward my mother's not so happy expression.

I couldn't help it, I laughed too. Mom, on the other hand, clearly didn't appreciate our shared humor and pursed her lips, shooting Gran a dirty look.

"Your mother fell out of bed when your great-great-grandmother Ivy dropped by unexpectedly for an early morning chat."

My mother's lips parted, her eyebrows knotted into a dubious frown. "Morning chat? It was three a.m., and I was fast asleep. What did you think would happen? The woman hovered

over me like some kind of reaper!" A piqued grumble left her mouth and she rubbed her bare arms. "You could have warned me, you know. I was only sixteen."

With a laugh Gran reached over and patted my mother's forearm. "What, and miss the awed panic on your face the next morning?"

"Anne Dederick Ekert, you really are an evil, old woman."

Gran burst out laughing, giving my mother's arm a decisive squeeze. "And where would we be if I weren't? White witches hardly ever get to play in the dark as much as we have this year, and it certainly keeps things interesting." She turned, her pointed gaze finding me still fidgeting. "Which brings us back to you."

"Me?"

She nodded, leaning over to reach into an oversized bag on the floor beside her chair. A soft thud followed an aged volume landing in front of her on the kitchen table. Our family bible.

"Like any reflective surface, mirrors are a portal."

Huh? Mirrors? I blinked at Gran's seemingly random statement, trying not to look as confused as I felt. "So you've said."

Her raised eyebrow was in direct correlation to my tone, and the single glance sobered my sarcasm.

"Of course, I've said it, and it's something you've heard many times, though never paid much heed to until now. You mentioned something wispy, either smoke or fog obscuring the face in the mirror."

I nodded, not wanting to venture another verbal wrist slap.

"Did you know fire can also be used as a portal? Water vapor is too delicate to hold a vision, but smoke and flame are a different story. Only the most accomplished of us master the art of fire. In fact, it's how the pious first got the idea to burn witches at the stake."

Pressure on my knee courtesy of my mother's slender fingers told me to stop fidgeting, but I couldn't help it. I wanted

to scream for Gran to land her damn plane already and get to the point. When it came to unwelcome visions, my track record proved they came in multiples and that meant another loomed somewhere in my near future.

"Historically, the hearth was the center of every home," she continued. "Fire was used for everything—warmth, cooking, cleaning—making the use of flame the least suspicious way to apply the art of summoning."

My ears perked up. Maybe we were getting somewhere after all. "Summoning? I thought fire was used primarily for scrying?"

I earned myself a closed lipped smile of approval. "Very good, Rowen. Certain gifted practitioners found the dancing flames could coax the sight and induce trances, thus giving them power over what they searched for in the physical world, as well as in the ethereal. Constant practice fed their skill, ultimately leading to the ability to breach worlds. It's a rare talent."

"So what has this got to do with me?"

With an eager expression on her face, Gran raised one finger. "This is what it has to do with you." She reached into her bag then withdrew her hand. In her palm was a tiny silver dagger attached to a black chord embroidered with silver thread, its beveled blade the length of my pinky finger.

I had to laugh. The pendulum looked like a prop right out of the *Harry Potter* series. "Professor McGonagall, unless that blade magically grows another foot, it's not going to afford much protection in the dark forest."

"Rowen!" My mother's soft admonishment left me mumbling an apology. Gran was never random, and guilt washed over me at being my usual bratty self.

Gran winked at my mother and then let the pendulum's blade drop from her lifted fingers. Its silvered edge suspended just above the bible. "Open the cover to the inside flyleaf," she instructed.

Sparing a glance for my mother, I turned the fragile book around to face me and carefully lifted the cover. Inside were sheets of vellum, hand stitched into the book's spine.

Familiae nostrae sanguinem. I sounded out the words. "That sounds like Latin." I recognized two words: family and blood.

Gran nodded. "The title is a broad reference to our maternal bloodline yet orchestrated so as not to arouse suspicion. Back in the day, a family such as ours needed to be beyond reproach. This record could have damned our line to dangle from the end of a rope or bound wrist and ankle to a pyre. It lists every powerful female in our family straight up to your mother and me."

She tapped the page, flashing a proud smile. "I brought this today because after this past year, I think we can safely add your name to the list."

I snorted. "Facing unseen evil should guarantee a fast pass to the head of the line."

Mom glanced at Gran and the two shared a moment before my mother's eyes found mine. "Everyone on that list had to face some sort of challenge, Rowen. Whether it was conquering prejudice or some supernatural menace. In many instances both proved to be just as insidious and evil. Besides skill, it's a question of courage and resolve that gets your name in the book."

Gran nodded. "Your mother is right, and yes, you've more than demonstrated those qualities despite your teenage bullishness, but you must remember the white arts will not work for you without a humble heart and pure objective. You must keep that covenant, always." She covered my hand with hers. "Congratulations, sweetheart, you're the newest hope of our future and possibly most important link to our past this family has seen in many generations."

Giving my hand one more pat, she turned her attention to the book. "This list dates to our family's origins in the sixteenth century. Of course, this isn't the original bible. The first one

came from Germany, migrating with our ancestors to the New World early in the eighteenth century. The names have been transcribed over the centuries, with more vellum sewed in as needed. This particular bible dates to the late 1800s." A single arthritic finger caressed the spine. "Now, let's see which witch decided to pay you a visit this morning."

She dangled the pendulum over the thin pages, mindful of how fragile and old their condition. The blade swung in a circular motion, 'round and 'round, picking up speed as she moved it slowly down the first page. The names registered in my head as Gran went through the list, but the varied ancestries left me with more questions than answers.

"The names are mixed."

Mom moved to Gran's side so she could see as well, her eyes scanning the looping script. "What do you mean? The dates are in perfect order."

I shook my head, the tip of my index finger tapping the edge of the list. "I don't mean the names are out of order. I'm referring to the nationalities represented; I knew we were German and Dutch, but this says English, Irish, and even a little Native American." Impressed, I raised a teasing eyebrow. "Kind of gives us a mixed bag of tricks, huh?"

Mom laughed. "I suppose so."

"Our ancestors were clever about not staying in one place long enough for anyone to accuse them of witchcraft. In fact, they avoided the hysteria like the plague. As bad as it was here in the late 1600s, it was worse in Europe," Gran added.

"But our family has been in Sleepy Hollow for generations. There are Ekerts buried in the Old Dutch cemetery and those grave markers have got to be two hundred years old at least."

The dangling blade hanging from Gran's hand stopped short, its sharp edges quivering over a single name. Of its own volition, the silver tip jerked downward, sinking point first into the fragile vellum.

Gran's lips curved into a knowing smile. "You're right, Rowen, and the reason we've been able to make our home here and not been too bothered by the pious populace lies with one woman." Nimble fingers underscored the impaled name and Gran tapped the vellum for me to read the one word written in faded black ink.

When I looked up, both she and my mother chuckled at the lingering doubt on my face.

"Hulda? As in the Witch of Sleepy Hollow? The same woman the Friends of the Old Dutch Church have listed on their tour?"

The two nodded in unison.

"She's real?"

"Oh, she's very real." Gran shrugged. "Her story is not well known, even to people who live in Sleepy Hollow. Hulda died on Battle Hill, leading a group of British redcoats away from a contingent of American militia. The exact year is a little hazy, but historians have the date narrowed to somewhere between 1777 and 1780."

"I thought Battle Hill occurred in White Plains, not Sleepy Hollow."

"At that time, the Hudson Valley was rampant with combat. The Battle of White Plains is the most famous because Washington lost the city to the British. Small skirmishes were commonplace, especially with each side raiding the other."

I grinned. "Cowboys and skinners, right? Cowboys being the redcoats who helped themselves to our cattle and skinners being the Americans who stole back what they took."

"Very good, Rowen. At least they taught you something at that high school."

I rolled my eyes. "Gee, thanks, Mom."

Gran waved us both off. "Hulda was a sharpshooter, and history tells how she picked off a good many redcoats before leading them on a wild goose chase. Of course, the British commander at the time wouldn't accept a woman singe-

handedly menacing his troops, so he made it his business to put an end to it and her."

She turned to the back of the bible, drawing out what looked to be an old newspaper editorial, and from the tight margins and close type, the article was nineteenth century if a day.

"This is a clipping from 1897, shortly after our latest bible was transcribed. All across the continental U.S., papers ran stories celebrating our country's history. Since Sleepy Hollow was a hot bed at the time of the revolution, one New York paper decided to run stories on the unsung heroes of the war for independence."

The edges were yellowed and creased, and Gran held the paper out to me with care. My eyes skimmed the document, squinting against the small, aged type. It told Hulda's story and then some.

"This stone belonged to Hulda." Gran lifted one hand, modeling the large moonstone on her left index finger. Like the emerald on her other hand, the ornate stone was one of her trademarks. "I'm not entirely sure how our family kept possession of the gem considering its value and the witch's history, but it has been passed from generation to generation as far back as anyone can remember."

Awe and curiosity must have warred on my face, because the next thing I knew Gran slid the silver clawed setting from her finger and held the ring out to me. "The heirloom will go to your mother first, but there's no harm in letting you try it on."

With a nod from my mom, I put the clipping down and took the ring from Gran's hand and held it up to the light. The ornate stone winked in the afternoon sun and imagination or not, I swear one of the silver claws caressed the stone's smooth surface.

"That's funny, for a second it looked like..." My sight blurred and indistinct images swam in front of my eyes. I dropped the ring, the metallic clink thick and distant in my ears as its heavy setting clattered to the kitchen table.

Heat sluiced up my arms and chest and sweat formed between my breasts. A loud buzzing deafened my ears, and I cried out, my hands covering either side of my head.

"Rowen!"

I knew my mother was up in a flash, but Gran's voice was what came through. "Sea salt and water! Now!"

The buzzing stopped and I was no longer in the kitchen. My mother and grandmother barely shadows on the periphery of my mind.

My sight cleared and I blinked against the rain pelting my face. A light wind blew curls of smoke into the raw chilled air, the white wisps rising from chimneys dotting the far landscape. Dark clouds obscured any trace of sun, and I shivered. This place was devoid of warmth, and my stomach clenched, knowing the bleak feeling came from more than just the foul weather.

Dirty water pooled on either side of the pitted, muddy road where I stood, each wind gust giving rise to the stench of barnyards and chamber pots. My head jerked sideways, pulled by the sound of shouting from a single rough cottage set back from the thoroughfare.

A woman stumbled backward out the cottage threshold, her coarse clothing sullied and torn and her fichu and cap askew on her head and shoulders as though manhandled.

"Please! NO!" she begged, slipping in the uneven sludge and falling to her knees.

A large man in a sweat stained shirt and dark breeches loomed inside the doorway. His ruddy face pinched in anger and his long hair fell in strands on either side of his face, free of the ribbon still tied at the nape of his neck.

"Begone, witch! Murderer! You killed my brother! Away w'ye!"

On her knees, the woman clasped her hands beseeching, "Please, Lars…I'm innocent, I pray!"

His eyes flew wide and his fists clenched at his side. "Pray?" He spat on the stone step. "Satan's whore! Spin yer lies elsewhere!" He yanked a small bundle from the frightened servant cowering at his side and flung the parcel into the mud. "Take yer yarbs and yer devil's tools

w'ye and go before I'm want of care and call the Dominee to have ye burnt!"

"Mama! NO!" A young girl slipped beneath the man's arm, her tearstained face puffy as she reached for the woman in the mud, her abject fear and sorrow the antithesis to the happy daisy-chain gracing her fair head "Mama! Please!"

"For the love of God, child! Avert yer eyes lest ye be lost, too! Wife, take her!" He shoved the wailing child behind him into the house, pausing only to rip the moonstone pendant from her small throat.

"No! Genève! Please, Lars! She's my child! Please... I beg of you..." The woman's choked sobs rose as she sunk farther into the mud.

My heart clenched and the pain in my chest made it hard to breathe. The woman's heart was breaking and with each ragged gasp, every ounce of her despair was mine as well.

"Get thyself up and take yer darkness from my door. Yer love for the child spared ye the pyre, but my brother's child has suffered enough from yer evil!" He hurled the necklace at her suppliant figure, one single daisy caught in the silver clasp. The pendant's weight landed in the muck with a muted plop. "And keep yer devil's talisman! Genève will bide a good Christian life even if it's at the mercy of my fist!"

"Lars!"

"Begone!"

The door slammed and the woman fell prostrate, her hands clawing the mud in her despair, her cries lost to the rain.

Chapter 3

I sucked in a breath. Freezing water pulled me from the vision, its icy fingers soaking me from head to toe and everywhere in between. Sputtering, I pushed my drenched hair from my face with a ragged pant.

"Rowen!" My mother's voice was two octaves higher than usual, her panic clear even as she wrapped a towel around my shoulders.

"I'm f-f-fine," I stuttered, blinking against the sting from the salt running into my eyes from my wet hair.

Gran held a cup to my lips. "Drink, sweetheart. It's hot tea."

I took a sip, choking on the bitter taste and shoved her hand away.

"Drink it, Rowen. It's dandelion root with clove. It will settle whatever it was you saw." She wrapped my fingers around the cup's porcelain handle.

I shivered involuntarily and took the cup from her hand only to pass it straight to my mother. "I don't need some weird brew to help me remember. The visions take care of that on their own when they blister my brain."

Despite Gran's objections, Mom walked to the sink and poured the tea down the drain. Gripping the edge of the stainless steel, she looked across her shoulder at my grandmother. "Did you know something would happen today? Is that why you brought the family bible and this new tisane?" She gestured toward the sink.

Gran shook her head, taking her seat again. "I wish I could say I did, but I'm as surprised as you." She lifted her hand and then let it drop to the table. "I brought the new recipe for you to try for the shop."

I snorted beneath the towel as I dried my now crunchy hair. "Not with that foul taste. Instead of brewing something to help me remember, why can't you two brew something to help me forget? And what's with the iced salt-water challenge? If I wanted a bucket dumped on my head, I would've done so for ALS."

"You know sea salt neutralizes spells. The cold water was to shock you out of your trance," Mom answered from the sink. "I grabbed the gallon pitcher from the fridge and dumped the salt in."

I shivered and then sneezed, wiping my nose and mouth on the end of the damp terrycloth. "I wasn't caught in a spell. It was just a vision." Large undissolved salt crystals clung to my hair like chunky dandruff and I sighed, wishing I had stayed in bed. "You'd think by now they wouldn't catch me so off guard."

"Bullshit."

I lifted the edge of my towel and peered at my grandmother. Expletives were not part of her usual vocabulary, however acerbic her tone. I blinked at her sharp expression and then shifted my gaze to the bible still lying on the table. "Is there a woman named Genève listed anywhere in that book?"

Gran slid her ring along the tablecloth and slipped it onto her finger. She clasped both hands together linking her fingers so both rings touched. "Could be," she replied shrewdly.

At her calculating tone, I shoved the towel onto my shoulders. "Just now, the woman I saw had a pendant that looked like very much like that..." I gestured toward the moonstone on her left index finger.

"What else did you see? Hear?"

My eyes focused on nothing. I pressed my lips together and inhaled through my nose, letting the pieces flood back. "It was heartbreaking…"

I told them everything. As I recounted the vision, the same desperation coursed through my body again, each word laced with vinegar as I described what I saw. Once done, exhaustion hit, and I found my fingers clenched on the table.

My mother pulled a chair beside me and sat, slipping her arm around my shoulders. I leaned against her, not caring how wet I was or if I ruined her blouse. "He took her daughter, Mom. The poor girl begged but he was so hell-bent and angry, he shoved her aside."

The pained look on my mother's face matched my own and she gathered me into a hug, squeezed my shoulders and got up again to grab another towel. "His name was Lars Staats, and that's not all he took."

With a loud derisive sniff she dropped a dry terrycloth to the floor, using her foot to mop up what was left of the water. Her motions were clipped, almost annoyed. "Hulda's family was part of the first palatine immigration from Germany. They worked like animals, enduring deprivation and sickness to pay off their passage and earn the right to land promised them by the English crown."

"So, the house and the farm I saw were hers, not his?"

She nodded, squatting to pick up the wet towel. "Witchcraft was a convenient felony employed by people of the time to exact revenge or cheat their neighbors without fear of penalty." She tossed the towel into the sink with a damp splat. "Lars threw Hulda out because the court awarded the land and house to her, not him, when her husband died."

"So, she just left her daughter? What kind of a mother does that?" I couldn't wrap my head around the thought. What if my own mother abandoned me after my dad died?

Gran leaned forward in her chair and pushed a wet strand from my cheek to behind my ear. "Rowen, you can't judge the

past by twenty-first century standards. Women had no real rights, and whatever allowances the law afforded them came to a palpable end when their husbands died. In this situation the poor woman had no choice, especially with a threat of witchcraft hanging over her head."

"Still…"

She shook her head. "No, still. If Hulda's brother-in-law officially charged her with witchcraft, not only would she have lost everything, but her daughter would have been shunned. Her lands would have been confiscated and her daughter orphaned with no future prospects the minute the gavel came down with a guilty verdict."

"What about the civil case she won? Wouldn't the judge have to consider possible grounds for a false accusation?"

Mom shook her head. "Like I mentioned before, witchcraft was a felony charge and as such trials required the governor to preside. William Tryon, the British authority at the time was too busy menacing innocent civilians to be bothered with provincial court cases, especially if they did nothing to sustain his thirst for colonial blood. He's the same bastard who sent his goons into Sleepy Hollow and the surrounding area to burn houses with women and children still inside.

"One lone woman accused of witchcraft was so far below his notice, Hulda would have died in prison awaiting trial, and Genève would still have ended up a pariah. She was caught in a web binding her as tightly as any hangman's noose. This was the only way out, the only way she could save her daughter and give her any chance for a legacy." My mother's voice softened, and she lifted her hand to my cheek. "You ask who would do that. Anyone who loved their child in the eighteenth century, that's who."

I wiped the sudden wetness from my eyes, and it wasn't from the salt water. "Now I really need you to brew something to help me forget."

Gran patted my hand. "Geneve's name is in the bible, albeit not until much later, but that's a story in itself for another time. My guess is she was forbidden to speak of her mother, let alone contact her, though she did manage to keep the bible which was a feat in itself, considering her circumstances."

She winked and pushed up from her chair. I knew Gran wasn't telling me everything, but then again when did she ever tip her hand?

Mom placed a cup of hot green tea with lemon in front of me along with a thick white envelope.

"What's this?" I asked, fingering the heavy stock.

"You asked for something to help you forget. I think this is just the ticket."

I turned the envelope over, but there was nothing on the other side except my name in gold calligraphy.

"Open it," she encouraged.

I wiggled the tip of my index finger into the space between the flap and its seal and ripped open the top. Inside was a single handwritten card.

"Jenny Beamer is inviting me for a weekend at her family's house on Cooper Lake." As my eyes scanned the gilt letters, I frowned. "Why in the hell would she invite me of all people? She hates me."

My mother made a face. "She doesn't hate you. I told you she'd eventually come around. Well?" She spread her hands toward the torn wrapper and the invitation in my hand. "It looks like she's had time to think and wants to move on. Britt said Hunter got one, too. It seems she wants this weekend to give everyone closure after what happened."

I slid the card back into its matching shell. "Not everyone." I thought my words were too soft to hear, but my mother's antennae were up and she wasn't about to let it go.

"Rowen, there's no postmark on that letter. Jenny dropped it by herself. She's invited everyone so you can finally put what happened behind you once and for all. No trash talk, no

innuendo to endure from the masses, just the kids who were there that night. She said she's planning a lot of fun for the group including a bonfire and rafting trip. I think you should go. It will do you good. Give you a clean slate before you start your freshman year at Binghamton."

I handed her the card. "I don't know, Mom. I have to think about it. With this latest crop of visions maybe it's better for me to stay close to home. What if I need you or Gran?"

Pfft. She waved me off. "Nonsense. You need this, Rowen, if only to finally say goodbye and move on. I know you think you've already done that, but you haven't. Not really. Your actions say otherwise."

I turned to my grandmother who was busy perusing the bible's lists on the counter next to her bag. "What do you think, Gran?"

"Hmmmm?"

My mouth fell open. She actually wasn't listening.

"Gran?" I prompted again, this time my tone a tad more forceful.

"What? Oh, I'm sorry, sweetheart. I was just thinking..." Her words drifted off and her eyes glanced back to the open pages in front of her. She lifted her hand and touched the vellum once, the movement uncharacteristically humble before she closed the bible with a muffled thud. She straightened, but still rested one hand on the bible even as her eyes found mine. "Yes. Your mother's right. You need to go. It'll do more good than you know."

Gran's distracted answer left me with an uncomfortable feeling.

Do more good for whom?

After what happened at home, I needed to get out of the house. I changed my sports top and terry shorts, trading them for a sleeveless floral and lace midriff and a pair of denim shorts. I shoved my feet into a pair of flip-flops and grabbed my sunglasses and Vera Bradley lanyard, slipping the pretty cloth case around my neck. Everything I needed was inside…money, phone, driver's license…not that I planned to drive anywhere. I needed to walk. *And think.*

I slipped out the front door, ignoring my mother and grandmother still in the kitchen. The sun was high and the temperature matched it degree for degree. The wind off the Hudson was warm, but at least the air wasn't stagnant. Loose tendrils freed themselves from the bun still tight on my head, but I didn't care. I had no plans other than a large iced raspberry coffee with milk and a walk to Patriot's Park.

For some reason the park was my go to place to think. It was situated off U.S. 9 or Albany Post Road as it was known since before the American Revolution. I often wondered what tales it could tell from everything it had witnessed over the centuries.

I walked up Beekman Avenue, stopping at the bakery for my coffee. Contrary to what the T.V. show *Sleepy Hollow* says in its dialogue, the real village of Sleepy Hollow does not have a Starbucks on every corner, nor does it have a population of 144,000. At the last census, we had 9,944 people in the village. But that's Hollywood, go figure. Most of my friends and I watch the show and like it, but we can't help but laugh every time the show's writers get it wrong.

"Hey, Rowen…what can I get you today? The usual?"

I smiled at Mrs. King, the bakery's owner. "Yup, but iced. It's too hot for anything else."

She smiled, reaching for a large cup with one hand and the raspberry syrup with the other. "Three pumps and low-fat milk, right?"

"You got it."

In went a large scoop of ice and she did her thing, clipping on the lid before giving the clear plastic a few good swirls. She handed the coffee to me across the counter along with a napkin and a tall straw. "Anything else, hon?"

I shook my head, handing her three dollars. "Not today, thanks."

"All righty, then. Stay cool," she replied before moving to her next customer.

I left the bakery and took the back roads through town, wanting to avoid walking past the high school. The houses along my route were modest, with attractive porches, clean-swept walks and carefully cared for gardens. Older residents, especially the townies whose families had lived here forever, took special pride in keeping their homes pristine. Flowers bloomed along grassy borders and along the curbs, the sidewalks darkened, wet from sprinkler systems and hand watering. I passed Mrs. Devescovi's place, waving to her in her apron and sunhat as she tended her tomato vines.

At the end of the block, I turned up College Avenue and entered the park through two stone pillars at the back entrance. I walked up the path winding its way through the grass and found my favorite bench.

The park was empty on account of the heat, but the noise and traffic from the shops along U.S. 9 filtered into the quietude as cars pulled in and out of parking spaces along the main road.

I set my coffee beside me on the bench, leaning my head back and lifting my face to the sun.

"I thought I would find you here."

I raised my hand to shield my eyes and looked at my best friend. "Hey."

"Hey? That's all you have to say after going M.I.A on me and everyone else but Hunter?"

"Chloe..."

She lifted her hand to stop me. "No, Ro... You've bailed on me one too many times this year and I'm not going to put up with it anymore." She reached into her back pocket and pulled out a thick white envelope, the same as the one I left on my kitchen table. "I stopped at your house. I know you got one too, so don't bother denying it."

"I wasn't going to deny it. I'm just not sure I want to go."

She folded the invitation and stuck it back in her pocket. "Well, at least it's not the adamant refusal I expected." She moved my iced coffee to the ground and wiped the condensation from the bench before sitting with a tired huff.

Neither of us said another word and the peace I hoped to find vanished when she finally exhaled a loud sigh.

"Out with it, Chlo. I know you too well to think you showed up here just because. You hate the sun."

She smoothed both cheeks with her hands as though wiping away the new freckles that had formed in the last couple of minutes. It was her trademark move when she had something eating at her.

"I used to think that, too," she said half behind her fingers.

"Think what? That you hate the sun or that I know you too well?"

My question was rhetorical and we both knew it. I was losing patience as well as my chance to think in peace, and I sighed just as loudly as she did. "Look, frowning at me is going to give you more wrinkles than the sun ever will. Spit it out already."

"What did I do to make you pull away from me as a friend?"

I gaped at her.

"Don't look at me like that. I know we all grieve in our own way, but *Jesus*, Rowen! You shut me out completely. You, me, and Talia...we were a team. When she died it nearly killed me

as well, but you went into your own little hole and had a pity party by yourself. The only person you bothered with was Hunter."

I opened my mouth to reply, but she cut me off.

"I know you two are *in love*..." She bent her fingers into bunny ears stressing the mocking tone to her words. "But didn't it cross your mind that I might have needed you, too? That I needed someone to cry with?"

I had no answer and she waved her hand in the air as though letting me off the hook. "I know there was more to what happened that night than what everyone thinks. I kept waiting for you to tell me, share it with me, but you never did."

"Chloe...I..."

She stopped me again. "Don't, Ro. It's over and I just want to put it behind me and move on." She turned to face me on the bench. "I think it would be good for us...all of us...to take Jenny up on her offer. After the horrible way she treated us throughout high school, if she wants to foot the bill for a weekend away, then great. She owes us."

I gave her a look. "Owes us?"

She shrugged. "Well, owes you anyway. I have no problem letting her pay."

I leaned down and picked up my melted iced coffee, holding the wet cup on my lap along with my gaze. "She's paid plenty, Chloe. Don't you think?"

I didn't look up, but her sigh told me she agreed.

"I suppose so, but Tyler was her problem from the beginning. She's the one who cheated on him, though they looked joined at the hip during the cemetery party. Then Ty got all weird. Who knows what kind of kinky stuff the two of them were into that lead to her attack."

Mouth open, I turned. "Chloe Abigail Martin, you take that back! The girl was beaten and raped. I don't care if they were into swinging from the rafters, no one deserves that."

Chloe's face was just as stunned. "Rowen! That's not what I meant! I mean she probably never thought Tyler capable of doing anything of the sort, regardless of how drunk he got. I mean, she knew him better than anyone, yet he still lost control."

I looked away and Chloe put her hand on my arm. "They'll catch him. It's just going to take time," she murmured.

I shook my head. "No, they won't."

She pulled my shoulder around forcing me to look at her. "You say that as though you already know. Have you heard anything? Is he dead?"

I shook my head again. "Let's just say he's not dead, but he's also no longer alive."

She let go of my shoulder and slumped back. "More Rowen Corbett double talk."

"Chloe, you don't understand. No one does, really. Sometimes, not even me."

"And that's supposed to mean what?" Her eyes sought mine, only this time her expression was angry, not frustrated or tired. "You know what, forget it. You're right. I never understood you or your family's weird ways and I don't want to. I want to put this all behind me. We start college soon enough and I intend to enjoy myself in the interim, and if that means a free vacation courtesy of Jenny, then what the hell. It'll be my kick off to summer."

"Do you really want to know what happened that night? Because if you do, I'll tell you. Not that you'd believe me."

Her lips pressed together in a thin line. I was pissing her off with every word that came out of my mouth, but too much had happened. Maybe now that Talia was gone, it left too big a hole to fill. Out of the three of us, Chloe was the hothead, Talia the drama queen, and me...I was the one who did her best to be inconspicuous. I didn't know what to do now. Whether we wanted to admit it or not, life had changed for all of us, but regardless, I wasn't willing to lose another friend.

"You're right, Chloe. I've been a terrible friend. You were there for me and I wasn't there enough for you. I wrapped myself in school work and Hunter and shut everyone else out. Hanging out with you and Benny was too much of a reminder. Hunter never questioned me. He just let me be whatever it was I needed to be…crazy, crying, angry, or heartbroken. I put him through the emotional ringer. So much that he had to get away, too. I know he told everyone he was visiting his father, but that was only half the story. Truth is, he needed a break from me."

She reached out her hand and ran a knuckle down my cheek. "You're getting sunburned."

I laughed. It was Chlo's way of saying, *"I already know all this, you big jerk, but it's nice to hear you admit it."* She took my hand and stood, pulling me up with her. "Come on, let's get out of this open air furnace. I'll let you buy me lunch and then we can plan our outfits for this weekend."

I tilted my head blinking away the wetness in my eyes, suddenly glad I wore my sunglasses. "I guess I don't have a choice, huh?"

She linked her arm in mine and steered me toward the path leading to the sidewalks along U.S. 9. "Nope, we're all going. You and Hunter, me and Benny, Jenny, Constance, Eric…even Hannah is coming."

I stopped in my tracks, jerking her arm back. "Hannah? As in Talia's sister?"

She nodded. "Yeah. It was a crap shoot. Jenny actually called to ask what I thought about it. Personally, I think it's a great idea. Talia was Hannah's role model and the poor kid still has a year left at Sleepy Hollow High School. She needs closure as well as knowing we're all here for her. I don't have to remind you how mean kids can be, and there's bound to be gossip aplenty." Chloe raised an eyebrow punctuating the truth of her statement.

"You're right," I admitted with a sigh.

A huge smile lit Chloe's face. "Good. Glad that's settled."

I smiled too, feeling more like my old self than I had in a long time. Chloe was a shooting star, exploding one moment then a streak of light the next.

We passed the monument commemorating the capture of Major John Andre, the British spy in cahoots with Benedict Arnold during the American Revolution. The town had it erected over a hundred years ago, marking the spot where three patriot militiamen stopped Andre, thus revealing Benedict's treasonous plot.

Chloe glanced up at the tarnished granite and laughed. "Do you know how much time Benny and I spent here and, in the library, trying to find something new about old Johnny here?"

"Something new?"

She nodded. "Yeah, for that stupid urban legend scavenger hunt Mr. Conniver had us do." She smirked my way. "You remember. It's the same project you and Hunter paired up on when you found out Tyler's ancestor was a lady of loose morals turned pious bigot."

I closed my eyes. "Don't remind me."

Chloe snorted, and I knew it was because the project was so lame, but I didn't want to be reminded because what Hunter and I discovered had more to do with what happened in the cemetery that night than Tyler's ancestors.

"Tell me about it," she went on. "The only thing interesting we found was a theory claiming the three militiamen touted were actually common thieves, skinners lying in wait to steal cattle and whatever else they could get their hands on. The fact they outted a serious plot was a complete coincidence. Funny thing though, no one knows how they happened to be in this very spot that morning. It's a mystery, even to this day."

"I'm sure that's not true. Someone had to know."

She shrugged. "Well, Benny and I couldn't find anything that said they were stationed here or sent here. I think the thievery theory is right and they were freelancing looking to score."

We both looked up at the monument again, but a horn beep from the street grabbed our attention. Benny waved from his new pickup truck, calling us over. Another smile took Chloe's face and she blew him a kiss.

"Looks like you're off the hook for lunch. Benny's buying."

I snorted. "Thanks, but he's your boyfriend. I've got cash and we can go dutch."

"Horsefeathers Pub?" she asked.

I nodded. "Always."

She gestured for Benny to park and then practically skipped toward the sidewalk. I guess we were good or at least well on our way to mended fences. Whatever she needed to say was said, and I was glad.

Maybe this weekend away wasn't such a bad idea.

Chapter 4

The sun sunk low on the horizon as I drove the hour or so to New York's JFK International Airport. After Benny dropped me at home, I took a shower and then spent the rest of the day organizing my room. If only to check up on me, Mom poked her head in sometime around four-thirty. She didn't say a word but was clearly pleased to see my mess disappear without her having to nag.

My conversation with Chloe weighed heavy on my mind, especially when I stopped cleaning to pick out an outfit to wear when I surprised Hunter at the airport. Things between Hunter and me developed fast and furious. He may never have said he needed a break from me, but what I confided to Chloe in the park felt like the truth, nonetheless, and a knot formed in my stomach at the thought.

Being my boyfriend was far from easy on a regular basis. I was difficult and I knew it. Top that with a sprinkling of supernatural chaos and the combination would make anyone a candidate for sainthood. Still, I was glad Hunter was coming home.

Thick traffic caused me to sit bumper to bumper on the Bronx-Whitestone Bridge and most of the Van Wyck Expressway despite being well after rush hour. I clutched the steering wheel trying not to let my anxiety about Hunter run away with my imagination. The last thing I wanted was for him to find me frantic and teary-eyed. He'd had enough of my crazy.

When I flung myself into his arms it was going to be for another reason.

I shifted my train of thought, glancing from the bridge to the skyline beyond the expanse of dark, dirty water. A twilight haze cast a ginger glow over New York and I chuckled to myself. *Sex in the city. More like stifling in the city.*

Manhattan held plenty of diversion, but I was happy to live in a village where everyone knew everyone, unlike my friends who couldn't wait to head into the concrete jungle.

Heeding the signs directing traffic toward specific terminals, I took my cue for JetBlue and pulled into the short-term parking lot, in the used Honda Civic my mother surprised me with after graduation. I loved it despite the fact it needed work and had been in the shop on and off for the past few weeks. Its bright red paint had a few dings and the odometer read fifty thousand miles, but it was mine.

I turned off the car's ignition and grabbed my purse before making my way to the parking garage elevators and the congested streets below.

After all the outfits I'd tried on and discarded, I finally decided on Chloe's white sundress--a woven knit with a fitted, sleeveless bodice. The hemline fell just above mid-thigh, and sexy three-inch t-strap heels completed the look making my legs seem long and lean.

She insisted I borrow them, and her ability to move forward and forgive made me even guiltier about how I treated her while in my grieving funk. I shook off the feeling and decided if she could get past it, so could I. True friends forgive each other as well as themselves.

I smiled to myself thinking about Hunter's fingers and a slow walk across my silky-smooth skin. Meeting him at the airport wasn't the only surprise I had in store tonight.

Hunter's birthday was a month away, and I promised myself the summer before college would be the time to graduate from everything, and I meant in *all* ways.

Despite my fears about Hunter's true reasons for leaving, his absence made me appreciate how much I needed him. Not just as a shoulder to cry on, but how much I wanted him. All of him…his conversation, his humor, his amazing smiles…hell, his physical presence to hold hands, to kiss, and hug. I knew without question I was in love with Hunter Morrissey and there was no room for denial or adolescent backpedaling. The time was right for us to move forward. I hoped.

Pushing my way through the terminal doors, I looked around to get my bearings then stopped to double check the flight's status on the arrivals board. The words next to the LAX flight read landed. He was here.

I got to the baggage area a little out of breath, embarrassed at how my heels clacked against the floor as I ran the whole way. There were four or five limo drivers waiting with placards, and I thought for a moment how cute it would be to have one that read *World's Greatest Boyfriend*. I almost asked one of the drivers if they had an extra card, but it was too late.

He stood at the top of the escalator and I watched as he yanked his carryon onto the moving stairs, his hand fishing in his pocket for something. The next second my own phone buzzed. I glanced down at the screen in my hand to see his name in digital letters as the incoming call.

"Hello?" I answered.

"Hey, I just landed. Man was it a long flight. I'm starving."

"Poor baby, you must be exhausted. Do you want me to whip up something special for when you get home?" It was all I could do not to laugh.

"Nah, I'll grab something here before I hop in a cab. My mother was supposed to pick me up, but one of her patients went into labor."

I couldn't believe he hadn't spotted me yet, and I bit the inside of my cheek. "Well, she is a midwife. That tends to happen."

"I guess. Listen, I'm heading toward baggage claim, I'll call you when I get closer to…" His words trailed off and then I heard "holy crap."

He stepped off the escalator, phone still in hand and a full-on gorgeous smile on his lips. Without so much as a word he walked toward me, dropped his bag and gathering me into his arms. His mouth found mine, hungry and demanding.

"God, I missed you," he murmured breaking our kiss, but he didn't back away. Instead, he held me against his chest pressing his lips to my temple.

All my misgivings melted away and I tightened my arms around his waist. He was home and he was mine.

"Get a room!"

We jerked apart as though someone threw water on us, and then we both dissolved into laughter. Neither of us knew who said it, but Hunter hugged me again, giving me one last squeeze before he picked up his bag.

"I'm parked across the street."

"Your mom's minivan?"

I shook my head. "Nope. *My* car."

He grinned, sliding his free arm around my shoulders. "You're just full of surprises tonight."

I met his smile with a secret one of my own. He had no idea.

Hunter and Britt Van Tassel Morrissey lived in the old Van Wart house, a nineteenth century Victorian home that overlooked the river. The building was listed with the historical preservation society and my guess was Britt was only permitted to rent the place because of her lineage.

There was an unspoken hierarchy in Sleepy Hollow between those who had been here since the Dutch settlers and those who were considered transplants. Either way, I thought the bias

stupid. Every generation produced its own crop of jerks, so who cared, really? Still, the house was tall and beautiful with gabled roofs, stained glass, and cute gingerbread trim. The yellow paint and white accents were pristine, but it was the front veranda facing the street I loved most, and I couldn't picture a better place.

I steered my car onto the gravel driveway and parked beside Britt's Jeep. Hunter's cobalt blue mustang was in the detached garage since he'd been away.

"So, you planned this little surprise all along," he said gesturing with his head toward his mother's car. Clearly there was no labor emergency.

"Maybe." I grinned, leaning back after turning off the ignition. "Are you sorry?"

His head shake was slow and deliberate, and he leaned across to the driver's seat to slide his hand into my dark hair. "Not a chance," he whispered into our kiss.

God, I wanted him.

"Hey, you two!" Britt called, waving from the porch. Hunter got out of the car, taking his bag from the backseat before going up the stairs to greet his mother.

"Hi, baby," she said, pulling him into a hug. "Good flight?"

Hunter towered over her and he bent to peck her upturned cheek. "Long." He slipped himself from his mother's hug and put his bags on the wicker loveseat behind her. "But worth it once I got to baggage claim." He offered with a wink.

She smiled, her hand reaching out to pull me into a side hug. "How could I say no to such a pleasant surprise for my baby?" She squeezed my shoulders.

"Baby? Really?"

She laughed. "Oh, get over yourself, Hunter. You're still my baby even if you have grown another inch since you left for the coast."

"I've only been gone three weeks, though it seems like forever."

A shadow crossed Hunter's face and Britt let go of me, moving to place her hand on her son's arm. She looked into his face. "That bad? Tell me."

The worry in her voice made my throat tighten and guilt washed over me for not asking once how his trip went. It's not like I didn't know there was trouble. But I was so caught up in my own romantic fantasy, I forgot. *Ugh. Chloe was right. I am self-absorbed.*

His fingers covered hers for a moment before gently disengaging her hand from his arm. "Stop worrying. Nothing happened I couldn't handle."

Her eyes searched his. "Are you sure?"

He nodded giving her another peck. "Positive. Dad's guilt trips don't work on me anymore, nor do his new manipulations."

Britt was clearly relieved, and she picked up the lighter of Hunter's bags and carried it through the open screen door. She may have missed it, but I caught the look on his face once her back was to him. He may have told her the truth, but it wasn't all of it.

I followed him into the hall and waited as he took his bags upstairs to his room. Hunter came down, kicking his sneakers off on the landing. I was barefoot, having left my strappy sandals on the foot of the stairs.

"You didn't have to take those off," he said gesturing to my shoes. "They look amazing on you."

I glanced at the floor and then toward the kitchen, past the credenza and the hall powder room. "I think your mom made a late dinner. I texted her you were starved while you waited for your other bag."

"Come and get it while it's hot," she called from the kitchen entrance. "Sit, both of you. I made linguini with pesto and white clam sauce. Your favorite," she said giving Hunter a smile as she placed a heaping fork full on a plate. "There's garlic bread in the oven."

The table was set for two, and I looked at Britt. "Aren't you eating?"

She shook her head. "Can't. I barely had time to wait for you to get here." She picked up a narrow piece of paper and shook it. "I was just finishing up a note letting you know I had to leave." She lifted one shoulder. "I may have told a white lie to cover for you at the airport, but Karma was listening. The hospital called for real about fifteen minutes before you pulled up to the house."

"Weird," I replied taking the serving tongs.

She sighed absently. "At least I managed dinner for you two," she murmured, taking the bread out of the oven and placing the precut slices in a basket on the table.

"And I for one am very grateful." He lifted his fork swirled with pesto covered pasta. "This is amazing."

"I'm glad you like it, sweetie."

"Do you think you'll be late?" Hunter asked, swallowing a mouthful.

She shrugged again. "Most likely. This one's a first-time mom, and they usually need a lot of attention." She walked to the table and put a hand on Hunter's shoulder. "I'll see you in the morning." Kissing the top of his head, she turned to go. "Have fun you two. Don't forget to wrap up the leftovers and clean up the kitchen."

The front door open and closed and suddenly it was just me and Hunter. I couldn't have planned this better if I tried.

He looked at me and my untouched plate. "You're not eating."

"Sorry, I was busy listening to your mom." I picked up my fork and pushed some of the pasta around on my dish.

"She missed you."

He smiled, wiping his mouth on a paper napkin. "And it got me a home cooked meal, too. Win-win." He winked.

"Don't be a jerk, Hunter." I flicked a small piece of garlic bread crust his way "Britt told my mother how worried she was about you out there in La-La land."

My dislike of all things Hollywood gave him a chuckle, but then his face softened. "I missed her, too. My dad can be overbearing yet absentee at the same time, if you get what I mean. He spouts the standard parenting bull, but it's empty, like he's filling a quota or satisfying some requisite script so he can tell himself he's a good father. Then without blinking an eye he disappears into his own world and doesn't give me the time of day."

I caught the same shadow that crossed his face when we first arrived. "Hey..." I started, reaching across the table for his hand. "Your dad's issues are his issues. Not yours." I hesitated, almost afraid to ask. "What happened? Why did you come home?"

He slid his fingers from mine, and I cringed at the abrupt feeling of being shut out. Chloe was right. The sentiment sucked.

Avoiding eye contact, he picked up a piece of garlic bread and pushed the crusty end into the sauce on his plate. "So, you're not happy I cut my trip short?"

I balled up my napkin and launched it at him. "Of course, I am, dum-dum, but that doesn't mean I don't care why." I waited for him to say something, but he didn't. "Are you okay?"

He gave me a noncommittal grunt. "Yeah, I'm fine. I told you my dad likes to pontificate. Well, he'd been on me about everything that happened last fall, and how it was best if I stayed out west with him and Clarice..." he stopped, realizing I had no idea who that was. "Clarice is my dad's new wife."

"What happened to Alison?"

"Divorced. Now it's Clarice. She's number three. He's definitely gone all Hollywood 'A' list collecting trophy wives. This new one is only twenty-three years old."

"Eewww."

He exhaled hard, shaking his head. "Tell me about it. And it gets worse."

"Worse how?"

He dropped his chin, and the look on his face left no room for doubt.

"No, she didn't..." I couldn't bring myself to say it.

He nodded, plastering a huge grin on his face. "Yup. She thought she might plead my father's case by paying me a little late night visit. *Wrong.* I was in such a deep sleep that when she startled me I nearly killed her. I punched her square in the chest."

"Oh my God! Did you hurt her?"

He chuckled. "Nah. She got the wind knocked out of her good, but she's fine. Though she did sound like a beached bull elephant seal." He mimicked a high, rough-pitched rasp.

I burst out laughing. "That's horrible."

He grinned. "But funny as hell." He glanced at his plate and pushed it away. His smile faded to a melancholy ghost and I knew then the incident had unnerved him, despite his jokes.

"She deserved it," I commiserated, trying to bring his smile back.

He lifted his eyes to mine. "After that, I knew I had to get out of there. The longer I stayed, the harder it was to breathe. Clarice thought herself clever, keeping her hand in Dad's wallet while planning to keep me around for kicks." He hitched up one shoulder and let it drop. "I know my father suspected something too, because he didn't argue when I called my mother to book me a flight home. He even paid for it."

"It was probably for the best. That triangle had *Bermuda* written all over it."

He raised an eyebrow. "What's that supposed to mean?"

I did my best to keep my expression deadpan. "Nothing, why?"

Unconvinced, he shot me a look. "Nice try, Rowen. You forget I can read you better than anyone, except for maybe your grandmother. There was no triangle."

Irked at being that transparent, I tilted my head and pursed my lips, weighing my own qualms against questions that might make Hunter more uncomfortable.

"Fine. You want me to play mind-reader, you got it." He exhaled. "First, you're dying to know what Clarice looks like so you can beat yourself up comparing yourself to her, next you're wondering if I was even the slightest bit attracted to her, and finally you're wondering if you weren't in the picture would I have gone for it." He raised an eyebrow daring me to tell him he was wrong.

Damn he was good. I crossed my arms in front of my chest. "I wouldn't have compared myself, but…"

"But nothing…" He smirked, leaning forward to pull my hands from their defensive vice grip. "Would you like the answers now that we know the questions?" He paused, waiting for the nod I wouldn't give.

"Fine…*One:* Clarice is one hundred percent Hollywood's definition of beautiful, but what did you expect? Her sole function, like everything else in my father's house, is for decoration and entertainment. Why else would he bother? *Two.* My friends think I was stupid not to nail her and be done with it, but I'm not that shallow, and regardless of what kind of relationship my dad and I have or don't have, he's still my father, and for better or worse, she's his wife, and finally, *three.* No, because vacuous and vain aren't my style or I would have jumped Jenny's bones last September."

The time for joking was over and he licked his lips in a self-conscious move clearly looking for me to say something. Anything.

"You're one of a kind, Hunter, and I'm one lucky girl." My voice was small, but my relief massive.

My reward for listening and not judging was a slow sexy smile that made my stomach jump.

Hunter lifted the pitcher of homemade lemonade his mother made and poured some in both our glasses.

"To a night full of the unexpected," I said, lifting my glass and tilting the rim toward him.

He raised an eyebrow at first, but then touched the edge of his glass to mine. "You always surprise me."

I took a sip and then put the glass beside my still untouched food. Butterflies had taken up residence in my stomach since we arrived, but they would soon be evicted.

"How about some music," he asked getting up to plug his iPhone into a speaker on the counter.

"Sure. Why not?"

"I saw *Florida Georgia Line* at the Staples Center in downtown LA. Except for hanging out with my friends at the beach, it was the only other thing I enjoyed about my trip." He pushed the arrow icon on his screen and stepped back with a grin. "This song made me think of you."

The sweet twang of a country guitar rose from the speakers and my own smile grew when I realized which song he chose.

Get your shine on…baby, get your shine on…

Hunter held his hand out to me. "Dance?" he inquired with a grin.

Unlike every other time he asked, this time I didn't argue. I stepped straight into his arms and slipped my own around his neck.

"Wow, that was easier than I expected." He chuckled, spinning me gently around.

"I said a night of surprises, right?"

I went up on tip toe and kissed him before he could respond. Our kiss deepened as the music swelled, and the two of us swayed, our bodies pressed tightly.

Hunter fisted the back of my dress and the hem rose slightly on my thighs. The feel of his jeans against my bare skin sent

tingles zinging across my exposed flesh. I deepened my kiss, the soft wetness of his tongue dancing and darting together with mine.

With a rough breath he pulled his lips away and dipped me over his arm. My head dropped between my shoulder blades, the arch of my back pushing my breasts up. "You're killing me," he murmured, letting his fingers skim the delicate skin of my neck, trailing the curves of my body to my waist.

As though in slow motion, he lifted me to my feet and both hands found my back, gliding to the small sensitive spot at the base of my spin. "Rowen…" he whispered, his breath uneven and full of need.

His palms skimmed the soft rounded top of my buttocks and then dipped lower, moving slowly, almost tentatively to cup its fullness. I gasped at the feel of his fingers kneading the flesh beneath my white knit hem.

Pressing my body tighter to his, Hunter moaned, and in a single, fluid motion he scooped me into his arms. He whispered my name again, this time his eyes dark with want and searching mine for the only answer I could give. Almost a year had brought us to this point. A full spectrum of emotion from everything we had been through culminated in that one beseeching whisper…desire and pain, grief and terror, and above all…love.

I wrapped my legs around his hips, and my arms around his neck. "I think it's time you showed me your room." My words were barely a half breath.

He carried me through the hall, his lips feathering kisses along the tender flesh beneath my jaw and ear. He took the stairs in a slow torturous pace, the feel of his muscled thighs against my bare legs making me want to scream. Only thin layers of lace and denim separated me from him, and the anticipation and anxiety growing the closer we got to the second floor left me more breathless than his kisses.

At his bedroom door he put me down, the fabric of my dress crushed between us. "You're sure?" His voice was gentle, though his hand shook as he trailed a single finger down my cheek.

Unable to form words past the lump in my throat and the butterflies in my stomach, I nodded. My body quaked with need and fear and I couldn't look at him. I focused instead on the flat muscled planes of his chest and the soft steady rhythm of his heartbeat.

"Look at me, Rowen." With his fingers beneath my chin, he lifted my gaze upward to meet his. "Are you sure? We can go back downstairs right now if you have any doubts."

Of course, I had my doubts. Anything to the contrary would be a bold-faced lie, but there was no going back. I didn't want to go back. "Open the door, Hunter. I want this, and I want you."

He leaned down and kissed me with a gentle sweet sweep of his lips. "I love you, Rowen."

I lifted my palm to his cheek. "I love you, too."

Hunter lifted me into his arms again and opened the door. "To a night of true surprises," he murmured and closed the door behind us.

Chapter 5

"Do you want another pillow?" Hunter bent to pick up one of the fringed squares from the floor beside the bed. The pillows had hit the carpet along with the comforter, neither one of us paying much heed to the mess we made earlier.

Watching him move around the room now, my eyes searched for any hint of awkwardness. If weirdness settled between us there was no one to blame but me. I had launched myself at him like a stealth missile. He didn't have a chance.

I pushed pause on the television remote, freezing Kevin Costner mid-stride as he danced with wolves. "Are you okay?" I asked, hoping Hunter wouldn't avoid the question and by extension, me. If he did, I'd have my answer plus a one-way ticket to Embarrassment City.

Pillow in hand, he leaned over and kissed the top of my head before stuffing the cushion behind my shoulders. "How could I not be okay? I have you."

Relief crawled up my cheeks along with a self-conscious heat I knew pinked to my ears.

"You're beautiful," he said brushing his lips over my hair again.

I was a tumbled wreck, but the look in his eyes made me feel beautiful, and that's all I needed. I patted the edge of the bed and he sat, but not before he took the remote from my hand and clicked the movie off completely.

"Look, you can stop studying me. I'm not going to self-combust, nor has anything changed between us because we..." He let his words trail off, doubtless because I had reddened to my hairline.

Kissing away my embarrassed high color, he love tapped my thigh. "Stop being a worrywart."

"How can you say that? We're in a different place now. *We're* different." I said, moving my hand back and forth between us. "Maybe it hasn't sunk in for you yet."

He shook his head. "We may be in a different place, but we're not different people. We've done nothing but take our relationship to another level, and now it's up to us to decide where we take it next."

I sighed.

"What? Buyer's remorse setting in already?" he joked.

I tossed a muffin wrapper at him from the tray of goodies he brought up earlier. "That's not funny."

"Then why the long sigh?"

I shrugged. "We just got to this place. I mean seriously *just* got here and already you're talking about taking things to the next level. Can't we enjoy where we are and figure things out as we go?"

Hunter laughed out loud. "You make me sound like a chick." With a smirk, he laced his fingers with mine and brought my hand to his lips. "Of course, we can stay right here. In fact, we can stay right here in my bed as long as you want." He let go of my hand and dropped his palm to my hip, a seductive smile on his lips as he traveled the length of my bare leg.

Hmmph. "I'll just have to think about that. In the meantime, I need the bathroom." I deftly moved his hand so I could get up from the bed.

I padded down the hall to the main bath, leaving the bedroom door open. The oversized tee-shirt I borrowed from him fell to my knees, and I felt a little naughty wearing it with

nothing but my panties underneath. He'd seen me in a bikini, but somehow this felt decadent.

Snapping on the bathroom light, I ran a hand through my curls, taming them into some semblance of order. Britt had a dish with bobby pins and hair ponies next to the sink and I helped myself to a blue scrunched pony to match Hunter's long blue tee. I gathered my hair in a high top knot leaving loose curly tendrils to frame my face.

I let the water run before rinsing my face, giving my slightly smeared make up a swipe. Tossing the mascara-tinged tissue into the waste bin, I closed my eyes and smiled to myself as images of Hunter and the entire night ran through my mind, especially the way he held me as though he never wanted to let me go. With a silent squeal, I hugged my middle and snapped off the light.

I walked back, wearing a secret smile only to find Hunter with a frown on his face. With his back against the headboard, his long legs stretched out on the bed. He held a torn white envelope in one hand and a thick gilt-edged card in the other. Jenny's invitation.

"We all got one," I replied before he could ask. "Chloe and Benny. Connie and Eric. Even Talia's younger sister…" I let my voice trail off. Hunter wasn't listening.

His face was inscrutable, almost as though he was listening to something or someone else. I watched his eyes scan the elegant calligraphy before he let the card slip to his lap.

"Hunter…" I didn't like not being able to read him.

He didn't answer.

"Hunter!"

His eyes found mine and their soft brown was dark and uncertain. "I'm sorry, Rowen. I'm not ignoring you. I was just thinking."

"About what?" Nervous adrenaline rushed through my body leaving a fine sheen of sweat in its wake. At least whatever

was preoccupying him wasn't a vision. One of us courted by the cosmos was enough.

He shook his head, lifting the invitation again to gesture with it in my direction. "I don't know about this, Rowen. You're just snapping back from what happened last fall. The deaths, especially Talia's, were so hard on you. Maybe this trip isn't such a good idea."

I climbed onto the bed next to him and sat back on my knees. I took the card from his hand and glanced at it. "Does that mean you don't want to go?"

"No..." He shifted onto his side to better face me. "That's not what I said." He paused, almost as though he wanted to say something but didn't know how.

"What?" I prompted.

He slid the invitation from my fingers and tossed it to the floor. *Weird.* An infinitesimal shake of his head told me he was arguing with himself. When he finally looked at me, he took my hand and held it just a little too tightly. "This is going to sound crazy, but with our history, crazy is a distinct possibility."

A frustrated exhale left my mouth and I knew I needed to rein in my impatience. Whatever Hunter was grappling with was serious. "Just tell me, okay?"

"I got a seriously bad feeling the minute I tore open that envelope and pulled out the card."

Bad feeling? My impatience left me completely and he had my full attention. "What do you mean by bad? An omen, a premonition or just intuition?"

He let go of my hand, raising his own in a confused gesture. "I don't know. A sudden chill hit me the minute my fingers touched the card. I was cold and literally started shivering. A feeling of despair came over me along with a sense of impotent anger. I wanted to shred the card, tear it into little pieces."

Our crazy was different than regular crazy, about that there was no question. But if I'd learned anything from Gran, it was to take the irrational with a grain of sea salt. Detached and

methodic were the only ways to navigate the churning waters of the supernatural, to never let emotions take over or you give whatever is messing with you an edge.

"Okay..." I was careful not to sound too patronizing. "Let's back up a bit." I chewed on the side of my lip, concentrating on keeping this from escalating into something it wasn't, especially in my mind. "You and I are connected in ways most people aren't. I'm talking about the fact you're a magnet and I'm a conduit for the supernatural. Our experiences are going to be more intense and therefore our scars much deeper. Don't you think there's a possibility what you experienced is just residual emotions tied to what we went through?

"Neither of us were able to help Talia or Mike, or even Tyler. We weren't able to prevent the fallout from bleeding over onto them. I carry my own guilt, and as you said, I'm just coming out of it now. Maybe you put off dealing with your own grief and anger because you had to keep me from imploding, and now that I'm okay this trip brought your grief to the surface."

He groaned. "Come on, Rowen. Psychobabble? Really? Okay, maybe I didn't acknowledge my feelings then, and yeah, I was worried you would take a header off the Tappan Zee Bridge, but I have since and I'm fine. I'm sorry, but after everything we went through, I am not about to dismiss my gut when it smells trouble."

"Trouble."

He threw a hand up. "I don't know. All I know is my body reacted as though something awful was sitting in wait, and to tell you the truth, I'm not up for another supernatural collaboration."

Awkward silence fell between us, and I leaned against the headboard tucking myself under his arm with my head on his chest. "It's ironic, you know," I said bouncing his hand up and down in mine.

"What is?"

"Both my mother and grandmother said the exact opposite. They agree the trip would do us all good."

A little warning nagged at the back of my head because that's not exactly what Gran said. I wondered if I should tell Hunter about my newest crop of visions, weigh the possibilities of a connection to his visceral warning, but I dismissed the idea. Now was not the time. He would go all alpha-male on me, despite Gran's assurances. I had planned to tell him, but I wanted to wait until he'd been home a day or so. It would keep. In the metaphysical sense, things were relatively calm regardless of Hunter's sympathetic nervous system spike, and I wasn't about to rock the boat. If neither Gran nor my mother were worried about my visions, then why should I?

"They didn't sense anything weird?" he repeated, sitting up so he could look at me.

I shook my head. "Nope." *My visions notwithstanding, but again they would keep.*

His expression was both pensive and relieved. "Well, there's no better barometer for metaphysical clearance than your grandmother. I guess it's okay then. The Catskill's aren't that far of a drive, about three hours. We'd have to leave Friday morning, though. Jenny wants everyone there by lunchtime."

I shifted around on the bed, sitting cross-legged so I could face him. "I talked to Chloe today..." I told him about her ambushing me at Patriot's Park. I went into detail about everything she and I discussed, except of course, my misgivings about him and our future.

"After everything she said, if I don't show this weekend, she'll never forgive me, but I won't go if you don't. We're a team, and Chloe will just have to deal."

"So you want to go..." His words were more statement than question.

I half shrugged, half nodded.

With a laugh, he grabbed me around the waist, the borrowed tee-shirt hitching higher up my legs as he pulled me

on top of him. He smacked my butt. "Then I guess we go, but you might need to coax me a little more just to be sure..." Chuckling, he slid his mouth over mine.

Friday morning dawned hot and sticky. Refreshing breezes off the Hudson had all but stagnated, and the Weather Channel called for severe thunderstorms and erratic conditions across the entire area. The Catskills would probably catch bands of whatever storms hit, but then mountain weather played by its own rules.

It was almost eight a.m. and an early start was just what the doctor ordered. Jenny wasn't expecting anyone until early afternoon, but Hunter and I told her not to count on us until much later. This way we could take our time and enjoy the scenic drive.

I wasn't a *jump in the car road tripin'* sort of gal, so Hunter suggested we make this an adventure and take the back roads. We could avoid traffic and the monotonous stretch of thruway while having fun exploring little towns and shops along the way. He even agreed to a bit of antiquing, daring me to separate real antiques from plain old junk.

Over the past forty-eight hours, my attitude toward this weekend had gone from trepidation to fluttery anticipation. I couldn't wait to get on the road. I was even happy Chloe insisted we go shopping for the trip. She loved makeovers and this weekend I was *Operation Live Doll*.

"I know we're going rafting, but if I know Jenny, she's got something else up her sleeve," Chloe said while tugging me from store to store. "She'll probably have the boat pull over at some posh lakeside chalet with music and dancing and she'll look like a million bucks while the rest of us look like drowned

rats. You've got to beat her at her own game, Rowen, if not for yourself, then for the other UPs of this world."

I rolled my eyes at her. Chloe's prediction was absurd, and her reference to the stupid high school slur for unpopular kids just as ridiculous. Old habits die hard against a track record like Jenny's, but as far as I was concerned, high school was over and done and its girl codes along with it.

Truth was I didn't think Jenny had anything untoward planned. The poor girl had been through hell and back, and I truly believed she wanted this weekend to make amends. After we lost Talia and Mike, our perspectives changed. We understood the need for tolerance and to be forgiving of each other and our short comings. Life was too short. A lesson Chloe needed to remember and one I gently reminded her of yesterday while shopping.

"Rowen! Do you want breakfast?" my mother called from downstairs, but I was too busy with last minute packing to answer.

My overnight bag was zipped and ready to go, and I put my daily personal items in a small buckskin backpack and slipped it over my shoulder. As I carried my overnight case down the stairs, the scent of chocolate and butter greeted me, and I dropped my bags at the front door, turning toward the delicious smell.

Hunter would be here soon, but the rich aromas lured me into the kitchen instead of the front porch where I told him I'd meet him. Who could resist chocolate for breakfast?

My favorite mug waited for me on the table, hazelnut scented steam rising from the top despite a dollop of cinnamon cream floating at its center. I spied a large clear Tupperware filled with homemade Toll House cookies, and on top of that, a plastic wrap covered plate with what looked and smelled like chocolate raspberry croissants. Blue and gold ribbon circled the entire package and I frowned realizing it was a gift. Chocolate for breakfast was too much to hope for in this house.

"I'm not taking those if I can't have one," I said blowing steam across the edge of my mug.

"Good morning to you too, sunshine." My mother's beautiful smile greeted me from where she stood working at the stove. "Those treats aren't for you, they're for Jenny."

"Not even one to go with my delicious coffee?" I teased, fingering the end of the plastic wrap.

She flicked her wooden spoon at me, splattering clear pine-scented liquid across the floor. "No samples! You can't show up to Jenny's empty handed, it's not right. She has gone to a lot of trouble to put this weekend together and I won't have my gift picked over."

Hand up, I laughed. "Okay...don't have a canary, I was just asking."

Mom's apron sported the Silver Cauldron's broomstick logo and the words *If You Can't Fly with the Big Girls, then Stay off the Broom,* silkscreened across the front. Funny as it was, that apron meant she was in full out work mode though it was off season for our shop. But, why?

"I made cinnamon raison bread yesterday. I can whip you up cinnamon toast, if you want."

She gestured to the wooden bread box next to the coffee pot, but I shook my head. "Hunter and I will probably stop for something to eat on the way. He should be here any minute."

"Knock, knock." As if on cue, Hunter poked his head in through the back door. "I've been waiting out front for fifteen minutes, is everything okay?" he asked looking from me to my mother and back again.

"Fine, sweetheart. Come on in. Would you like a cup of coffee?" Mom offered with a smile.

He shook his head. "No thanks, Mrs. Corbett. I stopped at the deli on my way over."

"No problem, you can help yourself if you change your mind. I even have disposable travel cups. Rowen, you know where they are in the pantry." With a nod she lifted the lid off

the large cast iron pot simmering on the front burner and gave the contents a stir.

"Between the chocolate and that woodsy wreath smell, it's like Christmas in here."

My mother touched her finger to her nose. "Very good, Hunter. Wild juniper has an earthy scent. I dried this batch from the berries picked last fall."

I rolled my eyes at them both.

"I saw that, missy. At least someone takes an interest in what goes on around here." My mother flashed Hunter a wide smile.

"What is that anyway," I asked.

"It's a potion to promote trance and prophecy." She ladled a small amount and poured it carefully into a small vial. "It's also good for safe travel," she added putting a cork in the top of the glass ampoule. "I'm thinking of calling it Transcendence. Pretty good, huh?" She held out the vial to Hunter and he literally took a step back.

"With all due respect, Mrs. Corbett, I've had enough communing with the spirits to last a lifetime and GPS has safe travel covered, so no need for a metaphysical map."

She laughed slipping the tiny bottle into her apron. "No worries, sweetheart."

"Why the sudden rush for new items? Between you and Gran, the shop will be well stocked months before the fall tourist season hits," I asked, dumping the rest of my coffee into the sink.

Mom lowered the flame on the burner before covering the pot with its heavy lid. "This batch isn't for the shop. It's for us."

I did a quick double take, ignoring the loud clink of my mug slipping from my fingers to the sink's stainless-steel grate. "Us? Why?"

She inhaled, leaning her lower back against the counter beside the stove. "Because Gran would rather us safe than sorry. The tisane she made the other day wasn't strong enough, so she

gave me the recipe to tweak. This is quite a brew now." She tapped the pot's weighty top.

"Has something happened?" Hunter's look was both questioning and accusatory. I should have told him about my newest visions when I had the chance, and now my sin of omission was about to bite me in the butt.

I opened my mouth, but Mom raised her hand, interjecting before I could say a word. "It's nothing, Hunter. Rowen has…visitations. It's not unusual for the women in our family."

He looked from me to my mother, disbelief creasing his forehead. "Visitations? That's what you're calling Rowen's visions, now? And you actually want to promote their occurrences?"

She shrugged, trying not to look guilty. "It's not what you think. In this instance the visions are limited to blood family, albeit dead ones. This potion enhances our ability to converse with our ancestors and in some cases breach the veil when necessary."

"The veil between what? The living and the dead?" he asked.

She shook her head. "No, not this time, although time is an important ingredient."

"Time is not an ingredient, Mother." Annoyed, I took the cookies and croissants from the table and handed them to Hunter. "Time just exists, and this *time* I think both you and Gran have slipped a cog."

I walked toward the front door for my bags, my mother close behind. "Don't leave angry, Rowen. It's not what you think."

I turned gaping at her. "Really? Because it sounds a lot like you and Gran have something in the works for me that I'm not going to like." I dragged in a breath, letting the air fill my lungs and drown out out my urge to shout.

"Rowen…" she began, but I cut her off.

"Look, I know you think this is just part of life as we know it, but this metaphysical connection we share with the cosmos has cost me too much already. I need a break."

Mom exhaled a tired breath. "It's too soon."

Her voice was barely a whisper and her eyes focused on something beyond. Her words weren't meant for me, yet I knew in my gut they were somehow connected to me. I searched her eyes and when she finally came back, she placed both hands on my upper arms.

"I promise, there is nothing for you to worry about." She kissed my cheek and then stepped back, her hands dropping to her apron. "Call me when you get there. Did you pack your iPhone charger?"

I nodded but then my eyes darted up the stairs toward my room. "Crap, no, and I don't remember where I left it."

With a small smile, she pulled the thin white iPhone cord from her pocket. "Turn around," she instructed and then unzipped the top of my backpack and stuffed the charger in alongside my wallet.

"See, the best laid plans of mice and men..." She didn't finish the quote, but I knew what she meant. Sometimes you still needed to trust your mother.

She walked onto the porch with us and before I could say anything, she pulled me into a tight hug. "I love you, Rowen. Remember that."

"I love you too, Mom, and I'm sorry I yelled."

She shook her head stepping back. "Doesn't matter, sweetheart, just remember who you are and where you come from, okay?"

I laughed. "*Jeez*, Mom. I'm not going to the Peace Corps. I'll see you Sunday."

She nodded, giving me half a smile but there was something in her eyes I didn't like.

"What?" I asked, not wanting to leave without satisfying myself she was okay.

She waved me off. "It's nothing. You two go have fun. Try to stick together, it's safer that way."

Hunter beeped the horn.

I waved to him to give me another minute, but my mother turned me around and gave me a pat on my butt. "Go. I'm just being silly. Consider this a nervous dry run for college move in day."

Relieved it was just a case of pre-empty nest jitters, I hugged her hard. "See you in two days."

She stayed on the porch until we pulled out of sight, and as her image grew smaller in the back window a shadow edged its way across my heart.

Chapter 6

No one was on the road and we made good time. We wound our way through quaint villages with imaginative names like Willow and Shady, villages that flanked the town of Woodstock, the icon of the 1960's hippie counterculture in America and the artistic hub of the Hudson Valley, and home to Jenny's summer place on Cooper Lake. As we headed north toward Ulster County, heart of the Catskill Mountains, we followed a scenic route, taking the long way around.

Hunter frowned, his eyes darting from the road to the dashboard. "We need to stop for gas."

"That's not funny. We've been in the middle of nowhere for the last thirty miles. Where are we?"

He shrugged. "GPS says Route 5 but if we turn onto 29A it will take us into the town of Hurley. I'm sure we can find what we need and grab something to eat."

We followed the road into town and sure enough there was a gas station at the end of the cut road. Hunter filled the tank and I went inside to use the bathroom.

"You kids lost?" the guy behind the counter asked looking up from his magazine.

I placed two iced teas and a large bag of pretzels on the scratched white counter. "Not anymore."

He rang up the items without comment. "That'll be four fifty."

I handed him a five dollar bill, noticing the real estate foreclosure listings hanging behind the register "We thought we could find a deli or a place to grab some lunch but there doesn't seem to be much choice around here." I put my hand out to collect my change.

He gave me a tired shrug. "That's for sure. Like everywhere else, the economy has hit us hard, but we'll snap back. Hurley is a tight knit community."

He moved a toothpick from one side of his mouth to the other before looking out the front display window toward the restaurant diagonally across the road. "You give the Roadhouse a try?" he asked with a chin pop in the eatery's general direction.

I shook my head. "The parking lot is empty. We assumed it was closed this early in the day."

A dismayed chortle said he wasn't surprised. "I've been telling the owner for years he needs to spruce things up to bring in more business. The place looks deader than a doornail more often than not, but I suppose he's doing the best he can, considering. Anyway, they're open for lunch if you're still interested."

"Maybe," I replied watching him put my things in a bag. "So, is there anything around here interesting to see?"

With a wink he turned and pulled a narrow white and red pamphlet from the desk behind the counter. "Hurley may be small, but we're big on American history." He held out the leaflet, and when I took it he pointed toward the hill that led up to the church steeple and beyond. "That's Main Street. Just follow it straight and you'll see what I mean."

I folded the pamphlet and stuck it in the bag with the snacks. "Thanks," I said, and with a nod, he went back to his magazine.

"This brochure says the women's rights activist Sojourner Truth was born in Hurley," I commented as we waited for our waitress to take our order. "Besides that, there are ten stone houses that date to the Dutch settlers, some as far back as the late 1600s and a few even played an important role during the revolutionary war."

He laughed. "Don't tell me. Washington slept here, too."

I made a face. "No."

Hunter waggled his eyebrows. "The dude certainly covered enough ground to have a little side action all over the eastern seaboard. Kinda gives new meaning to the phrase father of our country."

I smacked the side of his arm. "Not funny. Aren't you even the least bit interested? I mean, we're here so why not? Besides, the brochure also says there's an antique shop up the street."

He groaned, realizing I planned to hold him to his promise of treasure hunting.

"Hi, I'm Amy. What can I get you today?" A perky blonde in jeans, a white tee, and black apron asked as she waited with a spiral notepad and pen.

"I'll have a grilled chicken salad with lite Italian dressing on the side and unsweetened iced tea," I replied.

With a smile just a little too bright, she looked at Hunter. "And for you, handsome?"

I kicked him under the table, and he jerked forward.

"Are you okay, *handsome*?" I mimicked, batting my lashes.

With a quick glare shot my way he leaned down to rub his shin. "Yeah, I caught my leg on something unnecessarily sharp."

The waitress looked at me, her expression a little tighter than it was a moment before. "Do you need a minute, hon?" she asked Hunter.

He shook his head. "No, I'll have a cheeseburger, medium-well, with extra bacon, lettuce and tomato and double fries…with cheese."

"And to drink?" she asked with a ghost of a smirk.

"A chocolate milkshake and a glass of water."

She smiled brightly, tapping her pad once. "I'll put your order in right away."

"Thank you," I called after her and Hunter frowned at me.

"What?" I asked, fidgeting with a few sugar packets.

"You kicked me in the shin because a pretty girl smiled at me."

"Exactly. It was a flirty smile."

"How precisely does that qualify as my fault? If you thought someone deserved a shot, why didn't you kick her?"

I made a face. "You were closer."

The waitress came back with our drinks and put them in the center of the table. She noticed the leaflet sitting beside my napkin.

"Too bad you're not passing through town a couple of weeks from now. The stone houses will be open to the public then."

"What do you mean?" I asked picking up my tea.

She turned the pamphlet over, tapping on the advertisement gracing the back cover. "Stone House Day. The houses are only open to the public on the second Saturday of July. Once a year."

I picked up the pamphlet from the table and read the ad. "They're open only one day per year?" I repeated. "That's pretty cheap, don'tcha think? Sleepy Hollow is just as rich in history and tons of visitors pass through year-round. The local businesses make out like bandits."

The waitress sniffed, unimpressed, and we ended up waiting a long time for our food. She served it with markedly less enthusiasm than when she first seated us, and Hunter smirked when I finally admitted I was wrong for being over the top rude.

He took my hand across the table squeezing my fingers. "Nice tap dance there, fancy feet. We'll be lucky if she doesn't spit in our refills."

I shot him a look and dug into my salad. We ate quietly, talking about nothing and at one point I scrolled down my phone to check my text messages while Hunter signaled for the check.

"Chloe and Benny are just getting on the road now. I guess they're getting in late as well."

"Why?" he asked. "They aren't the sightseeing type."

I shrugged. "She didn't say."

We finished our food and Hunter paid the bill, the waitress giving him a wink and a wave as he turned with me toward the door.

Seeing my face Hunter grabbed my elbow and held the restaurant door open. The pressure in his fingers begging me not to make a scene.

Because he silently asked, I didn't say a word but looked daggers at her just the same, my meaning crystal clear.

"I guess we might as well head to the lake," he suggested as we walked into the parking lot. "Unless you want to drive to New Paltz and walk around the shops or explore the grounds at Mohunk Mountain House and do a little hiking."

"I don't want to be the first to arrive at Jenny's and New Paltz is south of here. It's too hot to go hiking, plus we've been in the car all morning. I want to walk around a bit. Even if those Stone Houses are closed today, we can still poke about, plus there's that antique shop up the street."

"Just inches from a clean getaway." He dropped his head back with an exaggerated exhale.

I held out my hand. "You promised."

He slumped for effect.

"Come on. We can leave the car here. Who knows, we might find something cool hidden in with the junk."

He took my hand, lacing my fingers with his. "Promise or not, you owe me, and I plan to collect later tonight." He lifted my hand to his lips and let their softness linger.

I sighed. This was a debt I was more than willing to pay. Just thinking about being with Hunter left my lower belly jumping in anticipation.

Intimacy was new to us, but it certainly wasn't the comedy of errors my friends all claimed their first time to be. Hunter was romantic and strong, gentle and sexy and we fit together like hand in glove. Maybe it had to do with everything we had been through or because he was a magnet and I the channel in our supernatural connection. Either way, it didn't really matter. It was perfect, and a secret smile tugged at the corner of my lips.

Hunter pointed out the blue historical marker on the front lawn. "Old Guard House. Lieutenant David Taylor, British spy, was confined in this house and hanged on an apple tree, October 18th 1777..." He opened the pamphlet to the center panel. "It doesn't say much more, just this place was used by the Continental Army during the Revolutionary War."

"They had spies during the revolution?" I took the pamphlet from his hand and looked myself for more information.

"Espionage isn't a modern notion, young lady."

Leaflet in hand, I jerked around to the old man sitting on a flat tree stump across from the house. On second glance, I saw he was significantly older than I first thought. He was thin, despite a small paunch, with long legs and a length of gray hair swept back from his forehead.

"Excuse me?" I was both intrigued and unsettled.

"I'm sorry, honey. I didn't mean to startle you or your young man." His smile revealed missing teeth, and his chuckle was wet and slightly wheezy.

"Do you know about this place?" Hunter asked, indicating the stone building behind us.

The man nodded. "Sure do. I know everything there is to know about Hurley's historical quarter mile."

Hunter gave the man a respectful smile. "That's pretty cool. Local historians are a godsend to students like me and Rowen." He slipped his arm around my shoulders. "We're from Sleepy Hollow. Last year we were given a very difficult research assignment. We wouldn't have made it through without help from people in the know."

I knew Hunter referred to the supernatural events that grabbed us by the throat last fall and not the AP English project that somehow managed to become entangled with it all. If it wasn't for Libby Scarborough, director of the Sleepy Hollow Historical Society as well as Gran and Mr. Grayson, the caretaker for the Old Dutch Church and burial ground, we would have probably joined Talia and Mike six feet under.

"Sleepy Hollow, eh? I'm from Cold Spring, across the river from West Point, so I know your neck of the woods, well."

"I'm sorry...you said you were from Cold Spring?" I asked.

Giving a hoarse chortle, he nodded. "I did. During the revolution, the village was part of Philipstown."

"Then how did you come to know so much about the Stone Houses here in Hurley? It seems like quite a distance for a hobby on such a hot day."

Giving us a short laugh, he coughed, lifting his shoulders in a casual shrug as the spasms passed. "I know I don't look the part, but I'm actually the unofficial photo archivist for the Putnam County Historical Society. I've been staying with my daughter in town for the past couple of months. I guess you could say I'm not one for being idle, so I made it my business to know everything there is to know about this village and its history. Pretty interesting stuff too, though not as interesting as what I could tell you about Cold Spring and West Point." He

reached into his pocket and pulled out a handkerchief to mop his brow.

He gestured toward the house, hankie still in hand. "British Lieutenant David Taylor was held here after he was convicted at New Windsor of spying near the Continental Army headquarters about thirty miles downriver. Sentenced to hang, the man was then marched north through hostile terrain to be quartered here while awaiting his sentence to be carried out. Taylor insisted he wasn't a spy, claiming he was a simple courier carrying information of no importance to General Burgoyne at Saratoga from British General Henry Clinton in New York City.

"Records say the general dashed off a quick note to Burgoyne on a thin piece of parchment tissue and then stuffed the note into a two-part silver capsule." The old man held his fingers apart about two-thirds of an inch to demonstrate the tiny size. "The two pieces were then screwed together to be easily hidden or swallowed if necessary. The capsule earned the name *silver bullet* because of its small size and shape."

"Hmmph, clever I guess," I added, impressed.

He nodded. "Sure was. During the revolution they had many means of incognito communications—hollowed out quills for hiding secret messages, coded alphabets, and even invisible ink."

Hunter's face was doubtful. "Invisible ink? That sounds made up, like something out of Sherlock Holmes."

The man turned his head toward the flag waving in the front yard of another stone house across the way. "A skeptic, eh? Well, if you don't believe me you can always poke around inside there," he said, motioning with his thumb backwards. "Ask for Margery. It may say Historical Society and Museum on the front sign, but it's also one of the most prominent antique shops in the area. She knows even more than I do, if you can believe that."

"Oh, Hunter is definitely one for needing proof, Mr...?"

He flashed another gap toothed grin. "Dunham. Name's Jan Dunham."

At that I burst out laughing. Seeing the old man's immediate reaction, I moved out from under Hunter's arm and took a step forward, holding up my hand against the unintended insult.

"I'm not laughing at you, Mr. Dunham. Please forgive me. It's just the assignment Hunter mentioned earlier required a great deal of research into the original Dutch families in Sleepy Hollow. There were so many named Jan we lost count. Many of them Hunter's Van Tassel ancestors."

Inadvertent affront forgiven, the man's eyebrows shot up and he looked at Hunter with appreciation. "So, your family is linked to Washington Irving's, legend, eh? Interesting."

Hunter shrugged. "Kind of."

I pushed on Hunter's arm. "Kind of? You know perfectly well you are a direct descendent."

Shifting my attention back to Mr. Dunham, I lifted my hand still trying to make amends. "Considering all the Dutch settlers we found named Jan, the fact your first name is the same makes our meeting seem almost fated."

The man laughed. "I see what you mean, miss…?"

"Rowen Corbett…and this is Hunter Morrissey," I replied.

Jan shook my hand and gave Hunter a nod. "Glad to meet you both." The man stuffed his handkerchief into a pocket and then reached deep into another to pull out what looked to be a collapsible cane.

"Can we help you get somewhere? Perhaps you could tell us a little more about the history of this place as we walk?" I offered.

He waved his hand, no. "Thanks, but I'm not as helpless as this stick makes me seem. I'm glad for the conversation, though. Not many young people share my love of history." He lifted the cane and pointed to the next street. "I was just heading home. It's not far, just up the road and then left." He looked at the two of us for moment and then swung the cane toward another

stone building across the street. "You two should really head over to Margery's place. I guarantee you'll find it interesting."

Hunter slid his arm around my shoulders again and we watched Mr. Dunham amble down the street, his stick tapping the sidewalk as he moved along.

"That was interesting," I said lifting my face to Hunter's. "Don't you think?"

"I suppose."

Not the reply I expected, I moved away from our side hug to look at him better. "What's wrong?"

He gave me a guarded shrug then pulled me closer and gave me a quick kiss before tucking me beneath his arm again. "Come on. Let's check out this museum antique shop or whatever it is."

Hunter was being evasive, but who was I to judge. I wasn't exactly forthcoming about my newest visions. I banished the gnawing worry starting to nibble in the pit of my stomach and focused instead on the warm sun and the comforting weight of Hunter's arm around my shoulders. It was all good, even if I had to force it to be.

We walked across the street and through the gate separating the natural wood picket fence. The path was light colored stone put together in a puzzle-piece design and curved toward a light blue door and matching shutters.

The door jingled an overhead bell when we pushed it open, but there was no one inside.

"Hello?" Hunter called into the empty shop.

Flat wood and glass cases lined the interior walls along with historic photographs and sketches from the town's long history. Displayed inside were artifacts of every kind, and I had the sensation of walking backwards through the twenty-first century to the American Revolution.

A plump middle-aged woman with graying blond hair poked her head through a side door off the main exhibit room. "Can I help you?" she asked, walking toward the center display.

"Hi. Mr. Dunham suggested we stop in. Are you Margery?"

A wide smile lit up the woman's face. "I sure am. Jan is a dear man. If he sent you, then I'm happy to be of service. Small town curators rarely get a chance to strut their stuff. What can I do for you kids?"

Hunter and I exchanged looks. "Nothing in particular," I answered, suddenly feeling a little silly for bothering the woman.

"We were looking at the Old Guard House earlier and ran into Mr. Dunham. He told us a little about its history, but said you were the local expert on the time period, especially when it came to revolutionary spies and their tools. He mentioned invisible ink, but to be honest it sounds a little hokey to me," Hunter explained, coming to my rescue.

"Hokey? I see..." she replied giving Hunter a close-lipped smile. "Then his sending you here was a good thing." She waved us over to one of a series of cases set in a horseshoe pattern around the center of the room.

"This might settle the question for you. In here, the museum has samples of correspondence from officers and tradesmen alike during the American Revolution where organic ink as well as sympathetic stain or white ink was used to hide military messages. Organic ink simply meant the writing compound was made of everyday materials: egg white, vinegar, milk, etc. Heat was then used to develop the ink. For example, once the message was delivered, the paper was then held close to a flame and the heat would turn the treated portions brown well before the paper itself was affected and thus reveal the hidden information."

Margery slipped on a pair of white gloves and removed two painstakingly preserved letters from the case and placed them on a white cloth draped across the counter.

"Washington, however, wanted something better, an ink that could only be revealed by a unique, specially formulated reagent. Sir James Jay, brother of American patriot, John Jay,

was a physician who dabbled in chemistry. In 1775, he created an ink for King George III which required one chemical for writing the message and a second to develop it, affording greater security than the organic inks. Jay never disclosed the recipe, and though he exported small quantities of the formula to America, it always remained in short supply. A correspondent would write a letter using the ink on plain white paper, and the recipient would apply a reagent in order to read it. George Washington dubbed the concoction *sympathetic stain* and used the code word *medicine* in his correspondence with James Jay.

"The stain eventually passed to the Continental Army's spymaster, Major Benjamin Tallmadge, who in turn provided it to the members of the famous Culper spy ring, including Abraham Woodhull and Robert Townsend. To avoid suspicion, Washington instructed his spies to write seemingly ordinary letters between the lines of their secret messages."

Margery spread her hands wide, inviting us to look but not touch, guiding our line of sight to the clearer portions of the correspondence. "If you look closely you can see the faded messages hidden in between the lines of the author's looping script."

Hunter stuffed his hands in his pockets, and I understood why as my own itched to pick up the delicate sheets and study them closely, as well.

"This is unbelievable." He leaned in to examine the pale writing, impressed awe on his face. "Look at this. You can still make out his words." His finger traced the air above the line.

When we were done, Margery's gloved hands placed the valuable letters back in their protected case. She removed her gloves and locked the display, but then moved to take another document from a separate exhibit, this time laying the sheet directly on the counter barehanded.

"Not only did Washington's men use invisible inks, but the spy ring devised elaborate codes. They used a numerical

substitution system developed by Tallmadge." She pointed to the document on the table.

"Spymaster Benjamin Tallmadge took several hundred words and dozens of names of people or places and assigned each a number from one to 763. For example, 38 meant *attack*, 192 stood for *fort*, George Washington was identified as 711, and New York was replaced by 727. American agents posing as deliverymen then transmitted the messages to other members of the ring."

She looked directly at me with another closed smile. "You might find this interesting. Female agents were used as well, and their code number was 355. In fact, a woman by the name of Anna Strong aided the cause by signaling the location of certain messages by utilizing a physical code involving laundry hung out to dry. A black petticoat hung on the clothesline indicated a message was ready to be picked up, and the number of handkerchiefs hanging to dry identified the cove on Long Island Sound where the agents would meet.

"There's another story as well, about an unidentified woman who was allegedly part of the Culper spy ring and worked behind the scenes, deep undercover, so much so to this day no one knows her true identity. Supposedly, she helped the American cause in the Hudson Highlands and ousted Benedict Arnold and his plans to sell West Point to the British. Through time, she's simply become known as Agent 355."

Doubtful, I made a face. "Agent 355? Sounds a little too Hollywood to me, like *Get Smart* and *Agent 99*. I find most of this hard to believe. Not the whole petticoat thing, but that the spy ring actively recruited women. Why? How? Women had no rights." I thought back to the vision I had of Hulda and what she went through at the hands of her brother-in-law. An angry flush crept up my throat and I glared at the parchment sheet on the counter as though it was to blame.

"Whatever holdings a woman possessed, however rich or small, were controlled by their husbands or whichever male

relative next in line was to lord over her. Very few were educated, and even then, it was never in military strategy or politics. I get what you're saying is historical fact, but I'm having a hard time wrapping my head around it. In my mind, it makes no sense. Women were basically possessions themselves, for decoration and breeding purposes. Why would an elaborate spy ring need to recruit women?" I stopped mid-rant and looked at her. "And please don't tell me it was to keep the men *happy*." I made bunny eared quotation marks with my fingers. "If that's the case, I'd rather not know."

Margery's eyebrows rose at my outburst, and she traded glances with Hunter whose own expression was just as baffled.

"It sounds as though you've been studying the period." Her reply was as hesitant as it was politically correct. "You're obviously very passionate about women's rights at the time."

I shook my head, a little embarrassed. "No, not really, although it is an interesting topic. We..." I gestured to Hunter, "...did research on a project last year that touched on women's rights during the eighteenth century — or rather the lack of them and what some had to do to survive."

She nodded. "It's true. The eighteenth century wasn't a time for independent thinking or free speech for anyone, let alone women, but lucky for them, men didn't listen overmuch to their opinions. It is part of the reason they were perfect for the position of spy. Men viewed women as notorious gossips who held the eyes and ears of a household and could easily report back, parroting what was discussed right in front of them. Men simply didn't see them as a threat to military security."

"Absurd," I mumbled under my breath.

"Indeed." With blooming appreciation in her expression, Margery held up one finger. She maneuvered around the horseshoe set of display cases to a long wooden and glass exhibit lining the far wall. She lifted the top and took out a small cracked leather pouch. "This came last week as part of an

anonymous endowment to the museum. It's right up your alley considering what we've been talking about."

The bag's threaded drawstring was surprisingly intact, but the aged leather flaked in the palm of her hand as she carried it to the counter. A quiet expletive left the curator's mouth as she carefully placed the pouch on the white cloth and again slipped on her gloves.

"Wow. Fragile, huh?" I whispered watching Margery move as if in slow motion.

"You think?" Hunter replied, rolling his eyes.

I refrained from poking him in the ribs, concentrating instead on Margery. She gently handled the bag's pulls, gradually coaxing open the old leather. Once done, she tilted the pouch toward her palm and out slid what looked to be an old-fashioned timepiece.

"Is that a pocket watch?" Hunter asked, leaning forward to get a better look.

Holding the antique between two fingers, she held it up to the light. "Initially, I thought so, too. The first time we opened the pouch I wasn't sure what we'd find, but this was more than I imagined. It's amazing, isn't it?" She put it on the table and took off her gloves. "The pouch is fragile, but I think the compass is in fine condition to handle bare-handed."

"Compass? Really?" Hunter repeated with undeniable interest.

She nodded. "Yes, it's an eighteenth-century pocket compass and sexton." Again, she picked up the antique only this time she held it by its fobbed end. "See this?" She pointed to a tiny button almost too small to distinguish within the tarnish. "It's a spring mechanism. If you push the release, the top opens like a pocket watch."

Margery demonstrated, and the top sprang open as she said. With the edge of her fingernail, she then lifted the circular sexton, so it sat perpendicular to the compass resting at the bottom of its metal case.

"The cotton felt around the inside was meant to keep it free from dust and water. The case is dull and tarnished, but it is pure silver, and once polished the piece is going to be beautiful, a real gem in our collection."

"It's gorgeous, Margery, but why did you want to show it to me in particular?"

She smiled, turning the compass over to show us the back side. "Because of the inscription. *"[Love] 'Tis in my memory lock'd, and you yourself shall keep the key of it. When sorrows come, they come not single spies. But in battalions!" —355*

"The quote is from Shakespeare or, so I've been told."

Still not understanding, I shook my head. "That's nice, but what has it got to do with what we were speaking of earlier?"

Hunter's eyes went wide, and he held out his hand. "May I?" he asked.

"Of course, but gently." Margery snapped the compass closed and placed it face down in Hunter's palm.

"Look, Rowen. It's not just one quote. There are two, and they're both from Hamlet, but from two separate acts. What's interesting are the numbers listed afterward."

I shrugged still not seeing the point. "Listings like that usually refer to a play's corresponding scene, page, and line number."

Hunter shook his head. "That's not what those numbers refer to. Don't you see what I mean?"

I looked closely at the small cursive script, but the engraving was all but obscured in the black tarnish. I leaned closer and then I saw it. My eyes found Hunter's and with a grin, he nodded. "355. This must have belonged to a female spy."

"Exactly." Margery nodded in agreement.

Hunter lifted the compass by the fob just as Margery had done and placed it in my palm. His fingers brushed mine, both our hands touching the antique silver.

In that moment the air was sucked from my lungs. A raw inward gasp left my lips and I gripped the edge of the case. The

room spun. Nausea gripped my stomach and spasms choked me until bile rose in the back of my throat. I forced it down, but vertigo took hold and as the wave crashed, my knees buckled, taking me to the floor.

"Rowen!" Hunter shouted grabbing me under my arms. He knelt on the floor holding me as Margery rushed to the front of the counter.

"Oh my God, is she okay? Should I call 911?"

I squeezed my eyes closed, clenching my jaw trying to will the vertigo away. I heard voices calling my name, but they didn't belong to Hunter or Margery. They were women's voices and the scent of wood smoke filled my nose. *No, not now. Not again...*

The voices grew louder and in my mind the wind blew, forcing me back. I stumbled in my own mind's eye and I knew I needed to fight whatever this was.

Course unseen across the night
Come to us as your time alights
Blood calls to blood in the hours hence
Come to us in the hours whence
Those who call through here and now
Bend light and sound and a century's vow
Be there no bounds to what you see
Blood calls to blood we summon thee.

I ignored their chant, shoving it to the bottom of my mind and forced my head between my knees so I could cover my ears without looking any crazier than I already did. At least I was still in control of my body, even if I was too afraid to speak. I knew at that moment I straddled two worlds and I needed to make a stand against whomever or whatever was messing with me.

In my mind I shouted the word *"No!"* visualizing slamming windows and doors closing inside my head. Whoever was trying to get the better of me was not going to win. I wasn't a novice anymore.

Laughter replaced the chanting and my head shot up as I heard my mother's voice the same as I did before Hunter and I left this morning. *"She's not ready..."* echoed in my mind, and I couldn't tell if it was truly Mom's voice or just spirits messing with my memories. Either way, I didn't care. I *wasn't* ready, nor did I plan to be. Ever.

"Rowen!" Hunter's voice was more urgent this time.

"I'm okay, just give me a minute," I ground out through my teeth.

"Are you sure?" Hunter asked, but his voice, like Margery's, was thick in my ears while the rhyme still played sing song in my head.

My eyes found Hunter's and his soft brown gaze was both worried and angry. This morning my mother had lied to him for me, and he knew it. He guessed something was up and I chose not to tell him.

The chanting and the scent of smoke finally subsided enough for me to sit up and take the cup of water from Margery's hand.

"Are you sure you're okay, sweetie? You went down like a cart of bricks."

I nodded. "My blood sugar must have dropped. It happens sometimes. I'm sorry, truly. Did I damage anything when I fell?"

She shook her head. "A toppled vase from the counter, but that's all. No harm, no foul. Why don't you rest a bit while I clean up the spilled water? There are a couple of dining chairs against the wall. They're antiques and for sale, but I don't think either you or your young man will hurt them any."

"Give her a little bit of that Belgium chocolate you keep in your desk, Margie. It'll help until we can get her something more substantial."

Both Hunter and I turned to see Jan Dunham standing in the doorway. "Hunter, help her up and let's get her settled. She needs a little sugar boost to get her even again, but that's not

going to last. He tapped a plastic square on his hip beneath his shirt. I'm diabetic, so I know what I'm talking about."

I straightened with Hunter's help and gave the old man a genuine smile. "Thanks, Mr. Dunham."

He waved me off. "No need to thank me yet." He gestured to the chairs. "Rowen, sit. Hunter, run down to the gas station and get some orange juice and a banana. Margie and I will keep Rowen company until you get back. This way you can get your car from the restaurant parking lot. I'm sure, given the circumstances Margie won't mind if you park in her driveway."

Water dripped in two lines from where I knocked over the vase, its summer flowers now prone in a wet mess on the counter. A single daisy had fallen to the floor where I collapsed, and I bent to pick it up before Hunter walked me toward the chairs. As I twirled the delicate bloom in my fingers, I had the strangest feeling this was somehow important. Symbolic.

Margery came back with a large bar of milk chocolate. She broke off a piece and handed it to me. "Of course, Hunter can park in the museum's driveway."

Hunter hadn't moved yet. He was still standing beside me when Margery glanced across her shoulder at him. "Go ahead, sweetie, your girl's in good hands with us."

I knew I was pale, and my hand shook as I took a bite of the proffered chocolate. It wasn't low blood sugar that caused my incident and Hunter knew it. He wasn't happy about being made an errand boy, but for appearances sake he had no choice. We'd be on the road quick enough and I'd tell him everything that had happened, starting with what I saw in my bathroom mirror two days ago.

Hunter lifted my chin and his eyes locked onto mine. "I'll be right back." His gaze held for another moment before he turned to leave. He didn't say another word, yet his message was loud and clear. *"I expect a full explanation and I'm not taking no for an answer."*

"Don't worry, honey. He's not going far, and you'll be right as rain in no time at all," Mr. Dunham commented, easing himself into one of the antique dining chairs.

"These aren't all that comfy, Margie. You might want to think about having the upholstery re-stuffed if you want to lure someone in to sit and look at your pretty face." His wheezy chuckle made me smile, especially when Margery rolled her eyes at him despite the pink tinge that flushed her cheeks.

With a shift and grunt, Jan made himself as snug as possible, pulling an old volume from that same deep pocket that held his collapsible cane earlier.

"Since you and Hunter were so interested in spies, I thought you might be interested in seeing this." He held the book out to me.

The pages were brown and yellowed, crumbling along the edges. The sheets were uneven and from breaks in the spine, I noted the binding was hand stitched. This was no ordinary book. This was a private journal, like one you'd find resting on a shelf in a literary museum or a rare-book store or even at a historical society.

"Ah, you've brought one of your great-grandfather's journals," Margery noted lifting her chin slightly. Her eyes were almost hungry the way they followed my hands as I took the book from Mr. Dunham.

"Six times great-grandfather, Margie...and yes, I broke out the big guns because this little lady and her young man impressed me." He leaned back in the old chair and lifted his hand, spreading his arm to sweep the room. "When's the last time you had anyone their age stop here of their own volition for any significant amount of time?"

Margery hmmphed.

"Just as I thought," he replied.

I looked between the two of them, confused. "I'm sorry. I must still be a little fuzzy because it feels like I missed something."

Jan shook his head. "No, it's fine. Margie has been trying to get me to give the museum here an exclusive on my six times great-grandfather's journals. Problem is I don't want the books here in Hurley. They belong in my hometown, Cold Spring, actually West Point to be exact. You see, honey, my ancestor James Thacher was one of the surgeons attached to the various field hospitals of the Continental Army's at West Point from 1775 until the end of the revolutionary war." He stopped and put his hand on the tome resting on my lap. "...and this is his daily journal, or one of them anyway."

I looked down at the book afraid to pick it up, that it might crumble in my hands. "Should I put on gloves?" I asked.

He smiled, taking his dark glasses off for the first time. His eyes were a milky blue, just like the graveyard caretaker Mr. Grayson's, and an unreasonable wave of anxiety passed over me they would change to a candy blue for an instant just like Mr. Grayson's had.

Jan patted my hand. "Don't be afraid to look at the pages. Based on what we were talking about earlier, I marked a few entries that might pique your imagination."

Tiny strips of white paper poked out the top of the journal. One had been noted with an asterisk and I carefully opened the book to that passage.

26th—At three o'clock this morning, an alarm spread throughout our camp. Two regiments from the Pennsylvania line were ordered to march immediately to West Point, and the whole army to be held in readiness to march at a moment's warning. It was soon ascertained that this sudden movement was in consequence of the discovery of one of the most extraordinary events in modern history, and in which the interposition of Divine Providence is remarkably conspicuous. It is the treacherous conspiracy of Major-General

> Arnold, and the capture of Major John Andre, adjutant general to the British Army. The army being paraded this morning, the following communication in the orders of General Green was read by the adjutants to their respective regiments:
>
> "Treason, of the blackest dye, was yesterday discovered. General Arnold, who commanded at West Point, lost to every sentiment of honor, of private and public obligation, was about to deliver up that important post into the hands of the enemy..."

I looked up at this point, and I knew my expression was a combination of awe and doubt. "Is this what I think it is?"

Jan nodded, his expression sober. "Yes. This is my direct ancestor's account from the very day the fort and everyone in it was informed of Benedict Arnold's treason and how he was a mercenary spy working for the British."

I read on, unable to truly wrap my head around the piece of history I held in my hands, literally.

> Such an event must have given the American cause a dangerous, if not fatal wound; happily, the treason has been timely discovered to prevent the fatal misfortune. The providential train of circumstances which led to it, affords the most convincing proofs that the liberties of America are the object of divine protection. At the same time that the treason is to be regretted, the general cannot help congratulating the army of the happy discovery. Our enemies, despairing of carrying out their point by force, are practicing every base are to effect bribery and corruption what they cannot accomplish in a

manly way. Great honor is due to the American army, that this is the first instance of treason of the kind, where many were to be expected from the nature of our dispute; the brightest ornament in the character of the American soldier is there having been proof against all the arts and seductions of an insidious enemy. Arnold has made his escape to the enemy, but Major Andre, the adjutant-general in the British army, who came out as a spy to negotiate the business, is our prisoner.

"This is amazing," I said still scanning the rest of the text. "So, this is exactly what was read to the troops on September 26, 1780, plus your six times great-grandfather's own personal account."

Jan exhaled, but his smile was proud. "Yup. Makes you want to stand up and salute, don't it?"

I chuckled. "Well, I wouldn't go that far." I thought for a moment, running my fingers over the page. "So, if this was read to the troops on the twenty-sixth, then that means Arnold was found out and escaped, when?"

"Everything unfolded on the morning of the twenty-fifth of September. Washington was supposed to meet Arnold and his wife for breakfast and then stay the night, but for whatever reason he was delayed. When he finally arrived, he found Arnold gone and was told he had gone to West Point ahead of the general. Washington went straight away to meet him there and was surprised when no one had seen the man. Washington didn't give it much mind and went ahead with the fort's inspection, fully expecting to meet Arnold back at his home later in the day, but when he returned, the reason for Arnold's MIA status was revealed. A messenger had already told Arnold of Andre's capture."

"In Sleepy Hollow…that much I know. We've got a statue in Patriot's Park commemorating the event."

He nodded. "Arnold was a real piece of work. Once he realized he'd been found out, he had a servant row him to the British sloop *The Vulture*, to facilitate his escape, and the bastard left his wife and child to face the music when Washington finally showed up for his visit later that day."

I looked at the artifacts surrounding us and what they represented, the people and the lives, and the thought occurred how many would have suffered if things had gone the other way. "Both men spoke of providence and divine intervention. It's almost as though they believed a guardian angel stepped in and changed the tide of events in their favor simply because they had right on their side."

His gap-toothed grin grew wide. "Well, isn't that always the way?"

I didn't get a chance to answer as Hunter came in carrying a bag filled with bottles of water and enough bananas and orange juice to open a smoothie stand but based on the look on Jan's face, I suspected the question was rhetorical anyway.

"Good job, young man. Now let's get your lady set and send you on your way. I'll bet dollars to donuts you didn't plan to spend this gorgeous day inside with musty old artifacts and two musty old people, enjoyable as it has been." Jan snorted, sneaking a glance at Margery.

"Speak for yourself, old man," she joked, patting her hair. "I can still roll with the best of them, now pour that girl some juice and let's talk about a prime spot for your remarkable journal."

Chapter 7

GPS took us as far as Route 212 to Cooper Lake Road and from there we had no choice but to follow the printed map on the back of Jenny's invitation. Most of the houses were small bungalow style homes situated across from the lake, but none of them fit Jenny's description. We knew we had to watch for a narrow gravel and dirt road on the right that would lead straight to the lakeshore.

The ride wasn't that long, about forty minutes give or take once we were finally on our way again, but not enough time to truly talk about what happened at the museum shop. Of course, that didn't stop Hunter from putting me on the spot the minute my butt hit the car's front seat.

"Well?" he began.

"Can I at least close the door?"

We both knew this was coming from the minute Jan made Hunter leave, but to be honest I didn't know how to begin. "What do you want to know?"

His fingers gripped the steering wheel tightly. "I'm not stupid, Rowen. I know your mother covered something for you before we left, so why don't you start at the beginning. After the episode in the museum, I can only assume there were more visions. When did they start again?"

I exhaled with a shrug. "Two days ago."

He pulled his eyes from the road to look at me. "Before or after you picked me up at the airport?"

I looked at my hands in my lap. "Before." At the sound of his rough exhale, I looked at him, watching the tension grow in his jawline.

"But they aren't like before, Hunter. There's no blood, no violence, just my ancestors messing with me."

He glanced sideways at me, again. "Messing with you? How?"

I shrugged. "I'm beckoned and then shown images from their lives. Gran called these types of visions, awakenings." My eyes found his and I reached out, resting my hand on his arm. "My mother didn't lie, Hunter. Awakenings *are* visitations and they're benign or at least that's what Gran and my mom think."

"Think? Don't they know?"

"Of course, they know. It's weird though. This latest vision didn't say or show me anything. It was strange. This time I heard chanting. Maybe a spirit is gearing up to show me a family ritual or a spell lost to time. My best guess is the visceral punch this time was stronger because you were with me. You know how that goes. According to Gran, you're the magnet and I'm the channel."

"How could I forget?" He made a face. "But why the compass? Why was that a catalyst?"

I shifted in my seat turning my body so I could face him better. "Your guess is as good as mine. Perhaps it was a metaphor and my ancestors are trying to guide me towards something. Who knows? I'm just glad the vision wasn't awful or violent, but it's safe to say no more antiquing for us—at least not together."

He laughed, nodding in agreement. "Now that's a promise I plan to keep."

We didn't talk for a while, and I plugged my iPhone into the USB port inside the console syncing my playlist to the radio. Jason Mraz filtered through the speakers and I watched the miles of unspoiled forest go by on the opposite side of the passenger window.

"Hunter?"

"Hmmmm."

"Are you worried?"

He looked at me. "About what? Your visions?" He shook his head. "If your mother and grandmother aren't worried, then I'm not either. Perhaps my bad feeling about this weekend had to do with you keeping things from me. Maybe on some subconscious level I sensed something bad and just didn't know what it was."

My eyes dropped to the console, guilt making my cheeks hot and my eyes sting.

"Hey," he said tugging on my hand. "Rowen, don't. It's done. Just promise you won't keep anything from me again. We're a team, right?"

I smiled. "Right."

"I think this is it. That's the turn off." I pointed to a tree with yellow and white balloons tied to a low branch.

"I certainly hope so or we're about to crash a birthday party." Hunter clicked on his turn signal and slowed to make the sharp right.

We drove half a mile and saw the start of an expansive lawn and small out buildings and sheds.

"Jenny said the property was big, but damn," I muttered.

"All this and yet we can't swim in the lake because it's a reservoir."

"I'm all for roughing it, but swimming with snapping turtles isn't my idea of fun, besides the house has a gigantic pool." I held up my phone to show him the pictures Chloe texted. "Plus, Chloe said there's a boathouse stocked with fishing gear, but if you're hell bent on taking a dip in the lake, I'm sure Benny would push you out of a row boat just to oblige."

"Ha, ha."

Another quarter mile in and the house appeared, looming large against the blue sky and the span of Cooper Lake. Thick

green trees lined the far perimeter on the opposite side of the water and the vista climbed majestically into the foothills of the Catskills and up.

"Wow, would you look at that," I said leaning forward. "And the house isn't bad either."

Hunter laughed. "I'm sure Jenny will be glad to hear that."

The house was a large log cabin style home built on a crest overlooking the water. A circular drive bordered well-manicured planting beds covered in a rainbow of flowers and ornamental grasses. A wide wraparound porch circled the entire house, and two-story windows flanked either side of the stone steps gracing an enormous chalet style façade rising from the porch and ending in a decorative pitched roof.

"If the house has this many windows in the front, I can only imagine how many overlook the water and the pool in the back," I murmured.

We pulled around the gravel semi-circle and parked next to Benny's pickup. As if on cue, Chloe came out onto the porch, waving like a mad woman. I barely had time to step out of the car before she barreled up, throwing her arms around my neck.

"You're here! Finally! I know you told miss prissy pants you'd get here late, but it's almost dinnertime. She's been stewing to say the least. Something about messing up her whole schedule." Chloe hugged me again. "So, what took you so long?" She eyed me with her tongue in her cheek as she wiggled her eyebrows up and down.

"Get real, Chloe. We're not the Motel 6 type."

Hunter laughed. "Hey, now. That's an idea."

I still had pretzels in my hand from our earlier stash, and I pitched one at him.

With a wink, he lifted the trunk and grabbed our bags, placing them on the gravel before slamming the top shut. "Lead the way, Chloe. Where do we drop these?"

Linking her arm with mine, she gestured toward the front door. "Just follow me. Everyone has assigned rooms."

"Assigned?" I asked looking past Chloe to Hunter. Maybe this weekend wasn't going to be as good as I hoped.

She gave my shoulder a light push. "Assigned, as in couples, so relax. *Jeez.* Put a lid on those hormones, we're not even through the front door."

Chloe held the door, and Hunter carried in the bags leaving my backpack and his guitar for me to carry. He took up playing again after Talia and Mike died, saying the music helped him deal with his grief. I envied him the outlet and part of me wondered if my previous fears were still a valid assumption and his music was an outlet for dealing with me, too.

Jenny came through a set of sliding glass doors that led out to the back veranda, a Mike's Hard Lemonade in her hand. "Well, you two certainly took your time getting here. Did you get lost?"

I shook my head. "Nope. We decided to stop and do a little sightseeing as we drove. There's so much history and natural beauty up here we couldn't resist."

She pressed her lips together. "I can't argue with that and I suppose once a history geek always a history geek." She smiled, raising her icy bottle. "Well, either way, I'm glad you finally made it. Welcome to the lake."

She turned to head back out, but then looked back again. "Oh, you two are in the third bedroom on the right overlooking the water. Drop your bags and then come on back. We're hanging by the shore where we're setting up for the bonfire. The grill is on and burgers and dogs will be ready soon, so don't be long. You have a lot of catching up to do." With that, she turned toward the back sliders again, this time dragging Chloe with her.

Hunter and I went up the stairs and found our room with no problem. The entire back side of the house was a giant wall of windows and the two-story living room had the same rustic beamed look as the outside façade and was capped off by a floor to ceiling river rock fireplace.

I opened the door to the bedroom, holding it wide so Hunter could carry in the bags. The room was large with polished planked floors. A thick area rug in deep jewel tones graced the floor, spreading beneath a four poster, queen sized bed. A triple dresser and armoire sat against the side wall next to the bathroom leaving the entire wall across from the bed for a state-of-the-art entertainment center and flat screen television.

"I guess we won't be bored tonight. It looks like Jenny's got the place wired for everything under the sun."

Hunter dropped the bags at the foot of the bed and in two strides swept me into his arms and deposited me on the embroidered bedspread. He crawled up beside me, gathering me in his arms. "I have been wanting to get you alone all day."

I ran my fingers through his hair, looking at the depth of brown in his eyes. "What do you mean? We've been alone since we left this morning."

A slow gorgeous smile spread across his full lips and he shook his head. "Yeah, but not this kind of alone."

I opened my mouth to argue, but he kissed me silent, his mouth demanding and hungry for mine. His hands untied what was left of the string tie on my blouse letting it fall the rest of the way off my shoulder.

Sliding his hand behind my neck he cradled me close, feathering soft, seductive kisses along my throat and collarbone, his lips grazing the top swell of my breasts.

"Hunter..." I breathed, arching myself closer to him. "Lock the door and close the drapes."

We both took showers and I was still in the bathroom when Hunter called through the door, he would meet me downstairs. I heard the bedroom door open and close and I sighed. How did I get so lucky?

I finished getting dressed, pulling on a pair of jeans and red cotton Horseman's jersey with Hunter's old football number. Tying my hair into a high pony tail I applied minimal makeup, trying to keep things casual.

"Not bad," I murmured as I gave myself a last once over in the mirror. I walked out of the bathroom and pushed my feet into a pair of black flip-flops and headed out the door.

"Well, look who decided to grace us with her presence?" Benny said, getting up from his chair next to Chloe. He gave me a theatrical flourish, and bowed deep. "Milady, please sit."

"Nice to see you too, Benny." I punched him in the arm.

"Ouch! What was that for?" he hissed, rubbing his arm.

"Love tap against whatever stupid thing you're going to say later once the beer kicks in."

"Ha, ha."

Glancing around the yard, I didn't see Hunter. Jenny was talking with Eric and Constance, and Benny was here with Chloe and me. That left Hunter and Hannah, and neither were anywhere to be found.

"Where's Hunter?" I asked, looking to Chloe for an answer.

She shrugged. "He and Hannah went inside for something. Maybe ice. The cooler was getting pretty melted."

I formed a silent *"oh"* and as if on cue the two came walking through the lower sliders, Hunter carrying two bags of ice and Hannah with a platter of what looked to be barbeque fixings.

Chloe slapped the side of my arm. "See?" She turned from me to tug on Benny's sleeve. "Babe, Rowen needs a drink. Can you grab us a couple of lemonades?"

Benny smirked, leaning down to peck Chloe's cheek. "What's in it for me?"

She shoved him away with a laugh. "Just do it. We can negotiate fees later."

He turned to head toward the coolers and I called after him. "Benny, wait! Real lemonade for me, okay? Not the hard one."

He chuckled. "Still, Rowen. Really?

I shrugged. "Once a light weight, always a light weight."

The barbeque went well, and everyone seemed to be getting along, though no one mentioned the reason for our getting together. That was up to Jenny, and if she decided she'd rather not, then I was more than okay with it.

"It's nice to see you again, Rowen," Hannah said, walking toward the fire pit. "Can I sit or is this chair taken?"

Hannah looked so much like Talia it hurt to look at her. They had the same pin straight blond hair and beautiful complexion. Even their eyes were the same shade of blue. The only saving grace was Hannah was shorter than Talia and she'd cut her hair into a bob similar to Chloe's. Somehow, that made it a little easier.

"Please, sit down. Hunter is busy talking with the boys, probably about what they expect to find at college come August. How are you, Hannah? How've you been?"

The young girl shrugged. "Okay, I guess. My mom and dad are still in bad shape. In fact, I'm surprised they let me come this weekend. They hardly let me out of their sight these days. If it wasn't for Constance, I don't think I would have seen the outside of my house since we buried..."

The girl's voice hitched, and she looked down at the red Solo cup in her hand. I reached out resting my palm on her forearm. "It's okay, Hannah."

As surprised as I was to hear Constance step out of character, I wasn't about to question it. During the year, I had passed Hannah in the hallways at school, but I was so caught in my own funk I barely acknowledged the girl. In that moment I was both relieved and grateful to Constance and planned to tell her so at some point this weekend.

The girl looked up at me. "I...I didn't want to upset you. Everyone knows you took what happened almost as hard as we did."

I inhaled, letting the air out of my lungs slowly. "Yeah, I suppose. But I'm better now. I can talk about Talia and laugh

about our silly fights and all the fun we had hanging out together. If you want to talk, it's okay. I'm here for you."

She nodded, but neither of us said another word about it. The topic was opened and shut that quickly, but at least the door was open for the future.

"Come on, everyone. The wood is ready and based on the weather we'd better get this bonfire started before the rain hits," Jenny called from the beach.

The guys grabbed the prepared torches and lit them in the fire pit before carrying them down to the stacked wood on the lake's edge. Watching them head single file toward the pyre almost seemed ritualistic. It was well past nine p.m., and the torches cast an orange glimmer in the darkness, illuminating corners and shadows. Hunter caught my eye and I waved from where I stood with my feet in the water. He looked gorgeous in the warm glow of the flames.

Jenny waved the guys over, and on the count of three they shoved the torches into the wood, lighting the twigs and dried brush and setting the teepee style structure ablaze.

She stood to the front on a small bank while the rest of us watched in a semi-circle as the flames grew higher licking at the wood. Jenny raised her red Solo cup and gestured for the rest of us to do the same.

"As the smoke rises, so do our hopes and prayers. This weekend we say goodbye to the past, to friends we've lost and to old ideas. We honor those missing tonight and cherish their memory, but we also must look to life and what's coming. So, while we drink to the past, we welcome whatever time brings and promise to make the most of our futures." She paused, looking around the circle to each of us. "Here's to hope and to new beginnings!"

Everyone cheered, mimicking the sentiment. Jenny caught my eye and I watched her wipe away the wetness from her own. She raised her glass to me mouthing the words, "I'm sorry."

I blew her a kiss and covered my heart with my hand, and in that moment, I knew we'd all be okay.

The flames reached the top of the pyre and we sat around listening to the sounds of the forest and the crackle of the wood as the fire claimed it. Hunter went inside for his guitar and we laughed as the guys took turns trying to sing the folksongs, he played in honor of the fact we were hanging out in Woodstock.

The air was still, not a breeze in sight. Even the smoke from the bonfire billowed straight up. It was only a matter of time until the weather broke, but Mother Nature enjoyed herself, teasing us for the next couple of hours with tiny drops and rumbles of thunder in the distance.

Benny stood and pulled off his shirt "I want to go for a swim. Come on, who's game?" He lurched over to where Chloe sat with me and Constance and took her hand, mimicking Hunter's trademark move and kissing her fingers. "Come on, Chlo, there's no one around. It'll be fun."

I reached up and punched him in the arm again.

"Hey!"

"I'm sorry, but you need another love tap for being really stupid. Can't you hear the thunder? There's a storm coming, plus there are very large snapping turtles hiding beneath that water and I don't think you want one of them taking a bite out of your private parts."

He actually looked down at his crotch, making Constance spew her drink across the sand. At that moment, the wind picked up, blowing paper plates and empty cups around the grass and into the sand.

"Crap! My parent will kill me if they find Solo cups floating around in the water tomorrow. Everyone, spread out!" Jenny shouted.

The wind gusted at this point, and lightning crashed, illuminating the beach and thunder followed on its heels which meant the heart of the storm was close.

The rain pelted us as we ran around cleaning up food and snacks, gathering whatever we could find. The guys threw sand on the fire, and between the rain and the dirt, it was out by the time we all stumbled into the house dripping and muddy.

It was almost midnight, and all I wanted was another shower and to crawl into bed with the remote control.

"Come on, Rowen, it's early yet."

"It's midnight, Chloe. Unlike you, I didn't sleep in until noon before jumping in the car. Hunter and I have been on the road since early this morning. Jenny said we're heading out for white water at eight a.m. and I don't intent to look like the walking dead in front of my boyfriend come morning."

She hmmphed, but I wasn't the only one heading up to bed. Constance and Eric were already upstairs.

"Let's go, baby," Hunter joked, pulling me by the hand. We got to the base of the stairs and without warning he bent, hitting me with a move he learned on the football field and threw me over his shoulder.

"Goodnight, Chloe!" he yelled over the banister and the sound of my laughter.

Chapter 8

Hunter rolled over taking the covers with him. His breathing was even and peaceful, yet I couldn't sleep. It was silly, but I felt myself giving his back a dirty look.

Disney's *Pirates of the Caribbean* was on the flat screen, but I wasn't paying it much attention. I sat up, looking around the room. The rest of the house was quiet. Even Chloe and Benny had thrown in the party towel, crawling up the stairs more than an hour ago.

I threw my legs over the side of the bed and sat staring at the rug. The storm seemed to have parked itself above the lake, and the accompanying thunder and lightning were directly outside our bedroom. I got up and walked to the window and pulled back the curtain. Nature was putting on quite a show. The rain hadn't relented, and that meant the white water we'd encounter tomorrow would be wicked fast.

Everyone had been rafting before, and Hunter and Eric had gone so often in the past they were considered experts. The rafting company gave us the option to switch courses come morning, but the guys were psyched for the test and there was no way they were going to let the females in the group punk out. Benny even went so far as to suggest Mother Nature had fist pumped the idea by sending such a kickass storm.

I chuckled to myself. One of these days we would have to record the boy when he drank so he could see how stupid he sounded under the influence.

I looked at the water and the fog swirling over the black mirrored surface. Either the air temperature had dropped, or the water was warm or vice versa, but this level of fog was odd in the summer, regardless. Squinting, I took a closer look and movement caught my eye. It wasn't normal vapor hovering over the water, it was something else.

I pushed the window open and leaned out, not caring if I got wet. Two figures formed in the ethereal white haze. From my vantage point they looked like white robed women. They lifted their arms, beckoning.

"Rowen..." they sang.

I waited, but the women didn't do or say anything else. Just sang my name, the unearthly tinkling carried on the wind.

This was getting more messed up by the day, and when I got home, I swear, both Mom and Gran had a lot of explaining to do. If neither had a clue what was behind this, then both would drop everything to help me figure it out. I was not heading to college with a line of weirded out ancestors in tow.

I closed the window and let the curtains fall back into place and headed to bed. I crawled under the covers and cuddled up to Hunter, spooning behind him. He sighed in his sleep as I slid my arm around his waist, and he looked so cute I couldn't resist blowing on the back of his ear.

He rolled over and opened his eyes.

"Hi," I said.

"Can't sleep?"

I nodded and he opened his arms, patting the side of his chest. Scooting closer, I settled against him and no sooner had my head hit his ribs than his breathing resumed the cadence of sleep. I snuggled in closer and concentrated on his breathing, letting the even rhythm of the soft rise and fall finally lull me to sleep.

"Ready to roll?"

Giving myself one last look in the room's full-length mirror, I turned with a sigh. "I suppose. Though why everyone thought battling rapids at six a.m. was a good idea is beyond me."

As expected, I was cranky after only three hours of sleep. Hunter slid his arms around my waist. "Who'd of thought my peach of a girlfriend is actually a prickly pear in the a.m." He lifted my hair, pushing it onto one shoulder exposing the side of my long neck.

"Think of this as an adventure, and we're doing it together so that makes it fun already." He pulled me close. "You smell amazing." Inhaling, he kissed my neck, his breath feathering out along my skin tickling my throat.

He kissed the tender spot beneath my ear, nipping my lobe with his teeth. "I have a surprise for you," he whispered.

Hunter released me and took a step back, digging into the front pocket of his cargo shorts. He pulled out a gold chain with a delicate heart dangling from the end. Undoing the clasp, he reached around and slipped the pendant onto my neck. "You already have my heart, but now you can carry it with you everywhere."

After he fastened the chain, I lifted the gold lattice heart, holding it in my palm. The design was custom made with our first initials entwined in the gold lace. I threw my arms around his neck. "It's beautiful, Hunter. Thank you!"

I squealed inside and turned to face the mirror. With a wide grin, I tightened the cinched waist of my blouse, so the gold heart sat perfectly in the tiny hint of cleavage showing along the blue embroidered edge of my shirt. The white bodice with its wide square neckline skimmed the top of my breasts and the effect was more than I hoped, the style making my waist seem tiny and my breasts full.

"I guess you like it."

I looked at him in the mirror, and I caught a glimpse of myself reflected in his eyes. I wasn't sexy by any means, but Hunter had a way of making me feel beautiful. "I love it."

He spun me around and held my arms out, taking in the full effect of my outfit and the flattering cut against my body. He didn't say a word. He didn't have to, his eyes said it all.

I scooped my hair up and pinned the heavy mass into a French twist securing it with two curved tortoise shell combs. "And that folks, is as good as it gets," I said smiling up at him.

He kissed my forehead and walked to the foot of the bed for our back packs, slipping mine over his shoulder the same way he did so often senior year.

"We're not in school anymore. You don't have to carry my stuff."

He flashed a smile and walked passed me on his way to the door. "I didn't *have* to carry it then, smarty pants, but you can certainly have your bag back if you'd rather carry it yourself."

I rolled my eyes and with a wink he opened the bedroom door. We headed downstairs where everyone was already waiting. I was surprised to see we were the only ones carrying backpacks. It's true, there wasn't much room in the boat but we each voted to take a small bag with our personal items. My buckskin pack was the perfect size—small enough to be low-key, yet big enough to hold all the Girl Scout necessities I packed just in case. A mini flashlight, small box of wooden matches, trail mix, a six-ounce aluminum water bottle—I don't know why I took them other than they gave me a sense of comfort.

I even stowed a piece each of Gran's tiger-eye and green ruby zoisite. One promoted balance and the other an appreciation for the blessings in your life. Lord knew I needed both these days.

Gran was weirder than usual when I went to her house for the stones, preoccupied, much in the same way she was after my vision in the kitchen. My mother shrugged it off, but I had a

nagging feeling Gran was keeping a lid on something while she worked it out, especially since she insisted on going over the basics of scrying, as well as giving me a primer on summoning. Between that and my latest vision, no wonder I couldn't sleep.

Again, I dismissed my uneasiness as unfounded, knowing neither would consciously place me in harm's way. I pushed my pack further onto my shoulder and reached behind to feel for my phone in my back pocket. It was fully charged, and I promised myself I would call them both when we got back from rafting to settle everything in my mind once and for all.

"Everyone ready?" Jenny looked around at the motley crew standing at the base of the stairs, yawning. "There's hot coffee already poured and in travel cups plus homemade chocolate raspberry croissants courtesy of Rowen's mom…"

Benny didn't even let Jenny finish before he pushed past the rest of us to grab a napkin and a handful of croissants. "I got dibs on any leftovers," he said already shoving half a pastry into his mouth.

"Eeww, Benny…mouth closed, please." Chloe's sunglasses were already on her face, and from her pale cheeks she looked as though coffee wasn't going to cut it this morning.

"All righty then, everyone grab and go because we need to get moving. The bus is here and it's not going to wait."

"Bus?" I looked at Hunter and he shrugged.

Jenny had arranged for a private rafting company to pick us up and take us to the launch point. We piled into what resembled a posh church bus and headed toward the Esopus River.

No one talked as the bus moved down the highway. Most simply finished their coffee and closed their eyes for a little more shuteye. We arrived thirty minutes later, and the rafting company rep greeted us with everything ready and waiting.

There was a slight chill to the air, not a crisp feel like in September when fall knocked on the door, but more the kind of

clean, brisk feeling after a storm. The humidity broke, and I filled my lungs with the freshness.

The rain certainly left the river level high, and the standard banks were submerged almost to the grassy picnic area where we stood waiting for instruction. Even from our vantage point on slightly higher ground it was clear the water was moving as a fast clip. Debris from the storm filed past us, branches and bits of twig still fully leafed. The water itself was a churning brown with white eddies just off the launch area.

We were each fitted with a helmet, a pair of water shoes and a specialized life vest to go over our clothes. The raft itself was bright yellow and could accommodate seven passengers plus a guide. I blinked doing a mental count. With a single raft, that left us one seat short.

"The raft isn't big enough for all of us," I said to Hunter while trying to get Jenny's attention. I did a quick head count, realizing then both Hannah and Chloe were missing from the group.

"Where's Hannah? Please tell me we didn't leave her back at the house?"

Constance laughed slipping her arm around my shoulder and giving me a friendly shake. "Now why would you think that?" she asked with a wink. She let go of my shoulders to take the equipment our guide held out to her.

"Hannah is fine, Rowen," she replied, resting her life vest against the side of her leg. "She just didn't feel up to rafting." Constance slipped her helmet on and frowned at the loose fit. "Someone is going to have to help me with this..."

"And?"

She smirked. "After last night, Chloe wasn't up to being bounced around, either. She tried to keep up with Benny and I don't have to tell you what an epic fail that was. She decided last minute to stay back at the house with Hannah."

I made a face. "I believe it. She certainly looked a little green around the gills before we left."

Constance smiled, pushing her loose helmet up from her eyes. "See? It's all good, and if I can get this damn headgear to fit properly this run is going to be classic."

The guide clapped a couple of times to get everyone's attention. "Good morning. I'm Xavi, and I'll be with you as we tackle the rapids today. As you can already tell, the water level is very high due to the heavy rain, and the rapids are wicked fast. I'm sure I don't need to remind you this is a dangerous run. Everyone needs to pay attention and do their part. If the raft gets thrown around, and it will, you need to lean forward and grab hold of the safety rope." Xavi had the yellow raft propped against a bench, and he reached over snapping the bungee-like cord that circled the top perimeter of the outside of the boat.

"You can leave your personal belongings on the bus...shoes, bags, whatever, but I'm obligated to say the rafting company is not responsible for lost or stolen items. You might want to consider stowing them though, as you will get soaked."

He pulled a rectangular box of quart-sized Zip-Lock bags from his own pack and set it on the picnic table next to the raft. "I brought these along, just in case. If you feel it necessary to bring your camera phones, this is the only thing that might stand between them and a watery demise."

The guide passed around the plastic bags and I took a few for myself and Hunter. Opening my pack, I placed my phone in one baggie and the few other items I had into another, sticking them both back in my pack.

Jenny was talking to Xavi, and it was clear the two knew each other prior to this outing. In fact, with the way she brushed his dark hair from his eyes and the other little touches they traded back and forth, it was clear they knew each other *very* well.

"Are we ready to roll?" the guide asked looking around at us.

Benny gave a loud *woop woop* and Xavi instructed each of us to take hold of the bungee-style cord and carry the raft to the

water's edge. With the shortened shoreline courtesy of the rain, it didn't take long.

Xavi had us place the boat only halfway into the water, and even then, the current was so strong Hunter and Eric had to stand at the bow to prevent the raft from being swept into deeper water. The two swayed along with the boat, the flux pulling on their legs at as well.

Hunter whistled for me. "Rowen! Xavi says we're ready to go!"

The guys pulled the boat farther into the water and struggled to hold it steady and secure while the rest of us climbed in, each taking a seat. With a nod, Hunter and Eric jumped into the raft with Xavi being the last aboard.

The seats were three and three, separated by a center aisle and Xavi took his position at the back of the raft, sitting higher to steer. I chose to sit in the middle seat with Hunter directly across from me.

"Everyone ready?" Xavi waited for us to man our oars, and then gave the signal to start paddling.

The current was strong, and the raft moved quickly down river into deeper water. Eddies thrust us back and forth and we hit the first set of light waterfalls about one hundred yards from where we pushed off.

They were easy to maneuver through, and Xavi made small talk with us, wanting to know more about Sleepy Hollow.

"The Catskills have plenty of folklore and history. Has Jenny ever told the story of Rip Van Winkle?" Hunter asked.

Xavi shook his head. "No, she's not much for talking when we're together."

Jenny turned every shade of red on the color wheel, and Xavi grinned. "But that's one of the things I like best about her."

The pace of the river quickened and that was the end of all chatter. We focused, and except for Xavi barking instructions over the roar of the water, no one spoke. We paddled hard and

sweat broke out on my forehead and under my arms and I wanted to peel the wetsuit jacket from my body.

"Watch out, in coming!" Xavi shouted, and the raft dipped low as a large wave crashed over. The water was colder than I expected, and I was grateful for the wet gear, all thoughts of stripping it off long gone.

Drenched, the river finally destroyed what was left of my French twist and the constant spray had me wiping my face and eyes with my sleeve between oar strokes, erasing any remnants of make up on my face.

We had been on the river for about an hour and had rocked back and forth between adrenaline-soaked paddle wars and an even, fast paced kind of drifting. When we finally came to another smooth patch, I relaxed my grip on my oar and rolled my shoulders. We were still moving quickly, but it was a well-earned reprieve.

My hair hung in ragged curls, half plastered to my face, and my clothes were soaked through to my skin. Chloe was right about us looking like drowned rats, but we all did at this point. Even Jenny.

"So, are we having fun yet?" I teased, finally taking a minute to look for my hair combs.

"There..." Constance tapped me from behind, pointing to where my combs had swept beneath Hunter's seat.

He reached under his bench and felt around, finally scraping both of them toward the aisle. Scooping them into his hand, he held them out toward me.

"You okay?" he asked, but before I could answer the raft lifted up and slammed down over another set of waves and Hunter pitched forward losing his balance.

"Guys stay in your seats. The water is unpredictable on this part of the river. We don't want any stupid mistakes, okay?" Xavi motioned for Hunter to sit back.

I answered Hunter's question with a wink and quick nod and stuck both combs inside the zippered front of my life vest.

The raft hit the edge of a fast whirlpool and spun, jerking wildly as Xavi had us paddle hard to push through. More waves broke over us, turning our yellow raft into a yellow submarine on a wild ride down a steep incline.

"Woo hoo! Get ready, kids, here we go!"

Xavi's tone was enough to make my stomach clench. I looked across the bow and my mouth dropped open. A raging torrent of white and brown erupted ahead as we raced toward a steep set of falls. The river forked and we fought like hell to guide the raft toward the calmer, less violent route.

No falls, no falls, no falls. The words became a mantra as we paddled, a Viking rowing chant in my head, *stroke, stroke, stroke.*

My shoulders burned and my mouth went dry despite the constant flood hitting us with each wave. My hands slipped on the oar and I cried out, struggling to regain my grip against the rush of water.

Water seethed and crashed in and over us, relentless, the waves breaking against rocks and tree limbs, tossing debris and anything else in its path into the air.

"Hold on!" Xavi shouted.

I could barely see for the spray as the raft bounded up, smashing down as fast and hard as the water pouring into the boat. It ran out the sides while the river tossed us around like a cat toy. We fought to stay on course, with Xavi strapped into the back trying to steer us away from dangerous rocks and rubble that impeded our route to safety.

A loud crack rang out and a large branch plummeted to the water, its line of descent directly in our path.

"Turn! TURN! NOW!"

Too late. The surge from the branch striking the swift, swollen water pushed us up and over, one side of the raft dipping low, almost capsizing. I screamed, my body jerking loose of any restraint and falling forward, my oar gone. Constance screamed behind me, pitching head over feet into the raft's center aisle.

Hunter's eyes jerked from me to what needed to be done to stop us from tumbling farther toward the falls, but his oar snapped, and the jagged plastic juddered back and forth threatening to impale him.

"Hunter!" I shrieked.

I scrambled for the edge of my seat, grabbing for the hem of his life jacket to yank him back from the serrated point. Another wave crashed and I was torn loose, my fingers losing their grip.

I hit the water hard, my back crashing into the torrent, forcing the breath from my lungs. A crushing pain spread across my chest as I went under, but another wave lifted me above the surface. I dragged in a hoarse breath carried on the upsurge, but my cries were lost to the roar of the water and the current sweeping me under again. The raft rose and fell above me, pushing me farther into the depths.

Panic rose and I struggled to pull to the surface, but the churning water tossed me about, tumbling my body in suffocating somersaults. Flung upwards, my arms crashed into the air and I fought to bring my head up.

"ROWEN!"

Hunter's voice was tinny and far away as I was pulled under again, spiraling in the water only to be thrust upward. Choking and coughing, my head broke the surface, and I dragged in a single breath before the rushing water swept me like a rag doll towards the falls.

The roar of the swift water intensified, tossing me against debris caught in the rocks. The words *you are going to die* rampaged through my head, but my mind rebelled against the thought. Adrenaline surged against the pain and exhaustion in my body and I balled myself up. With all my strength I uncurled, propelling myself like a bullet to the surface and sucked in a deep breath, pulling back into a tuck and roll position seconds before I went over the fall's edge.

PART II

Chapter 9

My lids fluttered open, but I couldn't see. My eyes and lashes felt sticky and crusted with something that smelled faintly of copper and mud. My nose wrinkled at the scent, and I turned my face earning a mouthful of what I just smelled. Blood and wet dirt.

I tried to lift my head, but shattering pain shot through my eye and the side of my temple, drilling me to lay still. My eyes stung, but no tears came. I was either too injured or too dehydrated to even cry.

Instead, I concentrated on the simple task of breathing. *In. Out. In. Out.* The basic motion scorched my throat, and my lungs revolted against the invasion as though the air was made of lead instead of oxygen. I wanted to sit up, to wipe my eyes and get my bearings, but I couldn't move. Surprised I survived at all, I wondered how long I would continue in this state if rescuers couldn't find me.

I had no idea how far I coasted with the current or where I washed up. From the pain in my head I knew I probably had a concussion. From the heaviness in my chest, maybe severe bruising or a few broken ribs. Breathing didn't feel like sucking air through a straw, so perhaps my lungs were intact.

My thoughts shifted to Hunter and my family. They had to be wild with worry. If I could only get up and get moving, I might be able to flag someone for help. The Catskills were well

populated this time of year, so chances were good I'd run into campers or someone fishing.

I lay in the mud listening. I tried to tune into anything, a twig crack or the sound of a reel cast, but all I heard was the water below the riverbank.

How did I get so high on the shore? The waterline this morning was so swollen it crested up and over the tree boughs. Could it have receded that quickly?

I dismissed the notion. I hadn't been missing that long. Or had I?

Finally, I heard people in the distance. I tried to pull myself onto my elbows, but I was so tired and weak. Gathering all my strength, I pushed past the throbbing in my head and chest and sucked in an aching breath, forcing myself to my knees.

Fresh pain tore through me and a raw cry ripped from my bruised lungs. I slumped forward onto damp grass. Cognizance wavered, and sound grew thick in my ears. I heard yelling and running footfalls, but I was going under again, only this time into dark oblivion instead of dark water.

The men rushed through the trees at the wrenching scream, their attentions shaken from their hunt. The expansive forest was the perfect backdrop for miscreants and deserters without qualm or conscience on whom they preyed.

They pushed through the scrub, the rotted foliage along the forest floor muffling the sound of their footsteps. One man moved ahead of the others, his steps sure and fast while another followed on his heels, his pistol cocked for cover. The other men in their hunting party dispersed, scouring the other directions for the source.

The first veered toward the water. As he approached the shore he slowed, stopping to crouch beside a thick copse of

evergreen to better survey the area. With slow, quiet movements he pressed a few young branches aside.

"What is it, Captain?" his superior asked, his voice barely a whisper as he came up behind the man.

The man's eyes mapped the inert form prone in the leaves and sparse grass. "It appears to be a young woman, sir."

The captain straightened, keeping his movements stealthy and his firearm primed and ready in his hand. He scanned the riverbank and the surrounding grounds for telltale signs of brigands or the remnants of a makeshift encampment.

"There doesn't seem to be anyone else around, sir. No footprints in the mud, no branches askew, or disturbed underbrush. From what I can surmise, the woman appears to have dragged herself from the river."

He waited for a moment before glancing across his shoulder to directly address his commanding officer. "Should I investigate closer, Colonel, or do we circle back and find the others?"

The colonel pointed toward the muddy bank, and together the two soldiers moved past the trees. On approach, the captain situated his musket against a fallen branch, far enough from wet ground to keep his powder dry but close enough to keep his rifle at arm's length. He squatted beside the prone woman's form.

"Is she dead?" his superior asked.

The captain shook his head. "I don't think so, Colonel. She's chilled to the bone and gravely injured, that much I can say for sure, but she breathes."

The captain lifted the girl's hair, moving the wet matted mess away from her cheek. At the sight of the blood on her face, he sucked in a sharp breath. "Nasty head wound, that," he muttered. Without hesitation, he reached into the front lapel of his blue uniform coat and drew out a handkerchief, carefully wiping the blood and dirt from her eyes and face.

The girl stirred and her eyes fluttered but never opened. "Hunter..." The word was scarcely a whisper before oblivion claimed her again.

Hunter? Puzzled, the captain looked to his commander. "Perhaps she's been attacked, or she's escaped petty thieves. She's a pretty little thing despite the nasty wound at her temple, though your guess is as good as mine in accounting for her manner of dress or the lack of it for that matter."

With an exhale, the colonel squatted beside his subordinate. "Such as it is, her clothing is too fine for a camp follower, and despite the wretched pallor and dirt, her skin is smooth and unblemished." He lifted her cold hand, turning it wrist up. "Her hands are without callus..."

The man's words trailed off and his expression grew introspective as he absently traced the soft pads of her palm. It had been too long since he'd last touched a woman, especially one as curvy and full as this in her odd yet revealing attire. The wet clothing clung to her, leaving little to the imagination, and he was torn between sampling her softness and covering her exposed flesh.

"She's a bonnie one, eh?"

The colonel nodded, taking in every inch of the girl's profile. "That she is, Barnes."

At his subordinate's smirking grin, the colonel cleared his throat, quickly recovering his professional mien. He reached out and gently pushed the girl's full upper lip toward her gum line revealing perfectly white teeth. "Just as I suspected."

With a deep inhale the senior officer pushed himself to his feet, wiping his hands on his thighs. "Despite her current condition, this girl has all the earmarks of affluence, Captain Barnes. I have no clue as to what brought her to this end, but one thing is certain, she has somehow run afoul of criminal action. With detachments of redcoats and deserters from both sides skulking the area we'd best take her with us."

"Sir," the captain began, "the girl's medical condition is precarious at best. Perhaps we shouldn't risk moving her until she regains consciousness and can be properly questioned."

The colonel looked toward the sky and then glanced down at the captain still squatting beside the prone girl. "No..." He shook his head. "I'll take the chance and the responsibility. These mountains have God cursed weather, and I won't leave an injured woman to the elements no matter what the circumstances. Besides, the closest doctor is hours away even on our fastest horse."

He unbuttoned the front of his jacket and shrugged it from his broad shoulders, rolling the cuffs on his linen sleeves "Morale is low and we've little to compensate it these days. I won't add unintentional murder to my list of sins. She's alive and I intend to do everything in my power to see she stays that way." He gestured for Barnes to get up. "Come...take off your coat. We'll build a litter so we can carry her out of this godforsaken forest. Dr. Thacher can ascertain her injuries and perhaps even her identity once we get her to West Point."

Hard, rough planking replaced boggy earth beneath me. I opened my eyes to the sky, moonless and dark as pitch. A scratchy blanket smelling strongly of horses was the only cover I had against the rain falling in fat drops, soaking my clothes— except I wasn't wearing *my* clothes. I was dressed in some sort of cotton gown with a thin, woolen cloak draped about my shoulders. It was heavy and wet, and I reached up to push its drooping hood from my eyes and winced. My head throbbed, rebelling against the effort as the lightning flashed overhead.

Sweating, I forced myself to sit up, fighting the nausea that accompanied the effort. In a flash of light, I saw I was in a wagon of sorts.

It had been pushed well off the road or what I supposed passed for a road. Someone had taken the time to hide the cart in the depth of trees. Between the new moon and the thick woods, I was lucky to see anything let alone my surroundings.

Flares of lightning showed me a few tents and a cold campfire with a metal tripod over the center. Hanging from the contraption was what looked to be an iron pot, similar to one of Gran's cauldrons.

There were a few men dressed in revolutionary uniforms moving around the tented area, and I gritted my teeth shifting my position to get a better look. Maybe this was a reenactment site. Even so, why was I in costume and who dressed me? Or undressed me was the better question.

Whoever they were, the personnel seemed agitated, moving in short, clipped actions. No one spoke, but the few people I saw seemed to keep watchful eyes on the far forest.

The river was to my left as was the muddy trail I assumed we were following. Whoever had brought me here was following the riverbank through a path in the trees.

Voices yelled in the distance, causing a flurry of manic activity in the reenactment camp. Everyone's posture turned urgent and heated. Fear spiraled down my spine. Where was I, and what the hell was going on?

My mouth was dry, and I wiped the crust from the corners with my sleeve. I had no clue how I came to be in this wagon dressed like an extra from a period movie, but I had a gut feeling I was about to find out the hard way. The sounds of yapping and growling followed the unmistakable *pop, pop, pop* of gunfire.

Most likely they were theatrical blanks, but maybe not and alarm flooded my veins. Stranger things have happened in our road-raged world. I pushed the cloak from my head to better peer into the darkness.

The last thing I remembered was waking up on the banks of the Esopus River and forcing myself to listen for the sounds of rescue.

This entire situation made no sense. It simply didn't add up, but I refused to let fear rob me of practicality. I needed to speak with someone in charge.

I listened again like before, trying to get my bearings, but how the hell could I figure out what was happening when I had no idea where I was or how I got here? It was like being dropped in the middle of someone else's life.

Gunshots sounded again, and from the volume off the trees, the shooter was not too far behind. I gathered my skirts and scooted toward the flat open end of the wagon. A hiss sucked through my teeth at the dizziness that hit along with fresh wave of pain in my chest and head.

Strange as it might sound, I welcomed the feeling. At least it was something recognizable, something that made sense from the events of my day. Warmth ran down my cheek toward my neck and the slick, metallic scent of blood reached my nose.

I lifted my hand to my temple and another wave of vertigo hit. There was nothing for me to grab onto to halt the dizziness, and I knew I was going down, hard. I lurched forward as the swoon took me and landed on my side in a muddy puddle on the ground. A chill seeped into my bones and I shivered, but at least the jarring pain kept me from passing out.

The cloak's hood had pitched forward again, flopping across the side of my face. It obscured my vision even more than the dark, but I sucked in a breath and tried to stand only to fall victim to my own retching stomach. I swallowed against dry heaves ripping past my gut, wiping my mouth on my sleeve.

Gritting my teeth, I got to my feet and turned to run, but stopped. Where would I go? Tears threatened and my trembling fingers went to my lips, but another hand shot from the darkness covering my mouth.

"Sssh...Don't move," a male voice whispered behind my ear. "Don't make a sound or we both die." The man held me tightly but was careful not to hurt me, and with a slow, decisive motion he pointed ahead to the far movement in the trees.

Lightning flashed again and my captor pulled us farther into the shadow of the wagon, but not before my eyes flew wide at what I saw.

Soldiers. Soldiers in redcoats. With real guns. Real redcoats with muskets and bayonets racing through the dark, darting between the trees not far from where we hid.

Their voices faded as they ran away from the river, and the man holding me released his tight grip. His hand came up and pushed the hood off my head to my shoulders.

"Who are you?" I croaked, looking into his deep set, violet blue eyes.

"I could ask the same thing of you, miss." The soft skin around his eyes crinkled and he inclined his head. "Lieutenant Colonel Alexander Hamilton, at your service."

My body stiffened. Eyes wide, I didn't make a sound as recognition and reality hit like another head wound.

"I see you recognize my name. Perhaps you would be so kind as to grace me with the same privilege. You are?"

He waited for me to find my voice, but a flurry of gunshots pulled his attention to his men. He flung me at the nearest soldier, shouting instructions for me to be moved to safety but guarded.

"Food and water and clean linen if she so desires, but do not let her out of your sight, is that clear, Sergeant?"

The man bobbed his head, practically dragging me bodily away from the exchange.

"I can walk, you know!" I snapped, yanking my arm from him. Nausea gripped me again and I knew I would retch if I didn't sit. Despite his grip, I sank to the ground gulping in air.

"I'm sure ye can walk, mistress, but considering the thump you're sportin' on the side of that pretty head, I think it's best if

ye let me help." He reached out his hand and waited, the whole time his eyes glancing past my shoulder at the smoke rising from the trees. "Come along then, lass. I won't have meself shackled or thrown in the stocks on account of one stubborn girl, hurt or no."

The terms *shackled* and *stocks* jerked my eyes upward to his. The sergeant winked, reaching forward to grip my elbow. "Aye, that's a good lass."

His brogue was endearing, if hard to understand, but there was a kindness in his eyes. The man looked war torn, with a grizzled beard and tattered blue uniform.

I shook my head trying to come to grips with what was unfolding before my eyes. My mind rebelled at the thought. This was a dream. I had to be in a hospital somewhere in a coma, and all the revolutionary nonsense Hunter and I talked about with Jan and Margery was causing delusions or subconscious rambling.

"Follow me. I'll put ye in the colonel's tent. It's the safest place considering ye've parked yerself in the midst of a wee skirmish with the local lobsterbacks." He grinned. "That and the men haven't seen anything as soft as ye in months. Best ye keep yerself hidden until himself returns."

Himself? The sergeant must mean the colonel. Damn, my subconscious was good. I had conjured Alexander Hamilton for this particular fantasy and my mind went ahead and made him young and good-looking to boot. Boy, Hunter was going to have a huge laugh at my expense once I woke up.

"Mistress…"

I jerked my head towards the older soldier. "I'm sorry, did you say something?" I might be in a coma induced dream state, but I could still be polite.

"Yes, I was telling ye this is not our usual camp. We're in route to West Point. The colonel is his Excellency's adjutant general and aide-du-camp and has been charged with helping General Arnold settle in to his new command."

"Wait, you called Benedict Arnold, his Excellency?" I almost laughed out loud.

The sergeant made a face. "No, ye daft girl. His Excellency, General George Washington." He waved his hand at me in a dismissive move. "I swear women have woolen stuff between their ears—anyway, ye were still visiting with the angels when the colonel and Captain Barnes returned from hunting. Provisions were getting low on the march, but we'll be at the fort soon enough, now."

"Fort?"

He issued an aggravated exhale and pushing open the tent flap, ushering me inside. "*Gah.* Haven't ye been listening to me? West Point."

The sergeant pointed to a chair and gestured for me to sit before moving to a makeshift cupboard. He filled a small round plate with cheese and bread and filled a cup with what smelled like weak beer from a bladder hanging from the colonel's chair.

"Here's the food himself promised. We have no meat, like I said, provisions and all." The man dragged a somewhat clean cloth from a pile beside a wash basin and ewer. Filling the bowl, he wet the cloth, ringing it so it was no longer dripping. "This will help with the mud on yer gown and yer..." he said, gesturing to the blood on the side of my face.

I glanced down at the serviceable blue cotton dress and its worn stitching around the cuffs and at the waist, wondering where my own belongings were in this madhouse dream.

I took the washcloth from his hand and cleaned the blood and dirt from my face and hands the best I could. "Can you tell me where we are?"

The man looked up from his duties. "We're about ten miles from West Point." He paused at my still questioning look, adding, "Five miles south of New Winsor where we found ye."

I remembered Jan telling us that the British soldier held at the old guard house was convicted in New Winsor. Chewing on

the inside of my lip, my eyes followed the man as he put the gleaming plate down beside my chair.

"That's more food than most of us get, so don't let it go to waste. Be thankful you're eatin' on fine pewter instead of a scratched wooden trencher." He gestured toward the plate, encouraging me to eat.

I picked up a bit of bread and took a bite. It was tough and grainy but at least it smelled fresh. I chewed slowly. I'd already suffered through dry heaves. If I did have a concussion, the last thing I needed was to make my condition worse by vomiting.

"You said New Windsor?"

He nodded.

"Wasn't a British spy hung in that town after the redcoats burned Kingston?" After the words left my mouth, I wished I could take them back. Did I have the dates right or had I just put my foot in it? It wouldn't be a far stretch for cautious chivalry to shift to suspicion if they believed I had advance military knowledge. Then again, why was I worried? This was my dream.

"Aye." His reply, hesitant. "But how do ye know of that, lass?"

"I once heard a story told about it."

"Ah...well, people do like to yarn about such."

I ate a little more and tried to keep my face impassive. This coma induced dream was astonishingly concrete. All my senses were alive and kicking, assailing me with every kind of sight and smell, especially the latter. The camp was rife with body odor and other hygiene deficient scents I didn't want to think about. I took a tentative bite of the cheese on my plate. It was surprisingly delicious and fresh. I must have looked stunned because the sergeant chuckled.

"Only the best for Washington's adjutant. Our rations may be scant, such as they are, but what we don't have in quantity the colonel makes up in quality."

I was suddenly ravenous and no longer shy about it. I made myself a small sandwich, causing the soldier to laugh despite a raised eyebrow and what must have seemed an odd manner of eating for a woman.

"I'm still a little muddled," I said chewing slowly. "Can you tell me the date?"

He looked at me queerly at first, but then his eyes dropped to the blood on the white linen cloth still on my lap and his expression softened. "Of course, lass. It's July the twenty-eighth."

I blinked. "And the year?"

Now he looked at me like I'd lost my senses, whistling low as he shook his head. "Ach, lass, whoever is responsible for knocking you senseless should be shot. It's a shame yer so higgledy-piggledy. The year is 1780, and just in case yer wondering, ye are traveling with the Ulster Division of the American regular army. If ye can keep from drawing attention to yerself, we will deliver ye safely to the fort where a proper doctor can care fer yer injuries. After that, word will be sent to yer family, I'm sure."

"Pinch me."

The sergeant jerked short. "Excuse me, lass?"

"I want you to pinch me. Hard."

The man's eyes bugged from his head and he nearly choked. "The colonel said ye were a lady, but I never..." He looked away, his lips pinched together.

I reached out imploring him. "Please. You don't understand. This whole situation..." I said swinging my arm wide, struggling for words. "I must be dreaming. It's too much...there's no other explanation."

My clipped words and voice broke, and the tears that refused to come earlier streamed down my cheeks. My face fell into my hands and soft sobs shook my aching chest.

"Yer head's bleeding again, lass," he said reaching for the white cloth. "That's explanation enough for why yer so

muddled." He squatted beside me and pressed the linen compress to the gash at my temple, issuing tender shushing sounds to comfort me.

The older man patted my shoulder but made sure to keep a proper distance. When my sobs faded to soft hiccups, he sat back on his heels and folded the bloodstained cloth before handing it to me.

"There's always a reason for the turns we take in life, lass. Take me, for example. When the war broke, I couldn't stop me boys from joining the militia. They were barely men, but their minds were set. Their mother, God rest her soul, had passed the year before in an Indian raid stirred by the British. Me boys swore vengeance and nothing short of an order from God's own lips would sway them." He paused, letting his gaze fall to the tent floor. "I lost both within a month of each other."

He stood, dragging in a sad breath. "At first, I wanted to die too, but I realized then I had a choice. I could sin before God and take me own life in sorrow and grief, or I could do something that would make me boys proud."

He turned back to me with a sad, close lipped smile and spread his arms. "So here I am at my grizzled age, fighting alongside boys not much older than me own, and there's no place I'd rather be. Life's turns give us pause, that's true, but God always gives us choice and it's up to us to ken which path is right."

The tent flap opened, and the lieutenant colonel walked in, the blue and buff of his uniform stained with mud, powder residue, and blood. His auburn hair had been blown back, the wind and exertion dragging it loose from the ribboned ponytail at the nape of his neck.

"Sir." The sergeant lifted one hand in salute, dropping the other to his side.

"At ease, soldier."

Hamilton tossed his tricorn hat onto his desk and walked straight to the ewer, then poured water into the basin to rinse

his face. The sergeant jumped to hand him clean linen and then went back to his spot, standing erect, feet apart, hands clasped behind his back.

Hamilton dried his face, rubbing the cloth over the back of his neck before he smoothed his damp hair, tucking it once again into place. His eyes found me, yet he addressed the sergeant "Everything well in hand here?"

The older man nodded. "Yes, sir. The lass ate a few morsels and managed to keep them in her gullet."

"It also looks as though she cleaned up a bit." Hamilton nodded. "Good." With an inhale he nodded again, distracted. "Thank you, Sergeant. You're dismissed."

With a wink and nod of his own, the older man left without a word.

Hamilton watched the exchange with a careful expression. He eyed me, walking around to the cupboard for a short pewter cup and filled it with weak beer from the same bladder hanging from his chair. Cup in hand, he leaned on his desk and lifted the hammered metal to his lips, his gaze studying my face.

"Our conversation was rudely interrupted earlier." He lifted his cup in a rueful salute. "My apologies. Unfortunately, the state of war has its own way of dictating time and circumstance, if not courtesy. You were just about to tell me your name, but I dare say there's no need. I already know who you are."

I swallowed hard. "You do?"

He nodded. "Yes. While I don't have the privilege of your given name, my guess is your sir name is Burritt. It's stamped into the top of the leather satchel we found washed up on the riverbank not far from where we found you." He watched my face. "Curious way of identifying personal items, but effective. My hat's off to whoever thought of the ingenious idea."

I followed his line of sight to the small camp seat opposite from where I sat. Atop the stretched coarse-twilled cotton was my buckskin backpack. It was in tatters, of course. One of its straps was missing having been ripped from its seams, but I was

more surprised it was here than at its condition. The torrent of water combined with the rocks and mud had ruined it, but there it was—proof I was not crazy.

"My satchel?"

He nodded, pushing himself away from the desk in order to retrieve it for me. He held it up, dangling it from its one remaining strap.

"Sad, really. Your haversack appears to have been of fine quality. It's rather dirty, so..." He put down his cup and proceeded to spread the same cloth I'd used to clean my face over my lap. "I don't want you to ruin your gown any more than you already have. The garment was hard enough to procure as it is, so I advise you to go gently until we get to West Point."

I took the pack from his hands and opened the top. Stamped into the leather on the inside flap was the brand name *Burritt*. No wonder he thought that was my last name. I pulled open the inner pouch and found a bundle wrapped in some sort of checkered cloth and my espadrille sandals I shoved into the bag when Xavi gave me water shoes, but everything else was missing: my phone, flashlight and matches...

Past and present warred not just in my mind, but in the jumble of material proof staring me in the face. I pulled the wrapper from the satchel and opened the soiled parcel. Inside were my white knee-length shorts and my cinched waist peasant blouse. They were tattered and stiff to the touch in places where the mud had dried. I rolled them in the cloth and moved to look at my shoes. They were damp and a little dirty, but otherwise unharmed. I had water shoes on when I went overboard, and they must have slipped off in the torrent at some point. My hand went to my throat. The gold heart Hunter gave me was gone as well.

"Recognize anything?"

I fingered the frayed edge of my gown's cuff, glancing from the rolled bundle to the colonel. "Just my clothes or what's left

of them." My face must have been a combination of confusion and accusation because Hamilton's expression hardened.

"I assure you, Miss Burritt, that while we did search your belongings, we returned every item we found, including the ragged clothing you were wearing when you washed up on shore." He stopped and turned, reaching for something on his desk. "Those items and these as well." In his hand was a compass that looked very much like the one from the museum shop in Hurley, and beside it was my mother's vial.

"The phial is of no interest to me." He held it out, gesturing with an indifferent flick that I take it from his hand.

At this point I would have burst into tears again, but I pressed my lips together refusing to cry. The colonel was gracious, but his body language screamed distrust and I doubted my tears would have fostered the same compassion in him as they did in the sergeant. Not that I was trying.

"You can stop looking so nervous. I had the good sergeant taste the phial's contents, and since he didn't keel over dead, I know it's not poison. But this...."

He held the compass by its fob, much in the same way Hunter had at the museum, and my heart squeezed. I issued a silent prayer he was safe and unharmed and had gotten to safety with everyone else.

"Miss Burritt, at least do me the courtesy of paying attention when I speak."

The colonel's deep voice brought me back from my reverie. "I...I'm sorry."

He frowned, but the displeasure didn't reach his eyes. It was almost as though he was more intrigued than annoyed.

"As I was saying, not a common item one would expect to find in a lady's reticule." He paused watching my face. "Then again, there's nothing about you that's common...is there?"

The ensuing question was almost an aside, as though spoken for his benefit alone. Whether intended or not, the two simple words were ripe with appreciation and a hint of want. His eyes

traveled my length and I knew he referred to more than just my curious possessions.

He recovered himself quickly, closing his fingers over the compass. "So, again, I'm obliged to ask. Who are you and what events transpired to lead you here?"

I opened my mouth to speak but closed it again. What could I say that didn't make me sound crazy? My gut told me to stick to the truth as closely as possible, but how could I explain what happened when I didn't understand it fully myself?

With every passing second, I realized this was no coma-induced fantasy. I was not unconscious and dreaming in some hospital bed. I had been dragged back in time.

Rebelling at the thought, I stared at nothing, my mind reeling at the implausibility. The word *impossible* rolled over my brain, but in a family such as mine that word holds a different connotation. I thought back to the events of the past few days, adding and subtracting moments. All the signs were there. How did I miss them? How did Gran and my mother? I knew without a doubt the chanting in my head at the museum was a catalyst, followed by the thunderstorm. How the compass resting in Alexander Hamilton's palm fit into this riddle I had no clue.

"May I see that, please?" I held out my hand for the device.

With a curious look he handed me the silver compass, and again, events mimicked what happened in the past or was it the future? Alexander's fingers brushed mine as he placed the compass in my palm as Hunter's had and I trembled, expecting the same feeling of vertigo, waiting for the chanting to start in my head, but nothing happened. Instead, a blurred image of an older woman's hand sliding the compass into my bag passed behind my lids while I waited for the onslaught. *Gran? Hulda? Who? ...and why?*

I turned the compass over, and my eyes widened. The inscription was missing. Had I imagined it there? Was I imagining this?

"Miss Burritt, are you feeling ill again? You seem out of sorts," he asked, taking a cautious step forward.

I looked up, shaking my head more from my own disbelief than anything else. The vial in my hand warmed, and whether it was from my own body heat or because the glass was charmed, I didn't know, nor did I care.

Lightning flashed outside the tent, and my eyes focused on the man standing just feet from where I sat. He was a real as me. I could feel his body heat, smell his masculine scent and watched as concern warred on his face with his sense of duty. He represented so much, not only to the past but to the future as well. Why then was I here?

As the question entered my mind alongside all the others, Gran's words came back. *It'll do more good than you know.*

In that moment, clarity replaced confusion and fear and my heart broke. The puzzle pieces knitted together, and I knew with complete certainty my own mother and grandmother were culpable. Gran especially. She knew I was meant to be summoned the minute her pendulum's blade hit home. I rolled the small glass vial in my hand trying not to cry.

"I, I…"

Queasiness rose and I couldn't speak. Indecision and mistrust warred in my mind. So much for my belief in the sanctity of family. There was no doubt the two women I trusted most had aided and abetted this insanity, but what I didn't know was why?

The realization I had been used as a pawn was too much to take in. For purposes yet to be revealed, I was a prisoner of time, with no idea why I was brought here or how to get home. Nausea gripped me and I pitched forward, vomiting the contents of my stomach onto the tent floor.

My head swam and numbness spread across my chest and into my throat, engulfing my head. Pins and needles pricked my skin until my eyesight narrowed. I knew what was happening and I dropped the compass to my lap along with my mother's

vial. The last thing I saw was the lieutenant colonel reaching to catch me as blackness took hold once again. Only this time, I welcomed the oblivion.

Chapter 10

At the sound of voices, my eyes opened, and I flinched at the bright light streaming in from the lead paned window. I blinked to accustom my sight, staring down at the white sheet and rough blanket covering the austere cot on which I lay. I was in a room with bare wooden walls and rough planked floors. It had no furnishings other than a small table hosting a coarse hand towel and a chipped blue and white floral ewer and washbowl. The only other decoration was a Chinese room divider with birds and flowers painted on its inner panels. It stood between my bed and the door, clearly something that didn't commonly belong in the room.

The smell of blood and old urine assaulted my nostrils and my hand flew to my nose and I wondered if the stench came from me. I didn't think so considering someone had changed my clothes, again. Gone was the heavy, mud covered gown, and in its place a light cotton nightdress trimmed in lace at the neck and cuffs. There was also a bonnet of sorts on my head, and I realized with a frown I was now part of an age where bare headed was not the norm, even while sleeping.

A tight bandage circled my head beneath the nightcap, and from the constricted feel across my back, sides, and chest, another circled my torso. I probed with my fingers and found the small, simple knots above my belly and under my breasts. No surgical tape or ace bandages here, but old-fashioned bindings.

I inhaled, wincing slightly at the pressure inside my ribcage and decided it was best not to move around too much.

"She's not fit to be moved, Alexander. Not for a few days yet."

My head jerked toward the voices coming from the opposite side of the screen and I winced with the effort, mouthing a silent *no shit, Sherlock*, at the estimation I wasn't fit to be moved.

I quickly wiped the sarcastic expression from my face, glancing toward the open window for anyone who might have seen. At least the paned glass had been lowered from the top, muffling the active camp, though from the smells in here I would have welcomed the fresh air regardless of the noise.

A muttered expletive followed the doctor's appraisal, and though I couldn't make out the voice I guessed from the name it had to be Hamilton. From the look of my surroundings and the authoritative way the other gentleman spoke, it was clear the regiment had made it to West Point, and I had been quietly consigned to the care of a field doctor.

Since my time-traveling epiphany back at Hamilton's tent, my sense of self-preservation kicked in big time. All previous assumptions had been effectively kicked to the curb. I still had no clue why the fates were jerking me around with my mother and grandmother switch-hitting as puppet master, but until I did, it was in my best interests to play dumb, at least until the universe presented both an explanation and a solution.

"She's been in and out of consciousness for a week. I can't in all good conscience send her on her way, wherever that may be." The doctor paused. "Is she the reason you weren't here to meet with General Washington on the thirtieth?"

I did a quick mental count for the date based on the information the sergeant gave. It was August seventh, give or take a day.

"Of course not. There were a number of skirmishes that delayed our arrival. I managed to send word, though.

Washington is aware of my situation and of the fact we now have either a refugee or a prisoner of war lying in that bed."

A rough laugh followed by a snort of indignation followed. "You can't be serious, Alexander. She's a mere slip of a girl."

"That may be so, but strange events have happened, and war makes for even stranger bedfellows. I've already obtained permission from General Arnold to move her to Robinson House. If she's not fit to be moved now, when is your best guess?"

"So, it's true, then. Washington gave the command to Arnold...*hmmm*. I wasn't sure if he'd go through with it considering the man's checkered past. I heard his wife's family is staunchly loyalist and that she had an eye for the British officers once they took Philadelphia."

"Really, James, if you spent more heed to the politics surrounding you and less time gossiping like a housewife you would know that General Arnold accepted the offer of command when Washington was here and he arrived on the fifth, some five days ago."

Okay, so it was August tenth. Maybe it took longer than three days to get to the fort.

"Hmmph. I have my hands full here at the hospital. The only thing I care about is keeping my supplies current and the camp's dysentery under control."

"Has General Arnold been here to see you, James?"

"No. He keeps away from the wards. As brave as that one is on the battlefield, he has a phobia of untoward illness."

"I gathered as much. When I told him that General Washington requested, he extend his hospitality to the girl while she convalesces, he had no issue as long as she was fever free."

"Can't say as I blame him. Disease is an unseen enemy that strikes with deadly stealth."

"James, I need your help. I can't reiterate enough the distraction this girl presents."

The doctor snorted. "There are plenty of women in and around camp, Alexander. Why would one girl's presence be any more of a distraction, unless, of course, the one she's distracting is you."

The doctor's tone was good-natured and followed by a quick chuckle. Footsteps moving toward the bed forced me to close my eyes, feigning sleep or unconsciousness.

I wanted to hear everything they had to say when they thought I wasn't listening. It was the only way to gauge what they surmised about my situation and perhaps give me a clue to their plans for me.

"She can't stay here much longer. Keeping her safe presents countless difficulties. Soldiers are like hounds. They can sense a woman's presence at two hundred paces, and the longer they go without one the more rabid they become…" He paused, and the short hush was broken by a loud thump. "Whose foolish idea was it to use this contraption to keep her hidden? This isn't a boudoir. Get rid of it."

"Keep your peace, Alexander. One of the nurses thought the screen would help keep her somewhat removed from the other patients."

The man replied with a tired sigh. "James, every patient in the field hospital already knows she's here, as do half the men in Fort Putnam, Fort Montgomery, and Fort Arnold combined. They know the circumstances in which she was found, and the rumor mill is turning with supposition and curiosity."

I watched Alexander from beneath the curtain of my lashes and when he looked straight at me, I thought he knew. He ran his hand distractedly over the boudoir screen's painted fabric. "Where in God's name did you acquire this Chinoiserie anyway?"

The doctor chuckled. "From Benjamin Tallmadge's quarters in the Red House. You are indeed correct, Alexander. This girl is most definitely a distraction. Even unconscious her mere presence has rendered you too diverted for singular thought.

Imagine what havoc she could exact on the entirety of West Point if left to her own devices."

I watched the interaction from beneath my lash line and had to bite the inside of my cheek not to laugh.

"Dr. Thacher, sawbones and resident wit." Alexander's scowl made the doctor laugh out loud, as well.

I nearly choked when the realization hit me. This was Jan Dunham's six-times great grandfather in the flesh.

The man circumvented the colonel, moving from the edge of the boudoir screen to the side of my bed. It was time for me to stop feigning sleep.

Except for his height, the doctor looked nothing like his six times great-grandson. Then again, Jan was an old man when I met him, and the doctor looked to be in his mid-twenties, a little older than Alexander if I remembered my history correctly.

Beckoning the colonel to my bedside as well, the doctor fished a pair of wire rim spectacles from the inside pocket of his loose-fitting vest. The weather was very hot, and even Alexander wore a blousy sleeved linen shirt with a simple cotton waistcoat, having left off his jacket, laying it on the cane-backed chair beside the window. Both men wore neck stocks, regardless of the temperature.

"Look here," the doctor began, turning my head slightly. "The bruising to her eye area and cheek is localized, which tells me her head wound was caused by some sort of blunt force. Perhaps a fall."

He removed his glasses, holding them folded in his hand as he continued talking. My guess was it wasn't proper for him to open my gown and present my chest injuries, so no spectacles required.

"Based on a quick probe, I can confidently surmise she has fractured ribs on her left side. There is a goodly amount of bruising across her kidneys, lower torso, and side. She has no fever and her pulse is strong, so there is no need for me to bleed

her. If she escapes internal grievance, the rest will heal with time."

The doctor paused in his appraisal and glanced at Alexander. "You said she was articulate enough for conversation, yes?"

Alexander nodded. "I left her in the care of my aide when gunfire broke out after we had made camp. He said she aggressively tried to piece together the circumstances of her scrape, but the recollection eluded her. He claimed the effort brought her to tears."

The doctor sighed. "It's a shame the degradations war brings upon the innocent, but I'm encouraged her mental faculties are intact. It's not uncommon, though, for severe trauma to exact its consequence in loss of aptitude or even memory. I wouldn't push her, Alexander. It's clear she's run quite a gauntlet."

"But she will recover?"

The doctor nodded cautiously. "Except for what I've already recorded, she seems in perfect health. I took the liberty of having my housekeeper bath her prior to my examination. Pretty thing, really. Who is she? Do you know?"

"I have my suspicions, but nothing that can be proved as of yet. I was hoping you could help with that?"

The doctor looked at the young lieutenant colonel. "Do you think me some sort of soothsayer? That I have the skill to examine the conscience as well as the body?"

Alexander frowned. "I'm speaking of clues that might help construe her identity. I understand your professional obligation in telling me not to prod her for information, but I have my duty, James. The war is at a precarious precipice. I am not at liberty to assume innocence when nefarious connections may be the reason behind her unfortunate situation. I have my own assumptions as to who she is and from whence she hails, but until it's verified, I had hoped you might find markings that could aid our search."

"Markings?"

Hamilton eyed the man. "Yes, telltale signs...*errm*...hidden, underneath." He slipped two fingers into the buttoned spaces of his waistcoat indicating he meant under my clothing.

The doctor frowned. "If you're asking if the girl was raped, my professional inclination is to assume not as I encountered no untoward bruising. And since you asked, she is also unmarked, meaning she carries no brand indicating past criminal behavior. She is well fed and her body well proportioned.

"The health of her teeth, hair, and nails is exceptional and her skin, if you'll forgive a young man's penchant toward poeticism, is like the finest porcelain. I am inclined to think this girl is a moneyed young lady who simply suffered an unfortunate accident."

That was my cue. I inhaled and slowly opened my eyes, hoping my performance was enough to keep me out of the colonel's suspicious line of fire.

The doctor's bright smile greeted me, his small blue eyes twinkling. "Well, well. Good afternoon, young lady. Welcome back to the land of the living."

Alexander stood with his hands on his hips, his buff-colored waistcoat framing his trim waist. "Miss Burritt." A clipped nod of acknowledgement was all he spared.

"If you will permit me," the doctor asked with a professional nod before untying the night cap strings beneath my chin. He removed the cap from my head, allowing my hair to tumble to my shoulders in a riot of curls.

He slipped his glasses onto his nose and lifting my wrist, timed my pulse before touching his fingers to my forehead. "Still no fever, and your pulse is strong. Good." His fingers cupped my chin and moved my head to the side, watching my eyes. "Excellent. Your eyes are clear and appear to follow normal function." He then unwound the bandage circling my head, clearly happy with what he saw. "The external wound has scabbed over nicely, there's no bleeding or fester and even in the short time since I first examined you, it looks as though the

swelling beneath the skin has receded." The doctor retied the bandage and patted my cheek.

"Excuse me, Doctor, but do you have any ice?" I asked.

Alexander raised an eyebrow. "Ice? It's summer."

I cast my memory back to the time my mother dragged me to the historic Muscoot Farm homestead. Was it the eighteenth century or nineteenth century that utilized ice houses? With a deep breath I nodded, hoping my guess was correct.

"I'm aware of that, Colonel, but I was referring to ice stored underground. I have a slight headache, and I remember hearing ice placed on a wound such as mine will help ease the pain and reduce swelling."

The doctor seemed impressed, taking his glasses off and tapping them in his palm. "Yes, my dear. That is true. It works just as well on strained joints and ligaments. Willow bark tea is also good for pain. I will send for both immediately. In the meantime, do you feel at all peckish?"

I looked from one to the other and seeing my confusion, Alexander smirked taking a step back from the doctor so he could mime lifting a spoon to his mouth. At the thought of food, my stomach growled, and I licked my lips hoping my infinitesimal nod was enough to acknowledge Alexander's help.

"I am a little hungry. Thank you, Doctor...?" I gestured with my hand just like I had with his six times great-grandson.

"Thacher. Doctor James Thacher." He inclined his head, giving me a quick wink.

I smiled at the young physician, but Alexander's eyes were on me as well.

"Excellent. Hunger is a good sign. I will have my housekeeper bring you a tray straight away," he said patting my leg. "In the meantime, you need to rest. Colonel Hamilton, will you stay and visit with our guest while I make the arrangements?" he asked, but didn't wait for an answer.

Both men knew my interrogation wasn't complete and fainting again wasn't in the cards. I knew where I was and I

knew the timeframe, but I still didn't know why, though I had faith whoever summoned me would reveal their reasons soon enough. Now I needed to concentrate on playing innocent so I could gain strength enough to wait it out.

Hamilton's head was cocked slightly to the side as he continued to study me. "I'm afraid I can't stay with our injured bird, James. I have other duties to attend to, but I will return. She and I have much to discuss." He paused. "We can begin with any further recollections that come to mind while I'm gone."

The doctor left with a wave, and Alexander took his jacket from the cane chair and slipped an arm through the sleeve, shrugging the rest onto his broad shoulders. He was an impressive figure in his dark blue and buff trimmed uniform coat, vest, and buff breeches. Gold buttons on his lapels and his rank's insignia were proudly displayed on his shoulder epaulets.

His legs were long and well-muscled despite a short stature by twenty-first century standards, and his uniform was fitted to his trim body, its cut accentuating the solid curve of his trim waist and strong thighs. He stepped back in a formal short bow.

"Until later, Miss Burritt?"

I blinked at him, earning a questioning look. Was I supposed to incline my head or do something formal, as well? Screw it. I was injured and had been through the ringer. My brain was too tired to play name that century when it came to correct protocol. I needed a bit of twenty-first century slack and I was going to take it while I could.

"Keep it cool, Colonel." With a careful scoot, I shrugged further into my cot and pulled the sheet up to the lace at my chin, not bothering to look up for the confused frown I suspected was aimed my way.

"Hello, love."

I opened my eyes, and lifting my head, I blinked across my shoulder at the sound. An older woman in a short-sleeved gown of lavender and white calico smiled down at me. Cotton lace covered her elbows giving the effect of three-quarter sleeves. Draped over her forearm was a small mound of clean linen, including something that looked very much like another nightgown or petticoat of sorts. With effort, I turned onto my back, wincing as tight bandages cut into my side.

"Oh now, do go slowly, dearie. I can't have you making yourself worse for the wear, especially not when Lieutenant Colonel Hamilton has set his cap for you to be aboard the first available bateau to Robinson House." The earflaps of her mobcap fluttered with each movement as she fussed about the bed.

"Bateau?" I croaked, hoping it wasn't something I should readily know.

She clucked. "Still half asleep, not that I blame you after what you've endured. The transfer boat, m'dear. He means to have you taken across the river to the hospital wing of Robinson House." She walked to the head of the cot and slipped her arm behind my shoulders. "Let's sit you up so this tray doesn't douse you altogether. I brought you some nice broth and a few scones I managed to sneak from the kitchen up at the Red House."

"The Red House?" I asked beginning to feel a little bit like a parrot.

She smiled, tucking another pillow between my shoulders and the bare wood wall. "West Point headquarters. It's where his Excellency stays when he comes to inspect the battlements and meet with his generals and their adjutants. It's also where many of the officers have their quarters, including Dr. Thacher and Lieutenant Colonel Hamilton."

I winced again, adjusting myself against the feather pillows. "It sounds like it should be called the Red Estate if so many call it home."

She laughed. "That it is. The land and outbuildings belonged to the Charles Moore family, but as what comes with war, the property and structures were appropriated because of their advantageous position along the river. The Moore holdings had many out buildings, and every square inch of space is utilized. I'm lucky. Since I'm housekeep for the fort's physicians and work as a nurse at the field hospital, I have a small room at the Red House myself. I used to share it with another woman, but she was recently sent packing for diddling with a married officer."

My mouth opened and she nodded gravely, but her eyes glowed. "Oh, there's plenty of that kind of goings on with so many men and so few women, so count yourself lucky the young colonel wants to move you across to the main hospital."

"I'm sorry, Mrs…?"

She waved me off in a flurry. "Oh dear, where are my manners. I'm Mrs. MacPherson." Her flustered smile broke and she looked at me with shrewd eyes, they narrowed a bit and she placed two fingers under my chin to better look at my bruised cheek and temple. "Did someone do this to you, darlin'?"

I shook my head. "I don't think so." I glanced at my hands and recalled the feel of the raging water and my fear. My inability to breathe and the sense I was going to die. I knew I couldn't tell Mrs. MacPherson the truth of what happened. She'd never believe me and instead of heading on a skiff toward rest and recovery, I'd be packed off to an asylum.

My eyes found hers and held. "My memories are broken. The jagged pieces come back in bits and I can't hold them. I do remember a storm, that part is clear. I was on a boat when the weather broke. Heavy rain fell, the likes I've never seen. It hit from blue sky and the water thrashed as though the devil himself stirred it. Fear gripped me as the water grew more

engorged. After that it's just bits. I remember the cold of the water and trying to breathe as the waves and eddies choked me. I must have torn my skirts..." I blinked shaking my head as though trying to hold onto a scrap of memory.

"Ssh now...calm yourself. You're safe." Mrs. MacPherson sunk onto the bed, taking my hand in hers as I told the tale, her eyes flashed with the suspense of it. She patted my hand urging me to go on.

"I remember screaming as the fierce pace of the water bashed me against rocks and debris from fallen limbs. The pain was almost too much. I didn't know what to do as the torrent smashed me to and fro like a rag doll. In the end I was so very tired and the last thought I remember was praying to God my death would be swift and painless.

"The sergeant who cared for me once I awoke said a hunting party found me washed up on the banks not far from New Windsor." I squeezed her hand and let every ounce of my genuinely confused fear flow into my face and voice. "Mrs. MacPherson, that's miles and miles of river. How did I get there?"

Tears pricked at having someone to talk to even though I knew Alexander had probably asked her to grill me for information. I squeezed my eyes closed and the tears slide down my cheeks.

"Oh darlin', don't cry. I'm with you now." She pulled me to her breast and held me close, and I found myself sobbing into her shoulder.

When my crying subsided to soft sniffles, she pushed my shoulders back, handing me a handkerchief. I wiped my eyes and she stood from the bed as though with a purpose.

"You are not to fret. You are going to eat this good food and gain strength back enough to go across the river, if not tomorrow then the day after. I'll go with you myself if I have to in order to see you're settled properly. General Arnold will be setting up housekeeping once his wife arrives, and I know some

of his staff already. There's a goodly woman, there. Mrs. Gerrittsen. She's a loving sort. Sad really, she lost her husband in a skirmish about thirty miles south of here near Tarrytown and has had to indenture herself to feed and clothe herself and her daughter."

"Tarrytown?"

She nodded. "You've heard of it? I was led to believe your people were from Vermont."

Before I could answer, another woman ran in calling for Mrs. MacPherson's help with another patient. She lifted the dinner tray and plopped it on my lap. "Eat...and that's an order. I'll be back as soon as I calm this tempest in a teapot."

She left in a huff, moving with quick small steps, her calico dress swaying back and forth with a soft swishing sound.

I picked up the spoon from the tray and dipped it into what looked like clear chicken broth with small, fat dumplings floating in the yellow liquid. I lifted the spoon to my lip, inhaling before I took a sip from the bowl.

My eyes rolled back at the delicious taste. It was even better than its amazing scent. I ate greedily, forcing myself to slow down so I didn't spill on the only garment I had to my name. In that department, I would have to rely on the kindness of strangers and whatever hand-me-downs they could spare. Even if I had money, it's not like there was a mall or even a town with shops anywhere near. I'd bet dollars to donuts every dress worn within a thirty-mile radius was handmade or brought in from a specialty dressmaker. Neither of which were an achievable option for me.

From what I could tell, there wasn't much here in terms of luxury. I'm sure the feather pillows and the cotton sheets that graced my simple hospital cot were courtesy of some officer at the Red House, and if Mrs. MacPherson was the duty nurse when I was brought in, then I know my relatively lavish accoutrements were because of her kindness.

I ripped a corner off a piece of bread and laid a slice of cheese and cold ham across the top, taking a small bite. It was heaven. *Jeez*, what had happened to food in the twenty-first century? Nothing tasted like this, not even the healthy, organic recipes my mother and I prepared.

I ate in peace for ten minutes or so, concentrating primarily on the food on my tray. Hunger satisfied, I slowed my pace, savoring the simple sugary bliss of the small berry scones Mrs. MacPherson swiped. I let my attention drift to the open window and the goings on outside. The small area of the fort I could spy was quiet except for a few passing soldiers, but my ears perked when I heard something said in passing having to do with me.

"She's a Burritt?" a nasal male voice asked.

Hearing the familiar name, I strained to listen.

"That's what I heard. I earwigged Hamilton telling the doc the name Burritt is a Vermont name. Ain't you from Vermont?"

"Sure am. I heard tell of the Burritt's, but I can't say as I know 'em. Had a cousin who worked for the family one summer. Farming family. Lots of land and lots of money."

A low whistle followed the last statement. "No wonder the lieutenant colonel wants her all to himself..." the man paused. "Hey, Jeb, you should tell him what you know about her family. Might get you extra rations or somethin'."

"Nah. I only know what my cousin told me. There were four brothers, and from what he said, one was a tory and the others, patriots, fighting for the cause like us. They had a passel of kids between them. A couple of pretty daughters, too. Headstrong. From what I heard, the one we got right here fought off attackers and ended up in the drink wearing nothin' but a pair of men's breeches and the top half of her shift. If that ain't bold, then I don't know what is. Wouldn't surprise me if she belonged to that Burritt litter like Hamilton thinks."

I heard a finger snap.

"Hey, I just remembered the name of the Burritt girl my cousin said was a real hellfire."

"Yeah?"

"Phoebe. I remember because he nicknamed her Partridge because she was plump. Had long, dark curly hair and dark eyes and a tongue as quick as a brood hen pecking at her mate."

I heard a hand slap and a chuckle. "Jeb, you lucky sombitch. You gotta go tell him…"

The two men walked out of hearing range. *Phoebe Burritt.* I nibbled on the end of my remaining scone. If that's who Alexander wants to think I am, then so be it. I won't confirm or deny it. It took weeks for letters of inquiry to travel back and forth even short distances, so for letters to reach Vermont and a subsequent reply to be sent, I earned myself a month or so before I had needed another viable story.

Amnesia was my friend until I could figure out why I was here. In the meantime, I needed to learn everything I could about the area, its people, and customs. Who knew how long it would be before I found a way back to my own time, if ever?

The thought sobered me, and I put down the scone. Angry as I was at my mother and grandmother, the thought of never seeing them again left an ache in my heart. Then, of course, there was Hunter.

My eyes stung at the thought of what he must be thinking or feeling, but I blinked back my tears. I didn't need anyone to tell me Hunter already contacted my mother and probably the police. He was probably beside himself, angry at being powerless to do anything but wait and hope. Mom and Gran had no intention of contacting me since they were part of the powers that sent me here in the first place. But Hunter?

I couldn't imagine my mother would let him suffer in ignorance, that she would betray her friendship with Britt. Then again, she betrayed me in not telling me what was about to happen.

I shook my head. I wouldn't allow myself to believe my mother would intentionally be that cruel. Yes, she knew I was to be summoned, and my guess was she had no choice in the

matter. It's why she grabbed me and hugged me so hard before Hunter and I left for Jenny's. It was why she took the time to slip that vial into my bag... Wait... *The vial.*

Maybe she couldn't contact me but slipped the vial into my bag as a way for me to contact *her*...if only to let her know I was still alive. Trapped...but alive, nonetheless. Like a prisoner allowed one phone call home. This new revelation stunned me. I pieced everything together again, adding and subtracting. It made more sense now than before—like Gran insisting on a crash course on scrying and summoning. They knew I was going to be taken and did everything in their power to make sure I had some tools of the trade with me to help.

I dragged in a deep breath and slumped back against the feather pillows, spilling a little of the broth onto the tray. I wasn't betrayed. Bone deep relief ran through my body. Even my chest hurt less and for the first time since I arrived in 1780, I dragged in a calm breath. They truly didn't have a choice.

At the thought, anger bloomed in my mind. Not anger toward them, but toward whatever power held this over my family in the first place.

Why? Why weren't we given a choice? What was so portentous that I had to be ripped from the twenty-first century and hauled back to this godforsaken time? It had to be something crucial, something that I would have knowledge of from a future standpoint that would affect events in the here and now. But what? Why me, and not some other witchy member of my family tree closer to the actual timeframe? Waiting two-hundred and thirty-four years for the right genetic predisposition seemed a little preposterous.

A scrap of memory tapped the back of my mind. It was part of a conversation I had with my mother last fall, right at the start of all the trouble with the evil in the Old Dutch cemetery bleeding into the first of my visions. At the time it was a nothing but chat, but now?

"Did this ever happen to you when you were my age?" I asked while washing my face and brushing my teeth.

"No, honey, I wasn't lucky enough."

Lucky? Through the crack in the doorway, I saw her as she went about straightening my room.

"I know right now you don't think of it as lucky," she added like she could read my mind. Tucking in the corners of my duvet she continued, "However, this shows how psychic you really are, and it's a blessing whether you realize it or not. Just think of what you'll be able do with your talent once you learn to harness it. No one in our family has this kind of sway with the veil separating the living and the dead, the past from the present. That's all time is really, a membrane as thin as a shimmer off the summer asphalt. I would bet of all our distinguished line, you're the one who could walk through oceans of time."

I laughed, throwing my hair over my head, trying to gel my curls into submission. "Uh, pass. Wanna trade?"

"Ha. Don't thumb your nose at the fates; you never know what might piss them off."

The wheels for this time-snatch had been set in motion nearly a year ago. Whoever was behind this had been watching, as well as waiting.

On the other hand, this was a Catch 22. Any historic knowledge brought with me from the future meant certain events already occurred. If I changed one thing, the future I returned to wouldn't be the same.

It was the ripple effect my mother talked about months ago—like throwing a rock into a cosmic lake and waiting centuries for the ripples to work their way to shore. If I was supposed to accomplish something here, then how was I supposed to know which events to change and which to leave alone? My cosmic handler needed to make an appearance a.s.a.p. and answer these questions pronto.

Chapter 11

Mrs. MacPherson never made it back and neither did Alexander. In the darkened ward I was dimly aware of voices barking instructions followed by footsteps running back and forth in the halls. Earlier that evening, a different nurse came to clear away my dinner tray, leaving what was left of my bread and scone wrapped in a linen cloth beside a jug of fresh water, and helping me to the chamber pot before I retired for the night.

That was an experience. I was tempted to ask her if I could toss the contents out the window into the dirt thoroughfare and douse the mess with alcohol and water, but I didn't. She simply closed the lid and offered to help me back into bed. When I asked for soap and water you would have thought I asked her to amputate my hands at the wrists. She eventually came back with a sliver of strong-smelling soap and I scrubbed my hands and arms as though I were readying myself for surgery.

That was the last I saw of anyone, and I eventually drifted off to sleep dreaming of Hunter and our last few days together.

"Mistress...Mistress Burritt...wake up, lass."

I forced my eyes open and peered through the darkness focusing on the face hovering over my side. It was the kind sergeant that had lost his boys at the beginning of the war.

"Sergeant? What's happening?"

"Small pox. We need to move you immediately."

I sat up quickly, wincing. "When? Where?"

"Straight away." He gestured for me to sit up fully and swing my legs over the end of the bed. "Lieutenant Colonel Hamilton has a boat waiting. He'll escort you across to Robinson House."

"But Mrs. MacPherson..." I didn't finish my sentence realizing I didn't have a choice in the matter.

He nodded as though he understood what I was referring. "She'll be accompanying the two of you as well." He turned and lifted a gorgeous dressing gown of deep persimmon from the cane chair by the window. "She sent this for you. Said she didn't want her girl traipsing through camp dressed in nothing but her shift." He held it up, gesturing with the garment for me get on with it.

I curled my hand around my middle and held tight to my ribs, pushing myself up to standing. A slight rush of dizziness took me, and I swayed a little on my feet.

"Easy now. I'll not have ye keel over on my watch." He grinned flashing a full set of blocky, yet slightly yellowed teeth between his now clean-shaven cheeks.

"You have kind eyes and a kind smile, sergeant....?"

That I bothered with his name at all earned me an even wider smile. "Campbell. Sergeant Douglas Campbell." He made a little bow, and then wiggled the dressing gown again. "We need to get a leg under us, lass, or it will be me that has to answer for ye."

With the sergeant's help, I slipped the dressing gown on and buttoned the double-breasted bodice.

"I brought this as well thinking ye'd want yer own things with ye across the river." He handed me my backpack and I wiggled open the inside pouch. Everything was as I last saw it, and I rummaged to the bottom and took out my shoes.

I sat on the end of the cot and lifted my foot to slip the espadrilles over my toes and heel. The gown fell open and my night dress scooted up my leg as I tied the ribbon laces.

"*Erm*, are ye done yet, lass?"

"Just about." I noticed the sergeant had averted his eyes, and it was then I remembered women's ankles and wrists were considered provocative in the eighteenth century. I almost laughed considering they could show as much cleavage as they wanted. I dropped my foot to the floor and repeated the process on the other. "All done, though I'm still feeling a bit weak in my knees. Can you help me up, Sergeant?"

He jumped to the task, gathering my bag from me and stuffing what was left of my supper, linen napkin and all, into the top before closing the top flap.

"Ready?"

I nodded. "Let's not make this a race, okay?" I asked, trying to be funny, but only earned a puzzled look in response.

"O. Kay?"

Now it was my turn to grin. "Sorry. It's a word I learned along the way. It's meant to inquire if everything is all right."

He lifted his chin, nodding slightly. "Oh, well then. O. Kay. No foot race."

I bit back a laugh but sobered when he passed me a ripped piece of linen, keeping another strip for himself. "Cover yer mouth and nose, lass. At least until we get outside."

He held my arm walking with me to the door, gripping my elbow the whole way as he steered me through the narrow corridor toward the main door. He went to wrap his fingers around the door pull, but I grabbed his arm.

"No! Not with your bare hands." Single-handed, I rummaged in my pack and ripped a jagged swath from my tattered blouse. The material was so damaged and worn from the water and rocks it shredded in my hand like so much gauze. "Use this," I said holding it out to him.

Again, he looked at me like I had sprouted horns, but he didn't argue, wrapping the torn cloth over the doorknob and turning it to open. We stepped outside into the cool night air and I gestured for him to drop the cloth. He did what I asked and took my arm again.

Torches burned along the darkened parade grounds, but the dirt paths leading between the out buildings were thick with blackness. "Step where I step, lass, and keep close."

We moved through the shadows hugging the corners until we hit the main square. I had to tug on Sergeant Campbell's arm to stop so I could catch my breath and fight off the light-headedness that threatened if we kept even a moderate pace for too long.

"How far is it to the boat?" I asked, feeling myself sweat under my arms and between my breasts. My head throbbed and I knew this was too much too soon, but I was grateful for their concern. Small pox was no small threat. The U.S. had stopped mandatory vaccination of school age children in 1972. Since I was born twenty-five years after the fact, I was as much a potential victim as anyone in the eighteenth century.

We crossed the parade grounds along the far side close to the stone battlements. With their castle-like gun turrets and catwalks they reminded me of fortifications of old. I had to laugh. They weren't old, not yet anyway. In fact, West Point was in its infancy, and Thaddeus Kosciuszko had been commissioned by Washington only two years earlier to design the fortification. Half the flurry of activity I watched from my hospital window was soldiers working to strengthen the forts, the batteries and redoubts of West Point.

I even knew about the 150-ton iron chain stretched across the river from West Point to Constitution Island, erected to hinder the British from assaults against the most strategic position along the Hudson. I smiled to myself. Dr. Thacher was dead-on. My mental faculties were as sharp as ever and Mr. Garrett, my AP U.S. History teacher, would be so proud. One for anecdotes and rich back stories, I hoped I paid enough attention enough in his class because lord knew I needed all the help I could get.

The dock was just ahead as were the dim figures of Mrs. MacPherson and Alexander. Pocket watch in hand, he glanced

down at his timepiece and then up the hill to where we were descending to the dock.

"Finally," he said reaching to take my elbow from the sergeant. "Campbell you can either stay, report back to General Montgomery or you can come with me. I'll be staying on the far shore with Miss Burritt and Mrs. MacPherson for the next few days. It's up to you."

The sergeant nodded already rolling up his sleeves. "I figure I'll take my chances with the dark water tonight. I didn't come all this way to die of the pox."

The colonel clapped him on the shoulder. "Good. I prefer it that way to be honest. General Arnold has much that needs to be coordinated from this end and I will be otherwise occupied. You can act as Miss Burritt's escort in my absence."

Campbell climbed into the boat first, taking Mrs. MacPherson's small travel trunk and stowing it toward the bow. The colonel held Mrs. MacPherson's hand and helped her step up into the boat, handing her off to Campbell to settle before doing the same with me. Alexander climbed in last and took up a set of oars as well.

Mrs. MacPherson and I sat back to back, with me facing Alexander and her facing the sergeant. We rowed in silence, and the soft chuff, chuff sound of the oars cutting the water combined with the unanticipated and premature exertion soon lulled me into a drowsy state.

"Careful, dearie, you're likely to topple over. Why don't you lean against me," she offered shifting around so her shoulder took the bulk of my lethargic weight. "We're going to be here a while, so make yourself comfortable, love." She held her arm out and I settled into her side embrace.

The men rowed in a steady rhythm, no one speaking, and I eventually dropped off to sleep.

"We're here, dearie." Mrs. MacPherson moved her arm, patting my cheek. "Wake up, love."

I opened my eyes to the dark river behind us along with the torch lit battlements of West Point.

"Oh, that was quick."

At Campbell's snort I immediately felt foolish.

"Aye, quick for ye, lass. Ye may have been carried on angel's wings while ye dreamed, but I worked up a midnight sweat and so did yon buck of a colonel."

Alexander grinned at the randy praise. "I was glad for the help, Campbell. The trip would have cost twice the time and twice the liniment for my aching shoulders otherwise."

"Colonel, best the ladies wait here with ye while I find a wagon or a pony. Mistress Burritt is not fit for the walk up to the house."

"Of course but be quick about it."

Campbell nodded and took off up the dark grassy slope disappearing into the trees.

"He's a dear man," Mrs. MacPherson said with a sigh, watching as his figure faded into the gloom and shadow. She turned gesturing for me to sit on the small trunk Alexander had hoisted from the bow. "I brought everything a lady of your station would need. Now, I know your memory is muddled, and that's quite all right. I've had a talk with the good doctor, and he assures us that your recollections will return out of the blue, but until then we are not to pressure you." She slid her eyes toward the colonel. "Isn't that true, Lieutenant Colonel Hamilton?"

Alexander mumbled something to the effect and then wandered up the path to look for signs of Campbell with some kind of conveyance.

Mrs. MacPherson smirked, waving her delicate hand at his back before turning to me. "Don't fret. The doctor told me

everything. Himself knows who you are, but he still needs to satisfy it for his own pride. There's a soldier in the doctor's employee..." she waved her hand back and forth as though trying to remember something. Finally, she shook her head. "I can't recall his name, but he doesn't matter. He's from a Vermont regiment and he told both Doctor Thacher and the colonel he recognized you from his home in Burlington. He said there was no doubt in his mind you were Phoebe Burritt."

"Mrs. MacPherson..."

She wouldn't hear me argue. "Pish tosh. I won't listen to your naysaying." She dropped her chin and gave me a stern look. "It's well after midnight and you're as wobbly as a child's top. The general is already here, and his wife is due within the next weeks. I don't know much about Peggy Shippen Arnold, but from the natter I hear she's not an easy one to please. They say she's a rare beauty, accustomed to turning the eye of every man she meets, but like a fleshy red apple that makes your mouth water thinking about its sweet taste, sometimes you take a bite and end up with a mouthful of brown mush."

"I don't understand."

"The woman is all show and as spoiled as week old milk. I think she married General Arnold to save face after shamelessly pursuing a British officer, or so that's what the gossip mill says. The general is old enough to be her father. It's not hard to ken what attracted him to her, but her to him? It all has to do with the fat jingle of gold in his pocket. The man faced a court martial not long ago for misappropriation of army funds trying to keep up with her lavish tastes."

Mrs. MacPherson spoke in a rapid hush with all the zeal of a fishwife and my head hurt trying to absorb it all. Right now, I would kill for my iPhone and a working Google App to get the historic low-down on these people and their lives. To Mrs. MacPherson, though, this was news of the day and listening to the older woman gossip dragged me into the story with gusto.

"A court martial? Yet they gave him command of West Point."

She nodded, but then lifted her finger to her lips as the men returned.

Sergeant Campbell towed a nag and a small hay wagon behind him, and he and Alexander hoisted the trunk into the front of the cart before helping both Mrs. MacPherson and me up and into the hay.

I sneezed, crying out at the sudden pain jutting across my torso from the jerking force. I rocked forward, my arm gripping my mid-section and the velvet of my dressing gown.

"Easy, now. Is the fodder an issue for ye, miss?" The sergeant asked with real concern.

I shook my head, having no choice but to wipe my nose on my soft sleeve. I made a face and scrubbed at the mark.

Mrs. MacPherson leaned in, patting my arm. "What did I say about worrying that pretty head of yours? I'm here, and I'm not leaving until I know you're well in hand and if that means staying until your own folks come south to take you home, then so be it. It'll be six weeks at least..." she lowered her voice and glanced surreptitiously to where Alexander rode with the sergeant. "I have it on good authority that himself isn't planning to write your folks just yet." She smiled and pitched my cheek. "He won't admit it, but the man is smitten." She slid her eyes his way once more. "I wonder what his girl will say once she finds out."

"His girl?" I asked, my own curiosity piqued.

She nodded. "Elizabeth Schuyler of Albany. She's the daughter of one of Washington's minor generals. It's a good match, though," she acquiesced with a sigh. "She's not overly pretty and not much of a wit, but she comes with a fat purse." Her eyes found mine, and her resigned complaint turned into a satisfied smirk. "Of course, my girl trumps that in spades. From what I hear you've got a nice dowry of your own waiting on the right gentleman. Add to that beauty and brains plus fortitude to

make any man proud in such uncertain times. How else could you survive what you did?"

"Luck and God's grace," I replied.

"Pish. You had the strength of mind and character to fight instead of letting the water swallow you whole. Didn't you say yourself how tired you were?"

I nodded quietly, but when I opened my mouth to respond she waved me off.

"I know I shouldn't refer to you as my own, but my husband Richard, God rest him, was never able to give me a child. It's clear your own father hasn't noticed one of his chicks is missing from the coop or if he has, no long-reach inquiries have been made thus far." She sniffed, straightening her shoulders. "Until he does, I've decided to make you my charge."

I didn't know what to say. Was this woman as generous and loving as she appeared, or was she a psychopath?

She cupped my cheek. "I haven't gone 'round the bend, dearie." She paused, her eyes soft and a little wet. "When you cried in my arms, I felt you shudder with fear and uncertainty, and it broke my heart. No one, especially a young girl, should ever have to feel that alone. You touched my heart." She let go of my cheek, her hands dropping to smooth the front of her lavender calico. Then she glanced up with a wicked grin. "...and from all accounts, you're as much of a hellcat as I am when it comes to what's right. With Peggy Arnold on her way it's going to take both of us to keep that shrew tamed, if not for her husband's sake, then for the sake of her servants."

I didn't comment but took the older woman's hand and laced my own fingers with hers. She was a font of knowledge, that much was clear. For some unfathomable reason she bonded with me, but who was I to look a gift ally in the mouth? I needed a friend, and one who appreciated a free spirt and independent thought, even better.

"Do you think Mrs. Arnold will accept me into her home?"

The older woman looked at me. "Well, if she sees you as a threat, then it will go hard for you. I'll do what I can to deflect any impatience, but I'm a servant and she will dismiss me as such. You, though, are a well-bred young woman not much younger that Mrs. Margaret Arnold herself.

"The general will keep you as long as the bonnie colonel wants, and since Hamilton has Washington's ear as his adjutant and aide-du-camp, it's a safe bet you'll be made welcome no matter what tantrums come. Peggy Arnold may be able to henpeck her husband into the poorhouse, but she won't pit her will against his when it comes to military obligations."

The large house loomed, and the cart slowed. Two young servants met the wagon at the base of the back-entrance steps. Their young dusky faces in shadow and half asleep.

"Bring Mistress Burritt's luggage to the guest room and then see the horse to the barn before going back to bed." Alexander's instructions were direct but somewhat clipped.

Their dark springy heads bobbed up and down, despite their dozy bearing. I caught the eye of the smaller of the two boys and smiled. "Thank you so much. I'm sorry we disturbed your rest."

The boy's puzzled expression led me to think perhaps he didn't speak English, but then he smiled back, nodding once before helping his brother with the heavy trunk.

The men didn't notice, preoccupied with the business of unhitching the horse from the wagon, but Mrs. MacPherson greeted me with a soft smile as I carefully climbed from the back of the cart.

"Beautiful, smart, *and* a compassionate heart. Our lieutenant colonel will never hear the shot until the ball hits him between the eyes."

Chapter 12

I slept like the dead at first, then spent hours waking and drowsing for what seemed like a full day and night. My only recollections were Mrs. MacPherson walking me to the privy and Dr. Thacher checking to make sure I hadn't reinjured myself.

I ate little, instead opting for the escape of sleep. I used my injuries as a stall tactic, and I knew it. Eventually, I'd have to get up, but Mrs. MacPherson's ramblings plagued my thoughts.

If I was as well-bred a young woman as they alleged, then I would be expected to have certain skills. None of which I possessed. Needlepoint, music, dancing, as well as language—I vaguely recalled passages I'd read about how these were considered standards in the proper education of a young woman.

I could barely sew a button. I was a decent cook, but I had no clue how to work a colonial kitchen. And music? Hunter was the musician, not me—and as for dancing, I didn't think freestyle was going to cut it in the era of the minuet. Luckily, I spoke decent enough Spanish, courtesy of my high school's foreign language department, but I had a sneaking suspicion the language the texts referred to was French.

I had been an unwilling guest of 1780 for more than two weeks, and thus far the fates had yet to tip their hand. Not a tremor across my skin or a whisper at the back of my mind. Perhaps they were waiting for me to regain my full strength.

Marianne Morea

I was better, but I would still give anything for an industrial sized bottle of Advil. The willow bark tea Mrs. MacPherson ladled down my throat helped, as did the ice and hot stones intermittently wrapped in soft cloth.

I needed to understand my purpose here and get on with it, and today was that day, even if it meant using the contents of my mother's vial. If the fates wouldn't come to me, then they were getting a collect call from the eighteenth century.

I woke fully, and morning found me in a large four poster bed not unlike the one I shared with Hunter at Jenny's house. Mrs. MacPherson was nowhere to be seen but considering her normal duties she was doubtless up and around at dawn.

My bed was twice the size of the small daybed she occupied. Her narrow bunk was wedged into a window alcove across the room, undoubtedly drafty and damp. Insulation wasn't a standard of the day, however, recent nights had been warm and dry so I didn't worry for her the way I did with Gran and her arthritis. Mrs. MacPherson was most likely decades younger than my grandmother, though you wouldn't know it to look at her.

People in general didn't age well in the eighteenth century nor did they live long. Poor hygiene, malnutrition, and overcrowding were some of the issues I witnessed in the short time, and my guess was they were more to blame for the spread of disease and death than casualties from the war.

I had every intention of trying to change that course for the people who were slowly become dear to me. How? I had no clue.

Reaching over my head I stretched out my arms and legs, surprised I didn't wince with the effort. I sat up and swung my legs over the end of the feather mattress. So far so good. No dizziness and almost no pain.

I padded to the privy for my morning business. Last night I was pleasantly surprised to find the bathroom in this house was actually a *bath* room, with a deep copper tub, a dressing table

and mirror and an armoire with folded bath sheets and linen shifts because no proper lady actually bathed in the nude. The commode was a completely separate room from the bath, and I finally understood where the term water closet originated.

Opening the narrow-slatted door to the privy, I lifted the lid and held my breath expecting every sense to be assaulted by overnight filth, but the bowl was surprisingly clean.

Before Sergeant Campbell made me a refugee from the field hospital, I stuffed my sliver of lye soap into the drawstring pocket of my backpack. Now I placed the tiny bar beside the fine red floral basin and ewer in the bathing room, making sure to wash my hands thoroughly after carrying the pot outside and burying the contents in the dirt by the front flower bed. I earned myself a few furtively puzzled glances from the servants, but I waved anyway, barefoot and in my nightgown.

I came out of the privy to find Mrs. MacPherson waiting for me with a scolding expression.

"What?" I said, drying my hands on a soft hand towel.

She pursed her lips. "What, you ask? The entire household now thinks you're mad as a hatter, carrying your business to the garden and burying it as though you were a dog or a cat. What in heaven's name were you thinking, child?"

"I wasn't thinking anything except to remove the filth from our room. Leaving it there to fester spreads sickness, not to mention the nasty stench. I won't live with filth and you shouldn't either."

"Darlin', I don't understand how a chamber pot spreads sickness, but we have a chambermaid to see to disposing all that. Promise me you won't do it again, and especially not in just your shift."

"I'm sorry, Mrs. Macpherson." I dropped my eyes and left the towel to dry on the back of a chair. "I didn't mean to embarrass you or myself. I just wanted to feel clean." My hand went to my hair and I lifted the heavy mass from one shoulder.

"I haven't had a proper bath in what feels like weeks. My hair is greasy, and my body feels crusted and I smell."

She walked to a trunk and opened the top. "I can take care of that well enough. A little hot water for the basin and some rice powder for your hair and you'll feel good as new." Reaching into the center of the trunk she took out a covered wooden box and what looked like a miniature bellows.

"Couldn't I just take a bath in the copper tub and wash my hair? The hot soak might help me move around better and then perhaps I could venture outside for some fresh air?"

She straightened, box still in hand. "A bath?"

I nodded. "I know it would take a few trips to fill the tub with enough hot water, but I'm willing to carry the pots myself. I really want to take a proper bath."

I was half way to bouncing up and down like a toddler pleading pretty please for something in a toy store. Mrs. MacPherson eyed me, not quite knowing what to make of my request.

"Perhaps we could manage this one time, it being for medicinal purposes, but, darlin', it's such a cost in time and effort. The staff has much to do today. Couldn't it wait?"

The last thing I wanted was to seem peevish and uncooperative, but I couldn't stand the feel of my grime and my scalp itched. All I needed was a case of lice or fleas and I'd go bananas.

"I certainly don't want to be a burden. Could I at least have a few pitchers of hot water so I can give myself a sponge bath and wash my hair?"

With a smile of appreciation, she nodded, replacing the items in the trunk. "Sensible girl. I'll see to it myself." She left without another word, leaving me to investigate the room.

Mrs. MacPherson told me the Robinson house belonged to General Beverly Robinson. He was a childhood friend of George Washington, but he sided with the loyalists once the war broke out. The house was confiscated once the Americans took control

of West Point, and the Robinson family had to escape to British occupied New York City.

I found it funny in an ironic sense that Tarrytown and Sleepy Hollow were considered neutral territory between the British held lower Hudson Valley and the American held northern counterpart. Yet both sides made free with raids and thought themselves entitled to whatever they wanted from the neutral zone. It was the story of cowboys and skinners, of Governor Tryon burning patriots out of their homes, and frightened residents, bartering their daughters to the British and Hessians to protect their farms. The neutral zone wasn't so neutral.

I walked around the room admiring all the rich touches. If these furnishing belonged to the Robinsons before they left, did that mean they now belonged to the Arnolds or were they the property of the Continental Army?

The quality of each item, from the embroidered bedspread and fine linens to the Chinoiserie curios and oriental plum flower wallpaper and all the furniture spelled gentry with a capital G.

I hadn't forgotten Mrs. MacPherson's trunk. The lid was still up so I didn't think a little peek would hurt. Inside was a full complement of toiletries. Hair brushes and combs, ribbons, strips of plain white rags and small round glass pots of different sizes.

The door opened and I jumped, feeling guilty at being caught snooping.

"Here's your water darlin'," she said ushering two maids carrying pitchers and dry toweling. The girls placed the steaming jugs in the bathing room on top of the vanity and the left with a bobbed curtsey.

"Do you want me to help or can you manage around the bandages yourself?" she asked.

The knots were very small and very tight. "I don't suppose you have scissor in that box of treasures?" I asked with a small guilty laugh.

She pursed her lips, but her sternness melted into a sideways grin. "I knew your curiosity wouldn't hold out. Why do you think I left the top open?" She waved me closer. "Come, that water needs to cool, or you'll scorch the skin right off your bones. Let me show you what I brought with me."

She practically giggled, taking out layer after layer, tray after tray from inside the compact truck. It was like watching Mary Poppins's carpet bag and I half expected her to bring out a tape measure to gauge my personality.

"I knew you'd have nothing of the necessities needed, so I gathered what I could from my own belonging and what I could procure from the other ladies in camp. We pooled our resources, but remember I told you about the woman who used to share my room at The Red House?"

I nodded, but didn't say a word, not wanting to interrupt her.

"The married officer she diddled with may have been a lout of a husband, but he was generous to a fault with her. He showered her with gifts that she kept hidden in a trunk beneath our bed. When their affaire de cœur was discovered and she made to leave, she realized he would force her to dispose of everything on the off chance it could be used as evidence against his character.

"She was proud to the end, refusing to part with one ribbon. Instead, she gave the lot to me with instructions for the goods to be parceled among the girls in the camp once she was gone. I was about to do so when Lieutenant Colonel Hamilton came tapping at my door the night they brought you to the field hospital at the barracks.

"You were in such a pitiful state. Beaten, filthy, and covered in vomit. I couldn't in all good conscience let you stay in that

condition. Dr. Thacher let me have my head, and I bathed you and put you in one of my own nightgowns."

I exhaled, relieved. "I was afraid it was one of the soldiers, again. I'm sure you know I wasn't wearing that grimy dress when the colonel found me. I don't know how I'll ever be able to thank you."

She smiled, holding up one finger. "There's more." With a gleeful grin she bent over the trunk, reaching toward the very bottom. Out came a set of stays or the colonial version of a corset, two knee-length shifts, two fine cotton petticoats, one a deep rose color and the other a rich peridot or dark celery green with wool embroidery along each bottom and finally two gowns to match the petticoats."

I had no idea what to do with any of the items, but that didn't mean I couldn't appreciate their beauty or the fine work they represented.

"They're gorgeous. Are they a gift for the general's wife?"

Mrs. MacPherson blinked at me. "They're for you, you ninny. Now let's get you washed and coiffed and out into the sunshine. It will do you a world of good, and maybe we can convince the colonel to take you for a walk, if you feel up to it."

She reached into the second tray and selected two glass pots and a narrow, cobalt blue bottle with a bronze cap and painted birds on the glass.

"What are those?"

"For your toilette. Soap and perfumed oils."

She followed me into the bathroom and helped me with my nightdress. For some reason I didn't feel ashamed as I stood in front of her half naked. I was more concerned the bandages had gone dingy around the edges just from being on my body for so long.

"Do you think I should change these for clean ones?"

She shrugged. "That's up to you, dear. I see nothing wrong with them, but you seem obsessed with idea of clean."

She left me to my own devices, handing me a short towel and one of the shifts she brought with her. I waited until she left before I sniffed the garment. It smelled like perfume, but at least it didn't smell like body odor.

I wet my head and scrubbed the best I could with the liquidly soap from the first pot. Rinsing proved to be a disaster, and I ended up calling Mrs. MacPherson for help. Once the soap was out, I gave my hair the squeak test. The watery shampoo Mrs. Macpherson gave me smelled nice, but it was very strong, and my eyes watered from the residual that ran from my wet head onto my lashes. I rinsed my eyes a number of times, until I could open them without burning.

I wrapped my head in the short towel and then lathered up the hand towel I used earlier. I washed everything from head to toe and everywhere in between until I stood in a puddle on the wood floor. I dropped the towel from my head to the ground to absorb most of the wetness.

I sighed, looking at myself in the vanity mirror. My bruises had faded from black and purple to a greenish yellow. Across my cheek and temple, the coloration gave me a sickly look, and I wished my cosmetics had survived the trip back in time along with my other things. *Crud. Other toiletries.* What was I supposed to do when my period showed up? It wasn't like I could run to Walgreens for tampons.

My head jerked toward the bathroom door. The white cotton strips in Mrs. Macpherson's trunk. They had to work double duty as sanitary pads and toilet paper, or they would if I had anything to say about it.

I toweled my hair with the one dry corner left after I mopped up what remained of the water on the floor. Slipping the shift over my head, I finger combed my hair and hung both towels over the edge of the copper tub to dry. I opened the bathroom door feeling more like myself than I had since before I fell overboard.

"Oh, don't you look as fresh as a daisy." Mrs. MacPherson called me over, telling me to lift my arms to the sides so she could lace up the stays around my waist. "I'll not pull you too tightly. I don't want to re-break whatever inside that's started to knit."

She laced up the back of the corset and then draped the petticoat over the shift, fitting it to my waist with a pull of a drawstring. "I'm sorry I don't have a hoop for you, but there was just none extra to be had."

My eyes bugged and I was glad she was standing behind me. *A hoop on top of all this.* How did women not die of heat exhaustion?

"Give me your arms, sweetheart, and let's see if this gown fits or if I need to alter it. Though you are tall for a girl, you're about the same size in hips and waist as Hester; she's the girl I talked about earlier. "Let's see." She held the dress open and I slipped my arms through the sleeves realizing the dress had no real front, only sides and back skirt.

She turned me around and did up the laces in the back, leaving them tight, but breathable. "A perfect fit!" she said with a clap. "Turn, let me see the whole effect."

I spun slowly watching Mrs. Macpherson's face as her hand clasped together at her breast. "You look beautiful, and the peridot color is perfect for a summer day with your dark hair."

I laughed. "Well, it matches the green pallor on my left cheek, that's for certain."

Mrs. Macpherson's mouth dropped open and her expression fell. "Oh, dear, I didn't think of that. Perhaps we should change you into the rose."

I shook my head. "Not necessary. Everyone knows what happened to me. It's no secret, so I have nothing to be ashamed. I'm healing and that's all that matters."

With a quick inhale she nodded in agreement. "Yes. That's true. Now, let's do something with your hair. You have such

beautiful curls, so easy to work with and no hot irons required," she laughed.

She gathered the mass into a loose twist and then pinned the lot with two combs, arranging the top into an elaborate fall, securing the loose ends with hairpins. Holding out two ribbons for me to choose, the first the same peridot as my dress, the other a deep red trimmed in green, she gestured for me to choose.

"What are they for?" I asked.

"Why, your throat, of course." She replied with a curious look.

I chose the red one and she smiled as though I had passed some sort of test.

"All right, love. All that's left is a cap."

"No. No cap, thank you anyway." I said making her stop short.

"You have to wear a cap. It's just not done."

I shook my head, adamant. "No, ma'am. It's too hot. It's barley past breakfast and already sweltering in here. If I wear a cap, I will surely topple over from the heat."

She looked at me as though she wanted to argue but couldn't. She went to the trunk instead and pulled out a straw sun hat with a white ribbon around the brim and neck.

"If you won't wear a cap, then promise me you will wear this bergère if you go outdoors." She held it out toward me.

I took the sunhat from her hand. It was pretty and at least it would serve a purpose. "Of course. Thank you."

She nodded and the set of her mouth was like she'd won a battle. "Now," she said cleaning up the toiletries. "Let's get you fed and out into the sunshine."

I got my first real glimpse of Robinson House as we came down the broad, mahogany staircase. The foyer was wide with polished planked floors and a red and gold hand-knotted carpet that matched the runner following the length of the stairs to the second floor. The rooms were low-ceilinged, with large hand-

hewn joists and beams. I peeked in through the open doorways and saw each had a tiled fireplace and rich mantel. The walls were wallpapered in rich jewel tones with a chair rail separating the complimentary patterns dividing the top and bottom.

Bronze framed paintings and tapestries decorated the walls, while opulent furnishings graced each room, including a high gloss mahogany dining table with eight matching chairs, various tea tables, settees, and chintz upholstered chairs, cabinets full of shining china and glassware, vases, knickknacks and lace at every turn.

We walked down the stairs into the lower kitchen and the place was a flurry of activity. Maids and cooks and kitchen help of all kinds, men, women, even children scurried around thick, worn tables laden with vegetables and the fixings for bread and baked goods. I inhaled the familiar yeasty scent of fresh dough and almost sighed. From the smell, the preparations weren't much different from my mother's kitchen. Then again, we didn't do our baking in stone ovens above an open fire.

"All we have is warm porridge, but I can add fresh milk and honey to it if you'd like," the cook said with a smile.

"Thank you, but you look as though you could use another set of hands and eyes. I can help myself if that's all right?" I replied to her relief.

The woman shared a look with Mrs. MacPherson and the older woman smiled. "See, did I not say she was not like the others?"

The cook nodded with a wide smile, and I looked at the two of them. "Who's not like the others?" I asked, knowing full well they meant me.

"Why you, you goose," Mrs. Macpherson said shoving me into a chair and placing a bowl of porridge in front of me. "This is the cook I told you about back at the fort. Marta Gerrittsen. She'll be here for you once I leave to go back across the river. That is if I don't decide to stay here instead. From the look of things, they are going to need another set of hands, like you

said. Now eat or Dr. Thacher is going to have something to say about it later."

"I'm pleased to meet you, Mrs. Gerrittsen, thank you for the breakfast."

"You're welcome, love."

"Well, look at ye! Dressed up and as shiny as a new penny!"

The voice came from Sergeant Campbell standing in the doorway, and his smile greeted me with genuine warmth.

"Good morning, to you, Sergeant."

"And to ye too, love. How did ye sleep?"

I smiled. "Very well, thank you."

"Oh, good. I made sure to tighten those bed ropes 'til I thought they'd snap."

I looked at him queerly and then realized he meant the ropes supporting the bedframe beneath the feather bed. It dawned on me then where the phrase, *night, night, sleep tight* originated, and considering the lack of hygiene and overall cleanliness of the era, I also got where the next line came from as well. *Don't let the bedbugs bite.*

"I'm grateful, Sergeant. I'm also glad not to be consigned to the bedroom for the duration," I said sitting up straighter in my chair.

He frowned. "Why would ye say such a fool thing? Yer not consigned anywhere, but staying put is what ye should be doing, at least for the time being until yer healed."

"Consigned. *Hmmph.* I'll say she's not! Not after the work it took getting her to look so fine," Mrs. MacPherson sniffed.

Mrs. Gerrittsen waved her dishcloth at him "Out with you then, Douglas Campbell, unless you have a purpose for disturbing my kitchen, and you can stop your jawing and let that poor girl eat."

He put his hands up in mock defense, laughing. "Don't shoot the messenger, lass. Colonel Hamilton wants the dining room laid properly for when the general arrives after his morning inspections of the far troops. He said the man wants

his luncheon served in a correct manner before a much need rest after his long ride. Last I looked, there were still hay crates stacked in the corner of the dining room."

"For the love of God!" Mrs. Gerrittsen and Mrs. MacPherson jumped into action, neither paying any attention to Sergeant Campbell's noncommittal shrug. I watched them fly back and forth ramping up their orders to anyone within shouting distance. It didn't matter if the general was set to return in two hours or two days, the two were on a mission and God help anyone who got in the way. Including me.

I stood from the work table, pushing my uneaten breakfast away. "I want to help," I said loudly enough to earn another scolding look from Mrs. MacPherson.

I lifted a petitioning hand. "Not two minutes ago you were wishing for another set of hands. I hate being idle, let me help you."

She shook her head. "No darlin', you're a lady and a guest of this house. It wouldn't be seemly."

Nonplussed, I looked at her in disbelief, both at her refusal and her reasoning behind it. "Mrs. Macpherson, you've done so much for me, please let me do something to help you."

She shook her head, and from the set of her mouth I realized there was no brooking her in this. "Finish your breakfast and then go outside into the sunshine." She hurried toward the swinging kitchen door, still talking. "Stay close to the house, and don't over tax yourself." She stopped at the threshold and fixed me with another stern look. "Steer clear of the out buildings. The sick housed there are as sick as what we left at West Point if you get my meaning." With a firm nod, she plowed ahead taking over the house and the work to be done.

Chapter 13

I strolled up the grassy hill from the brick kitchens toward the front of the house. Gardiners and stable hands moved double time back and forth in various tasks, so much so, I had to jump onto the front steps to get out of their way. It was clear the kitchen and household staff weren't the only ones preparing for the general's imminent arrival. The entire property was in frenzy.

"Well, well. Don't you look pretty," Alexander said, climbing down from his horse. He stood beside the tall, handsome animal, gazing at me as he patted the horse's flanks before handing the reins to a stable boy.

"It's nice to see you up and about, but I must say it's even nicer to see you in something other than an old lady's night dress. Mrs. MacPherson is a generous woman no doubt, but that borrowed shift looked as though it could swallow you whole."

He looked resplendent in his full Continental uniform. Alexander wasn't very tall, only a few inches taller than my own five-foot-four inches, yet he seemed gallant as he stood beside his horse. I watched the way he moved around the animal instructing the stable hand. Confident and deliberate.

He turned to face me again and smiled as though he knew I was mentally sizing him up. He doffed his hat, presenting a short bow. "At your service, my lady."

"Really, Colonel, bowing? Given the circumstances of our acquaintanceship don't you think we're well past any such formalities?"

He raised an eyebrow, but his eyes danced with mirth. "Indeed." He patted the horse's rump as the animal clip clopped toward the stables. Alexander walked toward the front porch and stood with one foot on the bottom step facing me. "It's a lovely day, don't you agree?"

"Yes, warm but not overly humid."

He nodded. "Since you appear to be dressed for an outing, I would gladly request the honor of escorting you around the grounds but unfortunately both my hands and neck require a good scrub and I smell of horse."

I laughed, wondering if his sudden rush for soap and water was because he didn't want my company or because he truly cared if he stunk.

"That's quite all right, Colonel. I'll wait."

The man's lips twitched. "I'll be but two shakes of a lamb's tail."

Alexander bypassed the front door and headed down the slope toward the stone kitchen entrance, stopping by the well. Dropping the bucket with a muffled splash, he drew the water up and proceeded to mop his face and neck with a drenched handkerchief.

As I watched him in my peripheral vision, I had to cover my mouth with my hand not to laugh. Had I possibly hit the nail on the head and he actually cared if he stunk? Otherwise, why would he care what I thought if he had no interest in spending time with me? Talk about a contradiction in terms.

Then again, who was I to question? I was a living, breathing set of contradictions, so much so my brain hurt. A twenty-first century mentality trapped in the eighteenth century trying to convince everyone she belonged. Keeping pace with their formal manner of speech was becoming a fulltime job, forcing me to stop to think whenever I opened my mouth to speak. My

mannerisms were another headache altogether, but keeping proper deportment was necessary, if not exhausting.

Alexander waved when done, squeezing the excess water from the handkerchief and hanging the wet cloth to dry on a bush next to the kitchen door. He ducked inside, and when he emerged, he had a small basket covered in a white and red striped cloth draped over his forearm.

"Some provisions. I haven't eaten and chances are I won't get another chance once the general finishes across the river," he said as he joined me by the front steps.

He took my elbow and walked me toward the back of the house and the gardens. "Mrs. Macpherson had the cook pack this in short order, giving me strict instructions not to walk you off your feet. We are to keep to the garden, but no further."

We strolled down a soft grassy incline to a flat expanse overlooking the river. The breeze this morning was wonderful, and I yearned to pull my hair down and let it blow through my curls.

"The cut of that gown is very fetching on you, though I must say I'm surprised you chose to wear it with your coloring, such as it is."

I looked at him not sure if I should laugh or be offended. "Why is that?"

He pointed to my cheek and the side of my temple. Leave it to Alexander to notice my green around the gills bruising. I rolled my eyes and he laughed out loud.

"You are the most confounding woman. Do you know that?" The question was clearly rhetorical, but I gave him a curious look regardless.

"How?" I asked, not sure I wanted to know.

He took my hand and led me toward a columned gazebo covering a small patio. Holding my arm, he helped me up the single step onto the raised platform and gestured for me to sit on a two-person bench in the shade, but I opted for the sun instead.

"See, in just that. I direct you to the shade because that's what most ladies would prefer, but you rather the sun."

I laughed. "Is that I polite way of telling me I'm difficult?"

He smiled, pushing a small round wrought iron table closer so we could share the food in comfort. "Perhaps."

"Well, who wants to be a safe bet? Predictability is not necessarily a virtue. It rather denotes a lack of courage." At the look on his face I had to bite the inside of my cheek. Alexander's mouth parted but no words came out. I think I stumped him with my mad paraphrase from the movie, *Practical Magic*.

"Are you a betting girl, then Miss Burritt?" he asked, handing me a glass of wine before taking the cloth cover off the bread and cheese. There was even a small bunch of grapes in the carefully packed basket.

I took the glass but put it down, careful not to knock the stem over on the uneven table surface. "The table is a little unsteady, Colonel, did the cook pack coasters?" I asked purposefully avoiding his loaded question.

He gave me a curious look. "Coasters?"

I nodded. "Thin round or square shaped pieces of cork to be placed under glassware. Coasters prevent the glass from falling and protect fine furniture from drips or condensation." I felt like an ad for housewares and embarrassed heat crawled up my cheeks.

"Hmmm. Interesting and practical idea, and I can't say I ever heard of them. Sadly, though, no we have no such vehicle." He sipped his wine watching me. "Don't you care for Claret?"

I shrugged. "I've never tasted it before."

He reached across the table and lifted my glass, holding it out to me again. "Please, try it. It's exceptional."

I took the glass from him once again and lifted the crystal lip to my own. I took a small sip, nodding what I thought was appropriate approval. What did I know about wine?

"It's very good." I swirled the red liquid in the glass admiring the different shades of burgundy. I took a deeper sip,

too much so and I winced, scrunching my eyes as I forced down the gulp. I coughed into my hand, my eyes tearing. "Smooth," I croaked.

He burst out laughing, slapping his knee. "Miss Burritt, you amuse me like no other girl has in quite some time," he said with a genuine smile. "I only wish I knew more about you."

I put the glass down on the table again, still coughing. "That makes two of us."

His grin spread even wider. "I have an idea. Since we're both in a muddle about this identity conundrum, why don't I pick a pet name for you?'

I raised an eyebrow. "A pet name? Like for a dog or a cat?" I asked reaching for a hand full of grapes and a small piece of crusty bread.

He shook his head, pressing his lips together not to laugh again. "My God, woman, not at all. I meant like an intimate friend." His voice dropped an octave and his eyes met mine.

I flicked my gaze toward him, but just barely. "I suppose, but on one condition. You can give me a pet name only if I get to call you Alec."

His studied gaze relaxed, and his lips curled up on one side. "Alec?"

I nodded. "Short of Alexander."

"I gathered as much." He pulled at the seat of his uniform tailcoat and sat back crossing his arms, his lips pursed as he deliberated. "Agreed."

His gaze never wavered, taking on a considered feel. "You know, in the sun, your hair has an almost coppery hue in the depths of the chestnut brown. It's very fetching."

I rolled my eyes again but had a thought that might work in my favor. "Then perhaps you should call me Rowen. It's Gaelic for *Little Red One.*"

With a smirk he thought for a moment, but then shook his head. "No. The name doesn't quite suit you."

I choked on a piece of bread. *Really, dude? Maybe you should take that up with my mother!*

He waved his hand in the air dismissing the notion. "No...I think I'm going to call you Fifi." A short laugh punctuated the idea.

I blinked. "Uh, I don't think so. That's a name for a French poodle or some other silly, designer breed."

"What about Fia, then?" he asked, seemingly not noting the change in my manner of speech.

I shook my head. "How about Rose?" If he wasn't going to go for Rowen, then at least the first syllable of this was close enough I might actually turn when called.

"I think not."

"Then what?"

He shook his head, slowly. "Perhaps your name is meant to be Phoebe, as it should be."

I pressed my lips together and gave him a tight smile. "As you wish, Colonel, but that doesn't mean I'll answer."

Shrewd. The man knew how to play the game well and it appeared he lured me into this hand with a purpose.

He sat back with a satisfied smirk so I decided to turn the tables and change the subject as demurely as I could. "So, tell me about the general and his wife? Do they seem happy to be setting up house? I hear they have a new baby. I can't imagine planning a move with an infant. Poor Mrs. Arnold. This must be quite a hard journey for her, and so far away from her family, and to have to do most of the travel with her husband already here." I tsked, earning a raised eyebrow from Alexander.

He eyed me circumspectly, and I decided to clarify how I came to certain knowledge. "Mrs. MacPherson has been telling me about our soon to be mistress. I'm sure it was to ease any trepidation I might feel with the advent of her arrival."

He nodded, but his lips were tight, though I had no idea why. My question was innocent enough. Perhaps he thought the

general stupid or inept and that was the reason for his frown. Based on the history I recalled, Arnold was a bit of a blowhard.

"I can only assume the general is content enough in his commission. He's injured, and active field duty is beyond him though he's loath to admit it…as for his wife," he paused, and his expression shifted to a distinctly appreciative air. "She's quite beautiful and gracious, much the same as my present company."

He lifted the wine bottle, but I shook my head skimming my hand over the top of the glass. "No, thank you, Alec. One glass has made my head a little fuzzy."

I don't know why but I suddenly I felt very vulnerable, very much like my charade glowed in neon lights for everyone to see. I glanced down at my hands twisting the lace of my cuffs.

"Perhaps a walk instead? I know Mrs. MacPherson said to keep to the garden, but a surely a look at the river won't hurt."

I nodded. "I'd like that, but we'll have to take it slow."

Alec slid his knuckle beneath my chin lifting my eyes to his. "I would be honored to assist you in any way necessary." His fingers slipped across the curve of my cheek. "And slow is a welcome pace, especially when getting to know each other."

He got up from the bench and moved the table to its original place, packing what was left of our lunch into the basket. He left the wicker hamper where it was, saying he would send one of the kitchen maids to retrieve it later.

Offering me his elbow, we stepped down onto the path and wound our way toward the water where we settled on the grass above the bank.

"Allow me," he said spreading his uniform coat on the ground for me to sit.

The river was calm and gentle waves lapped along the rocks beneath the shore's steep drop. Across the river I watched soot-colored smoke waft and curl into the afternoon sky from the blacksmith and the foundry on the far side the fort. I thought about the great chain that rested submerged beneath the brown

water even as we sat, just waiting to split the hull of any British ship that dared make a move on West Point.

"I thought the Robinson dock was the only place with easy access to the water. Aren't you afraid someone could come ashore unobserved?"

He laughed. "What an imagination. And who did you think would maraud against a hospital full of small pox?"

"I was thinking more of the main house and all its finery. Don't you worry about deserters, and what about redcoats sailing the Hudson and anchoring across from the point? That has disaster written all over it."

At that he laughed out loud. "My dear, perceptive as your mind is, don't you suppose we've already taken measures to prevent exactly that from occurring?"

I glanced down, pulling a handful of long, yellowed grass growing between the cattails. "Of course, how silly of me."

He squinted across to the fort, his body relaxed back on bended elbows, his legs stretched out toward the water. "Silly is not a word I would ever use to describe you. To be honest, I'm both surprised and impressed the possibility of British ships invading even crossed your mind."

"You're attaching me too much credit, Colonel. However, anyone with eyes and a brain can comprehend whoever controls the Hudson controls the war."

He smiled at me before returning his gaze to the water. He lifted a hand to his brow, squinting. "Look to your right. Can you make out the large iron ring at the base of the battlements sitting slightly higher than high tide? The glare off the water is strong, but if you narrow your gaze you can just make out the shape."

I nodded. "I see it."

"Good. Now look across to Constitution Island. It's too far to see from here and the angle isn't quite right, but there's a sister ring directly across from the other." He slid his eyes to mine. "Do you know what spans the length between the two?"

I shook my head, though I already knew.

"Six hundred yards of chain made of huge iron links, each two feet in length and weighing one hundred and fourteen pounds. It stretches from West Point almost directly north to Constitution Island, a distance of fifteen hundred feet. At each end the chain is anchored to large rock-filled cribs." He paused. "See the log rafts bobbing just beneath the surface? They've been waterproofed with tar and oakum to help keep them from becoming waterlogged and both ends have been sharpened to give them less resistance to the flowing water."

"Amazing," I murmured, and I meant it. Erecting a chain of that length, girth, and weight without the help of heavy machinery was a feat worthy of praise.

"Picture an iron necklace left loose and curving downstream like the lovely curve of a woman's neck leading to the softness of her décolleté." He said running a finger down the edge of my arm. "The chain isn't stretched tight but rather loose like that. Large winches on either side help maneuver the length, but the hawser remains suspended in prime position to gut any ship that ventures too close to the point."

"Do the British know or is it a secret?" I asked as though from absentminded musing as I braided the long grass into intricate lengths one after the other while he talked.

"Yes. There was a similar one at Fort Montgomery farther down river, but this is a much more strategic position. See how the river narrows? Rough tides make it hard to maneuver as well, so ships need to slow their approach."

I smiled. "Tide, time, and chain, wait for no man, eh?"

He laughed.

"Alec?"

"Hmmmm?"

"Was a military career always your wish or was it mere ideology?"

He thought for a moment, his eyes taking on a million-mile stare. "My fervent wish was to be of great service, not only to

General Washington, but to the nation. Too many of us sit on the fence awaiting the outcome, ready to leap off in either direction regardless who carries the victory banner." He pulled grass from the ground, flinging pieces as though aggravated by the thought. "Those who stand for nothing, fall for anything."

I froze. I had read that same quote by him in Mr. Garrett's class and chills ran up my arm. "Surely you don't believe people are that fickle? If history proves anything, great accomplishments come from the banding together of like minds. Jefferson would never have written, nor would the Continental Congress have ratified the Declaration of Independence, otherwise. There will always be people who choose to straddle the fence, but don't you think it takes quite a bit of self-delusion to not see one's reflection for what it truly is each time they gaze in the mirror?"

He looked at me with the dawn of new respect, admiration in his eyes at being comprehended. "I do believe for the most part, man is a reasoning, rather than a reasonable, animal. However, you are right in pointing out people are capable of great things once convinced. Unfortunately, fear is an anathema to that and plays on base human nature."

Another famous quote or at least part of it. Two for two in one conversation, Mr. Garrett would have peed himself.

"Are you happy as an adjutant general?"

He shrugged. "As happy as I can be for now. I don't always see eye to eye with the powers that be. I guess you could say I have a passionate nature and also forget where I am and to whom I speak at times. All in all I will probably vie for a career in politics, but I could always practice law."

I looked at him. "You're a lawyer?"

He inclined his head. "Alexander Hamilton, Esquire at your service."

"That's good to know, though I hope I never face the need for defense counsel."

A high-pitched whistle caught us both off guard and we each jerked our attentions toward the sound. Whistling again from the top of the hill, Sergeant Campbell waved his arm, gesturing for us to come.

Alec got to his feet and swept the grass from his buff colored breeches before holding his hand out for me. "The general must be in transit. Time to go."

He helped me up and stood for a moment holding my hand, his eyes searching. "Phoebe, what a riddle you are."

Without warning he pulled me toward him and pressed a soft kiss to my lips and then to my injured temple. Whether or not he expected me to respond, I don't know but he stepped back slightly embarrassed, but recovered quickly.

With a wink he bent to brush the grass from my skirts, enjoying himself just a little too much in the process.

"Hey!" I said swatting his hand away. "I'm fully capable of taking care of myself, thank you. Though I have no clue how women do so in an effective manner wearing these infernal skirts."

He laughed holding out his hand to assist me up the steep slope. "Of that I have no doubt."

Chapter 14

I sat in front of the mirror in my shift, brushing my hair with a horsehair brush, another luxury from Mrs. MacPherson's travel trunk of treats. She left a scissors for me beside the red and white pitcher in the bathroom. After washing up I set about cutting the legs off what was left of my knee-length shorts, slicing them into serviceable strips for use as either toilet paper or for when my period eventually decided to show up.

Perhaps the fates would cut me a little slack and let me forego that little joy, but based on the crimpy feeling across my back, I was in for no such luck. In anticipation of the inevitable, I kept the top part of my pants intact, cutting the legs off as high as possible without compromising the crotch for use when the time came. With no tampons and no real maxi-pads, I needed something to keep the makeshift pads in place. Hopefully, this was just the ticket.

I'd heard some colonial women let nature take its bloody course down their legs, but I couldn't even imagine. The fact Mrs. MacPherson had her own stash of narrow white strips lead me to believe she was of the same mindset. Either way, I was going to have to figure out a way to barter for more soap or learn how to make it myself.

I felt better, but my time outdoors wore me out. My legs ached along with my throbbing ribs, and though Mrs. MacPherson hadn't fully laced me into my stays, taking them off left my body singing with relief.

My thoughts drifted to Alec. He was on the verge of becoming an epic mistake in this whole endeavor. I should never have let him kiss me.

I exhaled, not quite meeting my own gaze in the mirror. "He kissed me." I said the words out loud, but their false ring made me cringe. I tried to convince myself my partaking was born of fear for my safety, that I had no choice, but I knew better.

"If it looks like a duck, walks like a duck, and quacks like I duck..." I sighed, giving my reflection a razzberry. "You suck, Rowen Emmeline Corbett." I wasn't an innocent bystander, and Alexander's quote came back to bite me in the butt as I sat trying to justify my own acquiescence. *Men are more reasoning than reasonable animals.*

I was guilty of fully accepting that kiss and worse yet, I enjoyed the flattery. I liked the way Alec made me feel. Hunter was gone, and for all I knew I was never going home. I craved him though, and a small part reveled in Alexander's attentions because they reminded me so much of Hunter, so much so I nearly convinced myself it was tantamount to having him with me in spirit.

I put the brush down and turned away from my reflection. I had no time for regrets. I had to do what I had to do even if I hated myself for it. I would deal with the repercussions of my actions once I got back to the twenty-first century. All's fair in love and war, and I was in love with Hunter but fighting a war to get home to him. Would I ever have the strength to tell him? That wasn't the question to ask. The question of the moment was would I ever be given the chance?

As for Alec, I would deal with him as the situation progressed. In the meantime, I needed to invest in some fancy foot work to evade him in the short term, but perhaps once Peggy Arnold arrived, I would be off the hook. His wistful gaze wasn't imagined when I asked him what she was like. Clearly, the woman left a bevy of smitten suitors along the way to

marrying her much older general and Alexander was just one more in a long line.

With my hair brushed to a shine and my body as clean as it could be considering the circumstances, I took Mrs. MacPherson's advice and lay down for a nap. I stared at the ceiling from atop of the covers. The sun had dropped below the trees, yet the room was still sweltering. The concept of heat rising may have dawned on the colonials, but there was nothing they could do about the lack of air circulation. At least the bedrooms faced the river, so evening breezes cooled the rooms to a certain extent.

I hiked my nightdress up to my thighs, trying to think cool thoughts and coax sleep. I drifted off with thoughts of Hunter playing in my mind.

"Rowen! No! Swim, Goddamn it! Swim!" His terrified face hung well over the edge of the boat as I went under again.

"No! Hunter! Benny, grab his arms! Get him back in the boat!"

Choking and coughing they dragged Hunter back into the raft. He slumped back against the seat, his face buried in Eric's life vest. "She's dead. God help me, Rowen's dead."

I yelled for him, every muscle aching as I fought the water. "Hunter!" I shouted again, only to feel hands lock on my ankles pulling me down into the swirling torrent. I sucked in a breath as water engulfed my head, kicking at whoever had hold of me. I looked down and saw hundreds of arms and hands writhing and grasping toward me from the blackness. I screamed, but my voice was soundless in the cold depths. A hand shot through the water above grabbing hold of my arm yanking me up into the air and the light. My head broke the surface and I gasped, dragging in a painful breath, clutching at the arm that was my lifeline. I pushed the wet hair from my face expecting to see Hunter's soft brown eyes only to be met instead by a pair of violet blue. "No!" I sobbed. "I'm not dead! Hunter, please! I'm not dead…I'm not dead…"

"Wake up, dearie! Oh lord, please wake up!"

Mrs. MacPherson gripped my trembling form, her fingers digging into my shoulders. My eyes flew wide and I flung myself into her arms, crying.

"*Sssh,* now. You were just having a bit of a nightmare. It was bound to happen at some point after what you've been through. *Sssh…*" She rocked me gently, crooning soft sounds into my hair and she stroked my sweat sheened brow.

When I calmed enough, she pulled back to look at me. "Now would you look at what you've gone and done? You're all red and puffy and himself asking to meet you." She nodded with a huge grin as though she'd just imparted the best of news. "That's right! The general has requested you join him for dinner."

I was still half terrified, shaken that it was Alec's eyes that met mine, that saved me, instead of Hunter. What did it mean? Was I never getting home? Or was it just my subconscious beating up on me for being fickle?"

"Did you hear what I said, darlin'?"

I just blinked at the kind woman, not really hearing her.

"Phoebe Burritt, for Christ's sake get your wits about you, girl! You've been summoned!"

At that one word my fog dissipated, and I realized for the first time that Mrs. MacPherson had used my assumed name. I thought about telling her who I was for real and what happened to me, but she'd have the general pack me off to the nut house faster than I could say time traveler.

"Summoned?"

She went to push herself from the bed, her eyes on the ewer of water ready to dowse the cobwebs from my brain.

"Wait, don't leave me!" I cried, surprising myself at how much I meant it.

Her face softened and she sat, clasping my hand in hers. "I'm not going anywhere, love, and neither are you, except to get dressed to meet the general."

She went to get up again, but I held her hand tight. "Mrs. Macpherson, you called me Phoebe Burritt. Is that who you believe me to be?"

This time she sat, all urgency leaving her face. She smoothed the sweat panicked hair from my brow, her fingers caressing my cheek. "It is who you are, love. There's a soldier from Burlington at the fort and he recognized you straight away, why else do you think everyone has been so accommodating? You're a sweet child, but these are challenging times, and no one is to be trusted on their word alone. I know I said the lieutenant colonel was too smitten to send for your family, but the truth is they already know you're a Vermont Burritt, they just don't know which side of the Burritt family claims you as their own.

"Daniel Burritt is a staunch British loyalist and fought with General Burgoyne at the Battle of Saratoga, while his brothers are all patriots—one even fought alongside General Arnold at Lake Champlain and Washington himself at Valley Forge—though I'm not sure which. The point is the lieutenant colonel is loath to let the wrong side know you're here, afraid at this precarious point in the war it might trigger an allegation of kidnapping. They're hoping your memory will come back of its own accord, and it will. It's just going to take time."

I nodded, not trusting myself to speak. I knew it was the same soldier I heard outside my window that night who fed Alec and Mrs. MacPherson this load of horse manure. I also knew he did so at the prompting of his friend for personal gain. But what could I say? Their soldier is a liar and I somehow fell through time? Eventually time will prove this to be a lie, and my only hope of escaping a spy's fate was to never, ever admit to being Phoebe Burritt. Until such time as I have to account for myself, they could believe what they wanted.

I looked at Mrs. Macpherson's somber face as she nodded her believed truth in what she just said. "Thank you, Mrs. MacPherson. I understand."

She went to get up yet again and I stopped her one last time. "Mrs. MacPherson?" I began.

She looked at me, her eyes questioning what else could I want. "What is it, sweeting?"

"What is your Christian name?"

She smiled a beautiful, thoughtful grin and pulled herself up to her full height, all five feet of her. "Ferne. My name is Ferne...and you need to call me Mrs. Mac like everyone else."

I left the bedroom only after Mrs. Mac was satisfied my appearance was suitable enough for my first meeting with the general. I guess the idea of first impressions was as important in the past as it was in modern times.

She dressed me in the same peridot colored gown I wore this afternoon, but she changed the petticoat, swapping the plain day cotton for a vertical silk stripe of celery-green and lavender. She also managed a matching lavender ribbon for my throat and another to accent my hair, even stitching two light purple bows to either side of the gown's square neckline, perfectly tying in the new petticoat. In the twenty-first century, Mrs. Mac would either be a successful stylist or a kick-butt Hollywood costume designer.

Where she dug up the extra clothing and accessories, I had no clue, but I had a sneaking suspicion some of Peggy Arnold's trunks had arrived well ahead of their mistress, and Mrs. Mac had helped herself to their bounty, if only for tonight.

I offered to help clean up, but the older woman's raised eyebrow warned me off, so I made my way downstairs to the drawing room where the men waited with their aperitifs. General Arnold, Alec, and Dr. Thacher were my dining partners tonight, or so I had been told.

The men's deep voices and laughter drifted through the closed pocket doors leading into the drawing room. I hesitated

outside, but Mrs. Gerrittsen peeked in from the servant's doorway, gesturing for me to go ahead. I nodded, dragging in a deep breath and she blew me a kiss just as I knocked on the door.

The pocket door slid open to Doctor Thacher's smiling face. "Come in! Don't stand there shivering like a scared rabbit, Miss Burritt. Come in, we've been waiting for you." He laughed, sliding the pocket door the rest of the way open before offering me his arm. "Hamilton's been telling me you're almost completely healed. I'm thrilled to hear of your progress, although I see some lingering discoloration around that one eye and temple. Any more headaches?"

I shook my head. "None, thank you, Doctor. I still have to be mindful of sudden jolts or turns and I fatigue easily, but other than that I'm right as rain."

He kissed my hand. "I'm glad to hear it, and how's the memory? Anything yet?" he asked, tapping the side of his head.

I shook mine. "Not really, just dreams and pieces but nothing that makes sense."

He smiled. "That's a good sign. A wonderful sign, in fact. It means your recollections are coalescing. Eventually all the bits will form puzzle pieces you can then fit together, and voilà! Your memory will be as good as new."

"Well, Doctor, we all hope that happens sooner than later." The general smiled raising his glass. "Lieutenant Colonel Hamilton, why don't you introduce me to this lovely young lady?"

General Arnold stood by the cold hearth, leaning heavily on a carved wooden cane. His small brown eyes were shrewd, almost calculating, and I had the impression his gaze could decode a room and its guests with a single scan.

He was older and wore a richly powdered wig despite the heat and his forehead sported a faint sheen of sweat. His clothing was impeccable, his blue and scarlet uniform finely brushed and pressed and crisp in its fit. His light-colored

breeches and socks seemed new and the buckles on his black calfskin shoes shined.

Yet with all his obvious finery, the man's eyes seemed furtive. He smiled in keeping with a commanding, yet welcoming countenance but my gut told me it was a façade, that beneath his proud bearing were buried truths and hidden fears. There was an underlying bitterness that made the air thick with anger. No one else seemed to notice, but it was as palpable to me as the lingering humidity.

Alec beckoned me closer, and I remembered he said the general was wounded, suffering a career ending injury when his horse was shot at the Battle of Saratoga and later fell on him crushing his leg. He was hailed as a hero, but for all intents and purposes his glory days were over, and he was relegated to desk work and arbitration. From our conversation earlier, I got the impression Arnold's command of West Point was a result of partiality and pity on the part of Washington.

Alone, I stepped toward the empty fireplace and Alec moved to my side to take my elbow. "General Arnold, may I present Miss Phoebe Burritt. She is a refugee and guest of Robinson House at the request of his Excellency, George Washington."

I smiled doing my best to curtsey without falling over or tripping on my own skirts. "I'm pleased to make your acquaintance, General. I've heard so much about your bravery and intellect I look forward to sharing many a conversation with you while I am your guest." I held out my hand.

The man's eyebrows rose at the mention of Washington's request. I had no idea what Alec was up to, but my guess was he improvised knowing Arnold might not welcome the idea of another hen in his roost.

Chances were good Alec could notify Washington before Arnold even thought to do so, and perhaps already had. After all, being the adjutant to the head of the Continental Army had its advantages.

As protocol dictated, he took my hand, offering a short bow. "Well, my dear. It is certainly a pleasure to have such a pretty young thing under my roof and I'm sure my Peggy will welcome the company of another fine young woman once she arrives. She loves diversion and perhaps you can keep her entertained. Do you play or sing?" he asked taking a sip from his short-stemmed glass.

I shook my head. "Not a note."

He laughed. "Well, then do you sew?"

I shook my head again, and the general looked both astounded and amused. "My dear, every well brought up young woman has some talent in the finer arts. Are you telling me your family offered you no formal instruction?"

Alec's eyes watched me, as well as the doctor's as I considered my answer. I needed to be very careful of my reply. "I am somewhat fluent in foreign language and I have talent for cookery, or so I've been told."

The general seemed impressed enough. "And what language is it you speak so well? French?"

"No, Spanish."

He slapped his thigh and a grin spread across his thin lips. "Not a fan of the French, eh? Well, neither am I! Good, girl. Say something in Spanish for me. I love hearing foreign sounds roll from an American tongue."

I laughed, and glanced up to the right thinking. *"Mi querido, General , que fuera un gran hombre en el pasado, un hombre codicioso hoy, e será un traidor en el futuro."*

He clapped. "Excellent! What does it mean?"

"From language to language one can never achieve an exact translation, but paraphrased I said the general is a great, conscientious and tradition-worthy man, for the past, present, and future generations." Of course, I knew my words said he was a great man in the past, a one greedy in the present and a traitor in the future, but no one needed to know that but me.

"How nice." He rubbed his thumb absently across the thin stem of his pony glass, his expression was pensive. "You must sit beside me tonight at dinner." He drained his sherry and then glanced from his empty glass to where I stood, turning to Alec giving him a direct chin pop. "Hamilton, where are your manners? Pour the girl a glass of sherry."

I raised my hand. "That's quite all right, General. My constitution is ill equipped when it comes to spirits, but I would take a glass of water or sweet tea."

He looked at me curiously. "Sweet tea, eh? Have you ventured to the southern colonies, then Miss...?" He glanced at Alec.

"Burritt, sir. Phoebe Burritt."

The general's eyes widened for a moment. "I fought with a man by the name of Isaiah Burritt at Lake Champlain. A lieutenant, and a fine man at that. Good family. Well-to-do. Are you a relation?"

Before I could open my mouth, Alec nodded. "Yes, General. She is of the Vermont Burritt's, same as the lieutenant."

The general seemed to process this, but a shadow crossed his eyes, nonetheless. Perhaps he was weighing which side of the family claimed my allegiance as well. Loyalist or Patriot. Considering history painted Arnold as the revolution's biggest turncoat, it was no wonder the question carried such interest.

A footman opened the door announcing dinner was served. I sat at the general's right and Doctor Thacher to his left. Alec managed to scoot beside me on my other side, earning a knowing nod from the doctor.

The kitchen maids brought in platters of food, including carrot puffs and beets dressed in garlic, green bean braise, and Cheshire pork pie. Potato rolls, still warm to the touch, were set in a beautiful basket at the center of the table with individual crocks of freshly churned butter placed beside each dish.

Everyone was served and I took small bites to sample the fare.

"So, how is the food? You said another of your talents was cooking. How does Mrs. Gerrittsen measure up?" Doctor Thacher asked with a wink.

I gave the man a warm smile. "Mrs. Gerrittsen is a treasure and the food is everything it should be. I can think of nothing I would change or add to the meal."

A loud burp followed on the heels of my praise and I looked across at the general, fist to his chest and napkin to his mouth. "Excuse me, my dear. My stomach hasn't quite recovered from the travel and tavern food ingested along the way from Philadelphia, but you're quite correct. Mrs. Gerrittsen has been with me for years, and everything she serves is a delight."

"I'm sorry to hear you suffered on your journey, I sincerely hope Mrs. Arnold fairs better."

He smiled at that. "Yes, Margaret isn't one for arduous journeys and the lack of luxuries entailed with the prospect, but she will be cheered to see her house so well put together."

My smile was genuine, because I knew he was indirectly praising Mrs. Mac. "Yes, the staff has been wonderful, and Mrs. MacPherson has worked side by side with them to ensure Mrs. Arnold is pleased when she arrives."

"Mrs. Mac is certainly a force to be reckoned with," the doctor joked. His mirth-filled eyes found mine with a wink.

I addressed the general. "Mrs. MacPherson is Doctor Thacher's personal housekeeper at West Point, but I'm sure you already knew that. The good doctor sent her with me to aid in my recuperation."

The general glanced at the doctor, burping again behind his napkin. "That so, Thacher? Well, I should warn you, if my wife takes a shine to your girl you'll soon be filling the position of housekeeper with another set of skirts."

The doctor's grin turned downward, but an infinitesimal shake of Alec's head had the man wiping the unhappy expression from his face. "Time will tell, General. As Mrs. Macpherson is invaluable to me and is neither a girl nor one I

would refer to as a set of skirts, she is on loan to ensure my handiwork in mending Miss Burritt doesn't count for naught."

The general chewed thoughtfully. "You said she was a refugee. From what exactly?" He gestured with his head toward me.

I opened my mouth to speak, but this time the doctor beat me to the punch. "From the small pox outbreak in the barracks. The field hospital is rampant with it. I sent her here to protect her from infection. She was the victim of an unfortunate accident, thrown overboard on the river during a storm. She washed up on the shore, half dead, close to Lieutenant Colonel Hamilton and his militia."

Alec nodded. "I was in transit from a meeting with General Rochambeau and the French troops now garrisoned in Newport, but the doctor is correct. Her injuries were grave."

The general seemed to consider my face, his eyes narrowing slightly at the discoloration on one side of my face. "Yes, I can see the telltale marks." He remained quiet mulling over the facts or what was presented to him as fact.

The dishes were cleared, and dessert served, and as he spooned up sweet, thick bread pudding, his eyes watched, moving from one of us to the other. Finally he pointed his spoon at Alec. "Hamilton, why haven't you sent for her family? Surly the lady is missed and would rather be in the bosom of her own home than here on the outskirts of a rough army. I know, given the choice, my Peggy would have preferred to stay in Philadelphia."

Alec snaked his hand under the table and grasped mine. He gave my fingers a gentle squeeze, the whole while keeping his face professional as he caressed my palm, wrist, and forearm.

"A messenger has been dispatched, sir. We have yet to hear back. You know as well as I it may take a month before we receive word or instruction."

The general considered the man's words before he acquiesced. "Quiet, and with the upsurge in skirmishes along

the northern borders it may be longer still." He tossed his napkin into his empty dish and pushed his chair back. "Well, if word has been sent, Miss Burritt is welcome to stay as long as is required to see her safely home. We'll hear something at some point. Until then she is our guest."

He pushed up from his chair, using his cane for leverage. "What say you, Doctor, care for a brandy and a game of chess? Washington tells me you are quite the strategist."

It was clear dinner was over and Alec and I had been dismissed. I thanked the general for his hospitality and took Alexander's arm as he led me from the dining room.

"Would you care for a walk?" he asked. "Or are you too fatigued after today's exertions?"

After the dream I had, I didn't know what to do about my budding friendship with Alec. The images were too confusing, and I didn't understand their portent. Should I foster the relationship, or should I be wary?

This wasn't a simple case of boy meets girl, boy likes girl. Alec wasn't a typical young man in a twenty-first century sense of the word. Chronologically he was the same age as most recent college grads, but there was nothing about him that was still emerging. He wasn't on the cusp of adulthood. He was fully a man at twenty-three years of age. I'd have to be thick or stupid not to notice his interest or acknowledge where it could lead if I wasn't careful.

We stood side-by-side at the front door. The footman had left the entrance open to allow in the cool evening air. Lightning bugs were aglow in the garden, their luminescence sparking and then disappearing into the shadows.

"Look, Alec, how lovely." I purposely evaded his question so as not to put myself in an awkward position.

"When I was a little girl I would try and catch them in a glass jar to keep at my bed side." I walked out onto the porch and gazed into the gathering dark.

"And did you succeed?" he asked coming up behind me. His fingers swept the tendrils from my throat and he kissed the nape of my neck.

I held myself still. "Yes. Though they never seemed to last very long." To jerk away would insult him, and I couldn't risk that, not at this point in the game.

He chuckled, his soft breath fanning against my skin. "Something that beautiful and delicate should never be trapped."

I moved to step toward the door, but he held my arm. Trapped was the perfect word. It described my situation both here in 1780 and with him. My heart belonged to Hunter, yet he was gone from me. Maybe forever. What did the universe want? Unshed tears stung my eyes, and I blinked, grateful my back was still to Alec.

"Phoebe…"

I closed my eyes for a moment before turning to face him. "It's all right, Alec. I'm a little tired. I think I'm going to retire. The next week brings with it a second hurtle I need to conquer."

He looked at me queerly. "Peggy?"

I nodded.

He laughed. "That's ridiculous. The woman is vain and high spirited, but I wouldn't say she was unkind, at least not to her peers. You have nothing to worry about, sweeting." He reached out, sliding his hand around my waist. "Nothing at all."

He pressed his lips to mine, but there was no urgency in his kiss. My guess was our proximity to the house and the general kept his ardor in check more than anything else.

He stepped back, lifting his lips to my temple. "I did something tonight I never thought I would ever do," he whispered, pressing a kiss to my hair.

I pulled back so I could look at him, but he held me fast.

"What did you do?" I whispered back, suddenly nervous.

He exhaled. "I lied to a commanding officer." He paused as though weighing his words. Without warning he tightened his

grip on my waist, the effort almost beseeching. "I did so to protect you."

Alec dropped his head, immediately loosening his hold. I stepped back unsure of what to say or do, watching the muscle in his cheek work against the war of emotion on his face.

"Alec…"

He straightened, squaring his shoulders.

"Alec…" I tried again.

He shook his head and flashed me a charming smile, letting the corner of his lip curl in a *c'est la vie* smirk before pressing his fingers to my lips. "Goodnight, Phoebe."

Alec walked into the house to join the men, leaving me to ponder. He was clearly torn, but why? Was he angry with himself because he let desire rule his actions instead of intellect? What did Alexander Hamilton have to gain by protecting me?

I walked inside as well, pausing for a moment by the drawing room before heading upstairs. I lifted my hand to knock but heard General Arnold's loud voice through the closed doors.

"If all we have is one soldier's confirmation, I wouldn't be too quick to sign off on her identity, Hamilton. She's a pretty little thing, intelligent and innocently alluring, but that may be part of the ruse. My gut tells me she's hiding something. I want you to send a note to Benjamin Tallmadge. Ask him to investigate while we wait for word from Vermont. Find out if she's part of his Culper ring. She may be a 355…or worse, a British equivalent."

Alec's voice was low, but I heard his answer, nonetheless. He'd send the general's request to the Continental Army's spymaster first thing in the morning.

Chapter 15

A week had passed since my initial dinner with the general, and his wife had yet to appear. Life settled into a routine of sorts, but I found myself bored and restless. Alec hadn't said a word about letters sent or received. Of course, he didn't know I overheard the general's request, but each night we sat in the drawing room playing cards or discussing the day's events. I found it amazing how freely the different men spoke in front of me, as though I had faded into the floral wallpaper.

A round robin of dinner partners joined us throughout the week. Alec was always present, but the general kept the evening's entertainment new if not interesting by inviting various officers and adjutants from the forts. Often included were General Arnold's own aides-du-camp, Major David Franks and Captain Richard Varick.

I paid close attention to both, especially Franks. He was the one entrusted with dispatches.

Card games were a favorite way to pass the evening, and luckily, I already knew how to play Whist, having learned it at a living history day at school. I got pretty good over the past week, even winning a few rounds with Dr. Thacher as my partner. The general was even nice enough to allow Mrs. Mac to join us, with the understanding that it was just until his wife arrived and so I didn't feel like the only hen among the roosters.

The general, in fact, was extremely gracious and when I offered to teach them how to play Five Card Stud, he was more

than a willing student especially when he ordered Alec to give me a few coins that we might bet properly.

I laughed to myself as I wet a washcloth in the ewer and added a few drops of soap, remembering Alec's face once the poker game commenced. If there was an eighteenth-century word for hustler, I'm sure he would have thrown it my way.

No one uttered a word about my identity, and I could only assume that either no letters had arrived to the contrary or they had, and the powers that be were waiting to spring the spymaster on me unawares.

The days were beginning to blur one into the other. I still had no clue why I was here, but I was doing what I could to make the best of it. The house had gone from a frenzy of activity the day General Arnold arrived, to almost a calm before the storm.

As usual, Mrs. Mac helped me dress and I chose to wear the rose-colored gown today, with a creamy petticoat to offset the deep hue. The look was perfect against my skin. Eggshell lace graced the gown's elbow length cuffs and the same frills gathered in peekaboo fashion just inside the low scooped neckline.

Knowing Mrs. Mac needed to ready herself as well, I worked my long thick hair into a fishtail French braid that came around each side of my head, and then gathered the curled bottom pinning the weight up to give the style volume and height. To tie it all together I found rose colored lengths of ribbon in Mrs. Mac's box.

We came downstairs together, only to hear a huge crash coming from the kitchen. We both ran, expecting the worst.

"No, no, no! How many times must I tell you, General Arnold doesn't like it when the roast is cut too narrow! How am I supposed to stew a rump of beef when all you've left me are narrow filets? The cuts aren't even wide enough to hold the forcemeat! What am I going to do, now? He's expecting a roast!" Mrs. Gerrittsen ran a hand across her forehead and exhaled.

Marianne Morea

I walked through the door having heard the commotion. Mrs. Macpherson right on my heels. "The house feels all at sixes and sevens, yet herself isn't due to arrive yet for another week," she whispered. "Mrs. Gerrittsen is half way to apoplexy already. For sure she'll keel over dead before the mistress graces the front steps."

Mrs. Mac moved to my side and I leaned in to reply, "Alexander told me Peggy Arnold wasn't a mean sort. Why is everyone running around as though doomsday were upon us?"

The older woman returned my gaze and it was hard done. "Men only see what they want to see and that one was taken with Peggy Arnold from the moment he set his eyes on her. She has the look of an angel about her, so most men simply ascribe an angelic temperament to match the outer wrapping regardless if it is deserved or not. Peggy Arnold is as mean as a snake when it comes to those, she considers beneath her. Why do you think I haven't let you lift a finger in this house?"

I opened my mouth to argue like I had the day before, but Mrs. Macpherson held up her hand.

"No, love. The same reason I wouldn't let you help before is the same reason I won't allow it today. The general wouldn't notice if Martha Washington herself served his tea, but if Peggy Arnold gets even one sniff of you acting in a servant's capacity it will be all over for you but the requiem march. Servants gossip, and no matter how much they appreciate your willingness to lend a hand, it's bound to get back to herself, and you will be forever less than in that woman's eyes, and I won't have it."

"What am I to do then? I can't wander aimlessly until she arrives. Give me a task, anything."

She pondered a moment and then pointed to the counter. "All right then, today you can take that basket from the drying rack and gather fresh wildflowers and herbs for the table. Small task that it is, the general requires it. Says their soft scent calms the senses and lifts the spirit." She rolled her eyes. "Though it

sounds to me, the only soft thing he's yearning to lift requires his wife's assistance."

Feigning shock I burst out laughing. "Mrs. Mac!"

She nodded giving me an eyeful. "Men are fickle creatures, love, so I'd watch myself if I were you. When the cat's away the mice will play, and the prettier the catch the more they give chase."

Task assigned, Mrs. Mac shooed me from the kitchen, and I walked the grounds swinging the narrow, flat-bottomed rattan basket, enjoying the sun. My reflection played in the window glass along the back porch paralleling my movements. The mirrored scene felt like play acting, the way the characters do along Duke of Gloucester Street in Colonial Williamsburg.

From the upstairs bedroom window, I saw orchards in the distance and asked if they were part of the property. Mrs. Gerrittsen nodded, but didn't elaborate. The Robinson lands on this side of the Hudson were vast, and I decided to do a little reconnaissance.

The idea sounded stupid in my head. I wasn't a *Laura Croft* type, especially not in a gown and petticoats, but the necessity for me to know the property and its access to main roads, other homesteads or even places to hide was a grim reality. After hearing the general's words when he thought I was out of earshot, I knew I was on borrowed time.

I moved past the house towards a grassy slope that lead to the back orchards, grinning at the silhouette of the high, bergère hat and the wide flow of my skirts swishing along the path. Mrs. Mac believed hand-to-God that infatuation was the primary reason behind Alec stalling his inquiries regarding my identity. I knew better.

History had proven Hamilton a shrewd strategist, and everything pointed to him keeping his friends close but his enemies closer. He was the adjutant general to George Washington. If he wanted, he could have an answer from Vermont or Benjamin Tallmadge within a fortnight. Of course,

he would assume any subterfuge as my doing, even though I never confirmed or denied myself as Phoebe Burritt.

I was guilty of the sins of omission and deliberate evasion. In his mind I would be exposed as a liar, consummate manipulator, and possible spy. Alec would have an infiltrator in custody, but he still wouldn't know why I was sent or by whom.

I cringed at the thought of what was in store for me if that happened. There was no Geneva Convention to protect my human rights. I would be completely at the mercy of the Continental Army. Rape, assault, torture, they were all possibilities and I knew I needed a Plan B if the fates didn't ante up soon.

I continued on toward the orchard, eventually settling under the shade of a fruit tree some distance from the house. I munched on an apple picked from one of the branches, still lost in thought. It was mostly green and tasted like a granny smith, but perhaps its tartness was simply because it was too early in the season for picking.

It was nice to be able to just sit and think. I reveled in the idea of freedom. Not that I was a prisoner. Not yet anyway, and truth was there was really no place for me to run. No Emerald City for me to head to and click my heels together. With a resigned sigh I murmured, *there's no place like home* and tossed the apple core away.

Loath to dirty the dress with sticky apple juice, I wiped my hands on a few soft leaves. As my gown was raw silk, I did not want it to stain, especially since I might have to live in it for a while. The sun was high overhead and I wanted to get away from the bees buzzing through the green fruit and I had more ground to cover while I had the opportunity.

The moment Mrs. MacPherson sent me out alone I had doubled back to my room to slip my mother's vial into the pocket of my dress. Who knew colonial women had a completely separate pocket attached to a long string worn tied

around the waist above their petticoats for use as a purse? There was even a special slit in the gown to allow the wearer access.

Gathering my skirts, I lifted them enough for me to shift onto my bare knees. Mrs. Mac had no stockings in her bag of tricks, but there was no need, really. The weather was hot, and the dress covered everything, but aside from that I had salvaged my twenty-first century underwear, scrubbing them clean along with my hands that night in the hospital. I planned to wash and wear them until they fell off my body in shreds, the same as with the daisy dukes I fashioned from what was left of my shorts.

Still, based on the set of Mrs. Mac's jaw, I was sure a serviceable pair of over-the-knee stockings and matching ribbon-garters would somehow be waiting for me at some point.

I brushed leaves and loose grass from the back of my dress and looked across the orchard path. The trail was flat but slightly rocky and I was glad I had my own shoes. The ones I saw on the other women seemed thin soled, not to mention there was no difference between the left and right foot. I had enough aches and pains recuperating from my trip over the falls, I didn't need to add sore feet and a sore back to my list of complaints.

I followed the path for a while and eventually noticed the sound of running water. It wasn't the river though, that much I knew. The calm burble was so inviting I picked up my pace and traced the sound to a pool fed by a shallow brook. Smooth stones accounted for the soft rippling and I tracked the line of their incline to a waterfall coming from a rocky outcrop past a small, flowered clearing.

The place was beautiful, and the water perfect for my mother's potion. The pool was still despite the influx of water from the brook, and I knew I could kneel at its edge and scry from its depths. I looked up at the sun, tracking its place in the sky and frowned. I had been gone from the house a while. I'd have to come back, or risk being found and accused of

witchcraft. Cases were far and few between by the close of the Age of Enlightenment, but in rural counties old superstitions died hard. I couldn't take the chance.

I was about to turn back toward the house when I smelled smoke. Wood smoke like I did that morning in my bathroom. My body stiffened and the hairs on my neck rose. This was no vision, and it looked like I wouldn't have to place that cosmic collect call after all. The fates had decided to do this face to face.

I relaxed my shoulders and swallowed back my fear and turned around. The clearing was empty just a moment ago, but now a small wood hut graced its center and an old woman sat beside a campfire weaving daisy chains.

Okaaay. This wasn't what I expected. I was so used to visions of bloody heads and scorched crimson stained earth that I almost laughed.

"You find me humorous, Rowen?" the old woman asked, not looking up from her work.

I swallowed again. She knew my name. My real name. "Who are you? Are you the one who summoned me?"

She looked up at this point and through the smoke I saw the same milky blue eyes I saw in my mirror so many weeks ago.

"It's you, I'm sure of it." My voice was awestruck. I wanted to walk closer, to touch her, but I was frozen in place.

"You're so like your grandmother. Demanding and impatient. However, you're also like your mother and your great-great-grandmother Ivy. Kindness incarnate, with loving, open hearts. No hard edges, although there is a bit of stiffness forming around your aura. You've been through something terrible."

"I was forced over a waterfall after falling overboard, so yeah, I'm a little banged up but I survived."

She laughed out loud. "You survived all right. I saw to that. Then again, I'm the one who sent you into the water, but that's not what I'm talking about. I meant your dance with death last Samhain. You impressed me, Rowen. I know you had help, but

it was you and that young man of yours who put old wrongs to right." She eyed me. "You're going to be tested with that too, you know."

Tested? How? "I love Hunter."

She nodded. "I know, but you are going to have to put that aside to accomplish what it is you need to accomplish here."

I didn't like the sound of this one bit. "What do you mean? I know I'm in no position to make demands, but I would appreciate if you could just give it to me straight. I hate games and I hate riddles even more. If you were watching me last Halloween, then you know I've had enough mystery to last a lifetime. I have so many questions, and if you don't at least answer some of the more important ones, then how can you expect me to fulfill whatever destiny you envision here?"

She nodded again. "Fair enough, but first, come closer. No one will see or hear you as long as I am with you. They will only see the water."

As I walked toward the fire, I expected to feel heat and grime, but it was cool to the touch, like those mist stations amusement parks set up in the summertime.

She patted an old blanket near where she sat. I lowered myself to the folded square, careful of both my dress and my healing ribs, crisscrossing my legs beneath my petticoat. The old woman was dressed in clothing similar to what Mrs. Gerrittsen wore. A white shift, with plain, blue muslin stays and front laces and a matching jacket with a brown cotton petticoat and apron. Her mobcap was more of a bonnet. It had a puffed crown placed high on the back of her head, a deep flat border surrounding the face, and side pieces carried down like short lappets.

There were two daisy-chain crowns, one completed and sitting in her lap, and the other in her hand as she wove flower after flower into the circlet.

I found myself fascinated by the rhythm of her hands. She worked slowly but deliberately so as not to bruise or snap the

stems but also, so the petals fell in exact position, adjacent to the flower before it in the chain.

"Daisies are my favorite flower. So happy in their simplicity," she said with a wistful look. "I used to make daisy chains for my daughter." She looked up and her blue eyes met mine. "But then again, you already know that."

I balked for a moment but then remembered the little girl from my vision. Genève. She wore a daisy crown on her head. One of the flowers landed in the mud beside Hulda's moonstone, just like the single flower landed on my lap from the spilled vase at the museum.

"You're Hulda, aren't you?"

She didn't answer.

"Daisy chains take such patience to make. The flowers are so delicate, each twist in the weave must be precise or the circle will unravel. Such work to create, yet so easily destroyed." She finished the chain in her hand and held it out to me, her blue-eyed gaze shrewd.

I took the flowers, and a soft, reserved smile spread across my closed lips. She was right. They were a happy little flower. She nodded at the simple gesture as I placed the crown on my head acknowledging her daughter.

"You said you had questions, yet you've asked only one."

I inhaled, letting my breath out in a low rush. "And it's a question you still haven't answered."

Her now idle hands picked up a long white birch rod and poked at the fire. "Beyond the veil, names bear little significance, but I promised you no riddles, so yes, I am who you say."

"Why did you summon me? In this time, in this place?"

She looked at the fire "Our lives, our histories, are interwoven. Not just yours and mine, but all of ours. Lives bleed one into the other through fate. Each of us is separated by a mere hand's width in accordance to God's will."

"Six degrees of separation," I replied.

She looked at me, her head slightly cocked. A half smile crinkled her eyes a bit. "Explain."

I shrugged. "It's a twentieth century theory stating everyone is six or fewer steps away from every other person in the world by way of introduction. It talks about a chain of *friend-of-a-friend* statements that can connect any two people in a maximum of six steps."

"Ah...again a chain."

I didn't know where she was going with this philosophy, but I wanted answers not platitudes. "Okay, so we have daisy chains and the chain of life, what has that got to do with why I was summoned? I don't mean to be rude, but I've been through a lot and my gut is churning with an unspoken hunch it's going to get worse before it gets better. So please, land your plane and get to the point."

"There's that impatient, demanding stir, again," she said with a touch of rebuke. "You're here because I summoned you, and I summoned you because I need you."

"Need me for what?" I asked, not liking the sound of this.

She threw another small log on the fire and red sparks rose with the smoke. With the crooked end of the birch rod she pushed the fresh wood toward the center flame, absently smoothing the ash and dirt between the fire and the hearth stones.

She lifted the daisy crown from her lap and held it between her two hands. "Like this ring of flowers, our family line is unbroken and beautiful in its honesty and grace. Our history forms our circle of life, but one missed step, and the circle unravels." She pulled a loose stem and the circlet fell apart in her hands.

"I don't understand. Our family is fine. The considerable lineage listed in the bible is the proof."

With the end of the charred birch stick she drew three interconnecting circles in the ash. "Do you recognize this symbol?"

I nodded. "It's a Triquetra."

"Yes. I drew it to illustrate how the past, the present and the future are precariously linked. Our family is linked with events that are to happen very shortly, but it's not just our family that suffers if events don't transpire exactly. Everything is affected."

"Everything?"

She nodded. "The world as *you* know it."

I opened my mouth to ask what she meant by the world as I knew it, but she waved me off.

"You must fulfill what I can no longer do. The task is dangerous and there are variables that can sway the outcome, spelling disaster for all of us. You will have to go against your own nature, play on sympathies, manipulate and even hurt those who have showed you kindness. You will have to go against all that you feel is right, even against your own faithfulness to accomplish what needs to be done."

I was aghast. "And what if I refuse?"

She tossed the birch stick in the fire. "There will be no home, no family, and no love for you to return to. The life you know will be no more."

"I don't believe you."

She pursed her lips and gazed at the fire again for a moment. She raised her hand and the brook stilled as did all the natural sounds surrounding the small camp. The flames in the campfire sputtered as if sucking in oxygen, the blaze growing and receding until the center of each flame burned white.

"Give me the vial in your pocket," she said holding out her hand.

I reached into the small slit at the side of my gown and then down into the secret pocket. My fingers wrapped around the small glass ampoule and it warmed to my touch. I pulled it out and held it in my palm. "I wanted to use this to help reach my family. I wanted to let them know I was okay." My voice was small as I handed her the vial.

She wrapped her hand around mine as she took the potion, giving my fingers a squeeze. "They already know, sweetheart."

The vial passed to her hand and she rolled it back and forth in her palm as though mixing the contents. Her lips murmured a chant, and though I could only make out a few words I knew it wasn't the same chant I had heard in my head.

With a swift pull she uncorked the top, pouring half the contents directly into the flame. She handed the rest to me. "Drink it."

My mouth went dry as my eyes dropped to the small brown apothecary bottle and its pine scented contents. I knew it wouldn't poison me, but I also knew it would induce visions, and I wasn't sure I was ready for whatever Hulda wanted me to see.

"Drink," she said again, this time urging my hand up.

I placed the vial between my lips and tossed my head back, letting the liquid burn my tongue and throat. I coughed. The taste was bitter and a little oily, like chewing on pine needles covered in sap.

"Good. Now watch the flames and see what will come to pass if you do not accept your role in this drama."

The air was thick with smoke, and the battlefield strewn with dead. Blood coated the landscape giving the scorched black earth a slick crimson appearance. I walked, desolate. My heart breaking with the horrific scene. Bodies lay in charred carnage, and my stomach roiled with the smell of burnt flesh.

Cannon fire echoed in the distance and I heard and saw men running for their lives, others reaching for me from where they lay, begging for help or death.

Broken mortars pitted the earth, body parts flung wide with the impact. On a close hill, the American flag was tied to the feet of a dead soldier; the two hung upside down from a lone tree. Remaining soldiers surrendered, stripped of their guns and most of their clothes and slogged through the bloody mud in disgrace, their officers dragged from the horses of the British cavalry.

The scene changed. Boston burned; the historic buildings I knew and loved were gone. Faneuil Hall, the North Church charred to their foundations. Looters and mobs took to the streets of New York and Philadelphia, and countless men and women were tarred and feathered and paraded in front of what was left of the Liberty Tree, cut down and used for firewood.

Images flashed again, this time to the villages of Tarrytown and Sleepy Hollow. I stood ghostlike watching helpless as children sat huddled and crying, their mothers and sisters dragged off as trophies for the British soldiers, and even worse some of them were carried off, as well. I cringed at the sight, sickened at the debauchery and cruel inhuman treatment of one soul to another. Farms burned, and the Old Dutch Church stood in ruins, graves desecrated. Neutral ground had become a British free-for-all as lands were confiscated, families murdered in their homes, their belongings pillaged, and their women and slaves raped.

Free Americans were free no more. Forced to pay war reparations. If they couldn't pay, they were sold into indentured bondage until their debts to the crown were satisfied. There was no representation, no laws, no judge and jury, and no freedoms. Free-born former subjects of the British crown were no better than slaves bartered on the block.

The scene changed once more, and I recognized the parade grounds at West Point. Large gallows, erected in three tiers had been set at Execution Hollow, and as the dawn broke drums beat a solemn tempo. I saw myself shackled, made to watch as men as familiar to me as my own reflection marched from the jail. I screamed, but no sound left my mouth. Tears ran down my face and my heart clenched as Alexander, bruised and bloodied, lifted his face to me as he passed. The once proud young man full of life and vigor brought so low. Dr. Thacher, his frail form bent and broken, he could barely walk to his death…and lastly, George Washington himself, bound and gagged and carted to the gallows as soldiers pitched rotted fruit and feces at him. There was no honor in this, no chivalry. The British powers were either drunk with power or celebrating their victory on far shores, leaving punishments to be doled out with a blind eye.

The men were walked to the gallows and the ropes slipped over their necks. The sentences were read, and my fists clenched with rage and fear as the words rang in the silence. Alexander and the doctor were to be hung by the neck until dead, but Washington was to be hung until unconscious and then quartered, his near dead body tied to four horses and heaved apart.

The drum roll began, and without the benefit of benediction or blindfold the barrels kicked out from beneath the men. I screamed watching their eyes bulge and their bodies go ridged and then twitch until two hung still. Washington was cut down, his limp form dragged to the open grounds and his arms and legs tied to four separate horses. Water was thrown in his face until he regained consciousness and then the order given. The horses bolted and I squeezed my eyes shut, screaming no more...

The vision ended and my heart raced in my chest. Nausea gripped my stomach and I wiped my mouth and the fine sheen of sweat that clung to my forehead. I blinked against unshed tears and tried to quell the real fear blossoming in my gut with the knowledge this outcome would come to pass if I failed.

I truly was trapped.

"Was that true? What I just saw?"

She nodded.

"It's not just one possibility?"

She shook her head slowly.

"Why me, then?" My voice was barely a whisper.

She reached out her hand, and I expected an icy chill or for my skin to crawl in revulsion, but her touch was warm and soft.

"This is not castigation, Rowen. It's salvation. You are the only choice for this. I know it and your mother and grandmother knew it, too. Oh, they fought me. You are much cherished, my dear, as you should be, but they witnessed the truth of the situation. You possess the talent and the compassion necessary to see this through. There is no room for ego in this endeavor.

"You showed true empathy in the face of real evil that wintery day in the Old Dutch cemetery when you spoke to the caretaker. My grave is there, too. I heard what you said to him. I felt your heart break for your cursed friend. So many before you have had the talent but not the heart, or had the heart but not the talent, or they had both but were overrun with ego.

"I have waited a very long time for you, for a pure member of our line to safeguard these events to happen as they should. As they must. I have been trapped here on this plane for the past two hundred years. In what you called the Catch 22. History isn't merely a compendium of passages and anecdotes stored a textbook. It's as alive and full of promise as the here and now but exists on different planes."

She pointed to the Triquetra. "It's the same for the future. One link overlaps another and another. Events unfold over and over again, and if something alters one link, the ripple effects can be catastrophic."

"A rock thrown into a cosmic lake," I replied, the analogy truer now than ever.

She nodded with a sad smile. "I have reached past the veil in order to influence lives and certain events for centuries. I stayed bound to this time and place for my daughter's sake, so she could live and in doing so preserve our line. But I'm tired. It's time for my spirit to move on. You took care of the wronged spirit in the grave yard. Now you have to help set my spirit free by accomplishing this task in the flesh. Doing so will settle the history once and for all."

"What do you mean settle the history?" I asked.

She sighed. "I exist in the ethereal and any influence I exert over lives or events is as impermanent as I am."

"You have been influencing history?"

She nodded, not quite meeting my eyes. "You are flesh and blood, and once you ensure events follow the same path, I have set in motion for two hundred years, history will be set in stone."

"Set in stone? Isn't this against the Wiccan Rede and the bit about harming none, not to mention personal gain?"

"I did what I had to so our line could endure. Genève is caught, and the only way she will break her bonds and free her soul to take the path it was meant to is if you show her the way."

I sensed there was more to it than a simple visit to my however many times great-grandmother. "And?"

Her eyes met mine head on. "The only way you will convince her is with proof."

"And where do I find this proof?"

"It's hanging around the neck of the most self-centered woman you will ever encounter."

"Who?"

The witch simply stared at me, and when my mouth dropped open, she nodded.

"And what do you suppose I do? Ask her for it? Buy it?"

She shook her head. "You must steal it, but you must do so when she is desperate. When she has lost almost everything and is too terrified to care. It must be done in this way or the repercussions will find both you and Genève."

"And how do you propose I bring this about."

She blinked once, her gaze like flint.

"You'll figure it out."

Chapter 16

I walked back to the house lost in thought. *I'll figure it out?* Nice way to dump a little more metaphysical doo-doo in my lap. What did she expect? For me to have Peggy Arnold branded with a scarlet letter like in Arthur Miller's, *The Crucible*? I was more than a little out of my element, here. If Hulda wanted a feasible diversion, then she should have dragged my entire family back in time. I wasn't the A-Team. At least not by myself.

How did she expect me to manipulate a woman who by all accounts was a consummate manipulator herself? Especially when the playing field provided had a distinct home field advantage. I was a stranger in a strange land and Peggy Arnold was mistress of it all.

I didn't know much about the woman. On one hand, Alec said she was a kind woman, but the staff said otherwise. From all accounts she didn't sound particularly clever, though my guess was she liked to pretend so. She was adept at flirtation, using her skills to entertain and stage the officers she toyed with and then discarded like accessories.

I chewed on my lips. Perhaps I wasn't being fair. Everything I'd heard to date was hearsay, though why would Hulda lie if so much hung in the balance? She made it abundantly clear our family's continued existence depended on me and what I needed to steal from this woman. It hung around her neck. That limited the possibilities to jewelry, a skeleton key, or notes

hidden in carefully constructed containers like the two-piece silver bullet Jan Dunham told Hunter and me about at the museum.

I needed to think, but in the meantime, I hadn't picked one flower and the sun was already at mid-point in the sky. I caught a burst of orange beyond a small crest to the left of the orchard and climbed up the small knoll for a better look. The tall swaying flowers were tiger lilies and they grew along the edge of what looked like a marsh. I took off my shoes and hiked up my dress, tying it in a knot even with my knees and trudged the distance through overgrown grass wondering if deer ticks carried Lime's Disease in the eighteenth century.

I picked the orange lilies and marsh marigolds, wild irises and bell flowers and then I saw the prettiest flower shaped like a heart and thought, why not? I reached out to pluck the stem and pain shot through the underside of my fingers with a thousand hypodermic needles. I yanked my hand back and swore, stopping myself before I stuck the affected area in my mouth. Bad enough my hand was tingling with a telltale sign of an allergic reaction to the toxin in the flower's stem. I didn't need to ingest it as well.

An infection or rash in an era where treatment would most likely kill you either from sepsis or a doctor bleeding you dry was not a good thing. I squinted at the underside of my fingers and saw tiny glass-like fibers protruded from my skin. *Crap. Stinging nettles.* Why didn't I recognize the flower? My mother used them in spells for warding off negative energy. I snorted at the thought. Thanks, Hulda. My ancestor was queen busybody when it came to influencing outside events so what's to say she didn't influence this to teach me a lesson? News flash, this was not helping to rid me of my resentment.

Either way I had to find a set of tweezers or something sticky to pull these little hairs from my fingers or they would continue to swell. In the meantime, I did what my mother

taught and reached down to dip my hand in the mud. At least that would draw some of the swelling down.

I needed cold water and some sort of balm, but I had no clue what I could use. Perhaps Mrs. Mac would have an idea. I looked at the basket brimming with color. There were more than enough flowers for two table arrangements.

Fingers throbbing, I walked the rest of the way back to the house, managing with one hand to untie my dress and not splatter mud on the rose silk. I walked with my hand raised and the basket over my other arm, the burning and sharp sting increasing with each step until I picked up my pace practically sprinting into the kitchen.

"Heavens, child what in the world has gotten into you?" Mrs. Gerrittsen asked?

"Is Mrs. Mac in the house?"

She shook her head. "No, she's not. She went across the river with Doctor Thacher for supplies. She'll be back shortly, though."

I winced, placing the basket on the counter. "Here are the flowers for the table in the dining room and the drawing room mantel." My tongue itched and I swayed suddenly lightheaded and I prayed I wasn't headed into anaphylactic shock.

"Oh my! Here, sit," she ordered pushing a stool toward me.

I plopped down, trying not to pass out.

"What happened?" Mrs. Gerrittsen didn't wait for me to answer. She lifted my muddy hand and examined it from both sides. "Tsk, tsk. Stinging nettles. Didn't you know not to touch them?" she asked stretching for a bowl and placing it on the table beside where I sat.

Her question was rhetorical, and I knew it. "I wasn't paying attention and reached for the heart shaped flowers before I realized what they were."

She clicked her tongue a few more times as she moved around the kitchen gathering items. She opened a jar and left it beside the bowl.

"What is that?" I leaned over to peer at the powdery contents.

"Baking soda."

She didn't elaborate and walked to the windowsill for a small, folded piece of white eyelet cloth. From between the folds she drew out two green leaves and laid them on the table as well.

She examined me again, nodding to herself. "Putting fresh mud on this was a good thing. It's completely dried so we can brush the bits from your skin and hope they take the barbs with it."

Mrs. Gerrittsen reached into her apron pocket and drew out a small brush. With short fast strokes she made quick work of the mud and I had immediate relief.

"I think that took care of them. I need to go wash."

She pushed me back down onto the stool. "Not so fast, young lady, I'm not finished."

Filling the bowl with water, she lifted my hand and submerged it, carefully bathing whatever was left of the mud from my fingers, palm and wrist. She then patted my skin dry with a dishtowel, having me rest my hand palm up on the table.

She took both leaves and rubbed them carefully over the affected site, and I smiled realizing exactly what she was doing. I had seen Gran do this a hundred times, each time my mother worked with stinging nettles for a spell. She always got one or two stuck in her fingers at some point.

"That's jewelweed, right?"

She nodded with a smile. "Yes. I learned how to treat nettle stings from an old woman who lived on the outskirts of my village. She lived alone and most people were afraid of her, including me. But then my daughter got sick with the morbid sore throat, or so I thought. I prayed God wouldn't take her. We had no doctor at the time in Sleepy Hollow, and the women in the village were too scared to come and help me nurse her for fear of catching the infection."

My head jerked up at the name Sleepy Hollow. Mrs. Mac had told me where Mrs. Gerrittsen was from originally, but with everything that happened since, I forgot.

She continued as she rubbed the leaves over my palms and the tops of my fingers in case the rash spread. "I didn't know where else to turn. I was alone. My husband had been killed in a local skirmish months before, so I wrapped Lettie in a blanket and took her to see the old lady. The Dominee of our church condemned me from my own threshold as I pushed passed him. I didn't care, though. I would have sold my soul to the devil himself to save my little girl."

She stopped rubbing and patted my forearm. "Don't look so panicked. My Lettie lived and so did I thanks to the kindness of the old healer. Lettie was so ill we had no choice but to stay with Hulda in her hut." Mrs. Gerrittsen smiled, putting the crumpled leaves on the counter. "That was the old woman's name. We lived with her for weeks, though I knew the townspeople despaired for our safety. In the time spent there, Hulda taught me some of her recipes. She was a kind woman, though no one would accept her."

"How did you end up here?" I asked.

She shrugged. "When Lettie was finally well enough for us to leave, we returned to Sleepy Hollow only to find our house burned. The villagers were incensed, accusing us of embracing a witch. They forced us from town. I had no choice but to flee. I had no one. My husband was dead and not one soul in the village would defend us. Fearing a backlash on the kind, old woman, I went back to warn Hulda." She lifted the fabric that held the jewelweed leaves. "This handkerchief was hers. She wrapped food and a few shillings inside and gave the bundle to us before we quitted town knowing full well her selflessness might bring her danger."

"What happened next?"

Mrs. Garretson's face soured. "We moved south, thinking the warmer weather would keep Lettie from becoming ill again.

I began working for General Arnold as a housekeeper and cook. He was a widower and unlucky in his search for a new wife, though not from the lack of trying. He courted ladies from Boston to Philadelphia.

"Lettie was ten years old when we moved into the general's household. He was brash and brave, and we were happy there until he was gravely injured. He returned a changed man, and to my mind reluctantly accepted the appointment of military commander of Philadelphia, believing it to be a position granted more from pity than a reward for winning the battle of Saratoga. Unhappy, he took to living extravagantly, and soon after was besotted with Margaret Shippen."

"His wife?"

She nodded. "She enchanted him from the first, and he lavished her with gifts, spending money he didn't have. Young and spirited, she loved parties and formal dinners, dancing and music and the clothes...always new fashions. The general refused her nothing, but it wasn't until they married that everything truly changed for the rest of us.

"She badgered the general about the war and how inconvenient it was, and how she missed the chivalry and sophistication of the British. She compared Philadelphia now to when the British occupied the city, complaining it had lost its luster and elegance. She grew restless and short-tempered, and then out of the blue she was giddy again. Mrs. Arnold would wait breathless for letters sent by courier, and then take long rides out into the countryside. Maids would brush out her hair, finding leaves crushed into her intricate curls and grass stains and dirt on the rump and hem of her gowns and underskirts as though she'd been lying on the ground.

"One maid brazenly joked, asking if the stable was rubbing her saddle with grass and soil, and if she should ask them to stop for fear of them ruining another dress."

"No! That poor girl."

Mrs. Gerrittsen nodded. "The silly girl was dismissed from her post, of course. I had my own suspicions but kept them to myself. After all, a young vivacious creature like Peggy Shippen couldn't stay contented with an older crippled husband for long. It was only a matter of time before she took a lover."

"Did you ever figure out who it was?"

She shook her head. "I never got the chance to winkle it out. Mrs. Arnold became pregnant, putting an end to her riding and her clandestine letters. Living and serving in that household was almost unbearable. Mrs. Arnold was melancholy over her lost lover while at the same time miserably plagued with morning sickness.

"Thank God the nausea and fatigue was short-lived, but she grew bored and took her frustrations out on the staff. Utterly enamored with everything royal, she demanded each servant buy new uniforms after the style of the British royal household. Most of us couldn't afford the cost and were given the choice of either purchasing the uniforms or indenturing ourselves to her until the cost was paid off. She offered to indenture Lettie in exchange for my clothing, but I refused. I had one luxury. Another gift Hulda secreted into my bags before I took my leave of her. It was a bauble the likes of which I had never seen. Given no choice, I showed Mrs. Arnold the gemstone and the woman's eyes grew large and covetous."

Mrs. Gerrittsen glanced away, and a sinking feeling dropped into the pit of my stomach. I suddenly knew what I had to steal from Peggy Shippen Arnold. It was Gran's moonstone.

"What kind of a stone was it?" I asked, waiting for my suspicions to be confirmed.

Mrs. Gerrittsen smiled. "A stone of the most ethereal blue, with hues of milk and moonlight and of such a size. Mrs. Arnold took the stone from me and never asked for another penny. Two new head-of-staff uniforms were on my cot the next day plus two maid uniforms for Lettie." She sighed. "I wish I could have

saved that unusual stone for my daughter's dowry, but it wasn't meant to be."

Mrs. Gerrittsen took a small glass bowl and spooned two heaping portions of baking soda into the bottom of the dish. She added water and stirred the mixture until it formed a paste. With the back of the spoon she smeared it liberally over my palm and fingers.

She looked at me. "It's curious, though."

"What is?"

"When Hulda handed me the initial bundle she said something that has stayed with me ever since. She said, '*Do for your daughter what I couldn't do for mine. Keep her safe and loved. Take this and perchance we all will be better for it.*'"

I knew what Hulda meant when she spoke those words to Mrs. Gerrittsen so many years before the old woman met her untimely death. It was a foreshadowing of what was to come, of what I had been sent here to accomplish.

"Where is Lettie now?"

A broad smile spread across Mrs. Gerrittsen's lips. "Lettie turned fourteen in March, just prior to the birth of Mrs. Arnold's first child. She's the baby's nursemaid. I expect her when the family arrives."

Mrs. Gerrittsen steeped a pot of willow bark after wrapping my palm in strips of clean linen. She pushed a cup of the brew into my uninjured hand. "Drink this while it's hot. The tea will ease the pain and you need to let the poultice do its job drawing out the rest of the prickles. Go for a lie down and rest. I'll send Mrs. MacPherson up to your room when she returns."

I climbed the short staircase from the kitchen into the main house carrying the cup on its saucer along with a small plate of shortbread. The downstairs was quiet. Alec had duties to attend

to across the river, and the rest of the staff were scattered between the stables, laundry, and fields.

Most of the windows and shutters had been thrown wide to coax the light breezes off the river. Curtains danced, fluttering over sideboards and tea tables in the dining and drawing rooms, their doors propped open to allow fresh air to waft across to the small conservatory on the opposite side of the house. The general's downstairs library was a large office space facing the drawing room. The doors were usually shut, and the staff knew better than to enter without his leave.

As I passed, I noticed the door was ajar and I slowed my pace to peek in through the crack. The general stood behind his desk engrossed in a letter. His spectacles rested on the end of his long nose and he held the parchment so firmly both halves of the broken red wax seal looked as though they would crack again. A lit candle in a pewter holder sat directly ahead of him. Strange, I thought, as it was midday, and even from my narrowed vantage point I could see the sun streaming in through the open window.

"Do you wish to send a reply, General?" A male voice asked. It wasn't Alec's voice, nor was it any I recognized from the men who came to dine.

The general didn't answer, nor did he look up. His eyes narrowing as he scanned the looping hand.

"General?" the voice prompted again.

General Arnold looked up at that point and I stepped back out of the line of sight, listening. "What? Oh, of course. Forgive me, Heron. Yes, I will reply, but I need time to collect my thoughts. In the meantime, tell Joshua Hett Smith to meet me tomorrow at the base of the orchard after dusk. He'll know where."

I heard the scrape of a chair against the hardwood and I jumped back the hot liquid sloshing over the rim of the cup onto my fingers wrapped around the china saucer. I hissed, and the

sound must have been louder than I expected because the door yanked open.

The general stood in the door, his expression displeased and suspicious as my own attention jerked toward his library. Standing just behind the general was another man. He was dressed in common clothing that was dusty and travel-worn, but it was the fur trimmed hat in his hand I found immediately curious. I made eye contact with him for a split second.

"What are you doing skulking outside my door?" The general's words clipped short as I shook the dripping tea from my fingers, the cup and small plate of shortbread resting lighting in my other hand, bandages notwithstanding.

"Oh, my dear, I didn't realize you were hurt. My sincerest apologies. May I be of assistance?" he asked a little red faced.

I shook my head. "No, General Arnold, thank you just the same. I'm sorry to disturb. I spilled the hot willow bark tea Mrs. Gerrittsen made and scalded my hand." I lifted my fingers showing him the slightly reddening skin. "It appears good fortune has abandoned me this afternoon, for now I have two compromised hands," I said switching the plate and cup back to the lesser injured digits. "I guess we should all be grateful I'm not the one preparing tonight's supper." I lifted one shoulder in a sheepish gesture and the general's remaining irascibility relaxed into a soft smile

"Were you headed upstairs?"

I nodded. "Yes, Mrs. Gerrittsen's orders."

He smirked at that. "By all means then, carry on, my dear."

I nodded, bobbing a quick curtsey which had us both fumbling to steady my cup on its saucer yet again. I mumbled another apology and moved quickly toward the broad staircase outside the dining area.

The general stepped back into his library and I heard the door snick shut before my foot touched the first step.

I carefully opened the door to my bedroom and set the cup and plate of biscuits on my night table beside my evening

candle. Sinking onto the end of the bed, I untied my shoes and slipped them off my feet. A single voice spoke below my window, and I pulled back the sheer to look. The man I saw in the general's library stood alone on the back porch, and he seemed to scan the area before walking at a fast clip toward the back orchards.

I let the sheer drop back into place and sat on the bed. Why would he head toward the orchards? The only way out was the water. I mentally filed the question in the back of my mind. Since my corporeal vison with Hulda in the clearing, I needed to keep every scrap that struck me odd tucked away for future reference.

Clues were creeping up, but were they hints to the task I had in hand, or to events that simply coincided? Like most, I was well aware of Major General Benedict Arnold and what he represented to American history. Did he factor into Hulda's plans other than being married to the woman I had to rob for the sake of my family or was that just a coincidence as well?

Reaching behind my back, I loosened my laces and slipped the gown from my shoulders before stepping out of it completely. I had gotten pretty good at dressing and undressing myself in the clothing of the day, though mastering my stays still proved a challenge when I was alone. Every time Mrs. Mac had me hold the bedpost while she pulled my laces, the same scene from Gone with the Wind played through my head. *"You've simply got to make it eighteen and a half again, Mammie."* I had to bite my tongue not to laugh.

I shrugged off the rest of my clothes and laid them in a neat pile across the chintz chair beside the carved pedestal mirror before climbing up onto the bed. My hand stopped throbbing and I thought about unwinding the bandage but decided against it. I'd let Mrs. Mac do that later. Yawning, I picked up the cup from its saucer and drank the now tepid tea, wincing at the nasty taste. Two gulps and a grimaced shiver later, I returned the delicate porcelain to its place and lay back against

my pillows. Sleep found me before my eyes closed and I drifted dreamlessly into peace for the first time in weeks. I knew why I was here, and it was only a matter of time before I had a plan.

Chapter 17

I was in my favorite jeans and a tie-dyed tee as I walked up Main Street. A sigh of relief left my mouth at the familiar surroundings, but the closer I looked, the more my heart sank. This was home, but not.

Newspapers and trash gathered in corners and along the curbs. I shook my head. Sleepy Hollow would never allow that kind of litter. Empty cups and plastic bags blew down the street, picked up in a tepid wind gusting off the river. The air along the street smelled sour, like a mix of vomit and urine and I lifted my hand to my nose.

This was all wrong. Some of the buildings were boarded up and the place looked desolate. I shook my head against the images assaulting me. Main Street was always packed with pedestrian traffic, shoppers, and people sightseeing in town. Cars vied for parking on either side of the street and the public lots were always full.

I stopped walking, trying to find one thing unchanged. Plywood covered half of the front display window at Main Street Sweets, but the door jangled, and the familiar tinkling turned my head. My eyes widened. My mother stood in front of the ice cream parlor, her fingers on the glass as though trying to catch someone's attention.

"Mom!" I called running down the street, but she crossed to the other side and disappeared down a side road before I could reach her.

I ran after her, my lungs straining with the effort and the blooming discomfort in my chest as fresh as before. "Mom!" I yelled again. "I'm back!"

I stopped short in the middle of the street, and she stepped from the front garden of one of the houses. She looked around, her face hopeful and searching.

"Mom! Here! I'm right here!"

In that moment she turned, and my mother's beautiful smile lit across her face as her eyes found me.

She didn't speak, but I didn't care. Hot tears stung my cheeks even as I wrapped my arm against the throbbing in my ribs. I took a step toward her and sharp pain burst through my side and into my chest. Something held me tethered and the staggering drag refused to let go. I screamed reaching for my mother, but she shook her head, her face heartbroken as she vanished into the shadows.

"Ssh, love…it's all right…ssh…"

"Mom!" I cried out and sat bolt up, my heart banging in my chest. Disoriented I pushed at hands and arms trying to help me.

"Wake up, love," Mrs. MacPherson tried again. "You're fine." She took a firm hold of both of my shoulders and gave me a gentle shake. Her long hard-worked fingers brushing my hair back from my forehead.

I slumped back onto my pillow and inhaled a deep breath, letting it out slowly. "I'm sorry, Mrs. Mac. I was dreaming. I couldn't find my mother. She was there, but I couldn't reach her and each time I would call she'd wave as though I was far away and not coming back."

She patted my arm. "It was just a bad dream. It'll pass. Look at the bright side. Dreaming of your mother, even if it's disjointed, means your memory is edging its way back." She nodded. "Next you'll start remembering while awake."

I threw my arm over my eyes and tried to calm my racing heart. Was it just a dream or did it mean something else? Was this part of Hulda's warning that the future I would return to wouldn't be the future I knew? My mother seemed to know me, but not. Was I never born?

Mrs. Mac didn't say a word, just let me lay there and collect myself and she stroked my other hand.

Finally, I rolled over tucking one hand under my cheek. "What time is it?" I asked, squinting toward the window to judge the light.

"It's late." She got up from the bed and went right to the footboard to straighten the covers and a lump formed in my throat at how much she reminded me of my mother. I wanted to close my eyes and coax back my dream and make my mother talk to me. I missed her so much.

"It's after nine. You've slept away the rest of the afternoon and all evening." She gestured toward a tray on the dresser. "I brought you dinner. Mrs. Gerrittsen told me what happened with the stinging nettles."

She picked up the cup and sniffed the brown liquid ringing the bottom of the cup. "Willow Bark tea." She pursed her lips. "But my guess is she put something else in the brew to help you sleep. The pain from the nettles can be nasty."

I pushed myself up onto my elbow and reached out my hand for the cup. I sniffed the contents as well. The scent was undeniable. It was the same proprietary blend of sleep herbs my mother used whenever she wanted me to have a dreamless, peaceful sleep. I closed my eyes. My mother's mild mélange was just another family recipe passed down from Hulda and another reason for my being here. I reached over and placed the cup back on the saucer and lay back on my pillows.

"Should I get up and get dressed?"

She waved me off. "General Arnold knew about your injured hand, so he made your apologies tonight." She stopped, hanger in hand as she lifted my gown into the large mahogany armoire. "Did you have issue with him today? He seemed more preoccupied than usual and a little short tempered. In fact, his excuses regarding you were rather clipped."

I shook my head. "None that I'm aware of."

She eyed me again and I shrugged telling her about spilling the tea.

Lips thinning, she shook her head. "Silly man." She exhaled hanging the dress on the wooden roll bar. "All I can say is Mrs. Arnold better arrive sooner than later and do service by her husband. Judging by the curmudgeon he's become, he could use the welcome release." She turned eyeing me with a wicked grin. "Perhaps the lieutenant colonel should take the good general a-ridin' and I don't mean on a horse!"

"Mrs. Mac!"

Her mouth opened in feigned shock and her eyes were laughing. Feeling better, I couldn't help but smile myself.

"I shouldn't speak this way in front you, child, but truth is a good roll might steady the general's nerves and even his temperament. Lord knows we could all benefit from his relief."

I giggled. "Mrs. Mac, you are irredeemable!"

"Pish...I may speak freely in this room, but I'm not daft enough to repeat it elsewhere. Though lord knows everyone's thinking the same thing."

I pulled my knees to my chest and listened to the far sound of the river and the crickets singing in the mid-August night.

"Was Alexander at dinner tonight?"

She slid her gaze sideways. "Why do you ask?"

I shrugged. "No reason."

One side of her mouth curved up in a knowing smirk. "No, the lieutenant colonel chose to stay across at the fort with his men tonight. He sent word, but you were sleeping. Seems he's been recalled to meet with General Rochambeau in Newport. General Washington is rooted at his headquarters in Orangetown and cannot move. From what I've heard, the enemy is a scant ten miles from there and his Excellency is loath to leave his men so close to the hellfire. He's sending Colonel Hamilton as a replacement for Nathanial Greene. The man resigned his post as Quartermaster of West Point, and there

seems some other hubbub going on, though I'm not clear about the details." She laughed. "Not yet, anyway."

Mouth open I shook my head, stunned. "You are a venerable source of inexhaustible information. Surely you aren't the leader of some secret female sect of the Continental Congress. How are you privy to all this?"

"For one reason in particular, my dear." She lifted her skirts and gave me a deep curtsey. "I am a woman, and as such viewed as no more than a stick of furniture while men are deep in conversation, and if they be deep in their cups as well…" She laughed. "You forget where and to whom I am housekeeper. I hear much and listen to everything said. Ha! If I had a mind to, I could offer my assistance to the British and bring this war to a screeching halt, God love us."

At her words I froze, though Mrs. Mac went about brushing my gowns and straightening my ribbons and such. "You don't mean that." My voice was low, but my pulse raced. If Mrs. Mac was involved with Benedict Arnold and his dealings, it would break my heart.

"Ha! As though I would give a rat's hat for anything British at this point. I lost my husband to a lobsterback, and far too many young boys in the field hospital across the way found their final rest on Cemetery Hill instead of in a warm feather bed because of them."

I was relieved, but again I filed the information away just in case.

She smiled. "Are you hungry, then?"

I nodded and she brought me the tray, resting it on my lap.

"Don't fret, love. Alexander will be back at Robinson House tomorrow. I'm sure he'll tell you himself about his plans."

I woke to the sound of shouts, as though my erratic dreams weren't enough to set my nerves on edge. Worried the house was under attack I dressed quickly and ran down the stairs.

Dogs barked inside and out, and I had to jump to avoid a large beast bounding through the foyer, its pink tongue flapping out the side of its mouth. One of the black serving boys flew past me in a breathless huff, bobbing his head in the process as he ran after the animal.

I rushed toward the kitchen stairs, clamoring down as quickly as I could. "There's a dog loose in the house. It's got a long muzzle and a brown and tan pelt and nearly knocked me over as it bolted past me in the foyer."

"That was no dog, lass. That was Juno, Mistress Peggy's English foxhound."

I inhaled and held my breath knowing this moment might set everything in motion. "She's arrived, then?"

Sergeant Campbell shook his head. "No, thank heaven. Not with the state of things this morning." He looked at my rose-colored gown and delicate shoes. "You'd best go back upstairs, or you risk your gown in this mess."

I exhaled feeling like I had been granted a reprieve. I knew the woman was coming and I knew what had to be done, I just wasn't ready yet. I hadn't enough time to plan or think.

The kitchen was in a shamble. Flour and pieces of bakery crust, half eaten pies and broken cookery were everywhere, and on the floor beside the butchering table were scraps of bone and fatty pieces of meat that someone swept to the side. "It looks as though a hurricane blew through here, what happened."

Mrs. Gerrittsen hoisted herself up, holding onto to one side of the work table. "That demon dog you saw gallop past, that's what happened. Those fool boys were supposed to keep the animal on a run, but the lead snapped, and he loped in here after the foodstuffs."

"Where's Mrs. Mac?"

"She's gone to fetch the lieutenant colonel. He's familiar with the beast and can jail him properly."

An image of Alec in full uniform chasing after a giant hairy dog, hat and coattails flying was too much and I burst out laughing. A few mouths twitched as well, also recognizing the comedy of errors that transpired and some of the tension in the room seemed to dissipate.

"What in the bloody hell happened here?"

My snickering came to an abrupt halt as Alec and Mrs. Mac appeared in the back doorway.

"Nothing, sir," Mrs. Gerrittsen replied wiping her own laughter from her face.

Sergeant Campbell gave Alec a quick rundown of events and the two went out in search of the boys and the dog. I rolled up my sleeves and picked up a broom only to have it snatched from my hand.

"No, you don't, missy. What have I told you about servant's work?"

"But, Mrs. Mac, shouldn't this qualify as an exception to your rule?" I swept my hand across the broken pottery and flour dusted surfaces. "This is going to require all hands to set to rights and still get luncheon prepared for General Arnold and his entourage."

None of the kitchen staff said a word, but Mrs. Gerrittsen looked at Mrs. Mac and nodded. "She's right, Ferne, but just this once and only if she has something else to wear. I won't have the ruination of that rose silk on my head."

Clearly not happy, Mrs. Mac shooed me up the kitchen stairs. "Mind you, this is a singular treaty, and I'll brook no argument from you on that, my girl." She walked me into the bedroom and pointed toward the armoire. "Your original dress is hanging to the left. It'll do for today. I've mended the cuffs and other frays and added a bit of lace to the neckline making it a fine garden dress. The floral petticoat will go nicely against the

dress's royal blue cotton. Now, let's get you swapped and downstairs before I change my mind."

My quick-change rivalled a Vegas headliner and I was back in the kitchen. The staff had already made inroads, and I concentrated on what was left of the food. My big mouth had made claim to talent in the kitchen as one of my strong suits and now was my chance to prove it while I had people around to help and direct.

I washed my hands, causing more than a few eyebrows to head north in curiosity, but I ignored their stares and concentrated instead on what was left of the beef roasts.

"Juno did a fine job of tearing up this lot. There isn't enough to piece together into a roast even if we had all the twine in Philipstown." I thought for a moment and eyed what was left on the vegetable table.

"Have we any potatoes?" I asked.

Mrs. Gerrittsen nodded. "I can have one of the boys dig some. How many would you need?"

"Eight should do, and ask the boys to dig fresh carrots and celery root as well. We can make the general a rich stew of vegetables and thick cuts from the remaining beef. We can make aromatic breadsticks brushed with butter and sprinkle the loaves with toasted rosemary."

She nodded. "Stew isn't what I usually make in the summer, but it looks as though we don't have a choice. I'll see to digging the roots." She headed for the backdoor that led out to the vegetable garden but turned. "What are breadsticks?"

I smiled. "We don't have enough time for more dough to rise in time for midday. With what's left we can form narrow loaves that resemble long sticks."

She laughed. "Clever girl."

"What about a fruit crumble for dessert?" I suggested, causing Mrs. Gerrittsen to stop half way out the door again.

She shook her head. "No, love. Mrs. Arnold says crumbles are for peasants and taverns making the most of baking scraps

and near rotted fruit. The general wouldn't appreciate the effort."

I sighed looking at what was left of the pastry dough prepared earlier. "That may be, Mrs. Gerrittsen, but unfortunately that's the truth. All we have left are bakery scraps." I looked up searching the pots and pans hanging on a metal rack above the work table and saw what I wanted. "There! We can use those!" I said, pointing upward.

She came back in and followed the line of my index finger. "But those are for pasties and mincemeat patties."

I nodded. "Exactly, and they're the perfect size for individual fruit pies. We can make different varieties and serve the lot on a flat platter and let the general and his guests choose 'til their hearts and stomachs are content."

Mrs. Gerrittsen clapped. "He'll love the originality! Where did you learn all this, love? Cookery is not usually an art pursued by ladies?"

I smiled. "My mother. She learned to cook because she loved to surprise my father. From the time I was little she taught me her recipes and her love of creating with her own hands..." I stopped short realizing I had said too much.

Mrs. MacPherson's hand went to her heart and a huge smile graced her face. "Doctor Thacher said your memory would come back in bits and look, he was right! Oh, well done, Phoebe!"

I swallowed but nodded in agreement. Damn. I needed to watch myself more closely. Pats on the back followed, but Mrs. Gerrittsen set everyone to work lighting fires and stoking the ovens while I took down a large pan and various bowls to start my prep.

Mrs. Mac watched me work keeping me mindful of delegating the meaner chores to the kitchen maids. Satisfied I hadn't crossed the unspoken line between the classes she nodded and let me alone.

Once everything was set to simmer and bake, I left the final touches to the staff, smiling to myself as I turned to head up to change clothes for the day.

"Miss Burritt wait!" the sergeant called after me as he came through the garden door, shoving three fat partridges at Mrs. Gerrittsen. The birds were tied by their wrinkly pink ankles, their heads hanging limp.

"The lieutenant colonel asked that you meet him after you're done giving orders here. He'd like to take you riding."

I tried to keep my eyes focused on the sergeant, but I couldn't look away from the bird's lifeless black eyes.

The sergeant smiled, his chest puffed out. "They're a couple of beauties, eh, lass? They'll be succulent tonight, that's for sure. The general's got half the officer's club coming for dinner so ye'd better let Mrs. G have at it and not keep Colonel Hamilton waiting too long."

Mrs. Gerrittsen laughed. "Mrs. G, is it? All right then, out with you both." She laughed shooing me up the stairs and Campbell out the door.

Mrs. Mac nodded to me. "Let me wipe the front of that dress down with a wet cloth and get you a lace fichu for your shoulders. If you're going to be about on a smelly horse that blue cotton will do fine. At least it's easier to clean than silk."

I walked out toward the stables where Alec stood with the two boys, each holding the reins of a horse. The animals were beautiful, tall statuesque creatures standing at least sixteen hands. One looked like the classic black beauty while the other was a dappled gray.

I hadn't been on a horse in years, but I remembered every lesson at the Zephyr Farms in Putnam County where my mother took me to learn. I loved to ride and had trained English style which couldn't have been more fortuitous considering western anything wasn't even a sparkle on the horizon. This was a perfect way to scope the surrounding area with a

knowledgeable guide, and the fact I didn't suggest the jaunt even better.

The idea of the feel of the horse beneath me and the wind in my hair brought a smile to my face until I saw the saddle I was expected to use.

I slowed my pace, my enthusiasm waning with each step.

"What's the matter? Moments ago you looked as though you would take to the wind if I let you, now you look as if you'd rather wash up in the kitchen." Alec asked, running a hand down the black horse's neck.

"I was excited, but..." I didn't finish.

"But what?"

"I won't ride sidesaddle, Alec. I know it's not considered proper for a woman to ride otherwise, but I never have and to be honest the notion of sitting unbalanced on an animal that could crush a strong man let alone a woman, seems silly. Always has."

He guffawed so loud he startled the horse, setting the mare to snort and paw it front hooves.

"Alec, stop laughing. I'm serious and you're scaring the horse."

He waved his hand, catching his breath. "I know you're serious, and that's what makes this so delicious. You never cease to surprise me."

"Well, I suppose riding is out of the question for today. We could just take a walk then." I suggested a little disappointed.

He nodded. "I'm afraid I have no choice but to agree. Unfortunately, my time is so limited today as I have a meeting with the other commanders. Since both horses are already in full tack, by the time the grooms changed saddles we would have little time to enjoy any kind of a decent ride."

"That's fine, but if we do go another day I will ride astride or not at all. Okay?"

He nodded, lips pursing into a smirk. "Campbell told me about that odd word of yours. It's a funny sounding sort of

affirmation, but it suits you," he replied with a chuckle. "Agreed, then. Astride it is."

Alec handed off the two steeds to the boys and slid a blanket from atop one of the barrels just inside the stable and tucked it under his arm. He held out his elbow for me. "Another look at the river, perhaps, or a walk through the orchard?"

I nodded and took his arm, keeping Hunter's face in the front of my mind. Alec made his attraction clear. In fact, everyone in the house knew it, but this outing was not turning into an eighteenth-century version of beach blanket bingo regardless of how tenuous my position in the house.

"When is Mrs. Arnold supposed to arrive? It's been weeks already and the general seems anxious for her presence," I asked as he pointed to a large apple tree bursting with ripe fruit at the first row of trees. Initially I was tentative about the orchard considering, but I figured in the bright light of day it was a safe bet.

I nodded and we walked toward its shaded base where we spread the blanket over its roots.

He laughed. "Why is everyone so concerned when Peggy is set to arrive? Mrs. MacPherson had an unusually frank conversation with me earlier."

I coughed and he chuckled even harder. "According to Peggy's last letter to the general she arrives August thirtieth, or so it's been planned. From what I hear the baby was ill with summer croup and they had to wait until he was well enough to travel."

I had forgotten about the high infant mortality rate in this era and my heart squeezed for that poor baby and his mother, regardless of how much of a brat Peggy could turn out to be.

"I hope he's well. Infants are so delicate you have to be so very careful."

Alec sat with his knees up and both arms wrapped lightly around his calves. In the sunlight, his hair looked like burnished copper and the light stubble on his square jaw gave him a

rugged look. With his slightly disheveled ponytail, linen shirt, and waistcoat, he looked almost pirate-like.

"Captain Jack Sparrow," I murmured under my breath with a laugh.

"Who?"

I shook my head. "No one. In the sun you reminded me of a character from a pirate story I once heard. Very swashbuckling."

He chuckled. "If it's a story you favor, no wonder it's an adventure." He blinked at me, considering. "Do you like telling stories?"

I didn't know how to answer him. Was he asking an honest question or was he fishing for more information?

"Why do you ask?"

He picked leaves the way I had done with the grass the last time we sat together. "I'm curious about your likes and dislikes, your talents and your strengths." He shrugged. "While here you've not had much chance to spread your wings and I can't help but wonder if you're bored."

I laughed at that. "You mean like Peggy would be bored?"

He gave me a sheepish look and nodded. "I suppose. Yes."

I shook my head. "I'm not Peggy, of that you can rest assured. I have no trouble finding ways to entertain myself no matter where I am. I don't need to be fawned over and flattered or seek out dazzling soirees to find enjoyment. I am content enough in myself and find beauty and amusement in the people and places that surround me."

He inhaled, leaning over on one arm to face me. "That, my dear, is one of the things I am beginning to cherish most in you, besides your delicious mouth," he said dropping his head to steal a kiss.

I put my hand on his shoulder and edged him back.

"I'm sorry, Alec, this is just wrong. You are betrothed and I refuse to be commandeered by anyone for second rank."

He jerked back as though I scalded him. "Who told you I was betrothed?"

I raised an eyebrow. "Then you're not paying court to Elizabeth Schuyler with intent?"

Alec's lips pressed together in a fine line. "I haven't seen Elizabeth in months. We write, but..." His words drifted off.

This was my ace in the hole to keep this eighteenth century player at an arm's distance, at least for the time being.

"But what?"

He shook his head but didn't reply.

"Alec, if you're unsure of how you feel then you shouldn't risk what you have on an unknown."

His eyebrow cocked at the word unknown and I quickly raised my hand in defense.

"I wasn't referring to myself in that sense. I meant unknown as in what you perceive as blooming between us. You say you've been away from Elizabeth for ages. What if the lure you feel stems from a simple yearning for feminine company?"

His eyes locked on mine. "Oh, I most definitely yearn." His voice was low and husky, and he reached for me again, but my hand shot up just as quickly.

"Alec! I'm serious. I won't be a lonely man's plaything. Admit it. You long for Elizabeth and I am merely a reminder of her, a reminder of what you have waiting in the wings, but desire now."

"I thought that at first, but you occupy my waking thoughts. I am at a loss some days for the want of you. Just let me kiss you and hold you close and let you feel the force of my need."

"Need? Been there, done that, Alec, and I'm pretty sure the entire house knows we've locked lips. I won't have the whispers, nor will I have my rep ripped to shreds by cheap gossip and innuendo."

His brows knotted and he looked at me curiously. "When you rile, your manner of speech grows queer. Oft times I don't quite comprehend your words, even if I grasp their meaning."

I moved to get up. "I have no idea what you're talking about." I smoothed the front of my day dress waiting to see if he would get up as well.

"Phoebe..." he sighed as I turned on my heel to leave.

"The sun is well past the midday mark and we've missed luncheon. With the commotion in the kitchen this morning I've eaten nothing, and I'm famished. You can come back with me or perhaps use the time to think on what I've said."

He didn't respond, just looked up at me his face unreadable.

I sighed. "Alec, again this has nothing to do with my regard for you and everything to do with my regard for myself. I'm not a selfish girl, but I refuse to settle for second place in a man's affections."

He looked down at the blanket and then glanced up, his eyes full of meaning. "I've never met a woman of your equal, Phoebe. Remember that while you're thinking, yourself."

I walked up the path from the orchard's edge alone. Never met a woman my equal? I shook my head. His words might mean something if he had a clue as to who I really was and what I was meant to do here.

Alec originally said I was a distraction, and now he was on the verge of becoming one himself but not for the same reasons. I exhaled hard. I already walked enough fine lines on this metaphysical mission, and now the one I walked with him took on a much more complex layer.

Hulda's words haunted me.

You impressed me, Rowen. I know you had help, but it was you and that young man of yours who put old wrongs to right." She eyed me. "You're going to be tested with that too, you know."

Tested? How? "I love Hunter."

She nodded. "I know, but you are going to have to put that aside to accomplish what it is you need to accomplish here."

I glanced down the hill and looked at Alec's lean muscular form as he leaned back lost in thought. Was he my test? Would I

have to put my feelings for Hunter aside and use Alec to accomplish my task?

I shook my head. Covert cosmic task or not. No way. Spies may jump in and out of bed with whomever in movies and books and even real life if that is what's required of them, but not me. I couldn't do that to Hunter, and I wasn't ready to give up my hope that I would see him again.

Chapter 18

"Well, those partridges were absolutely delicious," the general announced, pushing himself back in his chair. Patting his stomach, he stood. "Shall we adjourn to the drawing room?"

I had changed into my rose silk again, and Mrs. Mac helped me with my hair. It was less formal than she had done before, and I was grateful to have the more relaxed feel.

There were ten at dinner tonight, including myself and Alec. He seemed moody and barely spoke, pouring himself glass after glass of claret and leaving the conversation to the other commanding officers.

My cheeks hurt from smiling and nodding, and I was relieved when the general suggested we move, hoping to slink back into a corner and become a piece of furniture, to use Mrs. Mac's analogy.

No such luck.

I walked unattended into the drawing room and saw the chairs had been rearranged to face one way with one single chair left at the center front.

"Are we to have entertainment then tonight?" I asked.

It was then Alec decided to pipe up. "Why yes, my dear Miss Burritt. You put the idea in my head this afternoon and I suggested to the general when I met with him and the rest of our esteemed guests tonight."

My face must have fallen, because the general patted my arm and then took my elbow to steer me toward the hot seat. He

seemed so eager he practically pushed me into the cushioned chair.

"There's no need for apprehension, my dear. A swashbuckling story, indeed! I'd love to hear you retell it, and I'd wager so would the rest of us. Why don't you make yourself comfortable and tell us the story? The lieutenant colonel says it's another of your talents."

I shot Alec a look, giving him a wide-eyed glare of my own before I scanned the rest of the room. Some faces were eager, others uninterested and some only looking to please the general. Alec on the other hand seemed smug as though he were punishing me for pointing out the obvious this afternoon.

If they wanted a story, then I would give them one. Every one of the Disney *Pirates of the Caribbean* movies was a favorite I knew by heart and telling the story two hundred years before the screenplay was written probably didn't constitute a copyright violation.

I fluffed the front of my skirts, smoothing the delicate silk before crossing my legs and leaning forward to start. "Gentlemen, our adventure begins at sea, aboard a British galleon making way for Port Royal and the colony of Jamaica. A ghostly pall blankets the water, the white vapor almost moaning with portent as the ship creaks and toils through the waves. A young girl stands at the bow, her thin voice singing...*Yo ho, yo ho, a pirate's life for me...Drink up, me hearties, yo ho.*"

Pleased with my pirate's accent, I paused for effect for more reasons than one. "And her name is...Elizabeth."

My eyes found Alec's and locked and his lips pushed sideways in a smirk. I nodded once as if to say, *nice try dude, but checkmate.*

"The fickle winds of fate are about to toy with this beautiful young girl's destiny, and so begins the tale of the pirate, Captain Jack Sparrow and the Curse of the Black Pearl..."

I made sure to keep eye contact with everyone in the room as the tale unfolded, leaving them breathless as I leaped from

my seat describing the eerie curse cast on the crew of the ghost ship. I felt a little like the character Anne Shirley from Lucy Maud Montgomery's *Anne of Green Gables* when the character gave her recitation of *The Highway Man* at the White Sands Hospital.

"So, this is the path you've chosen then, Elizabeth? After all, he is just a blacksmith." I mimicked the Governor's voice from the story.

"No…" I paused, sighing and love struck in the manner of the movie. "He's a pirate."

I made eye contact with Alec before I rose from my seat, curtseying low to let them know the story was at an end. The general stood clapping and a hearty round of applause followed from the rest in the room, even Alec applauded inclining his head acknowledging game, set, match.

"Well done! My word, Miss Burritt! Well done indeed! What a story! You must prepare a different one for each night!" The general slapped his knee. "Oh, how my Margaret will love this!"

The man loved his wife, that much was evident, and I felt a pang of pity for him and what I knew was to become their fate, but hey, they courted the devil and soon it would be time to pay.

"Mrs. Arnold enjoys thrilling stories, then, sir?" I asked.

He nodded emphatically. "My word, yes." His face grew pensive and a little careworn. "To be honest, I'm afraid my dearest will find Robinson House tedious as she is used to Philadelphia and all its diversions. Besides the officers you see here, we have only one close neighbor of the same ilk as we and I'm concerned Peggy will find living here tiresome. I'm sure you've heard how she enjoys a good party."

I nodded. "Then why not make her welcome in her own home and throw a party in her honor? Perhaps nothing as grand as a ball, but we could hire musicians and invite the local gentry as well as the officers from West Point. After all, you are in command of the fort and she is your lady."

The general's smile was genuine, and he reached out and took my hand in his. "That is a splendid idea. I will make all the necessary funds available to you immediately. You can organize everything starting tomorrow."

"Me? General, I have no expertise in planning such an important occasion. Isn't there someone we could hire? An event coordinator or professional party planner?"

He laughed. "Such humor and modesty. No, my dear. You will do a splendid job and I won't hear another word against it. You have a goodly amount of days to see it done."

Days! Jesus, did this man think I was Houdini?

I had no choice and inclined my head accepting the challenge. I had been outmaneuvered at my own game. He turned to leave, and I touched his arm. "Excuse me, General, but may I make a small request?"

Nodding once, he waited for me to pipe up.

"I would like to ask Mrs. MacPherson to assist me in this endeavor."

He waved his hand dismissively. "You may have leave to use all staff members to help as you see fit. This is for my dear wife and I want everything to be perfect. She arrives on the thirtieth and the party should be the week after, that way she may settle in first and rest." He looked at me. "Is there anything else?"

I nodded. "Yes. I wondered if I could have your permission to look through your library for a few books to read."

He raised an eyebrow, but eventually inclined his head. "You may, though with all your planning, I doubt you will have time to read a single word." He turned after that dismissing me outright and went to join the men and their brandy.

I retired about ten p.m., leaving the general and his guests well into their cups and deep discussion. I had neither the head nor the patience for listening tonight.

A knock on the door had me pulling my dressing gown over my shoulders. I opened the door to find one of the little houseboys holding out two long tapered candles and a thin stiff piece of cloth rolled in some kind of pine resin.

"Thank you," I said taking the bundle.

The boy bowed his head and mumbled a message about Mrs. Mac spending the night at the fort. Doctor Thacher needed her and with bad weather brewing she didn't want to cross the river.

He didn't look at me once while he spoke, but as I watched him head toward the stairs he peeked over his shoulder and when I waved, he smiled.

So, I was on my own tonight. That was fine with me, the time alone would allow me to think and plan. I closed the door and went to find the table lanterns on either nightstand. In each the candles were down to nubs, and I swapped them out with the new ones making sure to secure them properly. One of the chambermaids had lit a fire in the hearth, the first one since I had arrived at Robinson House and I bent to catch a flame on the end of the stiff pine scented cloth.

The night was cool, and the air blew in powerful gusts, knocking flower pots from the Parisian style plant stands on the back portico. I closed the window closest to the hearth and pulled a chair to the other side of the bed, setting it beside the open window.

I watched the lightning flash over the river, each flicker illuminating the clouds as the leaves and thin branches danced in time with the thunder. The trees moaned and their boughs cracked, but even with the cold stiff wind I was drawn to the spectacle.

No rain fell, though the gusts were as bad as the storm the night before this metaphysical madness started. I pulled the collar of the velvet dressing robe closer as a chill crawled over my shoulders. In the distance I heard faint music, a guitar playing soft and low and I strained to hear.

Odd. I hadn't seen anyone with anything resembling a musical instrument since I arrived. There were none in the house and no one I'd met so far, played.

The music picked up, the vibrations carried on the breeze, and though the sound was muffled, I picked up a portion of the melody. I swore it sounded like *Time in a Bottle* by Jim Croce.

Hunter had taught himself the music for that particular song this past winter, playing it for Gran on her birthday. She loved the thought behind the gift simply because my grandfather sang that same song to her when she gave birth to my mom, and then every year afterward on their anniversary until the day he died.

The haunting strains grew louder, and I heard Hunter's voice singing...*If I had a box just for wishes, and dreams that had never come true...*

In a clap of thunder his voice faded, the words drowned by a loud whistling moan from the gusts through the orchard.

I stood with my hands curling over the edge of the sill and leaned into the wind to try and catch the sense of it again, but it was gone.

My hair blew around my face, whipping my skin the same way it had in my very first vision of Hulda. Maybe what I heard was no more than wishful thinking.

"Rowen..."

My head jerked toward the wind. My name carried on the breeze as clear as a bell, the sound of chanting behind it. The same summoning I heard in my head at the museum in Hurley. My stomach knotted and adrenaline raced through my veins. Maybe Hunter had found a way to reach me. Wishful thinking? How about wish granted? If only...

My fingers clutched the belted velvet at my waist. *"Talk to me again, baby. I miss you so much, I can't stand it."* I kept my voice just above a hush, concentrating my power and all my intentions to send the message back along the same breeze. A channel was open somewhere, I felt it in my gut.

"Find me, Rowen...I'm waiting."

He did it. My breath hitched in my throat at the thought of seeing him again, touching him. Hunter figured out a way to reach me, and if he did, perhaps he also knew how to bring me home.

"Where are you? Why can't I feel you?"

"I'm stuck behind the veil. I can't reach any further. I need you."

The voice faltered and panic surged in my chest that I'd lost the tenuous link between us. I reached through the open window nearly toppling over onto the flagstones below.

"Hunter!"

"Follow my call, Rowen...there isn't much time."

Not caring who saw, I ran barefoot from the house, pausing for a moment to lift one of the lanterns from the front porch only to place it back on the step. It was too heavy and with the wild wind it wouldn't do me any good once the candle blew out.

I made my way into the pitch darkness listening for Hunter's voice.

"The trees. Make for the clustered trees..."

The only trees that fit that description were those in the orchard. I flew down the grassy hill, sharp rocks cutting my feet. I pitched forward over a raised root, catching the hem of my dressing gown on something in the shadows. My hem wouldn't budge, almost as if something was trying to stop me from finding Hunter.

I untied my belt and slipped the velvet covered buttons from their allotted holes and tossed the dressing gown on top of whatever held it hostage.

Gooseflesh covered my bare legs and arms as I ran in my thin shift. I tripped again, landing on all fours in the dirt. My

hair blew, the strands blinding me as I staggered forward into the center row of apple trees.

"Hunter!" I cried.

The wind stopped, almost as though my call ordered it to cease so I could find him.

Wood split and roots pulled from the ground, the cracking equal with the thunder rolling across the sky. The middle row of trees diverged, forming a clearing ringed by ominous reaching branches and rough bark.

Suspicion crept its way forward and my guard went up. I inhaled, swallowing back at oily tang of dark magic. The orchard had moved of its own volition and I knew only dubious spells screwed with nature.

I held my hand out and pulled every ounce of bloodline strength I had in my veins. "Show yourself!"

Hunter stepped from the shadows and I froze blinking to make sure I didn't imagine him.

"Rowen, thank God," he said and opened his arms for me.

The sight of him standing there in flesh and blood overwhelmed me, and I dropped my arms letting my command go. I ran to him. "Oh, my God! You're here, you're really here! I grabbed his face in my hands, not caring they were scraped and dirty. I went up on my toes, covering his cheeks and lips with kisses. "I love you! I love you! Hunter! You're real! You're really real! I can't believe you're here!"

Tears choked me and I clung to him, letting the stress of the past weeks flow out of me soaking his shirt. He stroked my hair, whispering against my ear. When I calmed, he lifted my chin and kissed me, his lips as cold as his breath.

I stepped back from him, unwilling to acknowledge the wariness tapping on the back of my brain. As if he sensed my inner caveat, he smiled, and it was my Hunter's gorgeous full on grin and my heart melted, dismissing my fears as unfounded.

Two shadows moved behind Hunter, catching my eye, and I took a reflexive step back.

"Don't be afraid, Rowen. The sisters are the ones who helped me get here, and they're going to help us both back through the veil."

I eyed them, and when lightning flashed again, I saw exactly who they were. The same women singing my name above Cooper Lake the night of the storm.

I shook my head and took another tentative step back. "Hunter, this whole thing doesn't feel right…and I still can't feel you. Something is wrong."

He smiled and reached a hand out toward me. "Come home, Rowen. I can't stand being apart from you. Your mother and grandmother did this to us. It's simple. You just need to drink, and everything will be as it should."

I looked at the cup one of the women held out toward me. It was a wooden chalice with symbols and runes carved around the neck and bowl. I recognized them. Binding runes to hinder free will and increase the magical bidding of the user.

The women were hooded in eerie, gauzy robes, and their hair and eyes were the same unnatural shade of white, just as they looked the night of the storm at Jenny's.

The one holding the goblet had dirty fingernails, broken and caked as though she'd clawed through a grave to get to the surface.

"Take the cup, Rowen. It's so easy, one sip and I can whisk you with me."

The wind stirred and I caught the unmistakable scent of blood coming from the offered goblet. I shook my head, unwilling to believe the truth staring me in the face. This wasn't *my* Hunter. My emotions had allowed this deception, my love for Hunter and my longing to be with him had played right into this charade. I raised my arms again, but this time anger flooded my body instead of adrenaline. No one jerked me around like that.

"SHOW YOURSELF!"

The wind howled, but it was my show now. The women screeched, retreating into the darkness but not before the false Hunter grabbed the cup from their hands.

"You will drink!" His face contorted to a skeletal form, the flesh dropping off in rotted chunks as he advanced.

The evil timbre of his voice was barley human; a rough growl laced with power forcing my arms to weaken. Alone, I couldn't hold him, and I screamed unable to move. My throat locked. I could barely breathe, producing only gurgles and harsh, strained whimpers as I struggled to free myself.

The being advanced, all resemblance to Hunter gone, even his clothes vanished replaced by a slick mottled film. He lifted his hand and forced my mouth open, lifting the goblet to my lips.

My mind rebelled and I mentally shouted to Hulda, summoning her with every ounce of my being, calling on our shared blood, our shared magic, entreating her to help me or all was lost. If she wanted me to save her daughter, our line, and the world as we knew it, she'd better get her ethereal ass here pronto!

She heard me and heeded my call and the old woman crept in from the north. Long wooden rod in hand, she raised it high. "Let her go!" she commanded.

The being hissed, its bony mouth clacking in a parody of laughter.

Hulda brought the rod down, pointing the end at the entity's heart. "She is not of your world and you are not of hers, be gone from here! Blood of my blood, I release you, daughter, and banish this evil to the darkest place beyond the veil." Turning the staff in her hand, the hilt struck the ground and the Earth rumbled.

In that moment, the being's hold shattered, and I crumpled to my knees. Hulda knocked the cup from his hand and as it

tumbled to the loamy grass, the ground opened, swallowing both the cup and its owner, sealing them from our plane.

Breathing heavy, Hulda crouched beside me. "Are you all right, child?"

I nodded, reaching for her but my hand passed right through her image, the substance thick and cold.

"What's happening?" I asked scrambling to my feet as panic suffused my body. If Hulda vanished before I completed my task what would happen? I would be left to fend for myself against attacks from either side of the veil.

"My time is growing short and your time is nigh. You must heed the signs. Do not allow yourself to stray from what you know to be true from history. Events must occur exactly as written, exactly as I have influenced. One change and all things change. You know this."

I nodded. "Yes, so you've warned..." I paused, looking at the ground that only moments before gaped as a portal to some place I didn't want to know.

"What is it, child?"

"What was that and what did it want with me? A demon?"

Hulda nodded. "The veil surrounding you is but a thin membrane. You are not of this time, yet your life force holds strong. It calls to those on the other side who crave more life. Our magical blood only enhances the temptation. It glows with the promise of power, like your aura. These beings are cunning and have learned to manipulate human frailties such as love and hate to attain their ends."

I shuddered, mentally chastising myself for being so easily fooled.

She shook her head. "You cannot waste much needed energy reproving yourself. Until your task it completed, you must resist anything that calls your true name, even if it sounds like your own mother's voice. I will seek you out if need be, and as you summoned me now you can summon me again, that is if I still have the strength to act."

"Who goes there? Identify yerself afore I shoot ye dead!" A gruff brogue called from the darkness, approaching from the direction of the house.

Sergeant Campbell ran forward, his lantern swinging wildly as he bounded into the clearing. "Miss Phoebe?" He stopped short, his mouth a gape as he looked at Hulda and the oddly positioned trees. "What in heaven's name goes on here? ...And why are ye out at this time of night in yer shift, lass?"

Hulda raised her stick and pointed it at the sergeant. The man straightened immediately, the hunched set to his shoulders stiff and his eyes vacant. She extended her rod and rapped on his shoulder once and he turned, greeting her with a smile.

"I'm going to need a little assistance, young man," she said returning his grin.

"No worries, Witchy Woman. I got you covered."

I gaped at the modern slang coming from the old Irishman's mouth and watched as he reached out and touched Hulda's shoulder. An ethereal glow engulfed the two, and her image thickened immediately, her strength returning if only for a short time.

The good sergeant, who was clearly no longer in possession of his own body, then helped Hulda relax out of her crouch. The old woman stood and stretched, and then smiled at me. "I did say I was on borrowed time, but extenuating circumstances prevail when one needs to borrow a little help, too."

Sergeant Campbell held out his arm, but she shook her head. "I'm fine. See to Rowen. She should be in bed at this hour."

Campbell turned to me and winked. "Ready?"

I blinked. The man's eyes were candy blue. Astonished, I opened my mouth to speak, but he raised one hand and blackness descended, enveloping me in a deep sleep.

My eyes opened to the sound of a rooster crowing from across the garden. I rubbed my eyes, and as awareness flooded back, I sat bolt up, scanning the room. Mrs. Mac was nowhere to be seen. That much I knew. My dress was where I left it, as were

the candles and the cloth match. The windows were both closed, and the hearth was cold.

I sank back onto my pillows. It was a dream. Just another bad dream. I stretched, yawning as blood ran into my resting muscles. For some reason I was sore, but that could be from sleeping on suspended ropes for the past few weeks. I yawned again.

One of these days I'd have a good night sleep without Mrs. Gerrittsen's brew to drug me into a dreamless stupor. God willing, it would be in my own bed in Sleepy Hollow.

It was time to get up, so I threw back the sheet. I stared in frozen disbelief at my shift and legs…both covered in dirt.

Chapter 19

"Well, you look like you had a hard night's sleep. Just look at the state of those bed sheets. What did you do, fight the devil himself?"

I stopped short, peeking out from beneath the towel I used to dry my hair. Dream or not, after what happened last night, I needed a good scrub, and if I could have scrubbed the images from my brain, I would have.

"*Hmmmm.* No words this morning, eh? Usually you are a venerable magpie."

I mumbled my apology and sat at the small mirrored vanity to fight with my tangles and curls

Mrs. Mac clucked at me. "Hand it over, miss. I won't have you tearing at that beautiful hair that has all the officers talking."

I glanced up at her across my shoulder and she nodded.

"Oh, to be sure, whatever performance I missed last night, it was certainly the talk of the breakfast table early this morning before they all left for their posts."

"I only told a story I knew. It wasn't as though I performed feats of magic."

"Well, magic it was, dearie, and they are all looking forward to the spectacle you're planning for Mrs. Arnold."

I made a face in the mirror and she yanked my hair.

"I'll have none of that. I'm here to help, and so is Marta Gerrittsen. She and the entire household staff are behind you in

this, so don't fret. In fact, a fat purse was left in safe keeping for shopping purposes with the promise of more if necessary. I thought we might take the carriage into Philipstown this morning and get a foot under us with the details. We don't have much time, and days will fly past if we're not careful with the allotted hours."

I swiveled around on my seat nearly knocking the woman over. "Philipstown?"

"Look who's got color back in her pale cheeks. Yes, love. We'll leave after breakfast, after we've made a list of what we'll need."

I ate quickly, running to the general's library for pad and a pen, only to realize there were no such animals and settled for a scrap of handmade cotton paper and a quill and matching bottle of ink.

The general informed me as I left the room, I should plan for at least one hundred guests. I bobbed my head and left trying to walk more carefully than I had with the tea, remembering India ink made for permanent stains and my clothing choices were very limited.

Mrs. Mac and I canvased the staff as to what foodstuffs and quantities were needed for a party of that many people, and then asked for suggestions in terms of entertainment.

"Miss Phoebe, if you don't mind my saying, don't leave the music up to the general. Miss Peggy hates military bands that play marches all night. She prefers music for dancing." Abigail, a shy kitchen maid, piped up, bringing my eyes from the paper to look at her painfully shy face.

The fact she spoke at all was a feat. The fact she spoke to *me* told me I was slowly winning everyone's affections. I nodded, thanking her for her help.

"Come, love, we need to make haste, or we'll never return in time for me to help with the supper. It's going to be a full table again this evening as everyone is breathless for your next story."

I turned, stunned. "They're expecting another story?"

She nodded. "Indeed. Didn't the general warn you to prepare?"

"Yes, but..." I stood, throwing my hands in the air. "How on earth am I to do everything expected of me? Who does General Arnold think I am? Walt goddamned Disney?"

Mrs. Mac tugged on my sleeve, her eyes wide with warning. "Calm yourself. You're muttering nonsense again, child." She put her hands on my shoulders and steered me toward the stairs. "We'll get your shawl on the way out the front door. It's a bit of a ride and we can use the time to think."

I sat in the carriage, lost in my own thoughts as the cart bumped and plodded up the dirt road. The methodic clip clop of the horse's lulled me into daydreams, dredging up the different stories I could tell tonight. Too bad I couldn't rework the Legend of Sleepy Hollow and regale them with the story of the headless horseman. I mentally shook my head. I wouldn't repeat Washington Irving's story as told. I couldn't, out of respect for the Hessian soldier whose wronged life and story Hunter and I finally set to right less than a year ago.

Perhaps I could rework Bram Stoker's Dracula. Yes...that might scare the pants off them and give me a break for a few days.

The carriage pulled into what I assumed was the village. The layout was nothing more than a strip of shops set along the side of the road. An inn that doubled as a restaurant and overnight accommodations, a blacksmith and livery, and a general store with a part-time apothecary, and finally the Black Bear Tavern. The general store, or so Mrs. MacPherson said, had a variety of items for sale including bolts of fabric and lace, men and women's ready-made shoes and hats.

The general's aid-du-camp, Major David Franks accompanied us instead of a footman, and he took hold of the purse given us for the excursion. Mrs. Mac wasn't happy about that, as she hoped she could bargain enough for what we needed to afford me a new dress for the party.

A regional tailor and seamstress passed through Philipstown every few months with new stock items for the store, and they spent a few days taking custom orders from the ladies in the surrounding area. Mrs. Mac learned they would be here for the next two days before heading south to their shop.

The area around Tarrytown and Sleepy Hollow was known during the American Revolution as a neutral zone, but for merchants it meant profitable business because both sides would frequent their shops without the worry of declaring sides. Of course, no man's land also afforded its own risks, as neither the British nor Americans felt obligated to offer protection from thieves.

Peggy Arnold was expected in two days' time and her entourage shortly after. The general personally invited well-to-do families from thirty miles around to join him in welcoming his wife to West Point, and that included those in the neutral zone. I wondered if he would be bold enough to invite his wife's British friends, but my guess was even he couldn't be that imprudent.

We walked from merchant to merchant with Mrs. MacPherson negotiating prices and delivery times for everything from the geese and turkeys to be roasted and served from carving stations, to the local bakery providing sweets and puddings to help Mrs. Gerrittsen with items for the dessert tables.

At the inn, she spoke with the proprietor about procuring extra serving staff, and lastly, she dragged me toward the tavern.

"With all due respect, Mrs. MacPherson, you have done a wonderful job helping Miss Burritt organize Mrs. Arnold's affair, but I'm not sure either of you should be seen entering this sort of establishment. It's quite a step from the inn in terms of gentility, so why not let me procure whatever it is you need?"

She eyed the man like a practiced haggler from an Arabian bazaar. "And what is it you think we need to procure here, Major?"

He shrugged. "Drink, possibly casks of wine and beer for the men."

She nodded. "Yes, the men and their drink. The general prefers claret at his parties, but Mrs. Arnold enjoys French champagne. Do you suppose the barkeep here will be able to procure either for us or will we need to head south for those particular items?"

He inhaled and considered her question, knowing full well Mrs. Mac was not one to be trifled with. "I think those items would be best sought back at the inn. The Black Bear is not the place for gentrified drink, but it is where we can acquire kegs of beer and all the whisky the men will want. I'll make the required inquiries."

"Thank you, Major," I interjected. It was one of the few times I had been able to get a word in edgewise all morning. Not that I would have interrupted Ferne MacPherson for the life of me. "Mrs. Mac and I certainly appreciate both your company and your service."

Inclining his head, he smiled. "Not at all."

Major Franks opened the door and Mrs. Mac grabbed my arm pulling me along behind her. She was not going to leave these negotiations to Major Franks, alone.

We were barely inside the main taproom and my hand went to my nose. The place was rank with body odor and the stench of stale beer and urine. Sawdust covered the floor and I lifted my dress to stop it from dragging through the muck.

"*Uhm*...Major Franks," I called, trying not to gag from behind my hand.

He turned from his initial conversation and when he saw us standing there, he rushed to my side. "Miss Burritt, are you unwell?"

I nodded unable to speak for fear of vomiting.

"Let's get you out of here and into the fresh air."

He ran to the bar and after a few words rushed back. "The proprietor said there are wooden tables around to the side. He's having his men put down flat planks for you to walk on as we speak. Why don't you and Mrs. MacPherson wait there? I'll be with you in just a bit."

With Mrs. Mac at my side I pushed my way through the door, dragging in a clean breath nearly sinking to the ground from the residual stench.

With a disgusted sniff Mrs. Mac rubbed my upper back "Damn foolish pride. I should have listened to the man." Her words were clipped, and she sniffed again. "And you nearly sick on the side of the road because of it."

I straightened, dragging in another breath. "It's not your fault. How could you know the place would smell like a cesspool?"

She didn't answer and Major Franks came out at that moment to lead us around to the side of the building. The tavern was the last structure in the row of shops. The building was set farther off the road with nothing but thick woods surrounding the back and right, affording us at least a better view than the horse droppings everywhere and the unmentionable puddles lining the street.

A visit to Philipstown was not the excursion I had hoped it would be, and my idea to lure Peggy Arnold here for a day of shopping and diversion were dashed to the nonexistent concrete. I'd have to find another way to foster a friendship with the woman in order to gain access to her belongings without suspicion. I had hoped she'd befriend me enough to loan me the moonstone.

The major gestured toward a small group of roughhewn tables and I followed Mrs. Mac, stepping where she stepped on the thin boards. It was then I looked up from my own musing realizing Hulda never said what she wanted with the stone once I had it in my possession. I had a sneaking suspicion any

conversation at this point would end with the words, you'll figure it out...again.

The small wooden table was set well onto a section of dry grassy ground. A barman placed two mugs of small ale down along with a plate of coarse bread and cheese.

"Drink the ale, but don't touch the food. Lord knows what's been crawling across it in a place that rancid."

I laughed picking up my mug and cleaning the lip with my cuff. "I think my obsession with cleanliness is rubbing off on you."

She clucked her tongue. "Nonsense, although it is nice to be around people when they don't smell like a privy." She leaned closer. "Marta told me the maids are all mimicking your example. They're washing their hair and keeping their hands and teeth clean. Seems they want to smell just as sweet."

A wide grin spread across my face. "I'm thrilled to hear it. I guarantee if you kept track, the level of sickness in the house will be significantly reduced, too. Now if we could only get the men to follow suit, perhaps the girls would gag less when kissed!"

She picked a crumb from the rough bread and threw it at me. "Such a sinful mouth on such a pretty girl!"

I laughed and Mrs. Mac busied herself were her lists of what we accomplished and what was yet to be done. I found myself drawn to the comings and goings of the people around us, and by the far trees I spotted something familiar. It wasn't just the cut of the man's coat or his gait, but something sparked my memory.

He walked towards us and sat three tables over. I glanced down at my fingernails, averting my eyes while at the same time trying to figure out how I knew him.

His already mud-covered boots were getting a fresh coat from the same muck squishing out from the sides of the planks put down for our benefit. It hit me then, and I was certain this was the same rough-cut man I saw in the general's study the

afternoon I burnt my fingers on the Willow Bark tea. He wore the same tricorn hat trimmed in raccoon fur I spotted on his head when he skulked off toward the orchards behind Robinson House.

My attention was drawn to the muffled sound of a horse's trot. Another man rode in from the back of the tavern, tying his horse to a rail near the back well. He was dressed like a gentleman, and as he walked toward the man in the fur-trimmed hat he balked at the state of the ground, gesturing for them to move closer to the planks and dry ground where I sat with Mrs. Mac.

The man in the unusual hat looked directly at our table and shrugged. Clearly, I didn't make much of an impression outside the general's library, and from his noncommittal gesticulation he didn't think much of me now.

The men moved over and leaned in to talk. Without trying, I heard every word, noted every gesture and facial expression. To be honest, I was stunned at how easily they dismissed our presence. It was Mrs. Mac's furniture analogy incarnate.

The man in the hat reached into his breast pocket and handed a letter to the gentleman.

"Joshua, the man at the point instructs this must get to New York without delay. Once you get there, impart the brevity of time and an answer is required as quickly as possible. There are means already in place for their reply to be transported. They should seek out his tender half."

The gentleman he called Joshua nodded and tucked the letter into his jacket. With a nod, he tapped his left breast and then got up to take his leave.

Feeling myself watched, I leaned in toward Mrs. Mac and joked about how Major Franks would stink from being inside the tavern so long we'd have to make him ride up front with the driver.

She snorted, and I caught the man's eyes on us from my peripheral vision and added a silly giggle for good measure. He

made a face at the coy sound, dismissing outright any late blooming suspicions. Without a word or another look he got up and left the same way he came.

For a second time in a week I watched the same man skulk off toward the woods, only turning when the tavern owner came out followed by Major Franks to greet us.

The man wiped his grimy hands on a dirty apron, and I rolled my eyes at Mrs. Mac. "Ladies, I understand from the major that General Arnold is looking for certain libations for his men, is that correct?"

I nodded. "Yes. This is a party to welcome the general's wife. That said, we are also looking for musicians to play. Good ones mind you. Professionals who can play other than just military marches."

The barkeep looked from me to the major and then back again and his eyes glinted over with greed. Major Franks saw it as well.

"I think these negotiations are over."

"What do you mean? I haven't mentioned one farthing to you."

Franks shook his head. "You didn't have to. General Arnold entrusted me to see we weren't cheated while making our preparations. I can smell the avarice on you along with every other foul scent from your establishment."

He pushed the man back giving Mrs. Mac and me room to rise from our chairs. "Ladies, if you please." He swept his arm out toward the street. "I will send a messenger on a fast horse to Tarrytown. I'm sure we can come to some kind of arrangement there for the rest of our needs."

The tavern owner was speechless, but he had tipped his cards and it was game over.

My eyes drifted toward the woods and narrowed. A message from the *man at the point* to British held New York City. That could only mean one person, especially with a response arriving via his "tender half." It seemed another set of cards had

been tipped my way and it was up to me to figure out how to play them.

I climbed down from the carriage holding the major's hand as Mrs. Mac instructed the boys and one of the footmen to bring the packages she picked up for the house and Mrs. Gerrittsen's kitchen. I had a small parcel wrapped in brown paper and tied with cord as well, an unexpected gift from Major Franks. I now had real soap and sweet-smelling shampoo and almost giggled with delight at the simple pleasure awaiting my toilette later today.

"Thank you, Major. You really didn't have to do this," I said gesturing with the parcel.

"Do what, Franks?"

We both turned to see Alec walking toward us from the direction of the stables.

"Not that it's any of your concern, Hamilton, but Miss Burritt was overcome today by the filth in town, and I gifted a small token to see her pretty smile again."

Alec nodded. "I see. Good man, Franks. Your chivalry is well noted, and I for one appreciate it. Miss Burritt is a fine lady. Where may I ask was she overcome? Philipstown is not the largest village, but the shops most women frequent are usually well kept."

Major Franks flushed and I knew Alec was baiting him into admitting he allowed me into the Black Bear. This was nothing more than a show of testosterone driven nonsense, and I was in no mood to deal.

"It was my own fault, Colonel. Major Franks insisted that Mrs. Mac and I wait for him while he negotiated the libations and music for the party with the proprietor, but you know how headstrong I can be. I marched into the establishment after him and the stench knocked me over. The place is beyond rife, and

as the major said I was overcome. To his credit he rushed to my aid and got me settled in the fresh air with a cup of small ale to steady my nerves and queasy stomach."

I placed my hand on the major's arm. "I can't thank you enough, Major."

The man straightened his shoulders before giving me a formal bow. "I am at your service, Miss Burritt." He looked up, meeting my eyes as he stood. "May I request the honor of a dance at the party, then?"

I nearly choked. "If your feet can stand the trampling. I confess I never learned to dance. Perhaps you'd do better asking Mrs. Arnold."

He laughed. "I and my feet will take our chances." With a nod to me and another to Alec, he took his leave.

I turned giving the colonel a narrow-eyed glare. "Jealous much, Alec?" I asked in my most coy voice.

Hmmph. "Why would I be jealous of an old man whose biggest claim to fame was paymaster to a failed campaign?"

"Wow, methinks the gentleman doth protest too much."

He made a face, but there was laughter in his eyes. "Educated women are a dangerous thing."

"Ha! Not a fan of Hamlet, I guess."

He snorted his reply.

I walked toward the front steps of the house, and he fell in step beside me. "Are you following me, Colonel?" I asked, glancing across my shoulder.

"I had every intention of asking you to ride with me once you returned but seeing as your sense of smell is so delicate perhaps being too near a horse isn't the best idea."

I smacked him with my parcel.

"Ouch!"

"You deserved that."

He rubbed his upper arm, laughing. "Touché."

I climbed the few steps onto the porch, my hand reaching for the door.

"Aren't you the slightest bit curious about the saddle I procured for you?"

I stopped and turned toward where he stood waiting on the gravel. "Astride?"

He nodded.

I squealed like a little girl. "Give me a sec to change my clothes and I'll meet you at the stables."

I didn't wait for an answer, instead rushing up the stairs, my hands already loosening my laces.

"Tag, you're it!" I yelled tagging Alec's thigh with my riding crop as I edged my horse into a full gallop.

"Slow down! Phoebe, you'll hurt yourself!" he yelled after me, but I ignored him.

This was heaven, and the horse Alec chose for me was strong and fast and responsive to the slightest touch directing him. I reached above my head and waved to Alec behind me, then pulled the combs from my hair, letting the wind take the curly mass, blowing it behind me like a dark curtain.

I gently pulled on the reins slowing my pace and waited for Alec to catch up. He'd left his hat behind, peeling his jacket off as well and stowing it in one of his saddlebags.

"Headstrong wench!" he grumbled, pulling his horse up short. "If you fell, I would be left to explain why and the fact I allowed you to ride astride would not go unnoticed!"

I laughed. "Stop being such an old, wet blanket. I've ridden astride my whole life. Nothing is going to happen." I kicked my horse and pulled up on the reins bringing him up onto his hindquarters. "Last one to the large oak straight ahead is a rotten egg!"

I took off full speed.

Alec growled something unintelligible, but he gave his horse a vicious kick and spurred him faster, overtaking my lead in

moments. He made it to the tree and dismounted with a single jump, leaning against the tree as I rode up.

"Show off," I teased sticking my tongue out at him.

With a lazy smile, he pushed himself away from the tree trunk and walked over, reaching up to help me from my saddle. With his hands at my waist, I slid down, my body following the length of his to the ground.

"Keep your tongue in that delicious mouth, little girl, or I won't be responsible for the kisses it elicits."

Hands on his chest, I was trapped between him and my horse. "I'll remember that, Colonel."

He took a step back with a flourish and I walked toward the large tree, grateful for the shade.

Alec opened both saddle bags and took out a blanket and the picnic lunch Mrs. Gerrittsen packed for us.

"Other than learning ladies don't belong in filthy wayside taverns, how went the rest of your day?" he asked, spreading the blanket beneath the tree.

I shrugged. "Fine, I guess. Mrs. MacPherson did most of the negotiating. We have all the food ordered and enough staff hired to run Buckingham Palace."

He cocked his head. "Which palace?"

Crap. Buckingham Palace wasn't built until Queen Victoria. What was the name of the castle now… damn it? Think.

"I meant Windsor Castle, although I understand mad King George purchased Buckingham House and has said it would be a grand place for his next palace."

I picked a few low hanging leaves and proceeded to pull them apart rather than make eye contact with Alec. I may have managed to pull my foot out of my mouth with that, but my face would give away my nervous embarrassment. Hunter always said I wore my emotions on my sleeve.

Alec set out the food and called me over to sit and eat. I picked up a cloth napkin and one of Mrs. Gerrittsen's chicken pastries full of succulent white meat, carrots, and potatoes. It

was a handheld potpie without the mess. I took a bite, watching Alec fill a plate with everything from fruit and cheese to pastries and a large slice of cold pork.

"Hungry?" I asked chewing slowly.

He nodded. "Famished. This is a treat today." He took a bite of a miniature apple pie. "Are you ready for your storytelling encore tonight?"

I rolled my eyes but didn't answer as we were interrupted by the sound of an approaching horse.

Alec put his food down and pressed his finger to his lips reaching for his pistol with his other hand, keeping the cocked gun flush against his thigh.

A gentleman on a dappled brown mare trotted toward us. As he got closer, Alec gently closed the hammer on his firearm placing it back under his uniform coat.

Stupid me, I didn't know he had a gun with him. Why wouldn't he, though? Everyone in the eighteenth-century owned firearms and could shoot. Everyone but me, that is.

"Jacob!" Alec called with a wave.

The man who rode closer was elderly, and he dismounted with effort and a grunt, tying his horse beside ours. "Alexander. It's good to see you," he said coming up to shake Alec's hand.

"Jacob, may I present Miss Phoebe Burritt. She's a guest of the general and Mrs. Arnold at Robinson House."

He inclined his head. "Jacob Mandeville, at your service, Miss Burritt."

"It's a pleasure to make your acquaintance, sir. Do you live around here? I've been staying at Robinson House for weeks and have yet to see neither hide nor hair of anyone other than the household staff and these rough-cut officers."

He laughed, rolling his eyes Alec's way. "It's just me these days. My children are married, and my dear wife passed a while ago."

"I'm sorry," I offered sincerely.

He smiled and glanced at Alec. "Don't be. I've been lucky in my life, and I've offered my house to keep some of the Continental Army officers, so I do know what you mean when you say rough cut." He chuckled. "So, you've been a guest at Robinson House. How is it you came to be there before the good general took command? Did you come with General Washington when he visited last month?"

I looked at Alec. "George Washington was here at the end of July?" I asked, and then remembered Dr. Thacher mentioning it that first day at the field hospital.

The man nodded. "He stopped on July thirtieth before heading back toward headquarters in Orangetown the next day or so."

"Phoebe hadn't yet arrived, Jacob. She suffered a boating accident and was under Dr. Thacher's care at the time. We brought her to the main house shortly after the general arrived."

"Boating accident, oh, my dear, I hope you're as recovered as you appear."

I smiled. "I'm fine now but thank you for asking."

Alec patted the blanket. "Join us, Jacob. The general's cook is a wonder and there's plenty."

The older inhaled and then patted his stomach. "It certainly smells wonderful, but Elisha Hammond is meeting me here shortly. I wouldn't want to impose the both of us on your picnic."

Alex waved him off. "There's plenty. Please sit, and when the quartermaster arrives, he may join us as well."

The old man doffed his coat and hat and I had to press my lips together not to embarrass him or myself and laugh at the lopsided set of his wig. I turned my head as he lowered himself to the blanket with a little help from Alec. He sat with an audible huff. I turned back just as he centered the white hairpiece on his head.

He shrugged, chuckling with the confidence of age. "Don't mind me, my dear, age is a delightful equalizer and affords me

many a liberty much younger men can scant afford." Without warning he reached out and tweaked my nose.

I laughed out loud, a genuine smile on my face.

"Behave yourself, Jacob." Alec scolded with a wink. "The pinching of young girls yet remains the domain of young men."

"Pish," I said mimicking Mrs. Mac and the two of them laughed.

The sound of another horse arriving brought Alec to his feet, and from the way the two men greeted each other and the nod of approval on Jacob's face, I could only assume it was Elisha Hammond.

The two walked toward the large oak. "You already know this old coot, but may I present Miss Phoebe Burritt. Miss Burritt, this is Fort Putnam's quartermaster, Lieutenant Elisha Hammond."

I held out my hand. "Pleased to meet you, Lieutenant."

He nodded once but didn't take my hand, just sat near the end of the blanket and took the glass of ale Alec held out to him.

"I'm glad I ran into you, Hamilton. I have to ask, how are things at Ft. Arnold and the rest of the Point?"

Alex nibbled the rest of his apple pastry. "How do you mean?"

Hammond took the proffered chicken I held out to him without acknowledgement, and after a large initial bite, he shoved the entire remaining half into his mouth. Cheeks stuffed, he picked pastry crumbs from his uniform jacket as he chewed, following it up with a massive gulp of ale.

I made a face waiting for him to burp, but he didn't.

"Aren't they feeding you at Putnam?" Alec asked, laughing as the man reached for another pasty.

"Just barely. I haven't had time to eat, not that I could with supplies at such a dismal level. Morale is almost at its breaking point. That's why I'm asking you about your observations."

Alec nodded, but his face was cautious. It was clear he wasn't comfortable discussing this issue here. "Now that you

mention it, I have noticed since General Greene resigned, matters have degraded some."

"Some?" Hammond shook his head, sitting back with one knee bent and his cup of ale resting on his thigh. "General Arnold has left the matter in my hands until Greene's replacement is appointed, but he won't release funds or give orders for replenishment. My hands are tied, yet I'm the one who has to deal with the day-to-day."

Alec looked at Jacob, gesturing toward him with his cup. "What about you, Jacob. Have you heard complaints among the officers at Mandeville House?"

The older man exhaled, lifting one shoulder and letting it fall. "Historically, there is always grousing between men-at-arms, but yes. The officers seem concerned about their troops and how liberally Arnold distributes their numbers, leaving their detachments scattered."

"What do you mean scattered?"

"Men are sent to bolster locales deemed less invasive thus leaving West Point pitifully undermanned. Repairs on the chain anchored to Constitution Island were never ordered, or so they've been told. There have even been grumblings leading back to Arnold's court martial for misappropriation of funds and confiscated assets during the Quebec Campaign, with some suggesting he's up to his old tricks and selling supplies on the black market for personal gain."

Hammond tossed his napkin down. "He's written to General Washington about the dismal state of affairs and lack of supplies, requesting more money. He even went so far as to claim, 'everything is wanting,' yet word around the fort is he's planning an extravagant party for his silly loyalist wife."

The man slid his eyes to me. "Are you planning to attend to party, Miss Burritt?"

I opened my mouth to answer but Alec shook his head. "Don't involve Miss Burritt in this, Hammond. She's but a girl and has no knowledge of the inner workings and intrigues of

war. It's not fair and I won't have it. She's a guest at Robinson House and it isn't seemly for you to question her about her host."

"Quite," Jacob interjected with a sharp nod. "I plan to attend the party, yet from your disdainful tone it's safe to assume you are not. Is that the case, Elisha?"

Hammond's mouth puckered. "I have more important things to attend to than frivolities with aimless young women."

Alec stood, a clear indication this matter was now closed. "As you know, Elisha, I am General Washington's adjutant as well as his aide-du-camp. I'm well aware of the letters sent and the discrepancies noted. If General Washington has concerns, he has yet to voice them, but I'm rest assured his Excellency has a firm understanding of the matter."

Hammond helped Jacob up from the blanket and the older man grimaced as he straightened. "Hamilton," the old man acknowledged with a nod, and then looking to me, he saluted. "I hope to see you again soon, Miss Burritt."

I smirked at the old man's clever tongue-in-cheek, especially when Lieutenant Hammond's faced soured even more.

"I sincerely hope you come to the party, Mr. Mandeville."

He winked, touching his index finger to his nose.

The two rode off leaving Alec pensive and me on edge. Clues were adding up. Between the morning's clandestine meeting at the Black Bear and now proof the general was undermining West Point's defenses, the game of treason was in motion and fast coming to a head. Yet his wife had yet to arrive. This party had evolved into more than just a vehicle to win trust. It was now the catalyst to ensure Peggy Arnold came to West Point sooner than later. If her husband's treason was revealed before she arrived, the woman would never come and Hulda's moonstone would be lost forever and my family's future along with it.

"Are you all right?" Alec asked, watching me chew my lip.

I nodded. "Yes, though Lieutenant Hammond was rather rude."

Alec exhaled. "That he was, and his table manners need polish, as well. I apologize, Phoebe. I never expected he'd be so irksome."

"You can make it up to me by ensuring that man doesn't show at the party. I want Mrs. Arnold to like me, not blame me for reminding her how rough and provincial the Hudson Highlands can be and that she's trapped here."

"Why are you still so worried about Peggy Arnold? I've already told you she's pretty and gracious."

I laughed. "That's all? She's pretty and gracious? I'm sure there's more to her worth than that. What does she do? What are her likes and dislikes, her pastimes, her talents?"

His expression seemed at odds, and he reached for more ale. "My, aren't we a buzzing little bee today."

I exhaled. "Alec, now you're the one being difficult. I may be under the general's roof, but everyone knows the true power running a household lies with the lady of the house. In a two days' time my life will be subject to Mrs. Arnold's dominion. It would be nice to know a little more about her than just *she's pretty.*"

I sat back in a huff, but then quickly leaned forward bringing my hand down on the blanket with a muffled thump. "My God, is that all men think about women? Mere decoration for the benefit of the male eye, to be paraded in public like prize horses?" I gestured to the two steeds munching grass not twenty paces from where we sat. Alec didn't respond, but then again, I didn't expect him to.

"To that end I voice an emphatic no thank you. Any man who hopes to win my affection would have to appreciate my figure and face, but also appreciate I have a brain and a tongue, with a discerning filter separating the two. He would have to welcome my ability to think and speak in a coherent and interesting manner and consider it a credit, priding himself that

my interests held a greater scope than simply hairstyles and fashion."

I exhaled, this time my eyes locking in Alec's intent gaze. "I want a man who not only wants my body, but wants and admires my mind, as well."

I plopped a grape into my mouth and chewed slowly watching different emotions shadow Alexander's face, realizing I had most likely gone too far, this time. I lifted a hand and let it drop. "I'm sorry, Alec, forgive me. I have a passionate nature and I sometimes forget where I am and to whom I'm speaking."

He got up from where he sat and moved next to me on the blanket. "Passionate, you say? Indeed, you are, and you take my breath away. I'm rendered nearly speechless in the wake of such fervor." He clasped my hand bringing it to his lips. "I've known you only a little over a month, but with each passing day you become more of an enigma. A beautiful, independent-minded mystery." Alec lifted my hand to his chest. "My heart is racing. How any man could want less than everything, your body, mind and soul, is beyond me."

He slid his arm around my waist and drew me close, pressing his cheek to mine. "You arouse me, my dear, in thought as well as in body. Whatever am I to do with you?"

I put my hands on his shoulders and pushed him back. His eyes searching mine and I glanced down in what I hoped was demure response and not the chicken-shit move it was at heart.

"I've embarrassed you," he said softly taking my hand again, but this time in a much more reserved fashion. "My apologies."

I shook my head. "It's me who needs to apologize yet again. My nature is often not as leashed as tenets require, and my words paint me as reckless, when in truth I'm not." I hesitated, not sure how to proceed.

"Alec, I'm not so naïve not to understand your interest and the passion that feeds it, though I'm not sure this is a path to be

pursued. I would hate to see you shower your affections on me and then find out I'm not who you thought I was."

He nodded, and I noticed a hint of suspicion creep into the depths of his violet eyes.

He inclined his head, and with that one practiced move, the mask of adjutant general was secured in place along with his gracious but distantly polite manner. "How could you be anything other than what you seem?"

"Alec, you're reading my words wrong." I lifted my hand to his cheek. If I had to play the coquette to get him to trust me enough not to send the pony express to Vermont for CIA purposes, then so be it. Hulda said I would be tried and here was the test, boldfaced and indifferent to my warring emotions.

I plastered what I hoped was a warm smile on my face and mentally apologized to Hunter, willing all my love across oceans of time, praying he would feel the ripples and know it was me.

"I'm going to say something that may stun you, especially coming from a feminine mouth, but men forget that women have feelings and desires in much the same vein as you. Your mood is mirrored in my own, but I need to feel secure in myself before I allow such emotion to take root. Do you understand?"

He nodded but didn't speak.

I let my hand fall to his and I wrapped my fingers around his bridle-calloused palm, bringing it to my cheek. I pressed it close, the same as I had seen done in old movies.

Alec took the cue and brought his other hand up, both cupping my face. He leaned in and I closed my eyes, imagining it was Hunter who was about to kiss me.

He pressed his lips to mine, one hand drifting down my arm to my waist while the other gripped the back of my neck. He urged me closer, hungry for more and though I tried not to respond, his mouth demanded otherwise. My hope for a chaste kiss evaporated as his tongue pushed its way through, claiming mine.

His kiss deepened and he pulled me down onto the blanket, his hard length against my softness. He broke his hold on my mouth, his lips trailing along the underside of my jaw to my throat, his fingers sliding upward toward the swell of my breasts. I put my hands on his chest and pushed him back, his chest heaving from the unexpected pause.

He kissed the tips of his fingers and touched them to my lips. "My unpredictable girl."

I glanced down at his waistcoat, not allowing my eyes to stray lower. An uncomfortable silence settled in and Alec eased farther back, letting his fingers slip from my waist to wrap around my hand.

"The party is just days away."

He kissed my fingers. "Yes, and I cannot wait to take you in my arms in front of God and the world and whisk you around the dance floor."

I chuckled. "I didn't say what I did to Major Franks just to put him off. I seriously cannot dance. I tried to learn the Allemande, but I'm afraid I'm hopeless."

I wasn't lying. I had tried to master the steps to the group dance when I belonged to the living history club. I had better luck with the card games and pitching a tent.

He laughed, giving me a quick peck before getting to his feet. "I'm sure over the next days, Mrs. MacPherson will think of something. She and I are of like mind in that we want our girl to shine."

He went about packing up and once the saddlebags were stuffed, he came back and the two of us folded the blanket together.

"Alec?"

"Hmmm?"

"Will you teach me to shoot a pistol?"

He stopped mid-fold and looked at me. "Why?"

I took the blanket from him and finished the folding before tucking it under my arm. "Because if West Point is as weak as

Hammond said, then I want to be able to defend myself if necessary."

Alec took two strides toward me and in less than a moment wrapped me in his arms. "West Point is not weak, despite what that blowhard says. You have nothing to fear, love. As long as I'm around no one will touch you."

I nodded taking a step back. "But you're leaving to meet General Rochambeau with General Washington, soon."

His mouth dropped open. "How did you..." He snapped his lips closed and made a face, nodding. "Mrs. MacPherson. She hears just a little too much at the Red House and shouldn't repeat it, especially not to scare you."

I shook my head. "She didn't tell me to scare me. She told me because she knew I'd miss you." As the words left my mouth, I cringed a bit on the inside because the truth behind those words stung a bit. I loved Hunter, but I had become very fond of Alec and would miss his company.

"I'm not leaving for another week. Not until after the party, at least."

"How long will you be gone?"

He shrugged. "It depends. I'm slated to set out to meet Washington on September seventh, but the general has scheduled his inspection of West Point sometime during the third week of September. He wants a complete report on the fortification before the first snow. I'll return with him then."

Chapter 20

Two carriages and various wagons laden with trunks pulled to the front of Robinson House. A dusty footman climbed down from the driver's perch and opened the door, letting the step down before holding his hand out to assist the passengers from the vehicle. A young woman dressed in a dark pink gown and large feathered hat stepped down from the carriage.

Her faced was obscured beneath the wide brim and delicate tilt of her hat. She lifted her head and I got my first glimpse of Peggy Shippen Arnold. She was breathtaking.

Powered and pink with fat blond curls resting daintily on her bare shoulders, she was a porcelain doll incarnate. Her waist was tiny and her breasts high, the tops of the soft mounds peeking devilishly from the folds of lace circling the low-cut scoop of her bodice.

She blinked but didn't say a word as we stood waiting for the general to emerge. The door to the second carriage opened and a full-figured woman in a dull gray jersey and a starched white apron, stepped down. She wore a floppy eared mobcap and had the most austere face I had yet to encounter.

The woman gestured impatiently for whoever was still in the carriage to make their way out, and in that moment a baby wailed.

"For the love of God, must you jostle Master Edward, so? Hand him over, he's probably hungry. You can change his

linens once he's done feeding." She waved her hand. "Come, come, Lettie. Move along."

She took the baby from a set of young arms and gestured again with a protracted sign for the girl to hurry up and climb down. A young face appeared in the doorway and I glanced at Mrs. Gerrittsen who beamed from ear to ear. It was her long-awaited daughter.

Younger than I expected, Lettie Gerrittsen stepped down to the gravel drive and sparred a small smile for her mother and the rest of the staff.

"Well, don't just stand there dawdling, gather the rest of the baby's things and come with me."

The woman carried the baby to her mother, who waved her hands at the governess. "Not now. I'm too tired, Rebekah."

"You must tend to him, Miss Peggy. We have yet to hire a wet nurse, and Master Edward has had nothing but sugar water and a cloth teat for hours now."

Peggy made a face. "Ugh, don't use those vile words in my presence. The baby will have to wait." She dismissed the woman and her crying infant and glared at the rest of us gathered on the stairs.

"Well!" she said, with a stamp of her satin shoe. "Can anyone tell me why my husband isn't here to greet me?"

The front door swung open and the general walked out onto the porch as best he could with his leg and cane "Margaret! Here already? I wasn't expecting you for at least an hour, my dear." He beckoned to her, unwilling to take the steps himself.

Peggy's mouth was a thin slash. "Benedict, you know I hate to be kept waiting. Where have you been?" She offered him her cheek which he pecked in a perfunctory manner.

"I've been busy with plans for the forts, my dear. There is much work to be done."

At the mention of West Point, her eyes and nostrils flared slightly. Maybe no one else noticed, but I did. In that moment I also noticed an unspoken transfer between the two.

"And we have a surprise planned for you, as well!" He clapped like a school boy. "A party!"

"I already know. Why else do you think I rushed all the way here from civilization?"

He balked. "You know? How? Word can't possible travel that quickly over something so foolish."

I smiled to myself. A few well-placed words at the inn and to the officers at the Red House and a flurry of letters to wives and girlfriends followed, sending word of the party tearing down the post road to the Shippen-Arnold household in Philly.

In fact, word got back to Mrs. Mac that Peggy had planned to push back her arrival yet another week, but my guess was the critical reply she carried for her husband from New York, and the lure of being touted as First Lady of West Point lit a fire under her butt to come north *tout suit.*

"You aren't the only one with a head for gleaning news, my love," she said with the very first hint of a smile. "Women have their own stratagems for winkling out information, and as for the speed of it, nothing burns the ears and the tongue quite like gossip. Now where is this mystery woman, the young girl everyone is chattering about?"

The general crooked his finger my way and I stepped forward. I had practiced my curtsey all morning and had it down pat. I lowered myself as though I was bowing to royalty and the woman's lips stretched with delight.

"No, my dear. Please. We don't stand on ceremony. After all, we're fighting a war to throw off those patrician indulgences, however charming they are."

She tugged on my arm and I straightened to my full height. Average for the twenty-first century, but a good four inches taller than most colonial women.

"My, my, aren't we a tall one!" She giggled, and took my hand wrapping my arm with hers. "Best not to invest in heels then my dear, no man wants a woman equal to him in anything, even height!" She laughed at her own joke. "Though I do love

that green silk you're wearing, so fetching in such a provincial way."

First dig of the spur. Her tittering laugh set my teeth on edge but ignored it. "Thank you, Mrs. Arnold."

She patted my hand, but then stopped to ponder the daisies I had Mrs. Mac weave into my curls. The delicate white and yellow complimented the celery green of my dress, not to mention they reminded me of Hulda's daisy chain analogy, keeping my mission at the forefront of my mind.

"Daisies. How charming they look against your skin and hair. Too bad they're such a drab little flower." She tsked, her expression patronizing. "Of course, I only meant my complexion is far too English rose for anything that...yellow."

Son of a b...what she really meant was something 'that common.'

I plastered a smile on my face. "You have beautiful features, Mrs. Arnold, I'm sure any flower would pale by comparison."

A satisfied smile spread across her pink mouth. "You must call me Peggy."

She flounced in through the door with me in tow and a sense of passing some sort of test crept over me. I realized then the test was to never contradict her. Ever."

She moved along the two short rows of staff lining the foyer, holding her hand out as though she expected them to genuflect when introduced. She smiled and nodded, but their names were forgotten the moment she stepped away. The only genuine smile she sparred was for Mrs. Gerrittsen, and only because the woman's cooking helped her hold sway over the general.

Peggy put one silk clad foot on the wide staircase but stopped when Mrs. MacPherson reached out to straighten one of my curls. She gave the older woman a covetous look and stepped down to address her.

"I understand you've been acting as head housekeeper, helping Mrs. Gerrittsen prepare the house for my arrival."

Mrs. Mac bobbed her head. "Yes, ma'am. The general asked if I could lend a hand."

Peggy pursed her lips. "I see, and I also understand you've been assisting Miss Phoebe, almost as her personal maid."

Mrs. Mac nodded. "I do so at the behest of Dr. Thacher. Once Miss Burritt is healed enough to return home, my services will no longer be required, and I will resume my post at West Point. I serve as head nurse at the field hospital under Dr. Thacher's administration, as well as head housekeeper to the officers of the Continental Army housed at the Moore Estate."

Peggy's lips pressed together. "Well, Miss Phoebe isn't going anywhere any time soon, is she, my love?" She turned addressing the question to her husband.

He cleared his throat clearly taken off guard. "Her family has been notified though we haven't received word back as of yet. Miss Burritt is certainly welcome to stay as long as she likes. I was hoping the arrangement would provide appropriate company for you, my dear."

Peggy slid her eyes toward me. "Indeed, and in the interim Mrs. MacPherson can serve us both."

Son of a beyotch, to the tenth power!

No one had introduced Mrs. MacPherson by name, which meant Peggy Arnold hatched this ahead of time. Poor Mrs. Mac. The older woman would end up shackled to this house because of her charity to me.

I watched Mrs. MacPherson's face tighten, but a thought occurred. *Three weeks.* If history followed suit Peggy Arnold will be gone from here and heading to Philly with her powdered head bent in disgrace, a traitor's wife.

General Arnold gestured for things to move along and he showed his wife the rest of the house, having the footmen take her bags to the master suite and the chambermaids unpack her belongings. I almost offered to help just so I could get a glimpse of her jewelry and where it was stored for my own purposes, but I didn't dare.

I expected the woman to spend the rest of the day giving orders and bustling around with me at her heels, but she was

too exhausted from the trip to come downstairs for anything, instead asking for a tray to be sent to her room.

By the time dinner rolled around, a wet nurse had been brought in from the village referred to as Garrison's Landing to see to the baby. At least he was well cared for, and his crying finally stopped once his belly was full. Mrs. Gerrittsen made arrangements for the wet nurse to room with one of the kitchen maids, letting everyone know the woman was to eat first before the rest of the staff to keep her milk supply healthy and flowing. Mrs. Arnold's orders.

The austere looking woman didn't stay long, thank God. She left in a coach straight away for Philadelphia. Mrs. Gerrittsen told us she was Mrs. Arnold's old governess, hired to help make the journey north before returning south to her position as governess in Peggy's sister's house.

No one seemed more relieved the grim woman wasn't a permanent part of the Arnold household than Lettie. Sweet girl, she reveled in that baby, cooing and playing with him while both his mother and father ignored him completely.

Mrs. Mac brought me a tray and I ate in the peace and quiet of my room, although I would have preferred to eat in the kitchen with everyone else. Mrs. MacPherson was adamant. Now that Mrs. Arnold was in residence, my days of fraternizing with the staff and making myself useful were over. It was just as well. More important things occupied my mind.

The officers and men-at-arms living in and around Robinson House made themselves scarce with Peggy's arrival, and that included Alec. My guess was at one point he was enamored of the delicate blonde and didn't want her to guess he had a change of affection.

Peggy Shippen Arnold was used to being the belle of every ball when it came to men. She would definitely not have appreciated the attention Alec sent my way.

Mrs. Mac handed my finished dinner tray to one of the maids and then closed the door. She brushed out my hair,

pulling the daisies from my curls one by one and laying them on the vanity.

"Common flowers, indeed." She sniffed.

I smiled at her from my reflection. "Mrs. Arnold is well schooled in the art of passive aggression. It's quite a skill to be that insolent yet couch your nerve behind a graceful smile. I understand her scheming, though. After every morsel she'd heard, it's no wonder she had a burning need to show me who was mistress of this house. If she were a dog or a wild animal, she would have pissed on my shoes to mark her territory."

The older woman's face scrunched, and she burst into a fit of laughter. She sat back on the bed, tears rolling. "Ah, love, that was worth a price above rubies."

"Well, you look splendid even if I do say so myself!" Mrs. Mac exclaimed turning me toward the full-length mirror.

Somehow, she managed to find an evening dress. I don't know from where or from whom, but I learned better than to question Ferne MacPherson in anything she did.

The gown was a stunning powder blue silk with a two-inch thick brocade of tightly woven gold edging its low-cut square neckline. A semi-sheer fabric accented portions of the bodice both highlighting yet camouflaging the gentle swell of the décolleté, increasing its sex appeal.

Mrs. Mac pulled four separate sets of strings attached to the bottom of the dress gathering the full skirt into sectioned puffs showing more of the floral petticoat.

An intricate array of curls and braids woven through with blue ribbon and pearls had been pulled into a sculpted style atop my head with a few ringlets left loose to highlight my long neck. White above the knee stockings with blue silk ties and a pair of matching silk, silver-buckled shoes gave my outfit a

polished dash, and the pearl choker and matching earrings were the finishing touch.

A professional dresser from Tarrytown had been hired to assist Miss Peggy, and I'm sure the idea was put into her head via the general who got the suggestion from Mrs. Mac. *Clever woman.* His wife would never have let her go in time to help me get ready, but the passive aggressive move was thwarted by the Peggy's own vanity.

The dresser worked for the same custom dressmaker we met in Philipstown when they were here for their rounds earlier in the month, and they jumped at the chance for an in at Robinson House.

"I can't believe this is me," I said gazing at my own reflection. I found her eyes in the mirror. "I know better than to ask, but I can't help myself. Where did you get this glorious dress? And don't tell me it belonged to your unfortunate friend."

Gazing back at me she dropped her eyes to the floor. "I stole it."

"What? No, you didn't! Mrs. Mac! Oh my God, we need to take this off me and return it to its rightful owner." Panicked, I reached around for the back laces and she laughed, halting my wrists.

"Do you really think with everything I had to accomplish today I had the time and inclination to find a horse, mount it, and ride thirty miles to the nearest dressmaker and steal one of their creations?"

She laughed so hard she had tears. She wiped her eyes on her apron and then sobered when she saw I hadn't joined her fun.

"Come now, child. You need some merriment. At least tonight there will be games and music. Perhaps the lieutenant colonel will ask you to dance, although from what I hear you already had your own gambol days ago at the base of a certain oak tree."

Heat marched across my cheeks and my eyes dropped to the hem of my dress.

"Oh, darlin', don't fret. There are eyes and ears everywhere 'round here, but every one of them was happy for you. He's quite a catch. Then again, from all accounts so are you, regardless which side of the Burritt clan you hail."

I looked at her and she pulled my hands to the front and held them loosely in her own. "If you must know who provided the dress, I'll tell you, though I was sworn to secrecy. You have to promise not to breathe a word."

"Of course," I answered.

"Good." She nodded once. "The gown, and everything with it, is a gift from Alexander. He sent for it yesterday. I don't know who he originally had the dress made for, but my guess it was for Elizabeth Schuyler. You remember, she's the girl I told you about when we first arrived."

I nodded but didn't comment.

"He is more than just smitten with you, love, and after tonight there's no doubt in my mind he'll be on one knee soon after." She sighed. "Now, that's enough of that. You look stunning. Miss Peggy's finery won't take away from the entrance you'll make with your natural beauty showing through."

She turned me toward the door and patted my rather wide gathered backside. "Off with you and mind your dress on the stairs."

Lanterns lit the circular drive casting dancing shadows along the trees and winding paths surrounding the property. Extra footmen were hired to direct carriages to the lower fields so as not to block the way to the main road, and special barges had been commissioned to ferry officers and their wives from

West Point. Local gentry filled every inn and household guestroom available for miles.

The inside of the house was a bower of fresh wildflowers and garlands of green. Dozens upon dozens of candles cast a romantic glow throughout the house, spilling out into the garden and the open-air tents erected for the occasion. The dining room was an elaborate buffet of small foods, with carving tables set out on the back veranda. Tables and low benches scattered the grounds affording plenty of space to eat and chat away from the music and noise.

Peggy hadn't made her entrance yet, but I didn't care. We spent little time together these past few days, but the time we did spend was mostly for her benefit, showing off her collection of dresses and furs. As expected, I smiled and oohed at everything she paraded past until I spotted what I needed most. Her leather jewel case.

The chest was at least two feet high and opened into multiple tiers. Her eyes caught me admiring its fine tooling and she brought it out of the wardrobe to give me a better look.

"Benedict bought this for me before we wed. The design is Spanish, which is probably why I can never manage the lock." She laughed with a dismissive wave.

She lifted the top, and there it was lying in the center tray. Gran's moonstone. I had to shove my hands into the folds of my skirts not to reach out and snatch it from the leather box.

"It's lovely, isn't it?" she said when she saw my interest. Hooking it around her neck, she caressed the stone in its silver setting, and I swore the damn thing glimmered. "I got it for a song." She flounced up from her tufted boudoir stool to model the piece in the mirror. "I don't even know the name of the stone, but I do know no one else has anything like it."

"It's called a moonstone."

She jerked her head around to stare at me. "You've seen this before?"

I nodded. "My grandmother had one similar."

She pressed her lips together, eyeing the piece in the mirror almost as though weighing if my words diminished the pendant's value. She shrugged. "No matter. No one *I* know has one, and that's what counts."

Peggy went on to babble about other fashion nonsense, lamenting there was no dress shop for miles. I nodded only half paying attention because I couldn't take my eyes from Gran's gem.

After that, she seemed to accept my presence in the house. We rode together as well, her in a rich riding habit and me in my blue cotton day dress, but once we relaxed into our strides Peggy's guard slipped and I watched an unexpected melancholy wash over her. I wouldn't say we were friends, but she looked so miserable, a pang of compassion tweaked my conscience.

"What's wrong?"

She shrugged it off at first, but then seeing my genuine interest she sighed, confiding how the general, while generous, only did so for position and appearance. That in the year since they wed, his attentions seemed to drift. He was preoccupied and unfulfilled in his career and seemed bitter, yet when she tried to share his interests and spur his ambition, he was dismissive.

At one point she realized she said too much and tried to backpedal as the conversation hedged toward politics and Arnold's military peccadilloes. The conversation swung back to the mundane and complaints of how he barely acknowledged her, even in the bedroom.

"The general spoke so highly of you, though. He worried for your comfort the entire time we waited for you to arrive," I offered.

She reached out her hand on took mine, squeezing it. "Thank you for that, but I have my own strategies planned to make Benedict see me again as the young conquest he had to have or die trying."

I cocked my head giving her a knowing look. "The green-eyed monster?"

She laughed. "A pretty woman's ace of hearts."

She was a perfect mix of both regret and excitement as she talked, as though there were two men she pined for: the one waiting in the wings, and the man her husband used to be. I know I shouldn't have encouraged her, but the truth was I felt bad for her. She was a trophy wife who had been placed on the shelf.

I dismissed my recollections and walked through the house determined to enjoy the party. The conservatory double doors were thrown wide and oil lamps lined the small downward slope that led to the tented dance floor. Torches burned with scented oil along the perimeters, their black smoke rising into the evening sky. From their perch on the gazebo, musicians played incidental music while waiting for the guest of honor to start the dancing.

People milled around laughing and talking, but other than a few familiar faces belonging to officers who attended dinners at the house, I knew no one. Mrs. Mac and the rest of the staff busied themselves serving and neither Dr. Thacher nor Alec had arrived.

I was about to turn back inside when I heard someone call my name or rather, my alias. I had gotten so used to responding to Phoebe, I had to remind myself in the mirror every day I was really Rowen Corbett.

Turning toward the double doors, I saw Jacob Mandeville standing beside one of the torches. He was dressed in a maroon striped frock coat with a solid waistcoat of the same rich burgundy, a set of cream hose to match his silk cravat and a crisp linen shirt. He carried a gorgeous, polished black and gold walking stick with a nasty looking knobbed head.

"That certainly looks as though it could thump somebody good," I joked as he walked toward me.

Marianne Morea

He lifted the cane, giving me a quick salute as he did when we last parted. "That it does, and that it has," he announced with a wink.

"I'm glad you're here, Jacob. I don't really know anyone, let alone people I feel at ease with."

He gave me a warm smile. "I'm happy to be of some use, m'dear, but I'm sure once Alexander finds his way to you, my usefulness will have run its course."

I laughed and no sooner did he say the words than Alec showed at the top of the crest. He made his way towards us, and I don't know why but I curtsied. Maybe it was because he looked so damn good in his dress uniform or because his gift was so generous. Either way I felt I owed him the acknowledged respect.

With a nod to Jacob, he walked right past the man and took both my hands in his, pulling me to stand.

"Phoebe, you take my breath away," he said turning my hands over to kiss my palms. "It's I who should bow to you."

The scene was right out of Jane Austen's *Sense and Sensibility* and I suddenly felt ridiculous. I burst out laughing. I couldn't help myself.

"You certainly know how to create a love scene, Hamilton." Jacob's chuckle was followed by a series of wet coughs, leaving the man gasping for air as he dug in his pocket for his handkerchief.

"Oh my God, do you need some water?" I asked taking a step toward him.

Jacob shook his head, finally drawing a maroon cotton cloth from his jacket breast pocket. Wiping his mouth, he sucked in a clear breath.

"Goodness no, water will kill you. I need a good glass of wine, and Benedict has some fine claret. I think I'll locate a bottle and not share it with anyone." He chuckled again, leaning in toward me with a wink. "Present company, excepted, my dear."

With a wave, the old man walked away leaving Alec and me standing alone in the middle of a crowd.

"Peggy will be making her entrance soon. Perhaps we should get a drink and find a spot where we can watch the spectacle," he said, gesturing toward the dance floor.

"Spectacle?"

He raised an eyebrow. "You've spent a week with her, yet you doubt her entrance will be anything less?"

I laughed, but what Alec didn't understand was Peggy's petulance and ostentatious displays were nothing more than her armor, and beneath it was a truly unhappy woman. Whether her discontent was of her own making or because she had no real choice in her life's path, I didn't know. My guess it was a bit of both. Maybe her involvement in Arnold's double dealings was a foolish attempt at saving her marriage.

The band played a resounding fanfare, and all eyes turned to the top of the slope. Peggy and Benedict Arnold made their entrance and it was nothing short of regal.

They were dressed to the nines, he in a dress uniform with gold epaulets, shining buttons and a dashing gold sash to match his sword hilt and scabbard, and she in a gown to rival Marie Antoinette of France.

Peggy's dress was of a rich crimson. Wide hooped with yard after yard of satin embroidered with pearls and tiny crystals covering the bodice and cinched waist and enough lace for a thousand doilies.

I caught her eye and waved. Her costume was pretension personified and was light years away from anything I would wear, but it suited her, and I almost flashed her thumbs up.

The two walked to the dance floor and the musicians played the opening strains to an Allemande. Peggy curtsied low and her husband bowed before he stepped aside, gesturing for Alexander to take his place with his wife for the dance. A shadow crossed the woman's face at the outward reminder of her husband's crippled state but was gone as quickly as it came.

Alec nodded to me, giving my hand a quick kiss before he strode onto the dance floor wearing a huge grin. I had to laugh because it was obvious, he loved the spotlight almost as much as Peggy.

Music swelled and the two took their first hold, arms linked over head as Alec directed their first steps in a promenade around the dance floor. They rounded the perimeter once, stopping as other couples joined, moving in and around each other in the lively Scottish line dance.

I clapped along, watching as the couples jumped and pranced until the music ended. After that, Peggy didn't want for a dance partner and Alec walked back, snagging two glasses of wine from a proffered tray.

"That was quite a show, who knew you were so agile and light on your feet," I said taking one of the stemmed glasses from his hand.

"My dear, I have many a hidden talent I long to share with you." He winked, raising his glass in salute.

We drank and laughed and talked, and I relaxed into people watching mode making fun of elaborate wigs and silly poufs. I lifted my glass, gesturing toward the orchard, and the few couples who ventured in so pristine, only to head out with their clothes askew.

After my forth glass of claret, the wine kicked in and I stood trying to mimic Peggy's mastery of the Allemande, only to trip on the hem of my petticoat.

"If you're going to dance you need to do so properly on the dance floor." Alec took my hand and pulled me toward the tent, but I stomped on his foot, making my escape through the house toward the drawing room.

He beat me there and cornered me by the stairs, pulling me into his arms. "You are the true belle of the ball tonight," he murmured.

"All thanks to you."

A small grin teased the corner of his mouth and he didn't seem angry Mrs. Mac had let out his secret. In fact, he seemed almost self-satisfied. I didn't mind, though. He'd been nothing but gracious and kind and I was honestly grateful.

Alec led me onto the front porch to one of the two person swings on either end of the portico.

"You're leaving tomorrow?" I asked, taking a seat on the swing.

He nodded. "At daybreak."

When I didn't comment, he sat beside me and took my hand in his. "Will you miss me while I'm gone?"

I looked across my shoulder at him. "You say the stupidest things sometimes, you know that? Of course, I'll miss you, and it's not because of the gown. It's because I enjoy your company. Besides Mrs. MacPherson, you're my only friend."

He gave a low, short laugh. "Friend?"

I nodded. "Yes. Friend. It's the way all good relationships start."

"True enough." His words were a soft murmur.

I pushed the swing back and forth and we rocked in silence for a while watching people mill around and come and go through the house. The thought crossed my mind to try dancing with Alec, but I couldn't do it. Dancing was Hunter's. Just like complete physical intimacy was his alone, as well.

Alec may have stolen a few kisses, and I was learning to deal with that from the point of view of necessity, but that was all it was. If I knew for certain I could never go home, that Hunter was lost to me forever, I would grieve and perhaps then there would be a place for Alec in my life.

According to record, Alec would marry Elizabeth Schuyler in December 1780. Three months from now. That's what the history books said, and hopefully by then I would be home and back in Hunter's arms.

"A penny for your thoughts?" he asked, lifting my chin so he could look into my eyes.

I smiled, enjoying the slight buzzy feeling in my head. "Nothing worth as much as that. Just the musings of a woman's heart."

He lifted our linked hands and grazed his knuckles down my cheek. "Oh, my dear, on that I beg to disagree." He smiled, letting our hands drop. "I have a small request to make of you, Phoebe."

I froze and my stomach flip-flopped. Whether it was from the wine or his unknown request, butterflies started winging in my stomach, and not the good kind, either.

"What is it?" I managed through the knot.

He looked at me so serious. "Kiss me."

I blinked. "I...I...don't understand."

He smirked, but his eyes didn't leave mine. "Until now our shared kisses have all been mine. You haven't taken the reins, as is proper, but..." He let his words trail off.

"Alec..."

He raised a hand. "I want to know your feelings mirror my own, so when I return, we can converse seriously about the future. The minute I taste your kiss on my lips, I'll know." He paused. "*Your* kiss. Not one I steal or one I seduce."

Jesus, had the man read my thoughts? This was exactly what I was trying to avoid. If I refused, then what? Would he understand and try again when he got back? Or would he go away angry and dismiss me outright? As cruel and mercenary as it sounded, I needed every ally I could get. It wasn't like he asked me to sleep with him, though lord knew he would if I let him. He's a guy.

It was just a kiss, right? When I got home, if I ever got home, my mother and Gran would help explain to Hunter. The question was could I explain it to myself?

Alec waited, watching my face. I didn't have time to make this into a great debate. Bottom line I needed to stack all odds in my favor.

I rested my hand on his cheek. "Come with me," I said, and stood from the swing, a little dizzy.

I took his hand, holding it so I didn't trip over my own feet and led him down the front steps to a wide bench under a small row of trees off the drive. The area was still in view of the party, but private enough not to elicit gossip.

We sat side-by-side for a moment before I turned toward him. Unsure, I reached up and slid my fingers toward the nape of his neck. I twisted my fingers through his ponytail and whispered his name, cupping the back of his head and urging his mouth to mine.

God forgive me.

I closed my eyes, focusing on the fuzzy, dizzy feeling in my head from the wine. Everything around me intensified. The feel of the silk and the pressure of the stays on my waist and breasts. Even the air was sensual, the breeze cool and tingly.

I opened for him, his soft lips and tongue dancing with mine. He moaned, his hands sliding around my waist to pull me closer. My dress crushed against his uniform as he held me tighter, mouths devouring mouths. I drew my lips from his and let my head drop back to drag in a clean breath, carelessly giving him my throat and décolleté. He groaned burying his face in the soft skin and swells.

With both hands I urged him up from the no-fly zone, desperately trying to keep this a simple kiss. I cupped his face and let my mouth take his once more before I broke our connection.

With a ragged breath, he gathered me to him. "Who would ever think a man could be roused to such heights? You're like an opiate and I fear I will forget myself. God's teeth, I won't sleep tonight or any other night until I can taste you again."

I eased his shoulders back. "I told you, women have the same passions and desires as men. All it takes is the right man."

Of course, I meant Hunter. The whole time I kissed Alec it was Hunter's face in my mind and heart. It was always Hunter.

Alec sat back with smug smile.

If he only knew.

"I think I need to call it a night, Alec. Everything is blurry and the ground feels like it's moving." I wobbled on my feet and had to grab the side of the bench.

He laughed. "Four glasses of claret will do that, you greedy goose. Let's get you inside. I'll find Mrs. Mac and she can put you to bed."

Leaning heavily on his arm, I snorted. "So, this is what drunk feels like. What if Mrs. Mac isn't around? Peggy's got her jumping through hoops, but that's not going to last long."

"Why not?"

Mrs. Mac came out on the porch and saw Alec half dragging, half carrying me to the steps.

"Lord Almighty, what happened?" she asked, clucking.

"The claret has taken hold of our injured bird," Alec answered trying not to laugh.

I looked at the both of them. "I don't feel so well."

Alec scooped me up in his arms. "Where?" he asked, and Mrs. Mac pointed toward the staircase.

"Top of the stairs and to the left. Second door. I'm right behind you. I just need to grab a few herbs from the kitchen."

Alec took the stairs two and a time and bent to open the door one handed. He walked toward the bed and gently placed me on the coverlet.

"Sit up, love. If you lie down the room will spin even more."

"Alec?"

"Hmmmm."

"Stay with me."

He sank down on the bed beside me and slipped his arm around my shoulders. I let my head fall to his chest and closed my eyes.

"I really like you, Alec. A lot."

His chest shook as he chuckled. "Well, I would hope so after that kiss."

"If kisses are what counts, then I'll wager you like me, too."

He shifted around toward me and lifted my chin, his eyes searching mine. "My dear, not only do I like you, I think I'm in love with you."

His hand still held my face, but I looked away. "If that's true then I need to tell you something. I owe it to you."

Mrs. Mac bounded into the room. "All right, that's enough of that! You, out...and close the door behind you. I need to get these herbs into her, or Miss Phoebe will have a whopper of a headache come morning."

Alec got up to leave, pressing a kiss to my temple. "Whatever you need to tell me can wait. I'll be back on the twenty-fourth."

He nodded to Mrs. MacPherson as he walked to the door. "Take care of my girl," he said and then blew me a kiss.

Chapter 21

I hissed through my teeth, trying to roll over without losing my cookies. "Close the curtains, please!" I said, jerking up the end of my sheet.

"What's wrong, dearie? The light too much for my little drunkard?"

"Not funny," I mumbled from beneath the covers.

She walked to the head of the bed and lifted the edge of the downy blanket, chuckling. "The day is fine and the general and Miss Peggy have been asking for you. If it's any consolation, herself missed breakfast as well, but now it's time for luncheon."

The thought of food turned my stomach inside out and I pushed her hand away. "Tell them I died."

She laughed. "I will do no such thing, however the one thing I will do is make you drink this." She pulled the covers back and held out a pewter cup with a foul-smelling concoction with bits and pieces floating on the top. "Come on, up with you."

"What is it?"

"Never you mind what it is. You'll drink it so the brew can clear the sticky cobwebs and cleanse the fur from your tongue."

I made a face.

"*Aah*, none of that." She sat me up and shoved the cup in my hand. "I'm not budging from here until every last drop is drunk." She crossed her arms in front of her chest, and I sighed.

Pinching my nose, I drained the cup with a grimace, shuddering as I forced the offensive liquid down my throat.

I slumped back and closed my eyes. In seconds, my lids flew open and I ran for the chamber pot throwing up the entire contents of my stomach. When I finally came up for air, Mrs. Mac held out a wet cloth and a cup of weak ale.

"Hair-o-the dog that bit you," she said urging both toward me.

"I don't think I like you anymore."

She laughed. "Perhaps not, but if you stop your complaining long enough to feel your head, you'll see the draft worked."

I sat on the floor and probed my temples. The pounding in my head was gone as were the barbs stabbing at the back of my eyes.

Mrs. Mac nodded with a knowing smile and handed me the cloth and the cup.

I cleaned my face and mouth and then took small sips of ale before rising to my feet to get cleaned up. Mrs. Mac closed the lid to the chamber pot and left me alone to finish.

When I emerged from the bathroom, she was gone but had laid out my clothes. Dressing quickly, I threw my hair up in a messy bun and went downstairs. Stomach still queasy, I didn't want breakfast, but I knew I needed to make an appearance. Maybe I'd get lucky and there would be hot coffee waiting.

Lunch was served on the veranda, a sunny alcove at the back of the house with tall columns and beautiful views of the river. Impressed, I scanned the garden and the gazebo. They were pristine. No one would know there was a party the night before.

I walked through the French doors and the general looked up from his afternoon correspondence.

"Well, well. It looks as though someone had a good time last evening." His smile was too broad and even Peggy chuckled from behind a piece of toast. "Would you care for a bit of potato leek soup?"

I glanced at the tureen and the chunky white liquid inside and my stomach clenched.

"She's greener than the bruises she sported when she first arrived!" He laughed.

"Stop teasing, Benedict. Can't you see she's all a sixes and sevens? Perhaps some coffee, sweeting?"

I nodded, accepting a cup.

"I was going to ask you to ride with me after lunch, but after seeing the state you're in perhaps you'd better stay put. I'll ask Major Franks to accompany me, instead." She turned to the general. "Unless, of course, you need him here with you, dear."

The general shook his head. "No, enjoy the day, please. I have other matters to attend to." He turned to get up, and as he walked around the end of the table he stopped and patted my arm. "The library is at your disposal, my dear. It's quiet, and no one will bother you if you wish to lose yourself in a book."

The library was overly warm, probably from being locked up most days. I walked to the window and opened it a crack for fresh air.

In addition, the general's large desk and the other rich furnishings, there was a telescope set on a high round table in front of the window to the left of the desk.

I scanned the bookshelves lining the far wall across from the hearth, looking for something interesting. My eyes drifted over the titles, many of which were in Latin and French, but nothing sparked so I moved to the two bookshelves behind his desk. They were divided by a large brass framed map and a small credenza holding a decanter of brandy, one of port, and various stemmed glasses.

My eyes moved across the titles and I was about to give up when I saw a familiar name. Nostradamus. *No way*. Chuckling, I glanced at the telescope again. Maybe Benedict Arnold was a fan of reading the stars or looking for portents about the revolution in the quatrains of the sixteenth century occultist.

I slipped the book from the shelf and leafed through it hoping the difficult eighteenth-century font wouldn't give me a worse headache than I already had. I laid the open book on the general's desk. The man had so much correspondence, it was hard to tell what was what, and I had the urge to sit on the floor and make organized piles, but I didn't touch anything. One piece of correspondence caught my eye from beneath a courier's pouch. It wasn't so much the paper itself, but the date listed on the top sheet.

September eleventh.

That date was a red flag for anyone who lived through the first decade of the twenty-first century. The day terror hit from the skies across the United States, bringing fear and death and a war with an unseen force being waged today. I remembered my mother coming to get me from Pre-K because the police evacuated the area around the Kensico Reservoir as federal troops moved in to protect New York City's water supply from a possible attack.

I slid the paper out wondering what our Revolutionary War generals would think about the events of that particular day two hundred years into the future. I dismissed the thought and arbitrarily scanned the letter's content.

I froze.

My heart pounded as I read the ornate cursive. The content had nothing to do with black market supplies or anything the officers at West Point suspected. It was much grander and much more insidious. This letter set the meeting for Benedict Arnold to sell West Point to the British.

The dispatch spoke tentatively of Sir Henry's interest in Arnold's initial naming John Anderson as Arnold's contact in negotiations. Of course, I already knew that to be the alias used by Major John Andre in his dealings with Arnold.

This was the reply Peggy had carried with her from Philadelphia. The letter was written to her from a Joseph Stansbury. I had no idea who he was, but he had to be a loyalist

in cahoots with Arnold. The core of the letter was harmless, but between the looping script and along the margins were brown notations, messages undoubtedly written in organic ink for Arnold's eyes only. Posts he clearly deciphered once Peggy delivered the document.

My hands shook.

The letter requested Arnold send a message to the head of British Naval Forces manning the Hudson River, confirming his arrival at the village of Dobbs Ferry to meet before final negotiations for twenty thousand pounds could be concluded with Sir Henry Clinton, British Commander and Chief in North America.

Twenty thousand pounds? The bastard was selling out his friends and allies for a measly twenty thousand pounds?

I needed to find Arnold's reply. This was not the way this was supposed to go down. Not only did I know the historic record, but I had read Dr. Thacher's eyewitness account in his journal, an account that hadn't happened yet, nor would it likely unless someone monkey wrenched the general's plans.

Arnold needed to supply British Naval Command with his means of transportation down river and the time of his anticipated arrival so British sloops knew not to fire. This was bad. *Very bad.* Arnold was supposed to meet with Andre in Verplanck, New York on September twenty-first, *not* Dobbs Ferry on September eleventh!

I knew the general had to have written his reply, but where? I hunted around for something, anything. An innocuous object, innocent on the outside but used to transport letters one didn't want intercepted.

Margery mentioned hollowed out quills as a common means used during the eighteenth century. Glancing around, I spotted a lone quill sitting on a small silver tray atop the ornate tea table. I picked up the long-feathered pen and turned the quill over in my hand. At first there was nothing about the instrument that seemed unusual, but the weight fest slightly off.

Bingo! I spotted a tiny notch just big enough for the edge of a fingernail between the nib and the shaft. Thank God my fingers were small enough to pluck out the general's letter and replace it with a blank sheet, instead. No information sent. No secure passage given.

I secured the quill and placed it back on the tray. Folding the incriminating letter, I stuck it in my pocket for now. There had to be other correspondence as well and while I had the opportunity, I was going to look. I searched the pile of broad letters on the general's desk, even looked inside the pouch and under other stacks of papers but found nothing, that is until I noticed a single uneven seam along the courier's satchel.

One of the buckskin panels had been carefully sliced, forming two thin layers and the leather meanly re-stitched. Inside, tucked between the folds of the hidden pocket were the other communications.

An earlier dispatch negotiated terms for compensation for intelligence given to the British about the anticipated arrival of the French fleet in Newport. That was six weeks ago.

Another offered the positioning of troops along with the illegal sale of supplies. So he was black marketing his men and their well-being.

Christ. This dude had been selling us out for months and I wondered if Alec or any of Washington's council suspected Arnold at all. The fact Arnold left the letters intact, albeit hidden, spoke not only of his arrogance, but his disdain for the country he supposedly loved and served.

Events were unfolding just as Hulda predicted, and the old woman's words came back. *...you must do so when she is desperate. When she has lost almost everything and is too terrified to care.*

I realized it was up to me to find the means to an end. I needed to create a desperate enough diversion to be the catalyst that put historic events into action precisely as they were meant

to unfold—just as Hulda had done for centuries from her ethereal place between the dark and the light.

I understood now why the fates had put the compass in my path. It was a physical metaphor. *I* was Agent 355. *Go figure.* No wonder the history books couldn't identify her... I hadn't been born yet.

Hulda was right. Time *was* a giant circle. A Catch 22.

God, I hated the universe sometimes.

I exhaled. Okay, fates, you win. But if I have to be Agent 355 the least you could have done was give me a cellphone in my shoe like *Get Smart* or a glowing finger like *ET* so I could phone home.

I put all correspondence back where I found it and picked up the book of Nostradamus's quatrains. After closing the library door, I walked down the stairs to the kitchen and grabbed an apple before heading into the orchard to read.

What was I supposed to do now? *Wait.* It was all I could do.

If the general was in a foul temper tomorrow evening, then I would know my little switcheroo worked, if not I would have to get a message to Alec and Dr. Thacher that a British attack on the fort was imminent. I patted the proof sitting in my pocket. Either way, I wasn't going to let Arnold get away with selling out people I had come to love and respect.

A chill had crept into the evening air with a nip of fall. Peggy and I sat in the drawing room playing cards while a footman tended the hearth. The smell of the fire and the sputter and pop of the wood as it caught flame, provided a universal comfort. I was teaching her to play Five Card Stud.

Loud voices drifted in from the hall and foyer and Peggy put down her cards and went to the door. "Whatever is the matter?"

Without a word, the general brushed past his aide and thumped up the stairs to the master bedroom, slamming the door. Both Peggy and I jumped at the antagonistic sound.

Major Franks shook his head. "My apologies, Mrs. Arnold. Our supply run down the Hudson was not as successful as we hoped."

"Why ever not? The scarcity of supplies is dire, not only at the house but at the fort, as well."

He nodded. "Yes, ma'am, but the redcoats fired on our sloop. We barely made it 'round to safety. Evasive maneuvers were necessary and I'm afraid we lost a few good men in the process."

"Oh my. No wonder Benedict is so upset."

Guilt slashed across my chest. People were dead because I took that letter. I closed my eyes. What else was I supposed to do? *Supply run, my ass.* If I didn't avert Arnold's meeting, hundreds of others would've died. I kicked off my shoes and tucked my feet under my legs. Never in my life did I think the words collateral damage would have such a firsthand meaning.

Peggy came back in and sat, absently picking up her cards. I understood why she was preoccupied. If things didn't go well, she and Benedict would have no money and the threat of discovery would linger ominously. They could lose everything. She was worried, but she wasn't desperate. Clearly the two hadn't yet played their best hand.

I glanced at the cards in my hand and almost burst out laughing—all aces and hearts—two threes and a five. *3-3-5.* Crappy cards for poker, but a winning hand for portent.

Peggy made her excuses and went up to tend to her husband. I nodded to the maid that came in to clear the dessert dishes and said goodnight to Major Franks pouring himself a stiff whiskey.

I climbed the stairs quietly, listening for loud conversation or the sound of crying. I knew this blow wasn't good for the general, and I hoped he wouldn't take his frustrations out on his

wife. I would talk to Peggy in the morning. Maybe I could glean more information that way.

The door to my bedroom was ajar, and my guard went up. This game was no longer a charade. My life, the life of my family and the world as I knew it...*I knew it*...lay in the balance.

Mrs. MacPherson was in the room. She cracked the window slightly and had laid a fire which snapped and sputtered in the grate. Her trunk was open on the settee at the foot of the bed and she was packing.

"What are you doing?" I asked closing the door behind me.

She looked across her shoulder. "I'm going back to the fort tomorrow. You're fine, sweetheart, completely recovered with a bright future ahead of you. Besides, the doctor needs me."

She seemed unhappy, and in the two months since I arrived, I had never known Ferne MacPherson to be downhearted about anything.

"What happened?"

She glanced at me again. She didn't say a word, just shook her head.

"Mrs. Mac, to use your own words, I will brook no argument from you, now tell me. What happened?"

"Douglas Campbell is dead."

"Oh my God, no. How? When?"

"This morning. He was aboard the sloop when General Arnold went for supplies. He was hit with gun mortar. They managed to get him back to the hospital, but the wound was in his gut. There was nothing Dr. Thacher could do."

The older woman dissolved into tears and sunk down onto the settee beside her trunk. I pulled the trunk from the small couch and sat beside her. Now it was my turn to hold her, to comfort her.

"He was such a dear man." She sniffed wiping her eyes. "Since being here, he and I developed a...a...friendship." She hung her head again, her shoulders shaking.

"I'm sure he was happy then. Who wouldn't be, knowing they were loved by you? I'm happy knowing that I've won a special place in your heart, and I truly liked the sergeant."

She looked up, her face wet and her eyes bright even through her tears. She patted my hand. "He was very, very fond of you, too." She laughed, wiping the end of her nose with her finger. "Whenever we talked of you, we both referred to you as 'our girl.' You were that special to him." She snuck her arm around my waist. "To me, too."

I sat with my arms around her for a while, letting her reminisce. She laughed and cried and, in the end, got up with her normal exuberance and pushed the trunk to the corner.

"I can help you finish packing later or in the morning."

She shook her head. "Alexander isn't back for another week and a half. The doctor can make do without me until then. Douglas wouldn't have wanted me to run like a scared rabbit. He'd want me to stay to make sure our girl had every chance to be with the man she loved. I know I would."

She smiled and opened her arms and I went to her. Ferne MacPherson was one person my heart would ache for once I got home…to the real man I loved. Hunter.

It was late. I had no idea where Mrs. Mac had gone, but my best guess she needed time alone to grieve. Either that or she and Mrs. Gerrittsen split a bottle and drinking away their sorrows toasting Sergeant Douglas Campbell away from prying, judgmental eyes.

I sat in front of the fire with my pack. I hadn't looked at it in weeks, not since I took my mother's vial with me into the orchard. My shoes and the leather pouch that held the compass were all that was left. I had used the shreds of my clothing for sanitary purposes, even giving a few of my unused strips to Lettie for her time of the month.

The leather pouch felt warm to the touch and I opened the top and pulled the antique from the inside. Of course, it wasn't an antique anymore. It was new and looked it.

The back was smooth. Not a scratch on it, and not a word in inscription. The last time I was in town, I saw the blacksmith's apprentice working on a piece of silver with what looked like a very, very sharp knife. I asked him what he was doing, and he said it was a wedding gift and the bride wanted the date added. Eighteenth century engraving. Who knew?

Maybe Mrs. Mac would come with me to town in the next day or so if I told her I wanted to have the metal case inscribed for Alec. With Sergeant Campbell's death, the last thing I wanted was to make her unhappy. Maybe it would be a project for her, and it would take her mind off her sadness.

Alec had been wonderful to me since I arrived, risking much. I had nothing to give him in return and wasn't about to give him the one gift he'd take in a heartbeat. No, the compass would have to do as a token from me to him.

I almost opened the metal case thinking to use the reflective inside surface to scry for Hunter, but Hulda's warning rang deep through my mind. What if who I conjured wasn't him? She wasn't around to help, I knew it. I felt it. I closed my eyes and sent my love out again into the cosmos, hoping he felt it on the wind.

The bedroom windows were closed, but the temperature had dropped outside giving the room a chilly feel. Fog rolled through the orchard and the slopes leading toward the river along the grounds.

I shivered, and closed the bedroom door behind me, swinging a knit shawl over my shoulders and tying it in front like I had learned to do with cotton fichus.

The dress I wore was a hand-me-down from Peggy, so it wasn't really new, but I liked it and with the weather turning chilly so fast, the heavier fabric made a difference in comfort.

The overskirt was a deep forest green, and the bodice and trim along the hem, a pretty green and blue plaid. I used the cream silk petticoat from my other dress and the outfit was complete. It had taken two months, but I was finally at ease in the long skirts of the day, and had come to enjoy the feminine feel of them

Heading toward the stairs, I stopped at the sound of crying. It came from the master bedroom and I hesitated unsure if I should knock or head to the breakfast room.

A door slammed and one of the servants ran from Peggy's door, upset.

"What's the matter? Is it the baby?"

She shook her head. "That woman is the devil." She didn't say another word, simply clamored down the stairs, tears on her cheeks.

I rolled my eyes and took a step down off the landing when the door opened again. I turned and saw Peggy standing in the entrance to her rooms in a pair of stockings and stays and nothing else. She looked awful. Almost crazy. Her face puffy and eyes red.

"Peggy, for God's sake, put some clothes on. Are you ill?" I climbed the stairs and marched over taking her by the arm to steer her back into her rooms.

She stood with half her junk hanging out, pulling at the hair on her head. "I can't stand this godforsaken war one more minute! Everything I want, all my hopes and dreams are gone because of it. Dashed!"

I got her dressing gown, held it out to her.

"No! Get that away from me."

I shook the robe again. "I will not talk to you or help you in anyway until you cover yourself and stop acting like a nut job!"

She stopped ranting and blinked at me. "What's a nut job?"

"Someone mad as a hatter. You are! Mad as a hatter."

She sank onto one of her plush chairs and laughed, but in a matter of moments her laughter turned to tears.

I tossed the robe at her and threw my hands in the air. "This entire house is under a dark cloud. First, Sergeant Campbell is killed, and Mrs. Mac is inconsolable, your maid swears you're the devil and runs sobbing from your rooms, and now you. It's an epidemic of sadness!"

Peggy wiped her eyes and her nose on the robe's sleeve.

I pointed at the trace of shiny wet she left in a line across the blue satin. "Peggy, that's disgusting. Look what you did to that sleeve." I stalked to her dresser and pulled open a drawer and dragged out one of a hundred handkerchiefs. Walking it over to her I unfolded it and flapped in in front of her face.

"Clean your face and tell me what is at the heart of this tempest."

She sniffed, wiping her face on the hankie. "Heart is right. Mine is broken."

"Why? What happened? I saw the general this morning and he actually seemed in good spirits."

It was not a lie, though his chipper mood did put my guard up. If he was in good spirits that meant something else was up. Time was growing short and I needed another metaphysical intervention.

"Can I ask you something, Phoebe?"

I nodded.

"Who do you want to win this bloody war?"

I considered her and her puffy face. It was bite the bullet time. "Why do you ask?"

She lifted her arms and let them fall. "Everyone I know is too scared to say what they think or how they feel. If you're a patriot, then you suffer at the hands of the British and if you're a tory you're considered a traitor to your own kind. But what everyone forgets is we are all British subjects. I like the comfort

of the crown and a rich motherland. I hate the unknown, and that's all this war offers if we win our freedom from England.

"The Burritt family is split. Five brothers—one loyalist and four patriots." She looked at me, her eyes searching. "Which side do you hail from?"

I inhaled and let out a rough breath. This would either hang me or save me. "General Daniel Burritt. He fought with General Burgoyne at Saratoga."

She slammed her hands on her lap. "I knew it! I told Benedict! Oh, thank heavens."

"Is that why you've been crying? Because of the war?"

She shook her head. "No, because of this." She got up, shoving her arms into her dressing gown and after tying the belt she moved to her desk and took a letter from the top drawer.

"My green-eyed monster."

I didn't understand at first, but then I remembered what she said about getting Benedict to pay her more heed.

"It's all right. You may read it."

I unfolded the letter.

My dearest love,

I ardently long to see you, but time is a clever thief and alas I cannot secure a safe place for our meeting. I have orders to travel north, and the path is arduous. In truth, my task will take me be but miles from you, but time is of the essence. I board the Vulture to sail for points off Kings Ferry on Wednesday evening next. I possess every hope to journey south again to New York by Thursday latest. If negotiations fail, expect another message, post haste.

Until we meet again, I remain lovingly thine,

J.

"I see why you're upset, but it's clear he loves you. Does Benedict know?" I had to ask.

She lifted one shoulder and let it drop. "Yes and no. He was an old flame of mine when Philadelphia was under British control. It was before Benedict and I met."

"He's a British officer, then?"

She nodded.

I knew before asking that J stood for John Andre or his alias John Anderson, and the sloop he was boarding was the Vulture. The same ship the Americans stationed at Verplanck Point would fire upon, thus leaving Andre stranded in Haverstraw at the house of Joshua Hett Smith during his negotiations with Arnold, the same Joshua I saw at the Black Bear Tavern weeks ago when plans for this meeting heated.

"Can't you write him? It's only the fourteenth. He says he's not leaving until Wednesday next. That's a week. What if you were to meet him on his way back to New York?"

She shook her head. "He'll be aboard the sloop." She chewed on the end of her finger. "I did write something, but I daren't show you."

I shrugged. "It's up to you, but you've trusted me thus far…"

She dug another letter from the drawer and shoved it at me.

My love,

My heart is broken. I can no longer endure the lonely days and the endless feigned love and respect for the man whose name I share. I have done my duty to him and my family and have borne him a son. My own spirit rebels against even the natural inclination of motherhood for the simple truth that the child isn't of your flesh. Oh, that he was. For a while I fostered hope that our couplings would have borne fruit that I might have a small piece of you, but it was not to be. The child belongs to my husband, of that I am sure.

I will come to you even though I walk through gunfire or worse, and when reunited, the gates of hell will open for my traitorous spouse. Arrest and death will be his due and then we can celebrate a true union of our own.

Your tender, PS.

I stared at the formal words, stunned. Finally, I looked up at her. I didn't know how to respond to such spiteful content. This wasn't love, this was obsession. A crazy, rabbit-boiling-on-the-stove fatal attraction.

"Well?" she prompted.

I lifted my hand still holding the note and let it fall to my lap. "You can't send this."

She snatched the paper from my hand, her frantic eyes scanning every word. "Why ever not? It's perfect."

I shook my head. "No, Peggy. It's not perfect. Do you really think this man wants to hear that you despise your own child? An innocent babe? Where do you think his thoughts will lead?"

She sank into a chair beside me. "That's true." She chewed on her finger again. "What am I to do, then?"

I covered her hand with mine. "Wait. He said he'll contact you again soon. I'm sure we will find a way to work this out."

She looked at me strangely. "We?"

I nodded. "Of course. You'll never convince the general to let you go anywhere unaccompanied. Just think of me as your wingman."

She laughed. "I don't know what that means, but I like the way it sounds. On wings we fly, wingman mine." She giggled.

Chapter 22

September 21ˢᵗ
Robinson House

"Phoebe!"

My door banged open and Peggy ran in waving a letter. She was practically panting, and tossed herself onto my bed, the dispatch pressed to her breast.

"Let me guess. A messenger came with private correspondence meant for your eyes only?"

She squealed and jumped up from the coverlet. "Yes, you goose! He wrote."

She ripped open the seal and scanned the few brief lines.

"What?"

She held up her hand and then her fingers went to her mouth.

"Is everything all right?"

She looked at me. "Yes and no. His task ran late, and he wasn't able to board his sloop to head back to New York. He had to spend the night in Haverstraw, wherever that is. He's traveling over land and sent this letter with the ferryman when he crossed from Stony Point." She paused. "Heavens, he was on the West Point side." She looked at me her face stricken.

"Is that bad?" I asked feigning ignorance. "Clearly he's fine or the letter wouldn't have reached you."

She nodded, and then glanced at the next lines. "He's traveling by horse and plans to stop in no man's land at Tarrytown for a fresh horse before traveling south to White Plains."

I didn't say a word, but I knew what was about to happen. He would be stopped by three skinners just a short distance from the safety of British controlled roads.

Peggy was intent on her letter, and I looked away, pacing. This was the only variable out of my control. From my place at Robinson House, I could keep tabs on events in the area, and through Mrs. Mac, make sure the men at West Point kept watch for anything out of the ordinary, like a certain British sloop loitering off Kings Ferry as far as Teller's Point.

In that respect, the hardboiled philosophy of, *if you see something, say something,* courtesy of the events of Sept 11, 2001 and its aftermath, worked as well in the eighteenth century as it did in modern times. I simply communicated that viewpoint to the officers of West Point in 1780. The fact Colonel James Livingston, ranking Continental Army officer at Verplank's Point, saw fit to fire on the Vulture proved how well the philosophy translated.

I walked toward her with my arms crossed and gave her a conspiratorial wink. "You know very well, even if the general doesn't shower you with attention, he still keeps up appearances and showers you with gifts."

"And?"

"So, what if you and I were to plan a shopping trip to a wonderful little dressmaker in Tarrytown at the same time your young man is set to be there to water his horse?" I nodded as the idea bloomed.

She clapped her hands together in delight. "When?"

I unfolded my arms and gestured wide. "Tomorrow, of course. We'll need enough travel time to head south and you'll have to meet with a dressmaker to keep up the charade. Your young man will probably arrive tomorrow evening, maybe

earlier if he's lucky and doesn't meet with any untoward delays."

She jumped up. "I'll speak to Benedict straight away." She ran to the door and then stopped. "Is there truly a dressmaker in Tarrytown?"

I nodded. "Yes, the same one who sent your dress the night of your party."

She clapped again. "I feel like Helen of Troy!"

Chapter 23

Afternoon
September 22ⁿᵈ
Tarrytown, NY

The carriage hurried down the Albany Post Road. Peggy, I, as well as Mrs. MacPherson sat quietly as the hours passed. Watching the scenery outside the carriage window I found myself amazed at how long this journey took. The twenty-five miles between modern day Garrison and Tarrytown would take four hours to travel by carriage when it was only a matter of twenty minutes by car.

Peggy pitched a fit when the general refused her no more than two horses. She flounced out of the house and took four of his best mares, basically thumbing her nose at him in front of the entire staff. Nothing was going to keep her from meeting her lover.

She chose the two footmen who would escort us, men I hadn't seen before. I asked Mrs. Mac if she knew them from West Point, but she shook her head no. Peggy had brought some of her staff with her from Philadelphia, so I chalked them up as part of her Pennsylvania entourage. Neither spoke, which I found unusual. The pair simply nodded whenever Peggy barked.

Four horses meant we didn't need to stop for long to water them. Even that short break brought out the worst in Peggy, her

impatience and anxiety gnawing at her and everyone else in the process.

Mrs. Gerrittsen packed Peggy's favorite lunch of cold chicken and apple pie. We ate in silence and by the time tea time rolled around, the carriage had parked in front of the Knightsbridge Inn off the Post Road in Tarrytown.

Peggy practically bounced out of the carriage, leaving the footmen to carry our bags inside.

"Isn't this quaint?" she exclaimed.

I rolled my eyes, and Mrs. Mac bit her cheek not to laugh. We could have stayed in a barn and Peggy wouldn't have noticed. The minute we crossed into Tarrytown a giddy euphoria came over her.

We signed the register and the proprietor showed us to our rooms. They were small and cramped. Peggy had her own, of course, while Mrs. Mac and I shared a bed that looked no bigger than an oversized twin and what I wouldn't do for a can of Lysol. Once I got home, I would never complain about chores again.

"I hope the mattress is fresh or we'll both sport bites galore tomorrow."

"What do you mean?"

"Bedbugs. Mrs. Gerrittsen and I have a schedule to ensure the rugs are beaten and the feathers maintained in the pillows and beds, but not everyone does."

"I think I'll sleep in the carriage tonight."

She laughed. "I thought as much knowing you, so I brought ticking and sheets from home. Herself can suffer her bites, alone." She gave the adjoining wall between rooms a dirty look.

"What time are you meeting with the dressmaker in the morning?"

I shrugged. "I'm not. Peggy made her own arrangements."

She narrowed her eyes at me. "We're not here for dresses are we."

I shook my head. "Peggy is meeting someone."

She frowned, dragging sheets from her small trunk. "I don't want to know about it." Her face was not happy with the situation, and she snapped the sheets, trudging around the bed as though all hell marched along with her annoyance.

"Mrs. Mac?"

She stopped, hands on her hips. "I'm not in the mood to talk now, Phoebe. I don't know what to make of your involvement with this liaison d'amour, but I don't like it."

"I'm not here to help Peggy cuckold her husband. Believe me. Her silly affair is just a means to an end. I can't explain, but there are important workings going on and I have to see them through. If I don't, the consequences will be so far reaching you cannot imagine. Many people will suffer and for a very long time."

She walked toward me and rested her hand on my cheek. "You're in trouble aren't you, my girl."

I shrugged, because I knew I couldn't answer her.

She nodded watching the emotions play on my face, speaking what I couldn't. "Oh, yes. You're not only in trouble, but you're in over your head."

I didn't answer and she didn't push the issue, just watched me closely. If I had to I would confide in her, telling Mrs. Mac the whole story and let the chips fall where they may. The thought of telling her filled me with a sense of relief. If anything, at least one person would know my real name.

The evening dragged on and Peggy could barely eat for her nerves. I reminded her she had to make at least some pretense of meeting with the dressmaker and she sent word, scheduling a visit at the woman's shop for eleven a.m.

I knew she'd never make that appointment. If everything went as scheduled, John Andre would be stopped and arrested at nine a.m. I would personally make sure Peggy heard the news. She never once told me her lover's name, so telling her a British spy was caught in town would seem innocent gossip. The hardest part would be getting her back to Robinson House,

so the last part of my nightmare could come to fruition and maybe send me home.

Wee hours
September 23ⁿᵈ
Tarrytown, NY

It was well past midnight when Mrs. MacPherson finally drifted off to sleep. I crept out of bed and dug in the bottom of her trunk for my pack. From the general's own closet, I stole a pair of black buckled shoes, a pair of breeches, a cotton shirt and jacket along with a plain tricorn hat. All I can say is thank God the man wasn't overly tall.

Dressing quickly, I French braided my hair and tied it with two ribbons, one at the nape of my neck and the other at the base of the tail. My waist was significantly smaller than the general's, but an extra-long piece of ribbon worked double-duty as a belt hidden under the dark blue jacket. I stuck the hat on my head and spared a glance for Mrs. Mac.

If all went well, I would be back in this room by dawn.

The worst tavern in town was a place called the Ferry House, or so Peggy's footmen said. Turned out they only shut up around her. No small wonder.

The tavern was close to the river and frequented by ragtag militia whose volunteer fighting status elevated them to a hair above highwaymen. I needed to find three specific men: *Isaac Van Wart, John Paulding,* and *David Williams.*

Historic record gave no clue what the men did the night before Andre's capture, but their own affidavits after the fact claimed they were skulking in the area. Every student in Sleepy Hollow High School knew the story of the three local farm boys and their claim to fame in helping bring down the blackest of

treasonous acts and saving West Point and even General Washington himself.

Everyone also knew the three were cut-ups, in fact, Paulding had done time in a British military prison for constant trouble with the Tories and Davey Williams had been run out of town on a charge of stealing cows.

Patriots, yes, but also most likely skinners. Paulding stated in his testimony they were laying by the side of the road for about an hour and half before Andre crossed their path. My gut said they were drinking all night and looking for a rich traveler to pluck, and the place to ready them for that was The Ferry House.

I slipped from the room, taking the pistol Alec left for me with a note to keep the gun by my bedside while he was away. I'd probably end up shooting myself in the foot, but hey. Having it was better than not, considering where I headed.

With the light of the full moon, the street wasn't as dark as I expected. I kept to the corners and the shadows working my way toward the river. Most of the homes were dark and the only sound, the call of ground birds disturbed by the scuttle of animals through the underbrush.

I walked on tip toe, covering my own mouth to stop from screaming when a pair of legs stretched out across my path from a darkened doorway. The sound of soft snoring followed, and I peered around the edge of the entry to see a slovenly man passed out, the flask still in his hand.

I closed my eyes and exhaled, issuing a silent prayer hoping that was the only surprise I'd encounter tonight.

Lights and music drifted from the bottom of the hill and I glanced ahead. From my vantage point, the moonlight on the river looked beautiful and I couldn't help but wonder if this steep slope was the origin of modern day Main Street in Sleepy Hollow.

The sound of men's voices grew louder the closer I got, and adrenaline slicked its way through my veins with a chaser of

unease and a steamy helping of self-doubt. I slowed my pace, but my heart still raced in my chest.

What makes you think you can pull this off on your own? You're a lone woman outside the eighteenth-century equivalent of a biker bar. What are you thinking?

I shook myself out of my uncertainty with the reminder if I didn't do this there would be no home and family to return to. The tavern loomed, its smell preceding it as I walked toward the front entrance. An arched sign with the image of a ferry and a mug of ale carved on its front swung from two chains. A light breeze from the river making it squeak as it rocked back and forth. Oil lamps on either side of the main entrance, smoked, sending curls of gray puffs into the chilly night air.

Hand on the door, I swallowed hard and entered the establishment.

There weren't as many patrons as I expected, but then again it was almost two a.m. I needed to find Paulding first, and then convince him to find his friends and take on this mission.

My eyes scanned the place. One row of dirty tables lined the far wall while another row took the center of the room. A scratched and worn bar stretched across one whole side, with large tap barrels stacked along the wall behind the counter. Dark bottles lined the spaces in between and a row of ceramic and pewter mugs hung from hooks along a long cord above the bar.

I walked to the counter and swallowed. "Excuse me. I'm looking for John Paulding."

The barkeep wiped his hands on his apron, and then picked up a mug before filling it from one of the kegs. He looked me up and down and then took a deep draught.

"What do you possibly want with Johnny…lad?" His eyes roved over me again.

His sarcastic tone wasn't lost on me, and neither was the way his tongue poked into his cheek. "Please, I need to speak with him. It's urgent."

He nodded, taking another sip. "That'll be hard considering he's dead."

I shook my head, disbelief edging into my chest. "I...how? When?"

Seeing my stricken face, he guffawed, slapping the bar's rough counter. "Yer face...laddie. Oh, if you weren't such a wheedling, I'd offer you a drink for giving me such a good laugh tonight." He wiped his mouth on his sleeve. "Now be off with you."

I turned from the bar realizing the bartender was not going to help and so it seemed no one else either.

"Were do you think yer headed?"

The question came from a rough looking lout standing directly in front of me. I stepped to the side only to have him step as well, blocking my path. I moved again and so did he.

"Stand aside, I'm here on business of grave importance. I need to locate a man named John Paulding."

He grinned at me. "I know Johnny. Come with me and I'll bring you to him...laddie." He winked at another man sitting at one of the center tables. He got up and gestured for me to follow him outside.

My inner warning bells were screaming for me to run. I walked toward the door, one of them in front and the other behind. This was bad.

We stepped outside and I turned to bolt, but a meaty hand shot out grabbing my jacket. My hat fell from my head and loose strands of hair fell from my braid framing my face.

"I..." My voice cracked and panic sliced up my chest nearly cutting off my air.

"Curious, Thomas, don'tcha ken? It squeaks like a lass but is dressed like a lad."

"Mayhap we should take a peek at what's hiding beneath those fancy breeches. Might be we'll get a nice furry surprise inside."

The telltale click of a gun's hammer sounded in the dark. "Leave her be or the only surprise you'll get is a bullet."

The men wheeled around.

Mrs. Mac stood, scowl on her face and pistol in hand pointed at them.

"Ah, look, it's the lassie's ma, well, yer welcome to join the party too, m'lady." The one called Thomas cackled. He grabbed me and Mrs. Mac lurched forward, giving the other time to grab her gun. The hammer hit and the shot rang out and Mrs. Mac crumpled to the ground.

"No!" I screamed struggling to get to her.

They left her on the ground in the mud to die, dragging me off toward the woods. She lifted one arm toward me and then slumped down. Tears stung my eyes, but I couldn't cry. I needed to fight. Fight or die.

In the dark of the trees, Thomas dragged me through to the base of a tree and a soft pile of pine needles. He tossed me to the ground and my breath left my body in a fast whoosh as my back hit the base of the tree.

"A young lass at a tavern in the middle of the night is looking for one thing, and a lass who shows up dressed as a lad is looking for even more and I'm gonna give it to you." He leered at me, peeling his coat from his shoulders.

I learned one important thing from Alec that day by the oak tree. Never show your hand. I clicked the hammer on my pistol and waited until both his arms were pinned inside their sleeves as he struggled to shrug his jacket from his bulk.

I lifted the gun and pointed the barrel at his soft middle. "This is what I came for!" I pulled the trigger. The gun exploded in my hand, my body jerking back against the tree, slamming my head. Hot pain shot through to my shoulder, my arm juddered and numb from the recoil, but my bullet hit its mark.

A wide crimson stain spread across the man's chest and thickset belly and he fell forward. I twisted out of the way and

gathered my wits looking for his cohort, but he was nowhere to be seen.

I scrambled to my feet and ran back to the tavern. Mrs. Mac lay in a puddle of her own blood, her body already cold. Hot tears streamed down my face as I pulled her limp form onto my lap and rocked her as she had done so many times with me.

I smoothed her hair away from her face and closed her eyes. "I hope you're with Douglas, now." I lowered my head to hers and wept until I had no more tears.

I needed to get up and find Paulding, Van Wart, and Williams more now than before. There was no way I was going to let Mrs. Mac die in vain. Forget all the other good it would do, I needed to do this for her.

I wiped my eyes and nose on my sleeve and got to my feet. I hoisted her body the best I could and moved her against the wall beside one of the tavern's front windows.

Patrons came out at this point, having heard the commotion but still taking time to finish their pints. Effing losers.

"Ah, no! Now the constable will be here along with the militia," the bartender said annoyed.

I whirled on my heels. "A good woman is dead because of you! You wouldn't help me when I asked!"

His face knotted and he lifted his knuckles as if to backhand me, but I took the butt of Alec's pistol and swung it wide smacking him across the temple. He went down like a sack of meal.

Chest heaving, I spun toward the rest. "Anyone else?"

A man stepped forward and I lifted the gun to strike again, but he raised both hands. "Please, miss. I'm John Paulding, and I am so very sorry for all this."

He turned and gestured for a few of the men to carry Mrs. Mac's body inside, waving for me to follow.

They laid her across a bench, and someone covered her with an old blanket. They left the bartender in the mud outside, no one caring to move him.

I sat with John at one of the tables and someone got me a pint of something cold and alcoholic. I drained half the cup, my nerves frayed.

"What do you want with me, miss...?"

I looked out the window and saw it was still dark yet. We had time and hopefully the rest of the night would make this sacrifice well worth the price.

"My name is of no importance. I am here because there is a plot to give control of West Point to the British." I looked at Paulding, and it was then I realized he wore the coat of a Hessian, the same blue coat I saw on the headless spirit in the Old Dutch Church burial ground the previous Halloween.

"You have been chosen to arrest the spy. He'll be dressed in civilian clothing and carrying papers signed by General Arnold. It's a conspiracy to get him through the American lines. He's managed to avoid militia patrols and bluff his way through any that questioned him."

He cocked his head. "And how does a slip of a girl in lad's clothing know all this?"

"I was just going to ask the same question."

Paulding and I both turned, and within a moment he was out of his seat giving the man a hug. "Ike, you devil. When did you get back?"

"Just tonight. So, is there a profit in this mystery, lass, or are you out tonight just for folly?"

I glanced at my cup. "Death of people you love is never folly, sir."

Paulding filled him in on Mrs. Mac and what happened with the men in the woods.

"I'm sorry for your loss, lass. Now tell us how you come to know this and why do you want John for the job?"

"And your name, sir?"

"Isaac Van Wart...Ike."

I glossed over the information and how I obtained it as best I could without letting the cat out of the bag. The last thing I

needed was for Arnold to get away sooner than expected. Everything had to be exact. Mrs. Mac's life was worth that much at least.

"You'll need a third person. I have a name and you tell me if you agree. Davey Williams."

Paulding nodded. "He's back as well and staying at his family's farm. We can get him before time and head over to where exactly?"

"Wylie's Swamp. It's almost dawn. The man you seek is set to pass at nine a.m. The man will be traveling under the name of John Anderson, but it's an alias. You'll find the papers in his boot. Lie in wait for him as I've said, just don't rob the man. He'll tempt you like the devil temped our Lord, offering you money and goods beyond measure if you let him go, but don't. We're counting on you." I looked at Paulding.

"You escaped from a military prison under British control. Imagine what will be in store for us all if West Point is given over. The war will be lost. You do this well and keep each other steadfast, you will be heroes called to give testimony to George Washington himself."

"What proof do we have this isn't some elaborate plan to discredit the local militia or drag Johnny back to prison?" Van Wart asked, skepticism edging his voice.

I inhaled. "How familiar are you with the intelligence workings under General Washington?"

The two looked at each other. "I've heard things," Paulding answered.

"Then all you need to know when the Continental Army takes your affidavit is that you got the information from a woman called 355."

The two looked and each other.

"When you bring John Anderson to town, you'll hand him over to the authorities, but they will try to send him back to West Point because of the papers he carries. You cannot allow

this to transpire. The head of this treasonous snake resides at West Point. Call in Benjamin Tallmadge."

Paulding sucked in a breath at the mention of the Continental Army spymaster.

I nodded. "Alert him immediately. He will know what to do and how to prevent this snake from slithering away. If Tallmadge asks how you know what you do, again tell him you were tipped by Agent 355."

I bid the two goodbye as dawn broke, asking only that they arrange for the men to help me bury Mrs. Mac and mark her grave until I could come back and have her properly interred.

Chapter 24

September 24ⁿᵈ
Albany Post Road
en route to Robinson House

"You haven't said a word since we left Tarrytown. Will you please tell me what happened?"

Peggy sat mute as the carriage trundled north. Of course, I knew what happened.

We were at the dress shop, Peggy pinned in a seamstress's drape when the uproar exploded in the square.

The seamstress's assistant ran into the street to find out what had happened.

There was John Andre, arms tied behind his back, sweating and dejected, clearly afraid for his life. People poured into the main street, the three local boys grim faced yet resolute that the man they had in tow was not only an officer of the Crown, but a spy.

The servant rushed back in, red faced and out of breath but with a voracious gleam in her eye as she recounted the story. Peggy was just as hungry for the news, gasping and flushed as the details emerged, that is until she heard the name.

"It's a lie!" she screeched, pulling the drape from her shoulders. She yanked me behind the curtain and ordered me to lace her immediately.

As soon as she was decent enough to step into the street, she gathered her things and bid the woman goodbye, shooting the assistant dagger eyes as though she was responsible for the angst now clawing at her heart. Little did she know the woman responsible was walking arm and arm beside her at a clipped pace back to the inn.

"Why did we race from the inn like the devil was on our heels? You wouldn't even wait for Mrs. MacPherson to return from her family visit."

"Mrs. MacPherson will have plenty of means to return to Robinson House. I left word and a purse full of money with the proprietor."

I exhaled. "I know that. I was there, remember? What I want to know is why?"

She clamped her mouth shut and didn't say a word for the next three hours.

It was well past dinner when we pulled into the circular drive. Peggy barely let the carriage come to a halt before she threw the door open and swept out of the coach.

A house footman rushed up to help with the bags and she grabbed his arm. "Where is the general? I need to speak to him immediately."

He shook his head. "He's across at the fort."

She exhaled hard, shoving loose strands of blond hair off her forehead. "Well, when is he due back?"

"He said not until very late. He's having dinner at the Red House and then they are going over preparations for General Washington's visit tomorrow. He's inspecting the fortifications and General Arnold wants the men to run drills until flawless."

She mashed her lips together and flounced into the house. At the door she turned to me standing on the gravel with the bags. "Have them bring my bags up but leave them in the hallway. I am not to be disturbed for anything short of fire or death."

With a flare of skirt, she marched inside and up the stairs, the door slam heard even from the front yard.

I went to my room alone and stayed there. After I undressed and washed up, I walked around the room picking up odds and ends. I just couldn't settle myself.

Every place I looked reminded me of Mrs. Mac. I found her mobcap and held it to my heart. She was the one person throughout this entire ordeal I could have trusted with the truth and I grieved for her, and for the chance I missed to tell who I really was.

I curled up in bed and tried to coax sleep, but it was a wasted effort. Grief and anxiety didn't make for relaxing bedfellows.

A soft knock got me out of bed, and I padded barefoot to the door with nothing but a shawl across my shoulders.

"Yes?" I answered, turning the knob and opening to the cold hallway.

"Can I bank the fire, miss?" the chambermaid asked.

I nodded, stepping aside.

She laid fresh logs on the grate and stuffed woolen strips and hay before lighting the kindling with the stiff cloth match and fire from the candle she carried with her.

Once done, she nodded and went to leave but stopped. "Oh, and this came today." She held out a letter with my alias scribbled across the front.

I closed the door behind the maid and went to sit on the bed. I ripped open the note and unfolded the paper inside.

My dearest Phoebe,

My heart races with the thought of seeing you again. I will be breathless with anticipation until I arrive at Robinson House tomorrow for breakfast with George Washington and the Marquis di Lafayette.

I sincerely hope you will join us.

My love and service await you,

Alec

He'd be here for breakfast tomorrow and so will I, but Arnold will be rowing his way to the Vulture and his life as an exile.

I took Mrs. Mac's mobcap and crawled under the covers and cried myself to sleep.

Morning
September 25ⁿᵈ
Robinson House

The sun rose over the horizon drying the cold dew and clearing the ground fog that swirled across the back of the house and lower orchards.

"It's only a matter of hours, now," I thought as I dressed.

I wore the blue cotton day dress Mrs. MacPherson sewed for me. I needed to feel her close, and though the fabric was thin and light, I could borrow her shawl again and wrap myself in her memory and her strength to see me through whatever the day brought.

I packed everything I could into her trunk, and stowed it beside the armoire before I headed downstairs to the breakfast room. Out in the hall I hesitated outside Peggy's door but decided to leave well enough alone.

The staff seemed skittish and strange looks were shot my way, so I decided to head down to the kitchen first to see what had happened.

"Good morning, Mrs. Gerrittsen," I said coming down the stairs into the workroom.

She looked up from her stove. "Ah, love. Good morning. Have you had your breakfast?"

"Not yet. Has Alexander arrived?"

She shook her head. "No, he stopped by earlier to say General Washington had been delayed and to go ahead and

start breakfast without him." She sighed. "All that prep and no one here to eat. We had special quail eggs brought in just for the Frenchie. I can't tell you how many of those delicate little eggs I broke trying to work with them." She laughed.

I gave her a half smile because I didn't have the heart this morning. One third of our mirthful morning trio was gone for good, and once Mrs. Gerrittsen learned the news she would be as heartbroken as I.

"Why don't you go upstairs yourself, love. Alexander was beside himself to see you and I had to threaten him with the gelding sheers not to wake you. He'll be here later and then you two love birds can go off for a ride in the warmth of the afternoon." She nodded, shooing me out of the room with a dishtowel. "Go on."

With a wink, she gave me a single nod and I headed back up the kitchen stairs toward the breakfast room.

It was quiet. Too quiet. The clock in the hall read nine a.m. Twenty-four hours had elapsed since I sent Paulding and his men to Wylie's Swamp to intercept John Andre, and the messenger bearing the news of his capture would be here shortly to warn Benedict Arnold.

I turned into the breakfast room. The general sat in his usual place at the head of the table, he eyes scanning a long letter.

"Good morning, Benedict Arnold," I said, flopping down into one of the chairs on the opposite side of the table.

He glanced at me above the edge of his correspondence. "It may be a good morning for me, m'dear, but it certainly isn't a good one for you." He folded the papers and tapped them in his palm.

"Do you know what this is?" he asked, gesturing with the letter before tossing it across the table in my direction.

"I'm certain I don't."

"For someone who is shortly to be arrested for impersonation and possible spying I would think the gravity of

the situation would be something you could most definitely comprehend."

I reached across the table and snagged the letter, opening it up to scan the content. "This is rather telling, I must say."

He sipped his coffee. "Indeed. You may have had the entire staff bamboozled including Washington's young lackey who thinks with his prick instead of his head, but I was not so easily fooled. As you can see," he gestured with his cup. "I had Benjamin Tallmadge send letters of inquiry about you. You are most certainly NOT Phoebe Burritt."

I shrugged taking a piece of toast from the bread rack and smeared it with butter and jam. "I, my dear General, never said I was."

I took a bite and chewed while he looked at me.

"That might very well be true, my dear, but you certainly let everyone believe you were Phoebe Burritt."

I shrugged again. "That isn't my problem. But ya' know what, Benny my boy, your own duplicity is about to blow up in your face and no amount of begging on your part or flirting on the part of your silly wife will get you out of it. YOU are the traitor, and you've been busted. Big time."

I crunched my toast and jam, watching the mottled color on his cheeks change from red to purple.

"How dare you! I welcome you into my home and you accuse me of heinous crimes!"

I laughed, wiping my mouth on a napkin. "Give it up, Benedict. They know—Tallmadge, Townsend, and the command of the lower Hudson. They have Andre in custody and it's only a matter of time before the letter with all the details reaches Washington. You are now an exile in your own country. The British will give you quarter because you did them a service, *but* West Point will *never* be theirs, they are destined to lose the war and the United States of America will become one of the world's super powers. England's power is waning and

within the next one hundred and fifty years will no longer be the empire it is now.

"England and its people will reject you for the turncoat you are, and you will live your life out in Canada, an exile from both America and England. You will die in June of 1801, a broken man, hated by the country you deceived. In fact, your name will become synonymous with the word *traitor*.

"Liar! Witch!"

I nodded, a smug smile on my face. "I was wondering when that word was going to be thrown at me. Yes, Benedict, I am a witch. I come from a very, very, long line of powerful women. As a matter of course, one of them brought me here...through time. You see, the reason you've been suspicious of me, the reason my manner and speech seemed queer at times is because I was born in the year of our lord nineteen hundred ninety-seven. Two hundred and seventeen years from now.

"I was brought here to make sure certain events took place as they should, and while it was difficult to accomplish, the fact remains I fulfilled my task. You made my job very easy. Your avarice and grasping need for money and power led you down this merry path, as did your ridiculous need to keep your vapid wife in high fashion.

"She must be quite skilled in the bedroom to have you so wrapped around her finger. You sold out your friends and allies, your self-respect and your good name all to keep that petulant sex kitten in the latest fashions. The sad irony is she will die in London three years after you, forced to auction all possessions to pay your debts. She dies a pauper—but if you want to dance with the devil, you eventually have to pay the fiddler."

He erupted up from the table, cups and dishes rattling in his wake as he stalked around to where I sat. Mouth twisted he raised his fist to strike me, but the door burst open and a messenger dashed in, an urgent communication in hand.

With a nod the man ran back out, leaving the general staring at the unopened letter in his palm.

"It's fiddler time, Benedict. I suggest you read the letter and decide what to do next. Of course, I already know what you'll do. Your cowardice is all over the history books, preserved for posterity."

He opened the letter and read every word, his face crumpling as the enormity of the situation took hold. He glanced at me, disbelief on his face.

I stood with my fingertips on the table. "It's hard to believe, I know. How do you think I felt when I woke up in 1780?" I gestured toward the door. "Peggy's waiting."

"Peggy?" I tapped on the outside of her door, but there was no sound from within. "Peggy, open the door."

The lock snicked from the opposite side and I turned the knob and let myself inside. She was in her dressing gown lying on her bed, a handkerchief in her hand, but surprisingly her face wasn't red and puffed with crying the way I expected.

"He's gone." Peggy sniffed.

"I know. He had one of the servants row him to the Vulture. He'll escape, though if I could change that fact, I would."

I knew events had to transpire exactly as recorded, but part of me wanted Benedict Arnold to hang alongside John Andre. At least Andre faced his charges like a man and didn't skulk away like a coward. Like Benedict Arnold.

"Johnny is gone, too."

At first, I thought she meant Paulding, but then I realized Johnny must have been her pet name for Andre. "Yes. Andre will hang on October second in Tappan, New York. Your husband will escape danger, but you both will live ostracized lives from now until the day you too, die. Unfortunately, your children will also bear the burden of their father's deeds." I

shook my head in disgust. "You've wrought quite a terrible legacy for yourself and your family, Peggy, and for what?"

She pushed herself up from the bed, staring. "Who are you?"

"Benedict didn't tell you?"

She shook her head.

"It's no matter now, anyway. I did what I came to do, except for one last detail." I walked to where she sat cross-legged on the bed and reached out wrapping my fingers around the moonstone hanging from her neck. One swift yank and the chain snapped, leaving the stone in my hand where it belonged.

"This," I said lifting my palm with the gem resting in its center, "doesn't belong to you. It never has and never will. You're a cheat and as much to blame for the downfall of your house as your husband. You deserve each other and the fate you've bought with your actions. You gambled and you lost."

"Witch!"

I laughed. "That's twice in the past hour someone has called me that, and you know what? I kinda like it. My mother and grandmother will be so proud."

"I'll ruin you! You won't be able to show your face in good society anywhere!" she screeched.

I dragged in a deep breath and then let it out quickly. "Well, I wish I could say I care, but I don't. Besides, that's kind of the pot calling the kettle black. You, my dear, are a pariah. No one of good society will ever embrace you or your husband again, and your father's money and influence in Philly?" I blew a razzberry at that.

"You'd better practice your acting skills because General Washington and his commanders will be here this afternoon, and that's when the shit storm is set to hit. He'll get his correspondence from the lower Hudson commanders with a full confession from Andre shortly after he arrives…and speaking of your liaison d'amour…I never told Benedict you cuckolded him with your old lover."

I stalked to the desk and took out the two letters she let me read a week ago and stuck them in my pocket along with the moonstone and the incriminating letter about me from Tallmadge. "For the sake of your child and the future children you will bear, I won't say a word to him as long as you stay away from me."

I walked toward the door. "If I'm slandered in any way after this, I'll attribute it to you, even if it's not. And these," I patted my pocket, "will be made public."

The door closed behind me and my shoulders slumped. I didn't need the papers in my pocket to tell the world what it already knew, but I needed to give the real Phoebe Burritt a little help. She had to live in the same era as Peggy Arnold, and I didn't want another innocent to suffer because of my time here. Sergeant Campbell and Mrs. Mac were more than enough for a dozen centuries.

I went to my room to finish packing. Now all I had to do was figure out how to get to Germantown and see Genève. I took the stone from my pocket and held it in my hand. It was cold to the touch despite being close to my skin for a while.

Hulda may have never said what to do with the moonstone once I had it, but she did tell me it was up to me to free Genève, and to do so I needed proof. At the word, the stone warmed in my hand as if agreeing with me. I had to give this to Genève and tell her about her mother, free her from the lies her uncle sewed and by doing so free our family to endure and prosper.

Knock, knock, knock.

My head turned toward the door and a slick of anxiety washed over me. The entire house was one big knot of tension, me included. At any moment I could still lose everything if I wasn't careful. I told Arnold who I truly was, but no one else and I doubted he would say a word. Tallmadge knew I wasn't

Phoebe Burritt, but my bet was he had his hands full with Andre for the time being and wasn't going to waste his time on an insignificant girl.

No one came down for luncheon, and as the afternoon waned, I heard footsteps back and forth between the guest rooms. Those footsteps became more urgent and were followed by shouts and doors banging open and closed. Of course, I knew what was at the root of all the noise and stress. Washington received his dispatch with the news of Arnold.

I walked to the door and turned the knob.

Alec stood in the doorway, his face a combination of delight and dark worry.

He put his hands on my shoulders and walked me backwards into the room before gathering me into his arms. He kissed my lips, my face, my eyes, my forehead, dipping his head to my throat and back again.

Taken off guard, I eased myself away and took a prudent step back.

"Aren't you glad to see me?" he asked sounding a little hurt.

"Of course I am, but something's wrong in the house. I can feel it."

He nodded. "General Arnold is a turncoat."

I let my lips part slightly as if speechless, but otherwise it was best if I didn't say a word.

"He's of the blackest mold, the blackest heart. He did all this and left his wife and babe alone to face the inquiries. Peggy is in hysterics." He shook his head.

"I should go to her, then."

He held my arm. "She wants no one at this point, but as much as it pains me to say, she's under suspicion as well. I don't have to tell you her family affiliations bring much of her activity into question."

I nodded. "Of course…"

"I must go, but I will be back. I am to debrief the three militia men who captured the spy working in cahoots with

Arnold." He turned to leave. "If I haven't returned by this evening, will you dine with me tomorrow night? There's much to be said, I think."

"Yes, of course. But I do have one small favor to ask, though I know the timing is inopportune."

He stepped toward me again and took my hand. "What is it, love? If it is in my power, I will do it."

"I need to make arrangements to go to Germantown as quickly as possible. There's a relative there I must see straight away. I was hoping perhaps you could take me, but if not, maybe you could help make other arrangements."

He smiled broadly. "A relative? Does that mean your memory has returned?"

I just looked at him. I didn't want to lie outright anymore. "Sort of."

He brushed my lips with his. "If I can get my debriefings done and General Washington can spare me, I will take you the day after tomorrow."

The carriage rocked back and forth, and drizzle left long wet streaks on the side windows. The weather had turned foul since Alec and I set out on our journey yesterday morning. Germantown was sixty-eight miles from West Point and the journey would take us two days to get there and two days to get back. Andre was set to hang on October second. I knew because of historic record. Alec knew because Washington had told him.

I have no idea how Alec managed to get a hall pass for the four-day trip, but I was grateful. After what happened when I ventured out alone the last time, I had no qualms about asking for help.

He thought it strange that all I had was a name and no address.

"I have never met this girl. She's distant relation, but I have something that belonged to her mother. Something I have to return."

"Where did you come by it? Every belonging you had to your name save what I found in that satchel was lost to the river?"

"I came across it recently when my memory began coming back in bits and pieces. It was in the haversack, just not where anyone could find it."

He looked pensive.

"What?"

He shook his head.

"No, what is it?"

"I told you I had to debrief the three men who stopped Major John Andre in Tarrytown on the morning of the twenty-third, correct?"

"Yes."

"I learned from the staff, you and Peggy were in Tarrytown that very same day." He took my hand. "What were you doing there?"

"Peggy had an appointment with a dressmaker."

Alec dropped his chin and eyed me closely. "No, you. What were *you* doing there?"

I didn't answer.

He sighed. "I don't see how either of us can move forward in this friendship if you refuse to trust me. When I debriefed the men, they gave a description of a young woman dressed in men's clothing who had intimate knowledge of Andre's whereabouts and his connection to what she referred to as the 'treasonous snake whose head resides at West Point.'

"They went on to describe the woman's features, who just so happened to have an uncanny resemblance to you. The one man, Paulding, said she was nameless except for a single code...355. That's the code the Culper ring uses for a female spy."

I looked at him. "That's an amazing story. May I use it on a cold winter night when I'm once again made to be the entertainment against my will?"

Alec made a face, but the driver wrapped on the roof door letting us know we had arrived. Alec instructed him to head to the nearest inn.

"We'll get settled, and then you can make your inquiries about your relation."

I nodded, grateful for the interruption. I knew the topic wasn't dropped, just postponed, but that was okay with me. Once I had seen Genève then the rest was up to the fates, and I would tell Alec the complete truth.

We pulled up to a wide log cabin style building with two stories. The sign swinging in the wind outside read *The Bull and the Bear.*

Alec checked us in, and the driver carried the trunks to the registration desk where he was instructed to take the two upstairs straight away. I walked in afterward and Alec handed me a key. "Adjoining rooms. Separate, yet close enough for comfort."

"Thank you," I murmured, knowing exactly what kind of comfort he meant.

I left him talking to the driver who was given accommodation in the barn. At first, I balked at the idea, but then decided to shut my mouth. I was in no position to pay for a third room and as there were other liveried employees doing the same, I didn't say a word.

"Excuse me," I signaled the proprietor at the registration desk.

"Yes, miss?"

"Would you happen to know a Genève Staats?"

He nodded. "Everyone in town knows Genny. She a friend of yours?"

I nodded. "A distant relative. Would you know where I might find her?"

He grinned. "Sure do." He dragged out a small card and a quill and ink and wrote her address, blotted the excess ink and then handed the card over.

"If you'd like, I'm headed that way in just a bit, I would be more than happy to escort you."

"That won't be necessary, thank you. We'll have our driver take us after we've had a chance to clear ourselves of road dust." Alec responded from across the foyer as though he had supersonic hearing.

I didn't want to wait. I had been waiting for over two months, plus I was in no mood to play cat and mouse with the colonel when I no longer had Mrs. MacPherson to run bedroom interference. I wanted to go home. I wanted Hunter.

"Alec, I'd like to go calling now, if you wouldn't mind. I'm nervous enough as it is, and if we wait, I'm afraid my anxiety will eat me alive."

He paused, looking at my face and then smiled. "All right. Just give me a moment and I'll be right down."

I sat on a low ladies' couch, waiting. The proprietor caught my eye and I gave him and smile and a nod.

"You know, it's best you see Genny now. Her uncle is at work."

"Lars?" I questioned.

He nodded, and it was clear it was with distaste.

"You don't seem like you care for the man, much."

He shook his head. "I don't. He's a wicked mean sort. I knew Genève's mother and father. Her pa was a hardworking man and he loved his girls something fierce, and when he died, Lars accused Hulda of unspeakable things. None of it was true, but superstitions are hard and people even harder sometimes. She left. It was the only thing she could do. I never spoke to Lars Staats again. Genève is a sweet girl, though she's not a girl anymore."

Alec came downstairs at that point and I nodded my thanks to the innkeeper and we set off. As we rode, the vision I had in

the kitchen with Gran and my mother came back full force, every nuance of the house and the farms, the muddy roads. I remembered it all, and before long it was right in front of me.

Chickens ran loose in the front yard and the outside of the house looked rundown. Lars certainly hadn't done much with the place once he stole it from Hulda. I pressed my lips together and opened the carriage door.

"Would you like me to come with you?" Alec asked.

I shook my head. "I think I'll be enough of a shock for her for one day."

I fisted my dress to keep the hem as far away from the muddy wheels as possible and stepped down onto the wet gravel. The rain only served to make the memory of my vision even more intense. It was raining then, and it was raining now. Fitting in the karmic sense to the nines.

I walked toward the entrance when a young woman in her early twenties came to the door. I stood in shock. She looked so much like my mother, I wanted to run to her and thrown my arms around her neck.

"May I be of assistance?" she asked.

I nodded. "Yes. Are you, Genève?"

If I could stand in the drizzle and absorb the rainbow of emotions cascading through me at that moment, I would have, but she looked at me curiously and I knew Alec was as well, so I needed to get on with it.

"I know this may seem strange, but I have something that belongs to you. It belonged to your mother."

She looked incredulous, almost as if her Pavlovian response was to cringe at the very mention of Hulda, but curiosity and latent love got the better of her and she invited me inside.

"My mother has been gone from my life a very long time," she said, sitting beside me on a small couch.

I reached into my pocket and drew out the stone. The poor woman gasped, taking it from my hand and turning it over and

over in her palm as though she couldn't believe it was a real, tangible item.

"Mama wore this every day. She said it was her talisman." Her voice an awed whisper.

"She's passed on, Genève, and I'm sorry. But she made me promise to come and give that to you and to tell you of her life. She never stopped loving you, and it killed her not to be with you all these years. She even taught me to make daisy chains the way she made them for you when you were a child."

"Did you know mama long?"

I shook my head. "No, but she was a very special woman."

I told her the story about how her mother died a patriot and a heroine of the town. How she endured for her beliefs but managed to find love and respect among the townsfolk. Her dying wish was Genève be the one to reap that hard-sowed reward. To live in Sleepy Hollow with pride and raise a family there.

The poor girl was crying, but she composed herself enough to beckon me to her small room. Beneath the floorboard in a woven pouch was our family bible. She managed to keep it hidden from Lars this whole time. She hugged it to her breast and her tears fell on the black leather spine.

"My mother catalogued our maternal line from Prussia, listing the strong women who fought and loved so hard. I was sure the line would die with my own weak will, but you've given me new hope and new strength. I'm free."

At those two words the window blew open and a soft wind gusted through the house. My heart soared and broke at the same time, and as Genève rushed to close the window above the couch, she stopped and bent to pick something up from the cushion.

It was a daisy.

I had fulfilled my destiny and saved my family.

Genève hugged me, and as I walked through the door to the front step, she stopped me. "You've given me such a wonderful gift and I don't even know your name."

I smiled. "It's Rowen. My name is Rowen."

Alec waited inside the carriage as the driver climbed down to open the door and help me scale the muddy, slippery step. He held my elbow and squeezed my forearm.

"You've done well, Itchy Witch. All is right on both sides of the veil, so stop worrying. I'm *happy* and I have a purpose."

At the name Itchy Witch my head jerked around, and the driver winked. My breath froze in my throat. His eyes were candy blue.

"Tyler?" I reached out to touch the driver's face, but he suddenly pulled back.

"Sorry, miss. Did you say something?"

The man's eyes were brown, and I blinked not sure if what I saw really happened, but then again, I knew in my heart it did. Tyler was okay. I wanted to laugh, to hug myself or throw leaves into the air, something silly and freeing. He'd said it. He was my messenger, and everything was right with the world on both sides.

"Is everything quite all right?" Alec asked poking his head through the door. He held out his hand and helped me the rest of the way in.

"Everything is wonderful." I threw my arms around him and gave him a hug.

He laughed pulling my arms down so he could look at me. "Clearly, and to use your turn of phrase, you are nuts."

I grinned. "So, I've been told."

The carriage started moving, the horses clip clopping at a moderate pace.

"I'd like to talk to you about something important, Phoebe."

I put my hand on Alec's arm. "Please don't."

He shifted in his seat, taking my hands in his. "Why? I love you and I want to marry you."

I shook my head. "I don't belong here, Alec, and I'll be leaving soon or so I hope."

"You're breaking my heart. I ache for you when I'm not with you. How can you say you're leaving? Where will you go?"

"Home."

He opened his mouth to argue, then closed it. Alexander wasn't one to beg, and he must have seen resolution in my face and simply nodded. "There's nothing I can say to convince you to stay?"

I shook my head. "It's for the best." I reached into my pocket and pulled out the leather pouch that held the compass. "I have a gift for you. Something to remember me by."

I handed him the pouch and he opened it, pulling the compass into his palm.

"Do you remember that? You found it in my bag when we first met. You said it was an unusual item for a young woman."

How the compass got into my bag was still a mystery, but in my gut, I knew it was Hulda's hand that held all the strings in this, just as I knew it was her hand I saw in the fleeting vision when Alec first handed me the compass.

He chuckled holding the metallic mechanism by the fob the way he had two months earlier. "Well, it's fitting as you are certainly the most singular woman I have ever met."

"Turn it over."

He turned the metal casing over and smiled. "Hamlet."

I nodded. "Methinks the gentleman doth protest too much."

"I remember." He laughed. "You were right, though. I was jealous."

"Read the inscription aloud, Alec. I chose it specifically for you."

"[Love] 'Tis in my memory lock'd, and you yourself shall keep the key of it. When sorrows come, they come not single spies. But in battalions!" —355

Alec's eyes widened.

Gunshots rang from the road and the horses reared, throwing the carriage back as they took off at full gallop. They charged, uncontrollable flying over the slick, wet ground. The coach careened and lurched, the wheels shimmying until one snapped, sending the conveyance rolling to its side into a ditch.

I screamed, feeling myself flung wild into the cold wet air until I hit the ground, and everything went black.

Chapter 25

"Rowen!" Hunter's voice yelled. *"Jesus, God…*Rowen!"

My body screamed in pain, even my hair hurt. Hunter's voice was thick in my ears, but I knew he was real this time. I could feel him. His warmth, his aura. Him.

"We should roll her over and do CPR!"

"Shut up, Jenny. Just call 911."

"Xavi's got it covered. They're on their way."

"Rowen…baby…can you hear me?" His panic calmed me. I was home, though I had no idea what day it was or what happened.

I heard sirens in the distance and people yelling. First responders. Yay for the twenty-first century!

They rolled me onto my back and clamped something stiff on my neck and then lifted my body. It was then I realized I was watching this, hovering above myself.

Oh, no effing way! I did not just save the American way of life and my entire maternal family line only to die in the process.

"It's all right, lass. Yer only visiting with us angels."

I whirled around from my airborne perch.

"Sergeant Douglas Campbell, at yer service, m'lady," he said with a smile.

Standing beside him was Mrs. Mac and she waved, slipping her arm around his.

I flew to her and she wrapped her free arm around my shoulders. "Oh, don't cry, love. It was meant and I wouldn't

have it any other way. I saved my girl so she could do what she was destined to do."

"But…"

"Pish. Butts are for goats…and no, I didn't feel any pain."

Sergeant Campbell leaned in, "Me, neither." He snapped his fingers. "Over in a flash."

"I had you both buried in the cemetery at West Point. I asked Major Franks to do so before Alec and I left for Germantown. It was quite a dance to explain to him, but in the end he did so out of respect for you both and because he felt guilt for working side-by-side with a traitor. He found out I was the 355."

The two laughed, but their images faded, and I reached out again to Mrs. Mac, but she shook her head.

"You need to go back and live the life you are meant to live. That young man is waiting for you."

Guilt slashed across my heart. The last time she used those words, they were meant for Alec.

She smiled softly. "Hush now. I'll have no remorse washing through this Godly place. Alexander lived as he was meant to. He and Elizabeth married and had children, and he accomplished great things in his short life as I'm sure history recounts, although his impetuous nature and his love for you never waned. It is as it was preordained to be, sweeting." Mrs. Mac sighed. "I wish I had known all along about this, what an amazing universe this is."

I nodded, with a laugh. "Even when it plays by its own rules."

They stepped back from me and I held out my hand. "I love you, Ferne MacPherson."

"I love you too, sweetheart. Live your life. I'll be watching."

The sergeant saluted. "Make sure that young man treats ye right." He sniffed, giving me a sharp nod. "'Because I'll be watchin', too."

A wave of power hit and flung me backwards, the air sucked from my lungs and forced back in. Vertigo hit and I spun and fell and fell…

I opened my eyes and saw my mother and Gran, both sitting on either side of my bed, their hands linked, and their free hands touched a part of me. Their lips murmured and I knew it was half chant, half prayer all rolled into panic and hope.

"Hi," I croaked, and they jerked their eyes open.

"Honey…*Oh my God*, Rowen! Thank God! You've been out for days!" My mother cried, her words clipped with tears.

She slipped her arms around me and hugged me tight and I winced, exhaling a grunt.

"Oh, baby, I'm sorry. Do you want me to get the nurse?"

I shook my head. "Where am I?"

"Phelps Memorial. We had you medivac'd in from the Catskills after you went over those stupid falls."

"I've been here the whole time?"

Gran nodded. "Of course, sweetie, where did you think you were?"

Confused, I looked at them both. "But what about all that stuff with ancestor awakenings and the vial of transcendence you slipped in my backpack?"

My mother and Gran exchanged looks. "Honey, you've been here for almost a week, and for the better part of that you've been unconscious." My mother took my hand. "The only thing I slipped into your bag was your charger. Whatever you *think* happened, was probably just a dream."

"Your mother is right, sweetheart. You *did* have an awakening and that was that unless there's something else you need to tell us." Gran raised an eyebrow and the set of her mouth was the same slash she always wore whenever her antennae were up.

I shook my head in reply. Maybe they were right and everything that happened was just a vivid dream. "Where's Hunter?"

"He's here. He just went down to the cafeteria to get something to eat. As soon as he gets back, Gran and I are going to take our shift. We haven't left you alone since you got here."

"Knock, knock."

I looked over and there he was in the flesh. No more dreams, no more substitutes. My Hunter.

Mom and Gran motioned they'd be back soon, my mother's hand lightly touching Hunter's as they passed in the doorway. He walked in and leaned over the bed and kissed me and my heart and body sang. I kissed him back with everything I had and didn't care if my mother and Gran hated the idea. I was home and Hunter was mine, and I was his.

He broke our kiss and sat on the bed beside me. "Wow, if that's the way you're going to greet me whenever you wake up, then we're going to have to spend many, many more mornings together."

I smiled. "That's a deal."

He smirked. "I have something for you." He dug in his pocket and pulled out the heart pendant with our initials entwined. "It was lying in the mud next to you when we finally found you on the shore. The chain was mangled, but I had it replaced. No one knows how you survived, but they don't know you like I do. You drifted about thirty miles downriver."

"Put it on me, please. I never want to be without it again."

He leaned over and clasped the chain around my neck. "I never want to come that close to losing you to anyone or anything again. I love you, my unpredictable girl."

I looked up at that, afraid it would be Alec's violet eyes looking back at me instead of Hunter's warm brown, but it wasn't. Was it all a coma-induced dream like I thought at first, like Gran and my mother said? Who knew? Did I care? Not

really, I was here, and I was with Hunter and that's all that mattered.

"Did you see all the flowers you got? Everyone's sent something and dropped by to see how you were doing. They'll be thrilled you're okay."

I inhaled. "They're gorgeous. Did you or Mom write down who sent what? I'd like to collect the cards so I can send thank you notes when I finally get out of here."

Hunter nodded. "Yeah. Every bouquet is accounted for except for one. No one knows who sent it."

"Which one?"

He got up from the bed and came back with a vase full of daisies. "This one…and the note is just as much a mystery, too."

I held out my hand for the card, my throat dry and my stomach suddenly in knots.

It is a mistake to look too far ahead.

Only one link of the chain of destiny can be handled at a time. ~H~

"I think the quote is from Winston Churchill." Hunter slipped the card from my fingers and turned it over with a shrug, and after a moment he looked up me. "But who's *H*?"

With a sly grin, I sunk back into my pillows.

Dream, my ass.

Note from the Author

This book is a work of fiction, though there are many elements of fact cited throughout the story. Like many authors, I was inspired by true historic events and motivation grew from there. Many of the characters are true historic figures, and the quoted accounting of events from Doctor James Thacher is true, but the story of Rowen Corbett and her time in 1780 is fictionalized.

Whenever I use historic events in a story, I take painstaking care to ensure the facts are correct. It is only then I allow my imagination to take flight. Here is some of the history that lent itself to the creation of Time Turner...

Hulda the Witch is a true historical figure who died in a skirmish on Hessian Hill, sometimes referred to as Battle Hill. The area where she lived and died is now part of the Sleepy Hollow Cemetery. It's true she was a woman who lived a solitary existence and was subsequently shunned because of superstition and fear, yet still offered help to those townspeople in need. She gave her life leading the British away from the local militia, giving the patriot army time to rearm and re-man. She died for her efforts, and is buried as written, along the north wall of the Old Dutch burial ground in an unmarked grave, adjacent to the unmarked grave of the Headless Horseman. If you'd like to visit Hulda or the Headless Hessian, the *Friends of the Old Dutch Church* have a map and tour waiting for you.

The Culper spy ring was a true Revolutionary War spy network inaugurated by George Washington and headed by Benjamin Tallmadge. Members, Anna Strong, Abraham Woodhull and Robert Townsend plus many others, are real people who served their country well. The unknown female spy known simply as *355* is also very real, and yes, her identity to this day is still a mystery.

Benedict Arnold and his wife Peggy Shippen Arnold resided at the Beverly Robinson House in what is now Garrison, New York. The towns of Garrison, Nelsonville, and Cold Spring together form the revolutionary township formerly known as Philipstown. The structure of the Beverly Robinson House burned in the late nineteenth century, but there is a historical marker delineating the land, as well as the path Benedict Arnold took when he fled to the HMS Vulture.

The iron chain that crossed the Hudson River from West Point to

Constitution Island is real as well, and what remains of it can be seen in a memorial on the grounds of the military academy.

The Old Guard House and the Historical Society and Museum can be found on Main Street in Hurley, New York, in the heart of historic Ulster County. Stone House Day is truly hosted once a year on the second Saturday of July.

The historic events surrounding those days in September 1780 unfolded in exact chronological order told in the story. Arnold did reschedule his meeting with John Anderson (John Andre's alias) after the initial meeting on September 11th failed. The rendezvous was held on September 21st at the Joshua Hett Smith house, and because the HMS Vulture was fired upon by militia stationed off Verplank, NY, events did force Andre to travel back toward British lines on horse.

The three unassuming men from Sleepy Hollow responsible for Andre's capture: John Paulding, Isaac Van Wart, and David Williams, were part of the area volunteer militia, but they all had individual scrapes with the law. Historians believe the men were actually skinners lying in wait for unsuspecting travelers and had gotten lucky when Andre stumbled upon them. To their credit, though, none could be bought with the bribes the British spy offered once they realized he was a spy and what was truly at stake.

Benedict Arnold did escape on the morning of September 25th, running from Robinson House and leaving his wife behind to face Washington, alone. Perhaps it was cowardice, or perhaps a decisively calculated move. Arnold knew his wife was a beautiful, beguiling woman, and what better way to distract Washington and his party than to play on their chivalry. Either way, we can only surmise.

Writing and weaving these historic events into the fabric of a fictionalized retelling has been an amazing experience for me as an author…exhausting…but thoroughly gratifying. I hope you enjoyed reading Time Turner as much as I enjoyed writing it!

Oh, and enjoy the pics!

Mar

Major General Benedict Arnold

Peggy Shippen Arnold and daughter

Alexander Hamilton
Bronze Statue Washington, D.C.

Sketch of the Beverly Robinson House
(Courtesy of the Putnam County Historical Society)

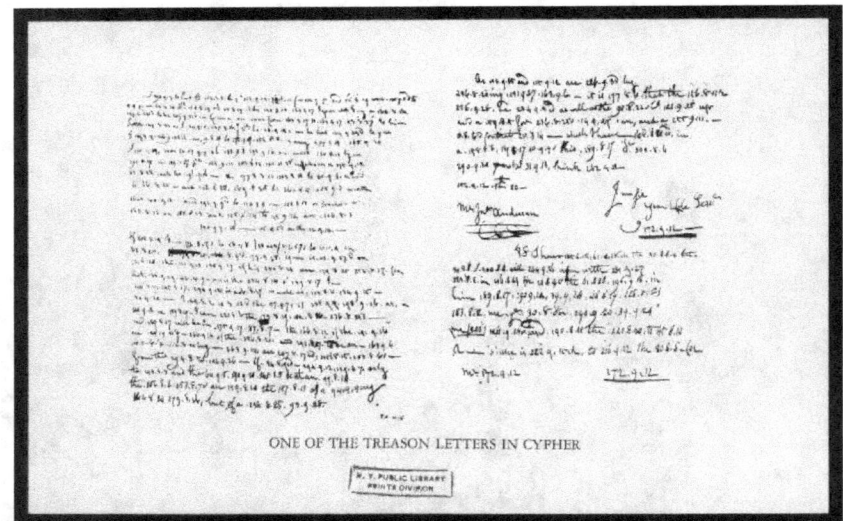

ONE OF THE TREASON LETTERS IN CYPHER

Sample of one of Benedict Arnold's treasonous letters in cypher

I *Benedict Arnold Major General*
do acknowledge the UNITED STATES of AME-
RICA to be Free, Independent and Sovereign States, and
declare that the people thereof owe no allegiance or obedience to George the Third, King of Great-Britain ; and I
renounce, refuse and abjure any allegiance or obedience to
him ; and I do *Swear* that I will, to the ut-
moft of my power, fupport, maintain and defend the faid
United States againft the faid King George the Third, his
heirs and fucceffors, and his or their abettors, affiftants and
adherents, and will ferve the faid United States in the office of
Major General which I now hold, with
fidelity, according to the beft of my fkill and underftanding.

Sworn before me this
30³. May 1778. at the
Artillery Park Valley Forge

Benedict Arnold's Oath of Allegiance to the
United State of America

Arnold Burned in Effigy
(Charcoal courtesy of Wiki-Commons Public Doman Art)

The Joshua Hett Smith House in Haverstraw, NY
(Photograph courtesy of Wiki-Commons Public Doman Art)

British Major John Andre

Marker from Patriot's Park, Sleepy Hollow, NY
Place of Andre's capture.

The Capture of Major John Andre
(Charcoal courtesy of Wiki-Commons Public Doman Art)

The hanging of Major John Andre
In Tappan, NY.

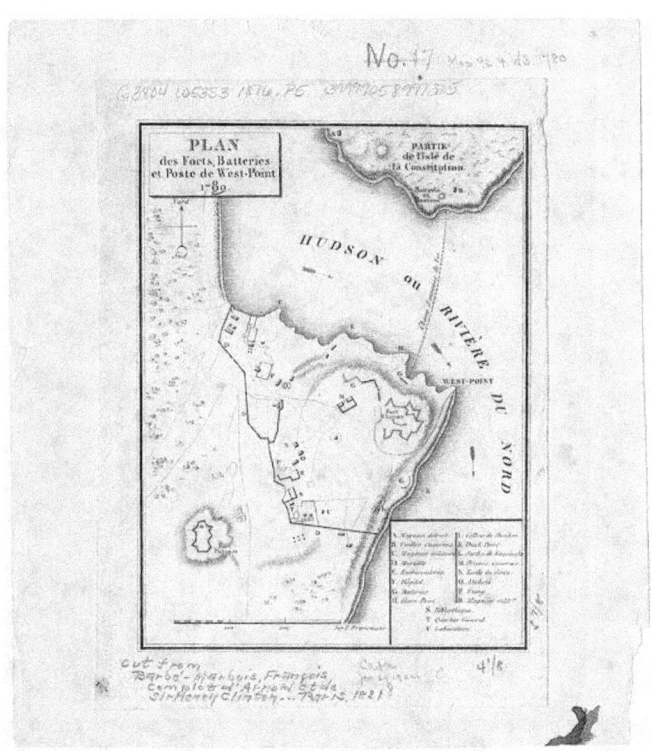

Map of West Point 1780

Stone House Row
Historic Hurley, NY

The Old Guard House, Historic Hurley, NY

Hurley Historical Society and Museum

Acknowledgements

Time Turner is the second book in the Legend Series based on historic events from my home in the historic Hudson Valley of New York. It is my eighth book to date, and a story I am very proud of. So many people have helped and encouraged me during the creation of this historic fiction.

My unbelievably patient husband, Bill, for putting up with the insanity and verbal barrages that accompany being glued to my laptop for hours. Our three kids for knowing enough to leave mom alone when she's writing, despite laundry piling up and pasta for dinner, yet again.

I need to send my gratitude out to the director and all the librarians at the Putnam County Historical Society and Museum. I can't thank them enough for their patient help during my research—for the historic books, pamphlets and genealogies they let me be privy to, and for answering my incessant questions.

I would be completely remiss if I didn't send my thanks out to Jan Thacher, photo-archivist at the Putnam County Historical Society and six-times great-grandson of Dr. James Thacher, surgeon in residence at West Point from 1775 through the end of the American Revolutionary War. This unbelievably patient man allowed me the privilege of handling his ancestor's daily journal giving me an exclusive glimpse into the daily life of revolutionary West Point, and in particular the treasonous days surrounding Benedict Arnold and his escape.

I was given the gift of a glimpse back in time to the thoughts and emotions swirling through the forts and the men once word reached them of Arnold's betrayal.

Meeting Mr. Jan Thacher was sheer providence, as the day was September 24th, 2014—exactly two hundred and thirty-four years to the date from when those historic and tragic events first unfolded. No words of thanks go deep enough, and the Putnam Historical Society and Jan Thacher in particular have my undying gratitude.

I need to send my appreciation out to Sara Mascia, Archeologist and Executive Director of the Tarrytown and Sleepy Hollow Historical Society, and Tara Van Tassell, Historical Society Archivist for the books and genealogies to help in the research of Hulda the Witch and her role in the American Revolution and for copies of the affidavits given by John Paulding, Isaac Van Wart and David Williams on their capture of John Andre. You ladies rock, and I'm grateful to call you friends and colleagues!

To my father and mother and my wonderful mother-in-law for their guidance, and my siblings for their support.

To all my hometown friends, especially Karen Marsh, Ginger Hardman and Ginny Ryan.

To my wonderful Street Team, especially my beta readers, Bonnie-Jean Aurigemma, Lisa Errion, Heather Gabriel, Ebony Laprocina and Patricia Statham.

I thank you *all* for reading, critiquing and for being the best cheerleaders anyone could want. And last but certainly not least, I want to thank God for all his blessings. The longer I live, the more I learn to appreciate what could very easily be taken for granted. God bless.

I hope you enjoyed the book.

Research Bibliography

Military Journal of the American Revolution
By James Thacher, M.D.
Surgeon in the American Revolutionary Army
Courtesy of Jan Thacher

Chaining the Hudson
By Lincoln Diamant
Fordham University Press
Pages 162—171

The Westchester Treasure Hunt— Treason in the American Revolution
By Julianna Free Hand
Caroline House Press 1980

Hidden Treasure of the Lower Hudson Valley
Stories from the Albany Post Road
By Carney Rhinevault and Tatiana Whinevault

Legends and Lore of Sleepy Hollow and the Hudson Valley
By Jonathan Kruk

The Kings Men: Loyalist Military Unites in the American Revolution
By Todd Braisted
Online   Institute   for   Advanced   Loyalist   Studies.
www.nyhistory.net/~drums/kingsmen_02.htm

Ghost Stories: The Other Legend of Sleepy Hollow
By Robyn Leary
New York Times, Sunday, October 29, 2000

Calendar of the correspondence of George Washington: Commander in Chief of the Continental Army, with the Continental Congress
Pages 453-458

Benedict Arnold: A Traitor in Our Midst
By Barry K. Wilson
McGill-Queens University Press
Pages 145-163

Year of the Patriots—
The Commemoration of the Three Captors of the British Spy
By James Caleb Beach

Hurley Heritage Society

http://www.hurleyheritagesociety.org/

Uniforms of the American Revolution
http://www.srcalifornia.com/uniforms/p41.htm

A Gothic Curiosity Cabinet
http://www.gothichorrorstories.com/behind-urban-legends/hiking-rockefeller-state-park-preserve-looking-for-spook-rock-hulda-the-witch-and-the-non-headless-horseman-origins-of-the-legend-of-sleepy-hollow/

The George Washington Papers at the Library of Congress
Time Line: The American Revolution—1780
http://memory.loc.gov/ammem/gwhtml/1780.html

Loyal American Regiment — 1777-1783
http://www.loyalamericanregiment.org/reghist.htm
http://www.loyalamericanregiment.org/beverley.htm

History of American Women
http://www.womenhistoryblog.com/2011/04/peggy-shippen-arnold.html

A Biography of Alexander Hamilton (1755-1804)
The Arnold/Andre Affair (September 1780)
http://www.let.rug.nl/usa/biographies/alexander—hamilton/the—arnold—andre—affair—(september—1780).php

Founding Brothers
http://foundingbrothersproject.weebly.com/alexander-hamilton.html

Ladies in Defiance
Agent 355–Her Name Might be a Mystery, but is Her Identity Really Still a Secret?
http://ladiesindefiance.com/2012/09/24/agent-355-her-name-might-be-a-mystery-but-is-her-identity-really-still-a-secret/

Spy Letters of the American Revolutions
From the Collections of the Clements Library—People of the Revolution
http://clements.umich.edu/exhibits/online/spies/index-people.html

About the Author

M.A. Morea was born and raised in New York. Inspired by the dichotomies that define 'the city that never sleeps,' she began her career after college as a budding journalist. Later, earning a MFA from The School of Visual Arts in Manhattan, she moved on to the graphic arts. But it was her lifelong love affair with words and the fantasies and 'what ifs' they stir, that finally brought her back to writing.

M.A. MOREA's Teen/New Adult Series!

**Wanna peek at Book Three,
Spook Rock?**

You got it!

SPOOK ROCK SNEAK PEEK...

Chapter 1

My cell phone chimed on the nightstand, its pleasant tones graduating to piercing, interrupting what was left of my broken sleep. Half awake, I hit the red snooze button and rolled over taking the covers with me to my chin.

Six a.m. Still dark.

"Hannah!"

Ignoring my father's bellow, I watched the ambient glow from the streetlights cast shadows across my bed through the curtains. I had another half hour before I had to get up and get ready for school. Not that I could concentrate. My mind already churned with what I dreamed last night.

Except I knew it wasn't a dream.

I closed my eyes again, but the image of Talia in my bathroom doorway wouldn't go away. Neither would her words. Her lips never moved, though I heard her loud and clear.

"I need you, Hannah. Find Rowen..."

"Hannah! It's after six!" My father's heavy footsteps echoed in the hall along with his voice.

"Please, Mouse..."

"Hannah!" A sharp rap sounded on my door. "I need to stop at the hospital before I drop you at school. Get up or we'll both be late."

I listened to his annoyed footfalls retreat and I pulled the covers over my head. "Leave me alone!" I groaned into my duvet.

Visiting hours for the psychiatric ward at Phelps Memorial were from six to eight p.m., but no one needed to explain why my father wanted to stop by a full twelve hours ahead of time. My mother was crazy and that meant a lot of paperwork.

"She's not crazy, Mouse. She sees me, same as you..."

I squeezed my eyes closed, shutting out the wordless conversation with my dead sister. Talia was killed on Halloween night almost a year ago. It wasn't long after that our mother started having visions. Problem was, I saw her, too.

Or did I?

Maybe crazy ran in the family. Except, I didn't really believe that, and that meant Tal was really here.

Or not.

Confused much? Yup.

"There are no such things as ghosts. It's just your imagination." I whispered my half-believed mantra and pushed the covers from my head, blowing the hair from my forehead. "Or maybe you're as lost as your screwball mother."

I stared into the clinging shadows, tears stinging my eyes. I was so tired of talking myself out of a daily nervous breakdown. I needed help, but who'd believe such nonsense when my own father wanted to have my mother committed for claiming the same thing?

"Find Rowen..."

My sister's voice trailed through my mind. I shook my head and exhaled hard. No. Rowen had enough pain dealing with what happened last Halloween. She was there front and center. The only difference was Rowen came from a long line of witchy women who were good with weird and didn't question the uncanny, while my father frowned on anything that cast aspersions on him or his cookie-cutter life.

He never approved of Rowen or her family and said as such every chance he got. It was Mom who stood buffer for us kids, taking the brunt of his ire over social slights and anything he deemed a hindrance to his upward mobility.

I smiled, remembering my mother's trademark eye roll when he'd go off about public image and guilt by association. She was not a typical politician's wife by any stretch, but she had money and connections. That much was made abundantly clear each time they argued, and he reminded her it was the only reason he asked her to marry. I knew the term *smooth criminal*, but never imagined it was a truth that fit my father.

Fresh tears pricked again. He'd have my mother committed all right and use Talia's death and its implied emotional import to manipulate his position with the town. I had to do something, but what? If Dad was as ruthless as he seemed lately, he'd have Mom and me in matching strait jackets if I so much as hinted at seeing Talia as well.

"Find Rowen..."

I threw my covers the rest of the way off and scooted my legs over the edge of the bed. I scrubbed my face with both palms and dragged a hand through my short blond bob, letting the pin-straight strands swing back toward my chin.

"Okay, Tal...you win." I wrapped my hands around my middle and squeezed, staring at nothing. "I'll find Rowen. But if you're really here, you gotta help me with Mom. We need you, too."

I wiped my eyes and slid off the bed to pad toward the bathroom, letting my hand trail over the doorjamb where I last saw Talia. I curled my fingers into my palm, sticking out my little finger. "Pinky promise, sissy?" My whispered plea sounded strange in the morning silence.

Coldness touched my hand and I jerked back from the door. There was nothing familiar or comforting about the feel. Goose bumps rose on my arm along with the hair on the back of my neck, and a knot formed in my stomach.

Cruel. Pitiless.

Those were the answering emotions buffeting my sympathetic nervous system. I knew one thing for sure.

It wasn't Talia that answered.

***

"Hannah, what are you doing here?" the charge nurse whispered from the doorway into my mother's room. She glanced over her shoulder and then stepped in, closing the door until it stood slightly ajar.

"My father is downstairs with the doctors and the hospital chancellor discussing my mother's care. I didn't think anyone would mind if I popped up to see her." I slipped my fingers into my mother's hand before turning back to the nurse.

The woman's concern softened. "Hannah, you've been here dealing with your mother's treatment both inpatient and outpatient for nearly six months. You need a break, sweetheart. Go out with your friends. See a movie. Your life can't be all school and a sterile hospital room. Everyone on the nursing staff is worried about you."

I gave her a soft smile. "I appreciate that, but right now this is where I need to be." Looking at my mother again, I frowned at the slack set to her jaw. "Why is Mom sedated again? She's not a threat."

"You're right, honey. She's not. Just a mom having a hard time letting go of a child she lost." The nurse exhaled a sad breath. "I wish there was something we could do, but doctor's orders say otherwise." She frowned again, her eyes growing hard as she glanced toward the sliver of open door. "At least the dose is mild."

"It's been almost a year."

The older woman nodded. "I know, baby."

My mother's fingers tightened in my hand, and a chill set over me. My mouth went dry and something squeezed my chest. I couldn't pull away from my mother's grip. A whisper jerked my gaze to the window and my voice locked in my throat.

Talia.

My sister's image reflected in the glass, but what I saw was different than before. Talia was graying, her face and skin, crepey as though decaying.

The temperature in the room dropped even more and my breath fogged out in white puffs. Crystals spread in an icy web across the panes, obscuring Talia from view. A foul stench filled the air and the fall mums I brought the day before withered and blackened on Mom's dresser beside the window.

My mother's grip constricted to painful, her nails digging into my flesh. Blood welled in my palm, and in that moment, the spidery web on the window dripped crimson, the rivulets pooling over the sill.

"Too late! Talia's calling! She needs me!" Peg Meyer bolted up in bed, eyes wild.

She jerked her head toward the glass, her fingers clawing at me. "Tell me you see her, too! Oh my God! The blood! All the blood!"

"Mom, please…"

"She's here!" she cried. "She's always here!" Peg ripped one hand away and flung it toward the bloodstained window.

"There's nothing there, Peggy." The nurse moved to her side and reached for a button attached to her IV. "It's a beautiful day out. Warm and sunny."

My eyes nearly bugged. Clearly, the charge nurse couldn't see what Mom and I saw. I bit the inside of my cheek and pressed my lips together to not give myself away.

Mom screamed, wrenching her head back and smacking it against the wall above her pillows. Laughter whispered over the sound of my mother's outcry and I tracked the sound to the window again. A bony hand clawed the pane of glass, ragged, torn fingernails scraping through the blood-smeared ice.

"Hannah! Help me—"

It was Talia's voice. Soundless, yet not. Her scream in the far distance was thick in my ears, and I squeezed my eyes shut. I ripped my hand from my mother's grip and bolted to the window, pulling the cord to release the blinds. They hit the sill with a muffled thud and suddenly all was quiet.

A soft keening came from my mother as she cowered against her pillows. I ran to the side of the bed, sinking beside her, smoothing her hair like I was the parent and she the child.

Her hands shook, but she was lucid enough to cup my cheek and look me in the eye. "I know you saw her, too. It's getting worse and time is running out."

"What is going on in here? Hannah! I told you to wait in the car!"

"Dad—" I looked from my father's scowl to my frantic mother's face and back again. "It's nothing."

"Hannah! Tell your father the truth. He can't deny both of us."

The medication in the IV was taking effect. Mom's last words slurred, and her eyes glazed into a sleepy stupor.

The nurse moved from the beeping monitor to straighten the bed covers, helping my mother relax into her pillow. With a sigh, Mom lifted a weak hand toward the window, but then let it drop to the bed.

"Dad—" I tried again.

He shook his head. "This defiance has to end, Hannah. I know you love your mother, but haven't we been through enough?"

"Careful, Dad. You might slip in public. Don't you mean *we* love my mother?"

"That's quite enough, young lady—"

The psychiatrist walked through the open door and my father shut up. With a frown, the doctor assessed what I was sure he assumed was another psychotic episode. He leaned in to whisper something to my father, and Dad spared a look for me before giving the man a nod.

"Wait for me outside, Hannah." Without pausing for me to reply, he took my elbow and ushered me toward the door. "The doctor and I need to speak with your mother."

"No." I jerked my arm from his grasp. "I want to hear what you have to say to Mom. She's sedated and can't be responsible for whatever you force her to agree to."

The doctor's head jerked from my mother's charts. "Hannah, no one is forcing your mother to agree to anything. I assure you that. At the moment, she isn't in the right state to make decisions about her health, so the unhappy task falls to your father. It's not easy, I know."

I ignored him, my eyes glued to my father's face. "I want to hear you say the words. I want you to look me in the eye and tell me how tossing my mother aside is for the best."

"No one is tossing anyone anywhere, Hannah. Your mother needs proper long term care. She can't stay here indefinitely, so placing her in a secure facility equipped to deal with her mental state is best."

I balked at the blatant lie. "Best for whom? Have you even tried listening to her?" I shook my head. "Of course not. That would require a leap of faith and we all know faith in you was broken long before we lost Talia."

My father's eyes flashed. "What do you want from me, Hannah? Have you forgotten how every day your mother ranted about Talia…seeing her, talking to her…please, honey…I hate that I'm the one forcing you to look at this with an ice cold eye, but your mother is very ill. Her mind is gone.

"There's no one to blame, except maybe Rowen Corbett and her crackpot family. I blame them for destroying us. If your sister had stayed away from her, like I warned, she might be alive today, and your mother wouldn't be lost to us."

"The operative word is *lost*. Not *gone*, Dad. Talia is the only one who's gone, and now you want to make my mother disappear as well." My hands shook as I lifted them to stop his imminent argument. Dad was a lawyer and an elected judge, but this was my mother and I'd argue with the devil himself to stop him from sending her away.

I took a calming breath. "I won't stand here and listen to you lie when I know the true motivation behind this. My mother and her troubles cast a long shadow across your political aspirations, a shadow your opponents can exploit. You want to hide her away and play the martyred husband and father so you can elicit sympathy."

My courage grew at the look of shock on his face, but there was no pleasure in the feel. "If you think I'll keep my mouth closed and stand by while you give speeches and shake hands when behind closed doors you maneuver to remove my mother from the picture, you've got another thing coming. I'm not a little girl anymore. One phone call from me and the press will eat this up with a spoon."

I steeled myself not to flinch as my father stared me down, his mouth an ugly line. Finally, the doctor cleared his throat. "Ted, perhaps this isn't the best time. A decision of this magnitude is hard for anyone to digest."

Dad was the first to break eye contact, turning to give the doctor a curt nod. "Of course." His reply was courteous and sure, but then he slid his gaze back to me, his eyes narrowed. "Hannah needs time to come to terms with her mother's illness. Time to realize it's for the best for everyone, including Peg."

I looked between the two and scoffed. "Think again, Teddy-boy."

"Hannah!" The nurse flinched.

I shook my head, still staring at my father. "You make a move against my mother and I will do everything in my power to ruin whatever life you envision without her. And you can bang the gavel on that, your honor."

Storming out of the room, I spared a glance for my mom. She had sunk into relaxed oblivion courtesy of whatever drug the nurse had added to her IV.

I felt sick as I fled down the stairs, not wanting my father to corner me by the elevators. It was bad enough I'd have to face him at home, especially when I knew my rant came off as something between petulant teenager and Joan of Arc.

Dad let me have my outburst, but in the end, we both knew I was outranked. He was right about one thing, though. I needed to think, and that meant school was out of the question today. If what I saw in that hospital room was to be believed, then we *were* running out of time. But for what?

Now more than ever, I had to find Rowen, but I couldn't face her. Not yet. I needed time to myself and there was only one place for that. Kingsland Park.

Chapter 2

"Mind if I join you?"

I turned wet eyes to find Rowen approaching from the slope behind. It was on my lips to ask how she knew I was at Kingsland, but when it came to Rowen and the rest of her family, those questions tended to be rhetorical. In the last year, she'd come close to rivalling her mother and grandmother in witchy expertise.

"I saw you pass the Silver Cauldron. I figured this was where you were headed."

She sunk down onto the grass beside me, and we both looked out at the Hudson's brown water with its soft lapping waves. The trees across the river were touched with gold and a kiss of crimson. I had always loved the fall, but since Talia's death, the colors and excitement for the season fell flat.

"This was always my go-to place whenever life's stresses got to be too much. Especially in high school. That's not to say the pressure from my mother and Gran to do right by our witchy roots can in any way compare to the weight you carry."

I watched Rowen's chin dip. Her shoulders were just as heavy as mine in this. "You carry it, too, Rowen."

She smiled softly and plucked a few long blades from the grass. "Hunter and I still come here when we get the chance. For some reason, the sloping grounds and the sound of the water centers us."

"I know what you mean. It's peaceful."

"Gran thinks the whole of Sleepy Hollow is a spiritual magnet, and not just at Halloween." She chuckled softly. "And Gran is never wrong, especially the closer it gets to Samhain." She looked at me at that point. "It's our word for Halloween. It's the Witch's New Year and a major fire sabbat on the wheel of the year. In fact, I was helping decorate the shop for the season when—"

I smirked, cutting her off midsentence. "When you *knew* I was here." I made bunny ears with my fingers.

Rowen grinned. "Guilty as charged."

"Sleepy Hollow is already crawling with tourists and it's barely the second week of October. You're a little late in the decorating department, don'tcha think?" I eyed Rowen with a crooked grin of my own. "'Fess up. How long ago did your mother ask you to help with the shop?"

"Three weeks ago."

I snorted. "Talia always said you weren't exactly into your witchy roots." I turned back to the water, my heart suddenly in my throat. "But that's all changed now, right? I mean, after what happened."

Rowen placed a hand on my shoulder. "What's the matter, Hannah? And don't lie to me. My Spidey senses are heading into overdrive the longer I sit with you. When

I saw you over the summer, you seemed better. Is your mom still having a hard time?"

Instant regret shadowed Rowen's face the minute her words left her mouth. The word *still* didn't belong in either of our vocabularies when it came to losing Talia.

"That didn't come out the way I meant it. I'm sorry, Hannah. What I meant was is Peg still seeing Tal?"

I nodded.

"And you haven't told her you see her, too?"

My gaze jerked from the shore to where she sat waiting for me to reply. "How…" I stuttered open-mouthed, but then pressed my lips to a fine line. "I get it. One of my mother's nurses knows Hunter's mom is a midwife, so they called Britt about my acting weird and she in turn called your mother, right? You came home from college because of me."

Rowen's worry softened into a small grin, but she shook her head. "That's a good hypothesis, but no. I came home because no one says no to Laura Corbett weeks before Halloween. She's still Sleepy Hollow's unofficial *official* town witch, and like it or not, I'm her appointed acolyte. Besides, the classes I've been taking are online. After everything that happened this year, both Hunter and I decided to defer our official start of college until January."

"Lucky. Right now, I would love to be able to go to school anywhere but here."

"I'm sorry things are bad for you at school, but I'm not surprised. Not with the pious bigots still clutching their crumbling hold on the village, but you haven't answered my question and I'd rather not assume. It's funny how you have the same knack for evasion as Talia." Rowen rubbed her bare arms as though a sudden chill crossed. "You look so much like her, it hurts sometimes."

Rowen's voice broke and I exhaled, hard. "I know. I can see the remembered pain in my mother's face whenever she looks at me."

"So, tell me what's up. I can always scry to find out, but I would rather you tell me. It cuts through the cosmic red tape, so to speak. I'm right, aren't I? You're seeing Talia, too."

I appreciated Rowen's attempt at humor, so I gave her a small nod.

"For God's sake, Hannah, why haven't you said anything? Even if your dad and the doctors don't believe your mother, you might give her the solid ground she's been grasping for."

Fat tears rolled down my thin cheeks. "I don't want to be crazy, and I'm afraid this makes me nuts like her."

"Why in heaven's name would you think seeing spirits makes you crazy? Hell, my family sees way more than that and we are saner than most people in town."

I opened my mouth to reply but closed it again. I glanced away, not wanting to meet Rowen's pointed gaze.

"Hannah, what?"

I shook my head.

"Tell me."

With a sob, I told her what happened in the hospital room just hours ago.

"Jesus." Rowen pursed her lips, resting her wrists on her bent knees, her fingers fidgeting with the Bridget Cross she wove from the blades of grass. "This is more than just Talia having trouble moving on. I don't like it. My gut says there's more at play than what meets the eye.

"Evil took its toll in blood a year ago, and I thought we exorcised the lot of it. Perhaps we have, but I need you to tell Gran about this firsthand."

"My dad said you and your family are the reason Talia is dead. He blames you for everything that happened last Halloween...Tal's death, Jenny Beamer's attack, and Tyler's disappearance. He doesn't buy the police report. He said your family's witchcraft called the evil to Sleepy Hollow. He even warned Hunter to stay away from you or he'd get sucked into your crazy as well."

Tears threated as I kept my gaze on the water, knowing I'd just hurt my sister's best friend. Rowen deserved the truth. Some of the obstacles facing us were flesh and blood.

"I know."

Mouth open, my head spun to face her.

"Don't look so surprised, Hannah. My mother got a phone call from your father after we all met for closure at Jenny's place this summer. He warned I was to stay away from you if I knew what was good for me."

"My dad threatened you?"

Rowen shrugged. "Not exactly, but he wasn't happy with my mother's reply."

I laughed in nervous relief. "I bet. He's lucky your grandmother didn't catch wind of it."

"Oh, she did. She had a few choice words of her own for his honor, Ted Meyer."

Rowen stuck the braided cross in her pocket. "Listen up. You need to tell your mother you see Talia. Do it quietly but do it—if only so she knows she's not crazy. Mom, Gran, and I can help, but not if your dad keeps Peg in a chemical coma. My guess is whatever is keeping Talia from moving on isn't done here, and you and your mom need to help her finish whatever it is that needs to be completed."

"Completed? Like what? Homework? My sister wasn't interested in anything but herself and Mike, and he got himself killed in the process, as well. What could she possibly need to complete?"

Guilt bit into my gut the minute the words left my mouth. It was hard to admit, but in the midst of my grief, I was angry. Angry at Talia for putting our family through this pain. It was irrational, but that didn't stop the feelings from bubbling to the point of choking me.

Tears welled and Rowen pulled me close, sliding her arm around my shoulders.

"I didn't mean that—at least not the way it came out." I sniffed.

"I'm angry with Talia, too. I can't share everything with you now, but there was more than what meets the eye in what happened that night. Evil is an entity that can punch a hole into our world, and often there's collateral damage in blood. I only wish we had figured it out sooner."

"You mean you and Hunter?"

Rowen nodded and a warm smile followed a tender million-mile stare. It was clear she was still very much in love.

"Hunter is a channel and I'm a magnet, or at least that's what Gran says, and together we seem to attract and repel what lies beyond the veil." Her eyes found mine. "I want him to weigh in on what's happening with you and your mom, too. He was there when evil broke through the first time, and he was the one who Gran bound to me to help send it back to hell. We might need his strength again."

"Do you really think you can help?"

Rowen shrugged. "I don't know, but we can certainly find out. That is if you can get your dad out of the way and your mom home. We'll need her in this as much as you."

I shook my head. "He won't listen. He's practically got the commitment papers signed."

"Don't talk to him. Talk to Peg. Since my family is persona non grata, maybe Hunter's mom can go with you. Britt's as witchy as we are, but your dad doesn't seem to notice."

I made a face. "He still carries a torch for that one. He thinks we didn't know. Tal and me, that is. But we did. You should have seen him when he learned Britt and Hunter moved back to town last year. He started going to the gym and using *Just for Men* to cover his grays." My frown deepened. "My mother tried to laugh it off, but I didn't because I saw how much it hurt her."

I snorted before continuing my rant. "And everyone wonders why Talia was so insecure. Why she was a slave to what people thought, especially Mike. If my mother was stronger and had more self-respect, Tal wouldn't have given that creep a second look."

"It's not your mom's fault, Hannah. Don't blame her for what she couldn't control. She has her own set of demons to battle, especially now."

"You think these visions of Talia are demons?"

Rowen shook her head hard. "No...oh, honey, of course, not! It's Talia you see. I feel it in my bones." Rowen pushed herself up and brushed off her pants "Come on. Let's go have some fun. My treat." She glanced up the hill, and a smirk tugged at her lips.

"Looks like I'm not the only one who knew how to find you." She gave a chin pop toward the path at the top of the hill. "Someone you know?"

I followed her line of sight to Angel standing fifty feet up the hill. "*Uhm*, sort of."

She chuckled. "Yeah, I remember when I *sort of* knew Hunter. I also remember that same awkward flutter and anxious look whenever I saw him, too."

Heat crawled up my cheeks. "I'm not fluttering and I'm certainly not anxious. I've known Angel for ages. He's a friend."

"Friend, huh? You sure that feeling is mutual? Guys don't usually happen by to check if you're okay unless they have feelings for you, either that or they have an ulterior motive." She glanced toward the top of the hill again and closed her eyes. A small smile sparked, and she nodded. "Definitely not an ulterior motive, and nothing indecent...yet."

"Rowen!"

"Okay...okay...relax. I promise I won't say another word, but if you don't stop fidgeting, he'll figure out you like him all by his lonesome."

"I am not fidgeting."

"Really? They why are you hell-bent on twisting the hem of your shirt beyond repair?"

I exhaled, untangling my fingers from my crumpled blouse and smoothed the material flat against my stomach.

Rowen reached and brushed the hair from my forehead. "I can't say as I blame you. He's kinda delish. Like Hunter."

"Rowen!" I objected again.

With a wink, she chuckled. "Listen, take your time hanging out with tall, dark and handsome, but promise me you'll leave before sundown." She glanced toward the water and inhaled. "My insides are doing the mambo, and that's a sure sign something is brewing and it's not good. Once the moon rises, it stacks the odds in whatever is out there's favor."

Leaning in, she pecked my cheek, pulling me in for a hug. "I know my mother and Gran have a fundraiser meeting at the Historical Society tonight, so let's plan to meet at my house tomorrow evening. I'll have my mom call Britt and I'll call Hunter. We'll get to the bottom of this. I promise. I'll ask Gran to meet us tomorrow as well and we can talk all you like, then."

I hugged her back, fisting her shirt in fierce gratitude. If my sister's warning to find Rowen was the omen I hoped, then maybe the hollow feeling in the pit of my stomach would go away.

"I promised Hunter I'd make pasta with tomato and feta tomorrow night, so I might as well cook for us all. Six thirty sound okay?"

I nodded, stepping back. "I'll be there."

"Good."

She walked up the slope toward the park exit, but I couldn't let her go like that. "Hey, Rowen!" I called after her. When she turned, I blew her a kiss. "Thanks!"

She nodded with a wave, and as promised, she didn't say a word as she passed Angel on his way down the hill.

"What are you doing here?" I asked as he closed the distance between us.

"When you didn't show for pre-calc, I knew something was up. We had a test, remember? And you *never* miss a chance to trounce my GPA."

"Ha! Not much of a challenge."

He reached out and tucked a stray hair behind my ear. "I was worried about you, Banana. When you went M.I.A., I figured this is where you'd be."

Angel Morales had been calling me Hannah Banana since kindergarten. Eventually he shortened it to just Banana, and while the abbreviated nickname irritated the crap out of me in the past, it now sent the butterflies in my stomach into overdrive. That and the way his chocolate-brown eyes took in every detail when he looked at me. Or maybe I imagined it. Wishful thinking, I guess.

I slipped and told Talia about it once. Big mistake. She said Angel was used to me following him around like a puppy and didn't want to hurt my feelings, because deep down he thought I was ridiculous. I loved my older sister and missed her like crazy, but sometimes—

I exhaled hard again, ignoring the bite of disloyalty in my gut.

"You okay?" he asked, tilting his head in such a way it made me want to kiss him hard.

"Yeah…I'm fine. Same old, same old." I sat back on the grass, pulling blades in silent agitation.

"You don't seem fine," he replied, plopping down beside me. He stretched his long, lean-muscled, soccer player legs out in front of him and rested back on his elbows.

"It'll pass." I cocked my head, giving him a sideways look. "So, you were sure I'd be here, huh?"

He lifted his face to the sky, squinting into the sun. "Yup. But only because you're so predictable."

I laughed, throwing a handful of grass at him. "Predictable? And the fact we've known each other since we were five years old has nothing to do with that, right?"

"Has it been that long? Doesn't seem it, somehow." He winked, tilting his head again and my stomach squeezed.

We sat literally arm against arm. His warm skin against mine in the fall sunshine. How many times had we been this close, but neither crossing the line. Ever. As if an unspoken minefield existed between us that neither wanted to tempt for fear it would blow our friendship into oblivion.

Angel was just over six feet tall with a lean, muscled body. His white tee-shirt clung to the flat planes of his chest and torso—well-defined and cut from thousands of hours playing ball. The light scruff on his jaw only added to his exotic appeal, not to mention the way his eyes flashed with easy humor. Much to my irritation, he dated half my clique of friends, but it never ended well, with him always the one to break it off.

How many times had I listened to my girlfriends cry and complain after the fact? Too many. In an uncharacteristic moment of sisterly bonding, Talia joked that Angel only dated my friends because he secretly wanted me. Of course, she laughed so hard afterward her caramel macchiato snarfled out her nose.

Angel was off limits and I knew it, no matter how good he smelled or how I secretly longed for him to make the first move.

Something had shifted between us in the past year, but there was no way I would take the chance and say something. Though, sometimes I swore he felt the shift, too. What if I was wrong? Not only would that qualify as an epic fail, but there was no coming back from that kind of awkwardness. From then on, it would hang between us like a giant elephant in the room. What friendship could survive that? No, thank you.

But something was different and not just because he was the only one of my friends who wasn't spooked by what happened to Talia. Even Miranda Beamer had bailed and if anyone could understand, it was her.

No, this went deeper with Angel. Like when you see a person, really see them for the first time without their high school façade. Angel was perfect, and perfectly named. At least to me. Not that I'd ever tell him.

He'd been there every day since the horrid, lurid details of how Talia died hit the hallways at Sleepy Hollow high school, when most of my friends fell off the face of the earth. I was in social Siberia, though I'd done nothing to deserve my fate. He made sure I still had street cred at school and saw to it I was invited to parties and games, though most times you could cut the awkwardness with a knife.

"It'll pass, Banana. You'll see. Right now, no one knows what to say or how to act around you, so it's easier to ignore the situation and you."

"You don't."

He smiled, slipping his arm around my shoulders, giving me a side hug. "A bruised Banana on my watch? Never."

Our fingers were side-by-side, but barely touched. He lifted his hand from the grass and curled his fingers into his palm, tapping his loose fist on top of mine. "You wanna talk about it?"

I shook my head. "Not really, but I appreciate the sympathetic ear."

He smiled, giving my hand a squeeze. "If an ear is all I can offer, then mine is all yours, piercings and all."

I turned my head to give him a smile, and in that moment, I knew I would either cry or kiss him. I let unshed tears wet my eyes.

Angel slid his arm around my shoulders and pulled me to his side. He held me close beside him, letting my head rest on his chest. To outside eyes, we looked like typical teenage lovers. *If only.*

"How about some ice cream? Main Street Sweets has cinnamon pumpkin spice. They just put the sign in the window. Remember how much you loved it last year? It's the perfect remedy to chase the blues from your baby blues."

I nodded, wiping my eyes and my nose on his tee-shirt.

"*Eeww.* Seriously, Banana? I offered a shoulder, not an invitation to make me a human Kleenex."

I snorted a laugh and lifted the hem of my cotton blouse almost as high as my lace bandeau bra to finish wiping my face. Angel's eyes flicked to my bare midriff and he licked his lips. However unintentional, I froze for a moment.

"You kill me sometimes. Why not flash the entire park while you're at it?"

Was that a flash of heat in his gaze or was it my imagination?

Recovering quickly, I yanked my shirt down, smoothing the front. "You offered an ear not a shoulder, and besides, I bought you that shirt so it's a wash." I tried to change the tone from awkward back to playful.

"Hannah..." he licked his lips again. "You never said why you came here. What upset you enough to ditch class? Is it me?"

All kidding aside, I searched his face. "Why in the world would you think that?"

He lifted a hand. "I don't know. I've been edgy and impatient lately, almost in knots. Even coach says my game is off."

"Why would you automatically connect your moodiness with me not showing at school? You know what's going on with my family. I tell you everything, Angel. You're my only friend."

A slash of guilt crested in my chest knowing that wasn't the case. I hadn't told him about seeing Talia, only that my mother claimed she did.

He shook his head. "That's not true."

I stared at him. The only other person that knew about Talia's visits was Rowen. There was no way he could know.

"Yes, it is. Do you see anyone else around? The closest thing I have to a girlfriend these days is Gianna Nichols, the freshman assigned to me on student sister day. Miranda is too busy campaigning for bitch of the year, and Cassie and Mel are so far up her butt you can't tell where Randi ends, and they start."

"They'll come around, Hannah, and if they don't? Screw 'em. You have me."

I rolled my eyes. "Yeah, and shoe shopping with me is your idea of a fun Saturday."

"It could be. It depends."

"Oh really. On what?"

"On whether you're buying sexy stilettos or orthopedic oxfords."

I laughed, nearly choking on my own tongue. "You are truly the last man standing when it comes to my friends. I don't know what I'd do without you."

His eyes held mine for a moment and then he quickly looked away, almost as though he wanted to say something but didn't. Confusion edged in and I shook my head. "What?"

He exhaled, keeping his gaze on the water. He opened his mouth to say something but then closed it again. "Never mind. Forget it."

"No, what?'

He shook his head. "It can wait."

With a grin he bent and grabbed me around the knees, tossing me over his shoulder. "But ice cream won't." I squealed and with a laugh he sprinted up the slope toward the parking lot and his car….

Intrigued for the rest of the story?
Spook Rock is available in paperback and ebook now!